CW00587883

THE CROSSING

Faith Mortimer was born in Manchester and educated in Malaya, Singapore and Hampshire. After training to become a nurse she switched careers and became involved in setting up and running various travel and sport related companies. On completion of Yachtsman examinations and a science degree she and her husband sailed their yacht across the Atlantic and enjoyed many years exploring the seas. They now divide their time living in the UK and Cyprus. 'The Crossing' is her first novel and she is currently working on her second.

THE CROSSING

Faith Mortimer

THE CROSSING

Olympia Publishers
London

www.olympiapublishers.com
OLYMPIA PAPERBACK EDITION

A CIP catalogue record for this title is
available from the British Library.

ISBN: 978-1-905513-68-0

This is a work of fiction.
Names, characters, places and incidents originate from the writer's
imagination. Any resemblance to actual persons, living or dead, is
purely coincidental.

First Published in 2009

Olympia Publishers
60 Cannon Street
London
EC4N 6NP

Printed in Great Britain

Dedication

To the gallant men of the Royal Navy Coastal Forces who served with such bravery and distinction during the Second World War.

Acknowledgments

I would like to offer thanks to several people for their support during the writing of *The Crossing*. I am happily in their debt. For Paul, a good friend who had preserved his father's story and shared it with me. He set me on Billy's and Richard's trails, and after showing me his father's wartime bible, DSM and photographs I was absolutely hooked on his riveting story. Although there are certain parallels, please remember *The Crossing* is a complete work of fiction. James Newby was generous with his advice and encouragement; he took my writing seriously and offered a model of hard work and commitment. My husband Chris provided me with a wonderful retreat in the Cyprus mountains, where the final chapters were completed and his thoughtful, sensitive and enthusiastic editing improved its final shape. For readers Margaret Street and Issy Blackburn and their helpful feedback and finally for my children Ross and Catherine who said, 'Go, Mum go!'

Prologue

Germany 1945

Billy collected his 'treasures' together and laid them at the end of his ramshackle bunk in hut 19. There wasn't a lot to account for three years incarceration at the hands of the sometimes-brutal Germans, but to him they represented his life and more importantly his soul. He thought about the refugees that had filed past the gates of his camp. Old people, women with children, babes in arms, the injured, burned, terrified, deranged. All were fleeing from the horrors. The Christians among them struggling to believe and reconcile their religious beliefs with Nazi cold-blooded excesses and mass murder.

He considered his pitiful little pile: Christmas cards from Penny, her heavily censored letters and her simple but evocative poetry, the hand-made playing cards, two unsmoked cigarettes, the German soldier's – Dieter's – belt buckle and Nathaniel's penny whistle. Nathaniel. Billy shook his head in regret and fought back the familiar choking feeling that arose in his throat whenever that memory arose. He thrust his dark thoughts aside and continued picking over his possessions. He would take as many clothes as he could carry. He had nothing heavy; he'd given his Bible away, hopefully to someone who would put it to better use than he. Gathering up his things, he tied them into a bundle with his faded and much darned pullover, and slung it over his shoulder. He straightened his back, lifted his head and stood as erect as his gammy leg allowed. I'll march out of here *proudly* he thought. Together with his comrades they formed into ranks and marched smartly up to the gates. The weak and sick were supported by their stronger colleagues, their spirits rising. They didn't know where they were going, but it had to be a better place than this.

B o o k   1

Chapter 1

The Atlantic 2005

Richard knew he had no choice. It had to be now. He'd never get another chance. Taking a deep breath he pushed off the heaving wet deck of his yacht and with sheer determination dived for the net. He hit the water, his lower torso disappearing into the black froth that fiercely clawed and clutched at him. Somehow, he managed to stretch out and grab the harsh net with one arm, feeling it tangle around him. The ship lurched and this time he was fully immersed in deep water. What seemed like minutes later he broke the surface, coughing and choking, the salt stinging his eyes. He clamped his other hand to the netting and clung to it like a limpet. The water roared and hissed around his ears, terrifyingly black. He knew he must climb the net fast as his energy was rapidly ebbing away and conditions were not going to get any better.

Moving one arm higher, he found a rung and hauled himself slowly up, grunting with exertion as he did so. His hands were bleeding from fresh cuts where he had smashed against the rough barnacles on the ship's hull. Fatigue was fast overcoming him. The past few days of untold stress and lack of sleep were taking their toll. Gritting his teeth, he managed to move up another foot of net and then slowly, by willpower alone, pulled himself up rung by rung. Faintly he heard the encouraging cries of the crew far above him. He paused and looked up and saw a line of faces peering down at him; his adrenalin surged and with renewed vigour he at last collapsed thankfully on the ship's deck.

Utterly exhausted by his ordeal Richard lay there not quite believing where he was. Water streamed from his body and he vaguely knew that soon they would all begin to feel the cold as it seeped through to their bones. Coughing and retching seawater, Richard sat up and became aware of the ring of sturdy looking sea boots clustered around him. He attempted to stand and felt strong arms supporting him. He braced his legs against the motion of the deck and looked round. A circle of anxious faces stared back; a stocky bearded fellow whom he assumed to be the captain, four or five crew members and an ashen-faced Toby.

The captain cleared his throat, about to speak. Again Richard looked around his surroundings and forestalled him by hoarsely saying, 'Where's Connie? Where's my wife?'

His voice wavered and he felt his heart thump wildly in his chest. There was a silence. No one spoke. All sounds drifted away from him. He was in a dreamlike glide and the reality was too strange to comprehend. The surreal took over. He felt as though his actions were slowing, as if seen in a slow-motion film, frame by frame passing by. Everything took an eternity, a raised hand placed on his shoulder, a sentence spoken by someone slowly, but everything seen with an achingly clear focus. All was sharply defined. He imagined her limp in his arms, her head thrown back and the curve of her throat, so beautiful. She was gone.

The slow world turned crimson red. It spun wildly on its axis, and then rushed up to engulf him as his head hit the hard deck with a thump.

***

Richard struggled to clear the mistiness away from his brain. As fast as he reached out and clawed at the blackness that engulfed him he was drawn back down again into his own violent hell. He tossed and turned in delirium on the sweat-drenched bunk where the crew had placed him after he had collapsed on the outside deck.

The ship's medic had quickly examined Richard's head wound and although it was a minor laceration he was more worried about the state of his patient's mind once he regained consciousness. As he observed Richard and listened to his feverish cries of anguish he could only guess at the nightmares that coursed around in his brain. The medic knew from Toby a little of what had happened on the yacht's fated voyage and he shook his head in pity as he again wondered how Richard was going to cope. He had had everything going for him he had been told, and now this. How the hell had it all gone wrong?

Chapter 2

Richard William Barker was hoisted a dizzy fifty-nine feet up in the air. A climbing harness cruelly encircled his loins; threatening to severely limit any last minute plans for fatherhood, whereas his chest felt decidedly crushed by the extra security rope looped tightly under his armpits.

'Up a bit more, more, more, that's it hold it! Stop!' He shouted down to Toby who was on the deck below, manning the electric winches. Toby took an extra turn of the rope round the winch and made it fast in the jammer. He then took up the slack on the second security line and secured it snugly onto a substantial looking cleat.

Richard could now change the tricolour bulb at the top of the mast and check the radio antenna at the same time. Toby gazed up at Richard and couldn't repress a slight prickle of fear. He remembered the one and only time he had gone up the mast himself when they were anchored off the Isle of Wight in the Solent. It had been a beautiful, hot sunny summer's day for once with very little breeze and subsequently very little movement on the water in the anchorage. That was until the inequitable jet ski roared past thirty feet from the yacht, its wash creating a sick making roll to the boat from side to side. The offending jet ski owner had laughed and jeered at his puerile jest and in panic Toby had clung to the mast, his eyes tightly closed. Toby thought he wasn't a coward at heart but he vowed never to willingly volunteer to go up the mast again if he could help it.

Right now he was perfectly happy to sit in the cockpit, take Richard's shouted down orders and maintain a watch on the safety lines. Soon as this job is done it will be too late to start anything else with a bit of luck, he mused. Just the right time to stop for a nice cold beer and decide where to go for tonight's dinner.

He stretched out lazily along the teak seating in the cockpit and looked around the Santa Cruz marina in Tenerife at the other sleek boats tied up alongside the pontoons. It was a large harbour and motorboats and other yachts surrounded *Ellentari*. They were all slowly bobbing on the slight swell. Although it had been a perfect day for a sail around the Canary Islands the majority of boats were snugly secured in their berths. The light breeze of about 8 knots ruffled the oily marina water and set the gaily coloured flags a flutter. Loose halyards tinkled against metal masts and gulls swooped noisily down to inspect debris floating in the water.

If you added up the value of all the moored boats it would run into many millions. Toby's accountant brain thought, what a waste. They should be used more. At least Richard was utilising his boat to the full. *Ellentari* was a beautiful yacht and clearly a sound investment. Toby knew good well-built solid boats kept their value well and this 45 footer was no exception. He leant back and looked up at Richard still aloft. With a bit of luck it was only a bulb that required replacing now and the radio antenna just needed to be more securely screwed in place. Better to check it here now in the relative calm of the marina than being tossed around 60 feet up aloft when at sea.

'OK. Can you turn on the tricolour now please?' called down Richard. Toby's reverie was broken as he climbed down from the cockpit into the boats saloon in response. The instrument panel was on the starboard side bulkhead and he reached over and pushed the appropriate labelled switch. A glowing red light indicated it was on.

'Great! That appears to be fine now. Turn if off and then you can slowly lower me down.'

Toby climbed the companionway ladder back into the cockpit. He adjusted the two lines holding Richard's life in his hands and slowly paid out the rope.

Richard landed safely on the deck, deftly untied the safety line bowline and eased himself out of the climbing harness, wincing as he did so.

'Thank God I've got that off, it's not exactly pleasant being trussed up like a chicken! Anyway that's a job well done and for a change relatively simple. Thanks for your help,' Richard said laughing, coiling and stowing the ropes away.

His thin angular face was creased in good humour. Straightening up he was a good six feet three inches, of slim build with a tanned muscular body. His straight hair was from a sun-washed blonde to light brown, flecked through with grey and cut fairly short. The tan looked good on him giving him a more youthful appearance than his 49 years. Women from 16 to 70 often gave him a second glance.

Good-looking bastard Toby thought, although he was himself attractive in his own smaller and darker way. Richard's got the money, the time, the boat and a kitten of a wife whom he doesn't appear to appreciate as much as he should. Aside from that though, he and Richard had been friends for 15 years now and he really didn't begrudge him his current good fortune.

'I think a beer or two onboard and then off to the Plaza to find a restaurant don't you?' said Richard.

'My thoughts entirely old boy, the sun must be well over by now. I expect Connie would like one too,' he agreed raising his voice a little.

As expected a tousled head appeared in the aft cabin hatch. 'I most certainly would. Just let me finish changing and I'll be right with you.' She ducked down and both men grinned at each other.

'Never misses out does she?'

'Only when there's dirty work to be done,' replied Richard dryly.

'You relax a bit. I'll go below and get the drinks.' Toby clattered down the companionway into the shady saloon. He was really looking forward to the sailing trip. Like the others this was his first Atlantic crossing. He was relishing the thought of blue waters, starry nights and glorious sunsets. Of course once across and established in the Caribbean he was sure that rum punches, bikini-clad beauties and reggae 'jump ups' would take precedence. No tedious commuting to town from his house in Esher and a break from the machinations of daily office parlance.

Richard had always had a lifelong dream of skippering his own yacht across one of the great oceans of the world and meeting all the personal challenges that would be thrown at him. He didn't know where this deep-seated yearning came from but for most of his life he had felt an almost overwhelming pull to go out, buy a boat and explore. Now the dream was just beginning; coming to fruition, as Richard and Connie finalised their preparations for their planned sail across the Atlantic. The huge golden orb of the sun was sinking fast, casting long deep-mauve shadows on the surrounding hills. It had been 'another perfect day in paradise' using the yachties' much hackneyed but true cliché. The temperatures had been in the high seventies, with a slight cooling breeze and a cloudless cerulean blue sky.

Toby reappeared in the cockpit with their drinks accompanied by Connie. Richard studied Connie with a familiar deep affection. Small, dark-haired and neat, described her outward appearance. She stood about five feet four inches in her bare feet with a slim build. Her legs were nicely shaped, rising to a firm little bottom, nipped in waist and medium sized breasts. Handful sized Richard would say, anything bigger would be a waste. She had recently had her hair cut short, as she knew long hair would be too hot and a pain in a tropical climate, besides, water on a yacht had to be managed. Her newly shorn hair was slightly curly from the salty air and not unattractive as it framed her violet-blue eyes. Connie enjoyed a refreshing Campari and orange juice; the ice cubes tinkling against her glass when she lifted it for a sip, relishing the slight bitterness of the fortified spirit against the sweetness of the fruit. Richard preferred a long cool local beer. He sat quietly contemplating the condensation as it slowly ran down the outside of his glass forming a small wet ring onto the coaster. He wiped it away with his hand. He was both excited and yet a little bothered at the same time. His excitement was caused by their almost imminent departure from Tenerife. In a day or so – all being well – they would have completed their tasks and boat preparations that they had set themselves in getting ready for a long extended cruise. They planned to leave the comparative safety of the Canary Island waters and sail across 'The Pond.' In other words, they had two thousand, eight hundred miles to sail across the Atlantic in a small boat. It was well known to be a vast, lonely and sometimes inhospitable sea, but it was an adventure that many an amateur sailor had undertaken without mishap, thoroughly enjoying the challenge and eventual achievement.

***

Richard's long-term plans had come together nicely. They now had all the necessary ingredients: the time, the money and a partnership that complimented each other for the majority of their time spent together. After a heady, passionate early marriage they had both settled down with only the occasional stormy row to punctuate their steady relationship. He loved Connie; there was no doubt about his feelings towards her, but as Richard was fairly undemonstrative he usually kept his inner feelings much to himself.

His business he had placed in the trustworthy hands of his manager besides which, with today's technology he could stay in daily contact if he wanted by satellite telephone and email.

Now, with almost everything in place Richard was eager to be off. There was no great hurry as the weather window stretched from now in early November to early February. The only urgency was Richard's own excited impatience to get going, set sail and make the Caribbean in time for Christmas. He sighed and took a swallow of beer. He still had this small niggle though.

Connie was not as passionate as Richard about sailing, and much preferred to be within sight of land. However, she had jumped at the chance of leaving her position as a surgical ward sister and was enjoying the newfound luxury of being her own boss. She found she actually had time for herself. Having enrolled in a dive class before they had left England she was looking forward to exploring the coral reefs around the British Virgin Islands as they were supposed to be fabulous. She had also rediscovered her old schooldays' talent for painting and looked forward to catching the colourful Caribbean on canvas. Their comfortable furnished aft cabin with its scandalously large double bunk had a whole locker dedicated to the paraphernalia that went along with her artistic inclinations. She meant to enjoy herself; the sailing would mainly be Richard's interest with her doing her bit. Richard thought back to a day or so ago when he and Connie had been alone on their boat. They had been relaxing at the end of a busy day. Connie was immersed in yet another doorstep of a book and Richard had been fidgeting on his seat before finally addressing Connie.

'You've clearly got something on your mind. I know you have. OK what is it?' She placed her bookmark inside the book and then laid it down closed on the cockpit table barely suppressing an irritated sigh at being interrupted.

He reached over for her left hand and imprisoned it within his.

'I do. I had a call from Toby earlier today with a request.'

'Uh oh. Why do I have this feeling of trouble I wonder?' She suddenly laughed, 'you know what he's like! Come on then. What does he want now?'

Richard took another swallow of his beer enjoying the sharp bitter taste and then proceeded to relate to Connie his telephone conversation earlier today with an excited and persuasive Toby.

In the early cool of that morning Connie had taken herself off the boat to buy some last minute provisions in the fruit and vegetable market. She particularly enjoyed the freshness of the local produce, knowing that it hadn't yet been irradiated for sale and storage in refrigerators abroad. She had probably overbought but they would certainly eat well in the next few weeks. Toby must have rung whilst she was out. She turned her attention back to what Richard had to tell her.

He had answered the call on his mobile telephone and inwardly sighed when he recognised Toby's clipped tones and cultured accent on the line. Toby didn't beat about the bush. It soon transpired that he had suddenly found himself with six months leave; nothing planned and wouldn't it be an excellent idea if he came along and gave them both a hand?

Richard had to think fast. As friends they had spent various weekends sailing together in the Solent and occasional trips across to France, with a couple of longer voyages in the summer weeks. Although Toby was only what you would call a 'weekend' sailor his sailing knowledge was good; he had done a few training courses and best of all he didn't usually suffer from the dreaded 'mal de mer.' He was certainly being very persuasive and knew with instinctive certainty that to convince Richard of his usefulness, indeed his highly significant inclusion to the party, was of paramount importance. He suggested that Connie was not perhaps as strong as a man and might not relish any heavy hardships encountered on the way. Richard couldn't of course retell this bit to Connie, as he knew she would be incensed. Instead he listened to Toby's suggestion that he would be a valuable asset and she could also enjoy (as they both would) shorter watch hours.

'I know she would. Three crew means that you and I, and her of course, could share the watches and we would benefit from shorter watch hours and a longer stretch of sleep. Much more civilised than with just the two of you. Don't you think?' he had enthused.

'Well I'm not sure. It's a bit short notice and we'll have to think about it. How about I let you know tomorrow after I've discussed it properly with Connie later.'

They had finished their telephone conversation leaving Richard to mull over this new idea. He was not 100 per cent certain, but he knew that Connie would be keener than he was.

So, they now had to come to some agreement over this new proposal. They both liked Toby; it wasn't that. They had each in their own way relished the idea of taking this challenge with just the two of them and without any other person's influence. This was an entirely different matter. As skipper, Richard had the final say. But he did realise the added bonus of another pair of hands. What if one of them was ill or injured? It was hellishly more difficult to sail solo than with someone else helping at your side. Maybe he wasn't being entirely fair to Connie either.

The discussion of the pros and cons continued over their dinner in the square in Santa Cruz. Connie was generally in favour and said so as they sampled the local tapas and a dozen oysters, followed by a delicious sea bream grilled simply with olive oil and herbs washed down with a crisp white *Marques de Caceres*; one of their favourites. They forego the coffee, preferring to stroll hand in hand slowly back across the cobbled square to their yacht, taking in the balmy cooling night breeze. They reached their pontoon and in the silvery moonlight *Ellentari* shone, her tall mast and spreaders thrusting loftily up into the blue-black sky.

They had decided. Toby could come for the crossing and, depending on how they all got along during this period, maybe, just maybe extend his stay for a short spell in the Caribbean.

***

Meanwhile, back in England Toby Ellis had already got out his sailing gear and was methodically sorting out which was appropriate for tropical climates and what was not. Definitely not the sea-stained heavy-duty waterproofs, better known in sailing circles as oilies. The expensive leather sailing boots could stay home too. He'd take his

25

own lifejacket and harness as they fitted him well and he felt comfortable in them. Deck shoes only for when they cast off, then barefoot would be the order of the day. He picked out lots of short-sleeved shirts and swimming shorts. Passport. In his bathroom cupboard he found a suntan factor 30 and a lighter one once he was more used to the sun. He'd need plenty of credit cards of course and some dollars for cash. Those he could pick up at the airport. Easy!

He *knew* that Richard would agree after talking to Connie. She had a soft spot for him and he found her pretty cute himself. But then he usually found most women pretty cute. They were one of his weaknesses. This thought led him to recall what had happened earlier that day at work and how he was now in this position, much to his satisfaction.

That grey, grim London morning Toby was reeling from the acid lash of the senior partner's tongue.

'For Christ's sake what the hell do you think you were doing?' he'd stormed. 'Michael's got enough trouble being married to a younger woman and trying to keep her satisfied without you rubbing his nose in it,' he jabbed a finger angrily at Toby.

'What's more she means everything to him and absolutely nothing to you. You only pursued her because you could and, frankly I find your behaviour disgusting!' he thundered.

He leaned back heavily in his leather swivel office chair and regarded Toby with open contempt. This time he had gone too far. As senior partner in Holmes and Benton, Chartered Accountants, Tom had to ensure that Toby grasped the significance of his misconduct. He couldn't actually force him to stop his affair with the unlucky Michael's young wife, but he could remove Toby from the day-to-day exposure to Michael.

'Michaels only got six months before he retires and I want him to enjoy his last six months with us. Furthermore I want him to enjoy his well-earned retirement. It's not been easy for him losing his first wife to a brain tumour and I think he deserves better than this. You, as far as I know have never suffered a serious heartache in your life. You go through women at a distasteful rate and never consider the consequences. Call me old-fashioned if you like but, I have built this company up from nothing and my long-standing partner deserves more respect than this. I place Michael in high esteem.' He paused and breathed heavily, he was clearly very irate.

Toby tried to remonstrate with Tom but the senior partner held up a heavy hand to stop his voice. 'No, I don't want to hear any of your protests. Michael is entirely blameless in this and has been caused enough pain already. This is what I am proposing and you have one of two choices. You either accept, or you decline and leave this company's payroll. Your work is good but as Associate partner you are expendable. However, I hope you do accept, as normally we have a good working relationship and you have talent and work well under pressure. Also unlike Michael you have a good few years before you retire. So, my suggestion is that while Michael works out his six months you take an extended leave during this time. A sabbatical if you like. Once everything has cooled down and Michael has retired you can return and resume your career. Well? What do you say?' he put his elbows onto his mahogany desk and continued to glare at him.

Toby was at first momentarily shocked at this proposal and wanted to argue his case but something in Tom's steely look stopped him. He was an old windbag, and what a fuss over some little bint. He considered himself not entirely to blame; she was no delicate young virgin and although someone else's wife had given him plenty of encouragement. But, he did like working for the firm and knew that Tom had a full partnership in mind for him later on. So, he held his tongue in check, managed to look contrite and nodded an acceptance.

Besides, he much preferred the chase and she had given in far too quickly. A piece of cake really. He fleetingly thought of how many other bored young wives there were; wealthy, spoilt and sitting alone at home. All in all he considered that he had got off lightly. What's more he had six fantastic months all to himself! Excellent. What a bonus, what fun could be had. He already had a plan formulating in his quick devious mind.

His friend Richard was at present in Tenerife, busily preparing his yacht for his forthcoming transatlantic voyage. He had spent and enjoyed many a weekend sailing with Richard and his sexy, beautiful wife Connie. What if he could inveigle Richard into letting him come along as the third crew member? Winter in the Caribbean would be tremendous!

***

Richard had enjoyed the sail down to the Canaries. He and Connie had left the Hamble River in September; rather late for a Biscay crossing but they had been lucky. The Gods had looked down on them and they had had a good trip down. For once the dreaded and notorious Bay of Biscay was calm with hardly any wind and they had motored half of the way across it. The slow swell coming from the southwest had gently buffeted *Ellentari* as she rose on each small wave and then slipped down into the green trough on the other side. The sea chuckled down her starboard side and left behind a long sparkling foamy wake. Early each morning they had breakfasted on deck and together they had gasped with delight at the huge pods of dolphins and Minke whale that tore across the molten sea towards them. Forty, a hundred, two hundred silver and steely blue, glistening bodies turning, diving, spinning and splashing, their toothy grins leering up at them, and then lazily flipping over onto their sides and gliding down beneath the meniscus of the deep.

They had put into a few ports down the west coasts of Spain and Portugal. They had enjoyed the heady, gaudy fiesta in Bayonna, eaten delicious seafood in Cascais and loved Oporto with its gleaming terracotta roofs. Lisbon was hot and listless and they had detested the foul smelling river full of effluent that poured out from the city's sewage system. Fewer dolphins escorted them now, nervously staying clear of the fishermens' nets that crisscrossed the waters down to Cape St Vincent. Rounding that corner paying off the main, *Ellentari* had seemingly picked up her skirts and screamed along at nine knots. Richard had roared with delight while Connie had snuggled down safely in the lee of the cockpit.

Lagos on the Algarve was great fun. It had been wall to wall with other yachts preparing for the 'ARC.' Every year about 250 yachts of all sizes from about 30–70 feet took part in an organised voyage across the Atlantic from Gran Canaria to the Caribbean to arrive in St Lucia in time for Christmas.

Richard preferred the more muted departure from Tenerife sharing relevant information and informal drinks parties with their immediate neighbours. There was less frenzy and commercialism than in Gran Canaria.

He was calm and capable, a good dependable sailor. He considered that with careful planning there was no reason that their voyage should not be straightforward and easily accomplished. He was in short a firm believer of the old adage that a good ship would always take care of its crew. This explained why he'd spent many years studying yacht manufacturers' brochures and specifications, visiting numerous yacht builders' premises, checking performance versus comfort and safety, and occupied countless hours crawling in the deep recesses of potential purchases.

In his younger years he had first learnt to sail dinghies on the Isle of Wight and then by badgering friends and friends of friends he'd inveigled his way onto various different yachts as crew. He remembered hours spent wet and cold and sometimes seasick. But, he maintained if you could sail in the Solent and cope with everything thrown at you from lousy weather conditions, ferries, tanker ships, idiot motorboat racers, sudden wind changes, huge tidal differences and the sheer large numbers of craft afloat then you could sail anywhere. Richard had always worked hard in ventures in which he was most passionate and this presently was sailing. He had set to hone his skills diligently and with perseverance. Years ago his father had been a sailor in the Royal Navy, but most of his experience had been gained during World War 2 and he had been largely reticent about talking about his own exploits. His only advice to Richard had been 'don't enlist yourself boy!' Even so maybe this was where Richard had got his first yearnings to sail at sea.

The senior William Barker – recently deceased – had been a quiet man, often lost in his own deep thoughts. He and Richard hadn't shared a particularly close relationship to which now Richard expressed some regret. His mother had died in the seventies at a comparative young age, leaving behind Richard in his twenties and a much older sister. William had doted on both wife and daughter caring for them with a fierce love and loyalty. When Richard was born it had been a shock to the little tight knit family of three. Although he was of course loved and cared for, he occasionally found himself on the outside; looking in as it were. Perhaps this was why he had found it hard to settle down to steady employment and forge a career for himself. He had drifted from job to job with only a handful of 'O' levels as qualifications. Eventually, after many false starts he had ended up working for a large removal company and became involved in the machinations of a staff buy-out. He had a good hunch about this and invested every spare pound he could lay his hands on into buying shares. His hunch paid off. With a new stock market flotation, overnight he had made a small fortune. He quickly sold his shares and reinvested most of the capital in something less risky. He was now at a loose end. He didn't particularly want to work for anyone else in some dead end job so he decided to renovate his tatty Georgian flat. He found the work satisfying and soon found himself buying another and then another rundown property to completely work over and sell for a tidy sum. He bought dozens of books on period property and taught himself how to renovate properly. And so, he suddenly found himself sitting with the title of 'period property renovator' around his neck. Now, some years later with some considerable funds in the bank, a row of discrete houses rented out to discerning tenants, he was able to buy his first large yacht and fulfil a long awaited dream. To cross an ocean, the mighty Atlantic!

.

Chapter 3

The morning dawned on *Ellentari* and on deck the excitement had been palpable. Nobody had slept much and one by one they had all risen and dressed within ten minutes of each other. Gathered on deck, a moist November wind ruffled Connie's hair. She looked alert and full of energy despite only about five hours sleep.

'I couldn't sleep, I'm too excited I suppose.'

She smiled at Toby as he came and stood next to her on deck.

'Me too. I thought I'd make some tea and sit on deck until the sun rose. Like some?' he asked.

She nodded so he climbed down below to the galley and filled the kettle. The slight phut and smell of camping-gas rose from below decks. The sounds of mugs rattling and the fridge box door being opened and closed filtered up to the cockpit.

Richard walked along the deck and stood at the front of the yacht. The tapering bow was gently rising and falling with the motion of the teal-coloured water. He gazed out in the direction of the harbour wall entrance and paused there, leaning against the stainless steel guard rail. A salty, fishy smell wafted up to him from where the water sucked and gurgled. After a few minutes he walked softly back to the cockpit and looked at Connie and smiled, the skin crinkling around his blue eyes. He was so excited; he could hardly catch his breath.

'Well today's the big day.'

She smiled back and hugging herself shivered slightly. 'I feel just like a child at Christmas. You know getting up early before anyone else has stirred, and knowing that today was going to be very special. Nobody else was up as early as me, except Daddy and he and I would sit and drink tea – mine was very milky. We would sit and whisper with our toes turned to the fire that he would relight. We ate chocolate biscuits, a special treat then, and waited until the other sleepy heads woke up and started screeching 'Merry Christmas'!'

Richard was surprised at this picture of her early childhood. She was always a very reserved private person, sometimes almost superficial. Her eyes glowed warmly in the half-light and she looked up at the lightening sky, neck outstretched long and tanned. She was quite pretty in an unusual way and her smile never failed to make him feel good even after their 14 years together.

'Tea's up. Who's for a bacon sandwich then? I'm making,' Toby reappeared with three steaming mugs and broke into their moment.

'Thanks,' said Richard. 'It's a good idea to have breakfast now. We'll do a few last minute safety checks and ease her out from her berth. No wind to speak of, so it should be dead easy.'

***

The engine had coughed into life and gently rumbled as Richard took the wheel. Toby and Connie eased the mooring lines and stood ready to fend off if the wind caught her. Richard drove her out of her berth and *Ellentari* slipped from the Santa Cruz marina and ghosted out beyond the harbour walls. The familiar chug of the 75hp diesel engine had rebounded loudly in the marina confines until they were clear and able to set her sails. Coasting along in the gentle early morning breeze they swiftly brought in and stored the fenders and mooring lines in deep deck lazarettes.

'You do realise that we won't be needing those for another two to three weeks don't you?'

'English Harbour, Antigua, West Indies, first stop!' they all chorused together. Tenerife to Antigua, nearly three thousand nautical miles as the seagull flies. How exciting!

Within hours the crew of *Ellentari* were experiencing the Atlantic at its best. A dark indigo blue sea with the slightest of swells was gently buffeting the starboard quarter. Thereafter each day the sun rose not long after the pearly dawn. A glimmering ball of seemingly dripping gold casting its long reaches across the sea. Sea birds had followed them until they were too far from land and now they only saw the occasional wing above the little crested waves, dipping and gliding above the surface hunting for a glimpse of moving silver. The days became hot, the decks smelling that beautiful warm smell of clean wood reminiscent of a sauna room. They were happy, relaxed and settling down to shipboard routine.

They knew the voyage could take them anything up to a month depending on the wind and sea conditions.

As far as Richard was concerned the boat was as near perfect as she was ever going to be. Everything that he could think of had been serviced, checked and replaced where necessary. Richard knew that he was quite a taskmaster and anyone who didn't realise the importance of good planning and preparation would even consider him pedantic. However, he was not concerned with what anyone thought of his running of his yacht. Richard had taken delivery of a new life raft, plenty of emergency flares, both short and long wave radios, and a special receiver for weather forecasts. He had also invested in a satellite telephone and an EPIRB that would flash their latitude and longitude position if activated in an emergency. Heaven forbid, he thought that they would need any of this equipment but it was better to be safe than sorry.

Ellentari was a 45-foot sloop with a deep fin keel. Her hull was white with a double blue stripe running along under the toe rail and the rigorous sea tests had pronounced her as a well-found yacht and extremely comfortable to sail and live onboard.

Now Tenerife was far behind and they had quickly settled down to shipboard routine. The conditions were kind; cloudless sunny days not yet too scorchingly hot, balmy soft-aired nights spent watching the amazing Milky Way with its numerous shooting stars. They had had good steady breezes giving them an average of six to seven knots and seas that were for the most part perfect: no huge waves or swell. Occasionally the wind would die away and they would slow down to a ponderous two or three knots. Then, the boat would develop a roll in the Atlantic swell as she rode up one long wave and then slipped down into the following trough. When the boat really slowed down they would rig a safety towline behind and take it in turns to take a swim off the stern, keeping a sharp lookout onboard for any sinister fin following their wake. The swims were exhilarating and refreshed both spirit and body.

The days seemed to slip away and no one seemed to experience any boredom. There was always plenty to do. Books were read in a day or two, meals to cook, crossword puzzles; Richard took his guitar up forward and lost himself in his music.

Connie was steadily turning a wonderfully lustrous shade of gold and loved nothing better than lazing in the cockpit book in one hand and a cold juice in the other. Work seemed such a dirty word and belonged back in cold depressing dreary England. Sighing in contentment she turned over onto her stomach.

'Can you rub some suntan lotion onto my back please Toby? she asked sleepily.

Toby was very happy. He relished the idea of triumphantly arriving in Antigua and then spending the next five months on *Ellentari* as she slowly weaved her way down the necklace chain of colourful Caribbean islands. He remembered a couple of eventful holidays spent in Jamaica and Barbados and looked forward to visiting Guadeloupe, St Kitts, Nevis, St Lucia, Dominica, and the tiny gems of The Grenadines.

Toby had come to terms with his banishment. He had been careful not to let Richard and Connie know the real reason for his six month leave and knew that he had actually done very well out of it ironically and he was enjoying the time spent in Richard and Connie's company.

He rubbed lotion over Connie's smooth skinned back. Especially Connie's!

Connie he was particularly fond of, which he found rather perplexing. Toby enjoyed most women's company but, he still regarded them as if not exactly inferior to men, certainly not quite *equal*. Connie he treated with much more care than he usually did most of the others.

His careless behaviour to his past lovers bore clear evidence to this. He enjoyed chasing women, bedding them and then ditching them when he was bored. Apart from that he didn't have a lot of use for them *per se*. He just didn't care enough for anyone more than himself.

So, it was to his surprise that he was drawn to Connie and enjoyed being in her company. Perhaps she was more immune to his very obvious charms and didn't fall for his usual sexual innuendo. A very confident woman, she would listen to his carefully rehearsed, well practised string of patter and then with a mischievous glint to her eye skilfully manoeuvre the conversation around to her own advantage. He playfully suggested, she teased. He never missed the opportunity to openly flirt with her and Connie appeared to enjoy the thrill of being in charge and on top. It was fun and the time passed miraculously.

The sun had climbed over a light blue sky and a sea shot through with sparkles. The yacht ran sweetly in her groove just before the wind. The song of the sea was running down her side and in the soft creak of the mast and boom. They had had a few hours of doldrums, the yacht lying melancholy with limp idle sails in a damp oppressive heat under a cloudy sky and rolling on a smooth swell with only a capricious breeze ruffling the surface of the oily sea. Most nights the heavens were lit from rim to rim with pinpricks of stars, held by the black warm velvet. The bloody moon rose until most high and, it seemed like the heat emanated from its imperfect globe.

They had been at sea now for six days and had logged about 875 nautical miles. They had experienced good sailing with very little periods of being becalmed. The skipper was happy with the yacht's progress. Richard knew that traditionally the Trade Winds kicked in stronger as they approached the western Atlantic, and they could then hope for an even faster passage. They were doing better than he had hoped for.

Today had been particularly eventful. The huge golden sun had swiftly risen in the early morning with a promise of yet another glorious day. Very soon the teak deck had warmed in the sun and the sweet wood smell permeated throughout the open cockpit. Half a dozen flying fish had been discovered marooned on the forward deck and had soon disappeared into the frying pan for breakfast.

Richard settled down at the chart table and using his Global Positioning System plotted their longitude and latitude course on the large Admiralty Atlantic chart in front of him. Their progress across the Atlantic could be seen by a series of 'fixes' taken at regular intervals daily and pencilled in on the sea map. The miles were being eaten up, Antigua beckoned. He thought about how sailing today compared to when his father had been at sea. Back then small boats had nothing like the electronic and safety equipment that you could buy now. It must have been almost an entirely different experience, especially during the wartime years. He wished that he had pestered his father into telling him a bit more about his early sailing life. It was too late now of course.

Both the mainsail and the headsail were up and fully laden with a good 17 knots of wind hard on the starboard quarter. That is, the wind was just behind their midships and on the right-hand side of the boat. The sea state was moderate and that fantastic deep inky shade of blue that is only seen miles off shore. They had had no dolphins for company for a few days, but they had recently passed through scores of turtles going the opposite way. One ship had been seen on the horizon and occasionally they would see the telltale slipstream of a jet far above in the brilliant blue sky. The temperatures were now rising; hot during the day and falling back down to a more gentle heat at sunset. It was true what the old sailors used to say, 'sail south until the butter melts and then turn right for the Caribee.'

Toby had the two fishing lines trailing behind the yacht. The boat came smoothly off a slighter larger wave and careered down the other side picking up another half knot. Connie was sitting idly watching him from the starboard teak seat at the back of the yacht. 'It's just like a roller coaster ride at the funfair,' she shrieked with laughter.

'Yep, only this is more impressive,' Toby agreed, letting out more line as he did so. 'Of course you can't get off though,' he continued.

'What?'

'Get off the ride my sweet,' he looked over to her and flashed a smile. His dark hair and tan contrasted heavily with his expensive dental treatment. He had lost a little weight in the time they had been aboard, and the daily exercise routine he practised on board was tightening up his slightly fleshy body.

'I don't mind. At the moment if the conditions stayed like this I wouldn't care if we went all the way to Brazil,' she laughed and ran her hands through her hair. 'Phew, it's getting hot earlier today though.'

'You wait until we really near the Caribbean. If the humidity is high then it'll be stonking. Would you like me to fetch you another cold drink?' he asked her.

'Ooh, yes please. I feel so lazy here in the sun. I know I should be doing something creative or cleaning something but sitting here is so much better,' she smiled up at him as he stood over her.

'Sitting here watching you turn a darker golden brown and trolling a fishing line is good enough for me too. And I especially enjoy watching you practise your yoga on the front deck.' he replied and took himself down below to fetch their drinks.

Connie smiled to herself. He really was a flirt. She hadn't known that he watched her when she went up to the forward deck for her daily yoga exercises. Having two men fancying her was a bit of a turn on. Although she knew Richard loved her he was sometimes too quiet and far too undemonstrative. She knew that Toby had loads of women friends and couldn't remember ever seeing him without some hot beauty attached to his arm. I wonder what he's like in bed, she mused. He's probably very good. Still I don't suppose I'll ever find out, not with Richard around anyway. She laughed to herself as her mind drifted off to consider sex in the sun, in front of the mast, or lying in the cockpit or stretched over the binnacle. Mmm. It was fun to play the tart sometimes!

Suddenly, the line trailing from the port quarter went taut and the rod wheel screamed as 200 feet of nylon was whipped out behind the boat. Connie jumped, bewildered for a moment and forgot her daydreaming.

'Fish!' she yelled, 'Toby fish!' She leapt up from her seat, 'slow the boat down.'

Toby rushed up into the cockpit and met Connie coming the other way; they collided with each other and Connie would have fallen if Toby hadn't put a protective arm round her.

'Easy my sweet,' he murmured.

Connie released the port genoa sheet and the sail bagged and flapped with the decreased pressure. Toby was releasing the load on the mainsheet and soon both sails were flogging badly and the boat had reduced her speed to a bare three knots.

Richard appeared in the cockpit, a questioning look of concern on his face. He had been forward in the side cabin immersed in the spares locker. What was happening? He hadn't given any order to slow the boat down. He noticed both Connie and Toby on the back deck, so both crew members were present and unhurt. That was a relief anyway. He then noticed a red-faced Toby at the stern; he was holding the rod in both hands and feverishly trying to reel in at the same time. The strain showed in his bulging arm and neck muscles. Connie watched with interest.

'It's a huge one! I saw it jump a minute ago. Look, there!' he puffed. The iridescent Mahi Mahi leapt four feet into the air way behind the boat. It was desperate to dislodge the treacherous hook from its jaw. 'Give us a hand will you, it's bloody heavy,' he continued, sweat running profusely down his face and soaking his chest.

Connie squealed in excitement as she saw the fish, while Richard hurried onto the aft deck. Together they heaved and reeled the fish closer to the yacht until it was near enough to gaff and haul on board. The fish lay there gasping from the struggle and fight it had put up. Its body was beautiful, glowing with all shades of blue, green and yellow.

Connie held the squeezy bottle of cheap spirits reserved for fishing and carefully poured a little into its gills. The sudden spirit seeping into the fish's gills caused it to die a quicker death instead of the twenty minutes or so of painful bloody thrashing around on deck. It flapped wetly a few times and then lay still, its eyes glazing over and the beautiful turquoise colours of its skin already fading to a darker murkier blue-grey.

'Must weigh a good six to seven kilos,' Toby said looking triumphant, 'have you room in the freezer?'

'We'll have some tonight and I'll make cerviche for tomorrow's lunch. I'm sure I have enough space now as we're eating well into the meat rations.' Connie replied, 'well done! Well done both of you for hauling it in. It looked like hard work.'

Toby grinned and nodded his agreement. 'I'll clean the fish for you and cut it up into fillets, OK?'

He swilled the remaining blood from the rear deck after gutting the fish. A lone shark swam stealthily behind *Ellentari*, its grey fin showing clearly in the boat's wake. It paused unseen and swiftly snapped at the dumped entrails before continuing on its journey.

Richard was reading a weather fax he had downloaded onto his laptop computer. Everything looked fine for their area. There seemed to be a blow some way to the south of them. The winds were strong and were going from a southeast to a westerly direction, but it was predicted to pass in front of them. Storms were not unheard of in November, but usually the weather was benign.

He decided to keep a close watch on it, just in case it crept nearer to their sailing area. It always paid to be prudent. If it did come closer then they could always slow down and let it pass on ahead. He made a few notes and then closed down the computer and stowed it safely away. A mention of the weather report was made in the log and then he decided to join the others on deck. He climbed halfway up the companionway ladder, the hot, bright sun hitting him squarely in the face forcing him to squint. Silently he took in a scene of Toby quietly massaging suntan lotion onto Connie's back. Still thinking of the weather report he was slightly mesmerised and didn't immediately react to Toby's hand lightly trailing across her browning skin. It was only when Toby slowly slipped his fingers under her bikini top that he realised what he was watching. He was rather startled and crossly climbed the remaining two steps up into the cockpit. What was Toby playing at?

Toby looked round at the sound behind him and swiftly removed his offending hand. He covered his movement by reaching for the suntan lotion. He didn't look discomforted in any way; instead he held the bottle out to Richard and drawled, 'Your job I think old boy.'

***

The wind had persisted around a steady 15 to 17 knots all day steadily from the northeast. During Toby's watch from midnight to 0300 hours the wind freshened and the boat heeled over at a steeper angle. Their boat speed increased and soon they were charging along at a good nine knots. The full main and genoa were still up and Toby wondered fleetingly if they had more sail out than was needed. Half an hour later and the wind had gone up a notch. Maybe it's a good time to reef down he thought. There's no need to wake the others. I know what to do. He carefully released the tension in the genoa sheet, slowly letting it slip on the winch. When the sail started to flog he immediately started to wind in the genoa deck line and the sail began to shorten. When it was about two thirds of its original size he tensioned up the sheet. The large mainsail was still causing them to heel over and the yacht's automatic pilot was finding it difficult to maintain her course. A reduction in this sail could only help calm everything down. Connie hated being heeled over; reducing sail would earn him brownie points.

The night was beautiful, a clear sky with no light pollution. The profusion of stars in the Milky Way was stretched out above his head and, with a gigantic golden moon hanging over the horizon he could see almost as clearly as if it were day.

The boat raced on with the water cascading down the portside deck, gurgling out the scuppers and over the stern transom. The boom creaked in protest and somewhere a metal shackle started up a rhythmic tempo against it. Wearing his safety harness and lifejacket Toby moved behind the large cockpit steering wheel and began to prepare the reefing line and mainsheet. The electric winch ground noisily and reverberated through the deck. A figure suddenly loomed at his side. Richard had awoken to the different motion of his yacht and with a quick glance took in the situation.

'We're going to have to bring her more head to wind to reduce the power in the sail to reef. It's impossible at this point of sail. When I say so, take her off auto and bring her around starboard about one hundred degrees and hold her there until I tell you to turn back onto our right course. OK?' He shouted to make himself heard above the increased wind.

'OK.'

Richard took over the reefing line. Toby stood behind the wheel and steered by hand, turning the wheel when Richard gave the order. The boat responded quickly and the motion immediately changed; large waves smacked at the bow and more water rushed down both decks. The boat shuddered and bucked with the force of the water as she came to a near stop. The lightened mainsail whacked and cracked as it hit the wind head on. Richard took in a third of the sail and gradually retightened the line securely.

'OK. Now start to bring her back slowly, I'll –.'

Bang! The boom shot across to the other side – the wrong side. Toby had turned the wheel the wrong way and had inadvertently gibed the mainsail.

'No take her back, take her back! Otherwise the headsail will back and we'll be in trouble,' Richard yelled urgently.

Toby stood stock still, confused. The boat continued to turn. Richard reacted by grabbing the wheel and turning hard to port; the boat responded sluggishly.

'Pull in the mainsheet or we'll gibe the boom again. MOVE!' Richard shouted frantically.

Toby woke up from the moment's panic and flung himself across the cockpit somehow entangling his legs in his harness safety line in his movement and grabbed the mainsheet with his left arm. Bang! The boom had swung across to its correct position, the mainsheet stretching out tautly from its outer end. There was a sudden crack and a scream from Toby as the rope tightened round his wrist and snapped it. He fell down into the well of the cockpit bellowing in pain, his arm trapped. Richard swiftly put the yacht back on its autopilot course, and bent down to help Toby. The boats' motion had calmed down enough for him to gently release the tight rope and secure it in the jammer. Toby continued to moan and clutch at his wrist while Richard carefully sat him up on the bench seat. Toby whimpered in protest, completely shocked and dazed.

'Connie,' Richard roared, 'Connie, we need you up here!'

Amazingly she had slept through the drama, her dreams probably only registering less heel to the boat and a gentle slowing motion.

Toby's face appeared deathly pale in the bright moonlight; an abrasion stood out clearly on his right temple. He opened his mouth to say something and promptly vomited on the cockpit floor. Connie appeared, clutching a thin sarong around her body. Richard filled her in with the last few minutes' events and she quickly got the message. He needed a plaster of Paris splint and an injection of 10mg Nalbuphine hydrochloride analgesic to help the pain.

A grim-faced Richard was left to clear up the vomit.

***

Richard was livid. It showed in his face and in the firm set of his jaw.

'Why the hell didn't you call me?' he thundered. 'You know it's always difficult to reef a boat this size on your own, and especially risky at night!'

Toby looked slightly abashed. He raised his head and the bruised temple stood out vividly. He had a moustache of sweat on his top lip and beaded perspiration on his brow.

'I thought I could handle it. We've done it dozens of time before,' he argued.

'You could have caused a lot of damage and endangered us all, apart from the injury to yourself.'

'Well I didn't and as you rightly say the only damage is to me. Now if you don't mind *Captain B* I'm officially off-watch and I'm going to bed.' Whereupon he clumsily heaved himself up with his good right arm and walked unsteadily forward to his cabin. He slammed the door crossly behind him.

Richard was shocked. Apart from the injury to himself, he could have seriously wrecked the boom or mast. Where would that have left them? A thousand miles from the nearest hospitable land, that's where. He knew the rules about calling for help at night. Richard had made it plain. *Nothing* was to be done without his say so. There could only be one captain on a boat and his word went.

'Arrogant bugger,' he exclaimed.

'Don't start. Stop being grumpy,' said Connie packing away the medication into the well-stocked first aid box. 'He feels bad enough about this I'm sure. It's just shock and the pain he's in. I'll go and speak to him.'

'Leave him for now. Bloody jerk. Let him sleep off his petulance. He's really annoyed me the last few days.'

'Oh why's that?' she looked over at Richard enquiringly.

'Well apart from tonight's little fiasco let me list the things.' He held up his fingers to count.

'He left the fridge wide open whilst he was fishing, spilt coffee all over the new Atlantic chart, left the forward heads shower dripping, broke the toggle on the radio, scratched my latest Stones CD, blocked his heads once – no twice now, *and* scoffed the last of the Bounty bars! He's just bloody careless and thinks of no one but himself. OK? Isn't that enough to make anyone grumpy? And now he's got you running around like the proverbial. No leave him to stew alone.'

'Oh for goodness sake anyone could have had bad luck. He's just a little accident-prone sometimes. Don't keep acting like Captain Bligh. You make us both feel uncomfortable sometimes. Even I have to keep making sure I don't break any of your rules.'

'I've explained there has to be rules.' He sounded exasperated. 'Safety is paramount on a small ship and there is only one skipper. It is my responsibility to ensure that my crew and yacht are safe at all times.'

'I know all that, it's just that sometimes you –' she stopped and shrugged, 'oh I don't know, you're just a little too intense sometimes. Anyway, I'm still going to look in on Toby, I just want to make sure he's OK. I've just given him a strong analgesic for the pain and to help him sleep. He is my responsibility as my patient. Have a good watch.'

With that she turned round and walked forward to Toby's cabin. She tapped quietly on the door, and then softly called out to Toby. On hearing a muffled response she went in and shut the door behind her.

Richard stood for a moment and glowered at the closed door. No sound came from within. His blue-grey eyes looked bleak and then gained a steely glint. With a sickening feeling of exclusion and misunderstanding he once more donned his lifejacket and climbed up into the cockpit.

***

Morning dawned. The sky gradually lightened in the east with streaks of pearly mauve and grey. The rising sun caught the tiny white cumulus high above and fringed the edges with gold. The sun suddenly burst over the horizon and soon the inky black deep was charged with golden bands.

Richard had stood a double watch this night, Connie hadn't relieved him and his pride forbade him to go below and request her presence on deck. He had moodily sat in the quiet of the cockpit, trying to read or listen to music. He was now a little cold and extremely tired. He needed a hot shower, breakfast and some rest. He presumed Connie had kept her vigil on Toby throughout the night. Apart from his broken arm, she said she wanted to ensure that the bump on his head was nothing.

At that moment she appeared in the galley. She too looked tired and dishevelled.

'I'm going to make Toby some breakfast. Would you like some too?' she asked.

'No thank you. What I really want is some sleep. So if you don't mind I am going to bed. Do you think you could stand watch for a few hours at least?' He watched her carefully.

'Sarcasm doesn't become you Richard, of course I can. Go to bed. I'll call you if I need you.'

She turned away and started the makings of breakfast. The bacon smelt delicious as Richard closed his cabin door.

'Men,' she thought. 'Why are they so childish sometimes? Talk about melodramas and amateur dramatics!'

***

For the rest of the day everyone suddenly developed either very good manners or sat with extremely long silences. Connie stood her watches and devoted a lot of her time to Toby. She was forever fetching him cold drinks, snacks, medication and meals. He had ventured out into the salon but Richard's all too apparent forced good nature soon had him scuttling back to the confines of his cabin. Richard had decided to bite his tongue and say no more about the matter sang-froid. Toby took the easy way out.

At present Connie was closeted in Toby's cabin, as Richard knew she would be. Injection time again it appeared. There was a little laughter from behind the closed door and then silence.

Richard gritted his teeth and chewed the end off his pencil in anger. He had just finished taking a fix and he now wrote the yacht's position in the ship's log. He had written a full report on the accident and was still very tired and badly needed a cat nap. He wished she would come out and he could go and have a sleep. Surely he wasn't going to have to go and get her? I bet there wasn't any lack of discipline during Dad's time on board he thought to himself sourly.

The cabin door opened and Connie slipped out smiling at Toby over her shoulder. He heard Toby say something and she let out a slight gasp and then a low laugh.

Christ! She actually giggled like a schoolgirl Richard thought.

Connie walked through to the salon, the spent syringe in her hand.

'What are you playing at?'

Connie coolly studied her husband. 'I've no idea what you're talking about but, I think I can guess. Stop looking at me like that. He's hurt and feeling sorry for himself. Can't you understand?'

'Hhmp! I understand that I need to sleep. It's your turn now.' Richard got up from the chart table and stomped off down into their cabin.

***

By day nine Toby considered that he'd probably wrung every last bit of sympathy out of the situation and calmly announced that he could resume his watches. He sat in the cockpit under the sun awning, sure of himself now and acting slightly cocky. Richard remained annoyed from his overall behaviour, but knew that they still had a long way to go and peace had to reign on his boat. An argument, annoyances, niggles and character traits all became way over the top if you let them in a closely confined boat. It was much better to let things settle down. Let everything blow over and try to get back to something like a status quo. After all, Antigua was what, a week away? As soon as they arrived Toby could see a doctor and then he was off the boat as far as Richard was concerned. He could do what he liked, but he was sure he'd have to fly home. Richard's responsibility towards him would then end and he could start enjoying being alone with Connie again. He was sure they could get back to the normal loving relationship they had had before Toby had arrived and upset things.

He was surprised how much the past few days had annoyed and unsettled him. He'd always felt Connie and he had a good, trusting and happy relationship. He didn't understand Toby's aggressiveness and Connie's seeming indifference to her husband's feelings. He spent more time on his own playing his guitar or reading. The boat claimed a lot of his time too as he maintained the yacht's equipment and keep a beady eye on the weather. The weatherfax had now changed the status of the 'blow' that was forecast into a late season storm. Thankfully it was not one of the huge catastrophic hurricanes that regularly beat down on the Caribbean islands and Florida during the summer season. According to the data Richard interpreted from his laptop computer it still looked like it would pass them by and they would remain unscathed. He'd get another weatherfax a bit later on that day and if necessary change the boat's course then if they were in any danger of running into bad weather.

What with Toby's injury and his wife's surprising behaviour *and* now this nearby storm, life wasn't quite so good as when they had first left Tenerife.

Chapter 4

They had now been at sea for ten days and were well over half way to Antigua. Morning dawned on a dozing Connie in the cockpit around 6 a.m. The sun wasn't the usual fireball rising in the east over the deep blue perfect skies that they were used to.

The complete horizon was hugged by a malevolent looking deep purple shadow. Above the horizon, the sky had amassed huge rolling clouds that were shot through with a strange pewter and copper hue. These clouds were speeding frantically across the sky in all directions. As the dawn continued to break, the air seemed to be full of charged static and a bolt of brilliant white lightning suddenly flashed ahead of the yacht and all around them. Off to the port side and far behind, there was the fierce growl of enormous thunder, cracking and rolling and gathering in volume as it travelled nearer. There was a strange up and down motion to the yacht on a sea that had now changed to an eerie colour of molten grey with steep irregular waves. The wind was rising and the sound through the rigging was alarming to listen to. Within a minute it had climbed to a nerve-jangling crescendo as the waves began bursting with a surf that crashed against the boat's hull. Somewhere a newly loosened stay was twanging in the wind and below there were the beginnings of strange bangs and thuds. Without warning a sudden deluge of warm rain dumped on the deck making it difficult for Connie to see and breathe. She climbed below and hurried aft to wake Richard. On reaching their cabin she saw he was already up and dressed, struggling into a lifejacket and harness.

'It looks bad,' she said. She hated rough weather and a tremor of fear ran through her.

'I can tell by the change in motion. It's come up quick. Keep your lifejacket and harness on, we're probably in for a blow.' He pushed past her in the galley. Toby appeared from his cabin rubbing the sleep from his eyes.

'The sound on the hull is bloody awful, it's impossible to sleep,' he said.

'Get your safety gear on,' was all Richard replied as he clipped on to the safety line in the cockpit.

As he climbed up the companionway ladder he was assaulted it seemed from every direction by wild blasts of hot wind. The thunder and lightning continued, cracking and flashing overhead. It was certainly wild out here.

He looked at the sea in amazement; it seemed to have grown to unbelievable steepness and the waves struck the yacht with an enormous force. The thunder rose in volume and filled the air with its bellowing. The roaring mass of rain hissed down on the sea's surface. Connie appeared pale and trembling in the cockpit opening as the yacht was hit by a huge wave and she was violently thrown to one side, smashing herself against the bulkhead.

'We've got to reduce sail,' Richard yelled.

Connie was frozen to the cabin's sole and rubbed her bruised shoulder. She didn't attempt to stand up or move from her position on the floor.

'You must help me,' he continued.

She shook her head, her face pale of colour. 'I can't,' she croaked.

Toby staggered over to the companionway ladder. 'I will!'

'Don't be daft, you've only got the use of one arm,' argued Richard. 'Connie! Get up here now!'

Slowly Connie climbed the ladder and looked around her, biting her bottom lip to stop herself crying out in alarm. The scene was now terrifying. Richard put an arm around her as he explained what he wanted her to do. 'Don't look out there. Concentrate on what I tell you. You can do it darling, you've never let me down before.' He gave her a reassuring squeeze and made sure she was ready before releasing the sheet.

The strength of the wind was now such that the rain and spray hit them forcibly in their faces, half choking them. Slowly, they managed to completely lower the mainsail and reduce the headsail to a mere scrap of canvas. The boat responded by calming down a little. She had less heel enabling her to remain more upright; now she gamely clawed her way on through the waves. The overhead thunder continued from one stunning thunderclap to another and the rain beat down mercilessly on the cabin roof.

'Any washing you need doing?' Richard said to Connie at an attempt to make her smile.

There was a sudden tremendous roar from the starboard side as a gigantic wave thundered into them. Richard and Connie were hit and the force of the water sent them tumbling and crashing across the cockpit; their safety lines pulling them up sharply, preventing them being swept overboard.

'You'd better get below,' he shouted as he helped Connie untangle her harness line and safely guided her down through the hatch.

Richard remained in the cockpit and looking at the side of the yacht he saw that part of the guard rail had disappeared. As they came up on the top of a wave he realised that it hadn't been torn away as he'd first thought, but that the sheer weight of the water had flattened the stainless steel stanchions. Looking further out across to the horizon he saw an enormous, heaving indigo sea laced with white streams of foam and broken water. They raced westwards. Somehow their yacht didn't seem quite so substantial out here now as she was tossed around on the furious sea. A fleeting thought of his father passed though him as he crawled below, gasping and wet through. Barker senior had had to put up sometimes with ferocious weather during his time in the Royal Navy. Richard put the washboard in its allotted slot to prevent the water flooding down the companionway into the salon below. Connie was sitting huddled on the floor crying; huge tears mingling with the salt upon her face, wet puddles around her. A concerned Toby was attempting to console her with a one-armed hug. The noise above and below was no quieter as the bilge pumps were going like the clappers. Gallons of water were being pumped out and gallons more were furiously being thrown right back at them.

It was obvious to Richard that they had caught the tail end of the storm and he had no idea how long it would last. The ocean heaved and the thrust of the wind drove the boat further and faster. The onslaught on the yacht continued. The wind howled in the rigging and monstrous waves crashed into the hull. White spume flew horizontally blinding him

The ghastly conditions continued all that day and the following night, relentless never ending, leaving all three of them feeling exhausted and anxious. Connie was nearly paralysed with fear and lay prostrate on the cabin sole; the narrow gap between the salon table and static seating confined her body and prevented her from hurting herself as the yacht was thrown around. Toby was sitting grim-faced wedged behind the salon table clinging to the grab rail with his right arm. He found it especially difficult with his still painful broken arm. Richard was seated; legs sprawled at the chart table, doing his best to get an up-to-date weather report. The thunderstorm prevented good radio propagation and so far he was unable to make any contact.

Earlier, Connie had been totally freaked out begging him to either turn back or radio for help, Toby adding his own voice to back her up. Richard thought that both ideas were totally over the top; they were in no danger of sinking and so long as conditions didn't get any worse they would be OK. He was exhausted. The last few days had really taxed him. Dark shadows ringed his eyes and his hair was encrusted with thick salt.

He had been covering all the watches as both Toby and Connie were incapacitated with seasickness and he was desperate for a rest. 'Toby, I have to lie down for a bit. I've checked the radar, there is nothing within a radius of 30 miles from us, so we shouldn't get run down or hit anything. Give me half an hour or so and I should be OK.' He didn't wait for Toby to agree or disagree but stumbled back into his cabin. He dragged off his uncomfortably wet clothes and dropped them on the floor. He crawled into his bunk and lay snugly against the lee cloth, safely keeping him within his bed. Thankfully he closed his eyes and sleep overcame him instantly.

***

He awoke some time later that day. It was quieter. It felt different. He felt a swell. Now it was a new regular up and down motion. Pulling himself together he dressed in dry clothes and entered the main cabin. The whole boat was a disgusting mess. Books, charts, games were strewn everywhere. In the galley the cupboard that usually contained the pots and pans was wide open; its contents disgorged. Coffee dregs were spilt onto the galley work surface and the sugar bowl had dumped itself into this mess covering the surrounding work surfaces and walls with a horrible sticky goo.

Richard hurriedly put as much away as he could. Anything heavy was especially dangerous if it was sent flying. Luckily the heavy steel cooker was still on its sturdy gimbals. If that broke loose they would soon know it. Connie and Toby were fast asleep, still in the same positions as when he had left them earlier. Richard had a quick scout around, checking that there were no other vessels around bearing down on them.

He was concerned about the weather. This could be just a lull and anything might happen. However, it was good to make the most of the respite and clear up the boat as best they could. Toby and Connie managed to force some salt biscuits and cola down themselves under Richard's insistence. He explained that the replacement salt and sugar was necessary treatment for seasickness. He made himself some thick corn beef and pickle sandwiches, which he devoured ravenously. He thought nothing had ever tasted so good. But, they needed something that was nourishing and hot; so he got out a large saucepan and into it opened some tins of vegetable and chicken soup. He placed steaming mugs in front of Connie and Toby and stood over them while they slowly sipped their way through the tasty broth polishing off two mugfuls himself with great satisfaction.

Later Richard went on deck to survey the scene outside. The sky retained its ugly, sullen colour but the sea now possessed a heavy molten slick overlying the whitecaps that sluggishly rolled down the waves. The decks were washed clean of dust and dirt and the drying teak gleamed golden. The genoa halyards were loose and needed bringing into the cockpit for easy access. The deflated dinghy was still amazingly secured on the stern push pit and the life raft remained in place on its mid-deck cradle. Apart from the crushed guard-rail stanchions there appeared little damage to the yacht and all the systems were working properly below decks. The little niggle of doubt and fear that had been with him for the past few days disappeared. They would be all right! The yacht was well built and would keep them safe, so long as they were cautious and kept their heads. He wasn't a religious man, but Richard thanked God for keeping them safe so far.

***

A few hours had now passed; they'd all managed to get some decent rest. As Richard finished making another entry in the ship's log he realised that the regular sea swell had begun to change to a strange uneasy motion. There was neither a strong pitching nor a heavy roll; instead every now and then there was a quick lurch that had no real direction. The yacht creaked in the rolls and lurches; when suddenly the wind came at them with a piercing shriek. The little scrap of genoa they were flying was torn from its foil; the boat checked and then lay heavily over on her side in a near broach.

Connie screamed, her mouth an ugly wide gape in her ashen face, 'I want to get off! I want this to stop now!'

The weather now had a direction and a meaning with the blasts passing to the north and west of them. These winds were succeeded by a pent-up southeast gale, which blew with enormous force causing a swell that could even have rivalled the roaring forties. They were now in a hard blow, a very, very hard blow with a dangerous following sea.

A sudden deafening crash on deck had all three of them look at each other. A panic-stricken and white-faced Connie turned to Richard.

'What do you think that was?' Her lower lip trembled and her eyes were red-rimmed from past crying.

'I don't know. I only hope it's not the life raft come adrift. That would be disastrous if it broke free. It could crash through a hatch or go overboard. I'd better go and check.'

He grabbed his wet waterproofs and dragged them on over his dry clothes. His lifejacket and harness were lying on the floor ready to don in a hurry. He finished dressing as fast as he could; the crashing on deck was becoming more urgent. Please, God let it not be the life raft! It was heavy enough to handle in calm conditions and would be a complete bugger during heavy weather.

Climbing out of the cockpit was difficult and quite terrifying. He tried not to notice the mountainous seas all around and crouched low on deck as he clipped his harness onto the safety line. Grim-faced and teeth clenched he edged forward; at times waist-deep in swirling green water as a wave hit the hull and cascaded down around him. The banging up front was now relentless. He reached the mast and immediately saw the offender. The spinnaker pole had broken loose from its attachment and was banging against the mast causing the racket below. The ropes were not taut enough and he needed some extra line to properly restrain it. He would have to retrace his footsteps and fetch some from the cockpit locker. It all took so long and so much energy. The wind buffeted and shook him as he crawled along the deck on his hand and knees, half-choking in the salty spray.

Below decks Connie was shaking uncontrollably. She wanted to get off this boat now. If not then she wanted to die. She had had enough. She couldn't think straight, she felt sick, weak and horribly ill. It was just all too much. Why oh why had she ever agreed to this? Damn Richard and his sailing. It was all *his* fault. She should never have listened to his exciting, enticing tales about the Caribbean. Right now she felt that she hated him. Damn. Damn. Damn!

Toby was slumped in his usual corner behind the saloon table, nursing his arm. He too looked stricken, his eyes bruised and tired. The yacht lurched and corkscrewed off a monster wave and Connie fell hard against the chart table. She shrieked with renewed fear and then heaved herself onto the bench seat behind it, wedging herself in. The red glow from the lights on the bank of electrical switches on the control panel was beside her. She quietly sobbed to herself as she lay her head down on the damp surface. She couldn't think about anything else except getting off the boat. As the noise calmed down above she stopped crying and sat up and glanced around her. She noticed the state of the cabin, with the wet streaked floor and the renewed mess from their possessions being thrown around them. She glanced at the battery state on the control panel and then across at Toby.
'How do you feel?' she asked.
'Ghastly.'
She again looked at the electrical panel overhead and her glance lingered on the high frequency radio set. Turning her head her scared eyes met those of Toby's. They looked at each other, the creaks and bangs going on all around them. Neither said a word. But, they knew what the other was thinking. That help could be just around the corner. Just with the flick of a switch.

Chapter 5

Out on deck Richard had his own battle with the spinnaker pole. Its weight felt tremendous under the heaving deck and he was thankful for his safety harness. He fleetingly thought of sea horror stories in the yachting press where harness lines had parted and given way. Their owners' bodies were often never recovered from their watery graves. He hurriedly dismissed the idea. Don't go down that morbid path. His equipment was in top condition. He frequently checked it. He returned to the problem with the pole. His hands were cold from the constant wetness and twice the pole had smashed down onto his knuckles, skinning them and drawing blood. He winced and swore and tried to block out the pain. It was imperative to contain the sixteen-feet long heavy lump of metal. It had already swung out alongside the deck and whacked against the starboard saloon window. If it continued to do so it could easily smash the Perspex and then they would have big trouble with the water coming directly into the boat. After what seemed like hours he got it under control and firmly secured it in its proper position on the mast. His chest was heaving with exertion as he crawled back, blood smearing the sopping deck, mixing with the seawater and running away through the scuppers. He rolled into the cockpit, utterly exhausted and feeling slightly nauseous with the pain and exertion. He lay there for a moment or two regaining his breath. Miraculously the autopilot was still coping with the sea. It could at least steer a better path than any one of them could for any length of time. Still, he had better check the battery state as by now they would be getting very low and would need a boost of recharging by the generator or engine.

Painfully he climbed down the lurching steps into the saloon. Here the relative quietness and calmness had a soporific effect. He leant against the steps and closed his eyes, relief flooding through him. A pulse beat in his neck and his whole body ached. Richard opened his eyes and took in the scene before him.

Toby had moved and was now sitting on the end of the settee hanging onto the chart table for support. He was studying his broken arm and didn't look at Richard; neither did he ask what the noise had been or whether everything was all right on deck. Connie remained at her place at the chart table, her hands clenching the edges, white-knuckled. She looked over to Toby. There was a certain calmness about her. She appeared more at ease although her mouth was still set in a grim tight line. She too neither mentioned the noise or the state of their boat.

Richard shook himself, annoyed at their apparent lack of either concern or involvement. Sometimes he felt that both of them could do with a short, hard slap to help them get a grip on themselves and perhaps lend at least half a hand. He took off the wet weather gear that was steadily dripping over the cabin sole leaving small salty puddles. He wondered about the latest weather reports. He needed to look at them to decide which course to take with this new stormy weather. How long was it likely to last and what wind speeds were they likely to expect? So far they had already experienced steady 55 to 70 knots of wind. Please God it must abate soon, surely?

'I need to have a look at the weather report. Can you please move Connie?'

He glanced at the electric panel ready to turn the SSB radio set on to download the weather report onto his laptop. He noticed the radio microphone was lying adrift on the chart table and the SSB was already switched on. He said nothing for a moment. Had he left it on from the last time he'd used it? No, he was a stickler for power saving. He looked at Connie and then Toby. Why were they so quiet? No weeping and wailing now. Furthermore, they both looked almost, well, guilty?

Connie stood up and made to push past Richard. He stopped her gently but firmly. He took hold of her arm and looked down at her. She stole a glance up at him and immediately he knew the answer from her eyes. He didn't want the answer. She disentangled her arm from his and moved over to join Toby on the sofa. Their close togetherness caused a jolt in Richard that he hadn't felt before. Connie took a breath, swallowed, faltered and then stopped. She looked afraid but then finally piped up with,

'Help's coming. It's on its way. A cargo ship is in the vicinity, less than 200 miles from here and it has deviated to pick us up!' she spoke quickly. Her face was suddenly suffused with colour as if the telling had forced her blood to race round her body.

'It's what? What have you done? You stupid bloody woman!' he asked quietly.

'But, they said they could pick us up! We're going to be alright!'

'We're already all right! This blow will pass and we are not in danger. How many times do I have to tell you this is a good sea-going yacht? Not a dinghy, not a racing surf board, but a well-found yacht. How dare you call up for help? On whose authority?' he finally bellowed at her, utterly furious.

'No we're not all right, we're going to sink and drown. And I have had enough of this and of you, you fucking power freak. I don't want to die!'

'I can't believe this. Call and cancel it right now!'

Furiously Richard grabbed Connie by the arm and dragged her back over to the chart table. He pushed the microphone at her. 'See if you can undo what you've done. Apart from putting another ship to trouble, we don't need them, for Christ's sake!'

Connie screamed an obscenity at Richard and furiously lashed out at him, hitting him across the mouth. He stepped back, shocked at her reaction. This was so totally alien to him, so unlike her normal controlled behaviour. He knew she hated bad weather especially gales, but she always calmly coped and moreover trusted his judgement. This was just not in her character and he felt that something else was underfoot. Perhaps Toby with his accident had convinced her otherwise?

Richard felt a strange unease pass through him. A strange feeling gripped at his heart. He again grabbed her arm and this time he roughly shook her.

'Pull yourself together. We've been in plenty of gales before, just try and treat this as being a little worse.'

She looked at him as if he was mad and screamed, 'No it's not, it's not! It's horrible and I can't stand it anymore. I'm so scared and so too is Toby.' She did look quite terrified. Her eyes were wild and her mouth was back to its thin white line. Richard could clearly see that nothing was going to convince her otherwise.

There was a sudden deafening crash against the hull and the yacht slew to one side as she careered down off another gigantic wave. Large pilot books cascaded heavily down from their shelf above the chart table landing with a resounding thump and hitting both Connie and Richard in their progress. Another lurch and they continued sliding across the table, catching the microphone cable still lying where it had been left, on their journey to the floor. The HF microphone was ripped from the set and joined the books in the wet.

'Shit,' said Richard as he dived to save it. 'Shit. It's too late. Now we can't call anyone to cancel. It's bust and I don't have another. You really have done it now. Satisfied? For God's sake why couldn't you trust me? I've never let you or anyone else down before. We've always got through everything together. Was this all your bloody idea or did you have a bit of help from friend Toby here?'

Richard looked furiously at the two of them. His body was held rigid and taut with his anger. He glared first at Toby and then back at Connie.

For the first time since they had been married Connie felt afraid of Richard and hesitated before replying.

'Well?'

Toby struggled up from his seat on the sofa, still clinging with his good arm to the handheld for support. He stood up straight and stared Richard squarely in the eyes.

'It was me – not Connie.'

Richard looked steadily at Connie as she took an intake of breath, her face going from white to pink after taking a quick glance at Toby. He turned away and looked at Toby.

'What?'

'I said it was me. Don't blame Con; she had nothing to do with it. Blame me if you like, but I had had enough, what with the pain from my arm and everything.'

He finished and stood there, quietly challenging Richard with his eyes.

'So?'

Richard shook his head in disbelief, not sure what to believe. He dragged his arm across his face and rubbed his sore eyes resignedly.

His look was sad and bleak. He then staggered from the saloon back to his cabin and closed the door. He didn't want to see either of them at that moment. A bright salty taste was in his mouth and he realised he had bitten his tongue.

Toby looked at Connie. Neither quite knew what they felt the most. Relief at the coming rescue or the slightly sickening feeling that they had both lost or at the very least antagonised a good friend causing him great anguish.

'You didn't have to do that,' Connie whispered, 'he wouldn't have hurt me. He's not like that.'

'Well I'm not so sure. He looked bloody murderous and he is so obsessed with his sailing skills and this boat,' he replied shakily.

'Yes but it's only when we're at sea. He becomes a different person with the responsibility of it all. It's quite common among skippers.'

'I'm sure it is. But, look at Captain Bligh and what happened to him!'

Connie managed a slight thin smile. 'That was a bit different. They were hard desperate men.'

Toby passed a hand through his unruly hair and seemed hesitant for a moment. Quietly he murmured.

'I love you. Leave him, come away with me.'

There was a pause. Connie raised her dark violet blue eyes to his.

'What?'

'I said I love you. I don't think I've misunderstood your signals lately either.'

Toby stretched out a hand to her and would have continued but, something in her eyes made him stop. He shook his head and looked away; he felt that he could hardly breathe. He again looked at her, waiting, hope in his face. Then, 'I know it's a huge decision but, I promise *I* won't let you down, ever.'

Richard reappeared quietly in the saloon. He took in the tight, intimate little scene around the table. He gave no indication as to whether he had heard Toby's words or not.

The storm continued to rage both outside and within.

Chapter 6

The crew of *Ellentari* were victims of the continuous vile weather. The sea and wind threw everything at them with a fierceness that they had never before experienced. This, and the personal deepening depression within the yacht's cabin made living aboard almost unbearable. Connie refused to speak to Richard and spent most of the time lying down on the saloon settee feeling sorry for herself. She had quietly overcome her seasickness, but steadfastly refused to assist Richard with anything to do with the boat. It was almost as if she had abandoned him as well as the yacht's well-being. Toby made small attempts to keep the peace and offered his own limited help, which Richard had gratefully accepted. He had managed to make a hot drink and a simple meal with his one good arm and was feeling less useless than before. He made small jokes about the cutting edge of his culinary skills and even managed to entice a small smile out of Richard.

The yacht continued gallantly on her way toward the west, the deep blue sea sluicing along her cabin topsides. She was a game little boat and despite the terrible conditions, was taking the battering better than most yachts would. In this Richard was right. Her hull design and build was extremely good. Despite this, the constant high winds in the rigging and relentless violent waves thrown against the hull would eventually take their toll.

The porthole above the chart table had now begun to weep seawater. Where the flailing spinnaker pole had smashed against the deck, it had caught the porthole frame and buckled the metal surround causing the Perspex to crack under the torsion. They had noticed the broken window and put gaffer tape over the, as yet, minute crack. The tape proved fairly useless and spare clothes had been stuffed around to help mop up the water. The water steadily dripped and then slowly trickled down the bulkhead, running behind the bank of the control panel which housed the navigational instruments, lights, bilge pumps and radios. The steady ingress of water caused the lights to flicker on the panel and there was a sudden silence from the main bilge pump. The second pump continued to work throwing the sea back from whence it came, but Richard knew that this pump was not as powerful as the inert one and it wouldn't be long before it either shorted or burnt out. Sod's Law of the Sea, he thought. The pumps had been a continuous drain on the 24-volt system and the batteries needed recharging. He didn't need to go out on deck yet again, receiving yet another dousing in order to start the engine, all he had to do was run the generator for power.

He pressed the pre-warm button. It came on with the familiar red glow. So far so good. He pressed start. Nothing. Not even a slight cough. The seawater had flooded into the control switch and had shorted out the power supply. To fix the generator he would have to remove the companionway steps to get into the small space behind. The steps were large and heavy, they could be secured safely but it was a difficult task on your own in a violent seaway. There was no other choice; he would have to use the main engine.

Once again he dragged on his uncomfortably damp salt-laden jacket and safety harness. Feeling thoroughly annoyed and dejected he staggered up the steps, holding tightly onto the heaving grab holds. The key was in the ignition but he had a premonition before he turned it. He couldn't believe it. It was a fine time to become a clairvoyant. *Of course* nothing happened. He tried again. In rage and despair he hit the wheel binnacle and yelled to the elements in frustration. Why this now? He'd done everything right. He'd spent hours servicing the engine so that it ran smoothly and sweetly. The weather at this time of year should be good and benign for a perfect Atlantic crossing. Was World Climate Change affecting the hurricane season, allowing a late storm to hurtle across their path? He'd so wanted Connie to enjoy this voyage. He knew that she hated rough weather, but he'd taken every precaution to protect her. It was so bloody unfair. No wonder she hated him at the moment. He had to get something right. True, help was on its way – 200 miles or so to the west – but they had to still be afloat when it finally did arrive.

Wearily, he clambered down from the cockpit ignoring the questioning anxious face of Toby below. Connie remained lying on her side facing the settee cushions. He opened the engine room door and surveyed the wet scene within. Water sloshed around the compartment, the problem obvious. Water had been sucked into the air intakes and flooded the engine. Normally it would be a fairly simple but grubby job in calm conditions but not now; there would be no chance of getting it dried out while the storm continued.

'Ah Richard, I – er think the radar's packed up.'

Toby was moodily staring at a blank screen. Richard groaned in despair.

'That's all we need. I can't get either the genny or the engine to start either.'

Without power both men knew that soon the instruments, GPS, lights, radio and the remaining electric bilge pump would shut down. The bilge pump was vital to them. There was no way that Richard could manually pump out the seawater they had taken on board for very long. His strength would eventually give up. He knew Toby was useless and Connie little better.

Feeling bitterly disappointed and full of anger Richard had to come to a quick decision. There was nothing for it now. The weather showed no sign of easing for the next few hours at least. The situation was becoming more desperate with each minute. They would all have to abandon the yacht and go aboard the ship when it arrived. Richard had earlier briefly thought of possibly offloading Connie and Toby and sailing on alone to Antigua. Connie could fly out and rejoin him later. To go solo now with everything failing and him feeling exhausted would be suicidal.

'Right you two. We'd better get our stuff together. We're definitely going to have to abandon ship now. So, I think, grab your essentials and put them with the passports and credit cards already in the emergency grab bag. Put your lifejackets and harnesses back on and we'd better keep a good lookout for the ship. I'll activate the EPIRB and the radio position given off from it will alert the UK coastguard who will relay our current position to the rescue ship. They shouldn't miss us then.'

Both Connie and Toby looked at each other in relief. Now they were in the clear over prematurely calling for help. Better still they were getting out of this hellhole. Soon the nightmare would be all over. They smiled and each thought about the coming ship. Toby dreamed of a hot meal of bacon and eggs and a stiff drink or two. Connie dreamed of a hot shower, sitting comfortably on a loo without being thrown off and a deep, long sleep in a soft bed. Richard was more prosaic; he knew that their ordeal wasn't over yet.

They had to somehow get onto the approaching ship.

* * *

Connie went aft to fix a support for Toby's arm. 'You need more strapping on that arm,' she had said more like her old self, 'then you'll be able to manage a bit better.'

Toby and Richard were left together in the saloon.

Toby looked rueful as he muttered, 'I'm sorry about all this.'

Richard frowned at him as he continued.

'I know how you feel about her. The yacht I mean, *Ellentari*.'

Richard was momentarily confused before he replied caustically. 'It's only a boat. If human lives are at risk then that must be the first priority.'

He was bitterly trying not to think about the past few days. How everything had suddenly changed. Their dream crossing turned into this mayhem. The weather, their relationships, the uncertainty of it all was gradually wearing him down. His whole world was caving in. He had to be strong for them all.

The yacht was threshing around, skewing her way down, up, down and through the waves. Simple things like gathering their few possessions for the grab bag were extremely difficult. Richard made Toby sit in the cockpit behind the spray hood keeping a lookout for any other boats. He eventually persuaded Connie that she too would be better off up there in the fresh air, ready to get off when help arrived. Together safely clipped on, they huddled under the spray hood, flinching whenever a particularly large wave crashed into the cockpit glass surround, and cascaded down onto them. The seas were still mountainous and the wind howled all around. Spume flew off the wave crests like treacherous frothy lace. Toby was astounded at the ferocity of it all and could only stare in horror. Being cocooned down below for the past few days he was unprepared for the sight that met his eyes. The enormity of what Richard had had to put up with finally got through to him. He cast his eyes all around him. What monstrous seas!

Suddenly, he noticed a loom on the darkening horizon. He rubbed his tired red-rimmed eyes excitedly, a pain throbbing behind his temple. It was! A ship!

'Richard! Richard it's here. The ship, I can see it on the starboard bow.'

He bellowed down to Richard below, straining to overcome the racket that was sounding all around him. Together, he and Connie watched the ship as she battled head on to the oncoming waves.

Richard seemed to fly up the companionway steps. He opened the cockpit locker and pulled out a red plastic container. Inside was a collection of their boat safety flares. He needed to alert the captain of their position; after all they didn't want to be run down by their would-be saviours. He took out a flare; a distress red-rocket flare and fired it into the wind.

***

The ship hove to their side, thereby given some protection to the comparative tiny yacht. The ship's bulk created a slick of calmer water in which *Ellentari* lay, and yet, her mast was still rising and falling with each successive wave that passed under her. The water surged and crashed as it sucked against her side. In the dimming late afternoon light they could just make out the scramble net that the ship's crew had thrown over the side. Somehow that had to be overcome and scaled. Richard knew he would manage it; Connie too was capable so long as she kept her head and didn't look down. But, the injured arm would seriously impede Toby.

Then, there was the problem of the yacht. It wasn't enough to simply abandon her. Left to her own devices she would be a hazard to other shipping and could cause serious problems. Richard had to make the heart-breaking decision to scuttle her. She would slowly fill with seawater and sink forever beneath the cold, deep water of the Atlantic. His heart felt heavy and full of regret; despite everything she had been a good yacht and only an accident with a loose spinnaker pole had caused her electrical problems. Something briefly nagged at the back of his mind. A story his father had told him about his own exploits during the war. He himself had had to scuttle a boat. He just didn't have time to think about that now!

It was agreed with plenty of sign language and bellowing down from the ship's captain that Toby would ascend first, aided by Connie. They had thrown down an additional line that Toby would knot in a bowline and tuck under his armpits. He could then half climb and be half pulled up the scramble net. Richard had to remain behind to knock out the seacocks to fully flood the boat. When he had accomplished this he would then take the grab bag on his back and climb to safety. Assured that the others understood everything, he went below to pick up his hammer.

Toby and Connie had positioned themselves on the lee side waiting for a comparative lull in the yawing of the yacht. They were poised ready to leap across the yawning black space to the ship and her scramble net. The ship's crew hung over the side above them, silently, anxiously watching. The yacht thrashed up and down, dangerously close to the steel hull of the ship. Closer, closer Connie thought; Toby leapt across the dark space and there was a howl of pain as he crashed against the hull. Steadfastly, he managed to crawl a little way up the net aided by the lowered safety rope, until he was clinging above the height of the hull of the yacht and avoiding being crushed as they smacked back together. He clung there panting and whimpering, sea spray blinding his eyes. He remembered Connie back on *Ellentari* and half-turned, yelling at her to jump as the hulls began to drift apart. She hesitated only for a moment then, survival being uppermost in her mind she closed her eyes and jumped. There was a small thump and a terrified scream passed her lips as Connie joined him clamped to the net, just a little below him.
'Good girl! Now climb, climb as quickly as you can.'
He gasped, and began pulling himself up by his one good arm. He slipped on the wet rope as his feet missed their foothold and he fell

away from the ship. Only the restraining rope prevented him from slipping back down into the waters below. As he crashed back to the hull he grimaced with the sharp pain that streaked through him. He had to somehow block it out, in order to survive. Taking a deep breath and with renewed energy, the adrenalin surged within him as he climber higher.

Connie struggled below, but slowly and steadily she made headway up the net. Toby couldn't believe it when he was grabbed by eager outstretched hands and unceremoniously dragged over the ship's side to the safety of her deck. He lay there sobbing in relief, pain and exhaustion. He was safe. He'd made it.

Connie was making better progress now. She was concentrating on finding her footholds in the deepening fading light and was more than halfway up the ship's side. She clenched her teeth and pulled herself another step upwards. She could do this.

The ship lurched and rolled. A sudden monster wave rose up between the yacht and ship and engulfed her. She screamed in sheer terror and panic, saltwater flooding her nose and mouth, choking her. Her cry was torn away on the wind.

Richard had finished the grisly task below and scrambled as fast as he could up out of the now fast filling yacht's saloon. Once on deck he saw with horror that the gap between the yacht and ship had widened. They had been parted by the monstrous wave and now the gap was eight feet or more. *Ellentari* went down and then rose up, the net maddingly out of arms reach. He had to reach it. Once more the yacht ploughed down in a trough and Richard waited, legs braced and stooped, tightly hanging onto the coach roof. The yacht rose and he could just see the lowest rung of the scramble net...

***

The merchant ship spent several hours crisscrossing the ocean in a tight figure of eight pattern searching for Connie. Back and forth they had searched the spume laden, frothy seas. After the ships medico had seen Toby and his arm had been re-strapped he had gone up to the ship's bridge. With his nose pressed against the rain-streaked glass he had vainly looked out at the wave lashed deck and the sea beyond. Once Richard had come round, he had refused any further medical aid for his cuts and had stood alone against the ship's rail hoping, just hoping for what he knew to be a miraculous chance that they might find her. After many hours under the now darkened skies the captain had to tell Richard that the search was futile. She was lost; drowned in the treacherous deep, blue-black ocean.

Richard felt numb. All the trusted clear channel markers of his life had been rearranged into chaos. He was in the dark on automatic pilot, floundering aimlessly in all directions and in constant danger of running hard aground on the rocks. He desperately needed someone he could talk to. He couldn't talk to Toby. He felt that he had betrayed his trust. He thought with regret of his father, now recently dead. He had lived a part of his life in the Royal Navy and he had lost many friends at sea during the war. He would understand Richard's loss and his abject misery at not feeling in control. Too late Dad. It's too late to talk to *you* and I was too late to save *her*.

The ship docked in Southampton and the coroner came aboard to take witness statements. A still stunned Richard gave his account through bloodless lips and afterwards sat silently watching the rain drizzle down the salt-encrusted windows of the wheelhouse. He'd been careless. Accidents happen, but to lose your wife was simply irresponsible beyond belief. The whole tragedy was compounded by his firm belief that she was leaving him for Toby. He'd overheard what Toby had said on that fateful day. His final words being 'I promise *I* won't let you down.'

Well, her *husband* had and nothing was going to change that. He was a complete and utter failure both in his marriage and in maintaining the safety of both of his crew.

One injured and one drowned.

The press were soon hounding him, once he was released from the ship and made his way through the docks. They were waiting vulture-like behind a thin veneer of solicitude.

'Just a few words, Mr Barker. What was it really like, on your yacht during the storm? What do you feel now? Could you have avoided the accident? What about Mr Ellis? How did he injure

himself? Did you not take enough precautions? What about the relationship now between you and Mr Ellis? Does he blame you?'

And on and on it went. The scarcely veiled accusations and insults. He had never before felt so utterly wretched, dejected and alone. His whole world had suddenly changed and collapsed around him. He had been catapulted from a life of comparative ease and uncomplicatedness to this. He had had a happy relationship with his pretty, self-contained wife, a very successful business and a beautiful yacht in which to pursue his dreams. With one cataclysmic heave all had come tumbling down; crashing around his ears and fallen broken, torn and in complete devastation.

Chapter 7

It had been snowing now for about four hours. Usually the winters in Hampshire were mild and often unseasonably warm for England. However, this year from January onwards the weather had been foul. There had been relentless freezing rain accompanied by a sharp icy wind, interspersed with only the occasional dry day. Now February was here with heavy snowfalls dumping all over the British Isles.

The thick fresh snow looked soft and pretty as it silently fell over the South Downs. Groups of children were making the most of an unexpected Friday at home, school being shut as all the pipes had frozen preventing the school heating from working.

Now, excited children well wrapped up in woolly hats and gloves were pulling homemade sledges alongside posher manufactured ones. Their eyes gleamed with glee and their noses were pink, sharp and runny with the cold.

In his house overlooking the hill and valley below, Richard had been standing at the window for nearly an hour. He'd watched as the children climbed up the incline and followed their paths as their homespun craft careered downhill. Their shrieks and whoops of delight carried clearly to him through the thin cold air. He wondered how different their life would have been if Connie had wanted children. His heart still felt as cold as the scene outside.

A sudden light breeze filled the air sending little flurries of snow from the branches of the trees at the edge of his drive. Around the tree trunks he noticed little uncovered clumps of snowdrops peeking through their soft white coverlet. For some reason he thought of his mother; they had always been her favourite wild flower.

He'd been back home in England for two months now. For him they had been two very long, miserable, lonely months. With bitterness he went back over and over that dreadful accident thinking, dying young could never be right. That is, is there ever a right or wrong way to die? Connie's death had definitely been a horrible way to die. She had been subjected to hours of abject terror, not knowing when and if it would all end and being completely incapable of helping herself to remove the object of incalculable fear. Her own horror had gone on and on for hours, a relentless, tortuous period, made all the more terrifying by the brief respite near the end; a slender hope of miraculous salvation. How must she have felt when, with the sheer relief in that moment when the ship appeared, only to have it cruelly dashed away with an unstoppable brutal assault as she was swept from the scramble net?

Richard shook as he imagined how she had felt as she had fallen, with the even more terrible realization that she was now alone, completely alone. Alone and afraid knowing there was to be no redemption. Nothing. No one would be able to save her. No one would hear her scream. No one knew where to look. It was as if she had simply vanished.

And then for Richard, it was hard to mourn for someone when there is no body. In knowing that the person's body will never be found. It placed an additional burden on the one left behind. Richard felt the total helplessness of failing to lay Connie to rest overlaid with pangs of guilt, remorse and deep despair. At the root of it all was the question torn from him. Why not me?

He had no heart for his business and besides his manager had all been geared up for running the company solely in his absence when he was off sailing. Although Richard was the boss and owner he was not welcome. His recent loss made the office workers feel uncomfortable, and frankly Richard was glad to let him get on with it.

Ellentari had been successfully scuttled and the insurance company satisfied with his testimony had settled his claim in full. Despite the money now being in his account Richard had no wish to set foot on another sailing yacht let alone think of replacing her.

The biggest void in his life was the hole created by Connie's death. It was fair to say that their relationship was no longer the passionate, breathless obsession of teenagers, but it had been steady, with good regular sex, and the longer lasting values of trust, respect, understanding and patience. Neither had made great demands upon the other, but they had fitted together like a lock and key. Now, the days were long and the nights far longer. Richard was finding that sleep was hard to come by. He dreamed and relived the last scenes when they had been at sea and these unconscious thoughts coursed through his mind. When sleep did come he would wake startled, sweating and trembling, that terrible journey racing behind his eyes.

In a peculiar way he also missed Toby. Despite all that had gone before them, they had once had a good, easy-going friendship. They had stayed apart on the sea journey to England, each deep in their own dark thoughts. At the time Richard considered that Toby had betrayed his trust and had made a play for his wife. Damn him! Neither had made any attempt to get in touch with one another once they had gone their own separate ways from Southampton docks.

As far as other friends were concerned he was trying hard not to be a burden. Everyone was very supportive; especially in the first few weeks after his return when it was still new and raw upon his nerves. As the weeks progressed however, he seemed to sense that they all somehow seemed to blame him. He thought that maybe they were judging him and it was entirely his own fault. Too bad to lose your boat, but to lose your wife! So he was now taking great pains to avoid them somewhat, not to lumber them with his desolation and so to avoid their censure.

He had never been an overly social animal. He enjoyed a few parties, concerts and suppers with really good friends, but he had never felt that he needed to go out of his way to look for entertainment. He was happy with his own company, Connie in the background doing her own thing, chatting on the phone to friends a glass of red wine in her hand. No, she was more the socialite. Recently he had tried the occasional pint in his local but soon found that there wasn't much fun drinking on your own. The pints had slipped down all too quickly and he soon found himself staring at the bottom of the glass. The locals all knew who he was from the press and he grew to hate their inquisitive stares and sidelong glances. Something amounting to paranoia raised itself whereby he knew that they were all judging and condemning him. It wasn't long before he felt that it was safer and less stressful at home. As long as he tried hard and didn't drink too much, he found himself beginning to cope again. He remembered his father's words spoken long ago when he was much younger and reckless. 'Take one day at a time. None of us can know what is round the corner, so tread carefully and treasure each good moment while it lasts. Nothing is forever.' A quiet man of very few words, Richard wondered what his father had been thinking of when he had said this.

Time however, was heavy in his hands. Daytime television was an anathema to him and so banal. Since when had we become a nation addicted to trivial imports, and afternoon tripe of game shows and contrived chat shows? They were nothing more than blatant advertising aimed at the gullible masses he thought as he threw the remote control down on the settee in disgust.

Perhaps he'd get a couple of cats for company. Better still a dog. Most days he found himself traipsing over miles of countryside and had rediscovered some quiet enjoyment in stumbling across hitherto unknown hamlets and empty valleys. A dog would give him every excuse to be out and about in the country and he liked the thought of unconditional love from a furry friend. Stop being morose and pathetic he told himself. It will get you nowhere.

Never overweight anyway, the miles of exercise had removed any surplus flesh that he carried. Now, his face looked gaunt and hollow-cheeked, with tightness around his blue eyes. Today he looked particularly grim as he had one task that he had been putting off: Connie's things. Not those lost when the yacht went down, but the stuff left here in their English home.

Her clothes. The trace of her scent still lingered. The silk of her underwear, neatly folded in the top drawer of her dressing table. Antique crystal glass perfume bottles forever stoppered. A hairbrush with fine dark hairs caught in the bristles. Rows of assorted clothing filled the suite of wardrobes. And her books! Row upon row of well-read favourite paperback novels and huge thick tomes of textbooks that she had collected during her nursing career filled an entire wall of the study.

Just what the hell was he supposed to do with it all? He couldn't as yet bring himself to bundle it all up in black plastic bags and take it to the nearest charity shop; nor could he live with it next to his own possessions. So, he had quietly moved himself and his belongings into another bedroom. This bedroom was smaller and cosier. The gabled windows looked out through a little coppiced area extending to the hills and valley beyond. At night he could hear the paired owls as they called to one another; the *terwit* followed by the mate's *terwoo*. He felt oddly at peace with such an ordinary but comforting sound. In May the nightingales would return together with the cuckoos. Spring would be something to look forward to.

For now he was happier in this bedroom that bore no memories. There was no great empty space in this smaller bed. Her stuff he could deal with later.

He hadn't yet realised that the true healing process had not really begun. Unaware that he was blocking something out, not all, but a few things went 'cloudy' when he went down that particular corridor in his mind. Whole scenes were obscured because of some primitive, numbing effect on those things too terrible to grasp.

***

February was slipping away and March was fast approaching. Richard remained at home, unsure what to do with himself. He was still unwelcome at work with his manager relishing his exalted position. Richard was considering how he was going to fill in the time on his hands. Friends still issued invitations to dinner and Richard accepted as many as he felt he could without becoming a burden as the 'token' single male companion to partnerless females. Connie's name was mentioned only when necessary and Richard didn't know whether he felt relieved or frustrated over this. He still felt that he existed in some sort of limbo and was now getting to the stage where he needed to talk or he would end up banging his head against a wall.

He had only recently realised that there was probably only one or perhaps two people to whom he could trust and let go to. These were his Aunt Mavis and his old sailing friend Stephen. Aunt Mavis was well advanced in years and with a no-nonsense attitude he had become close to her when his mother had died in her early fifties. His father had comforted his teenage son as best he could in his own way, but he had grieved sorely over his beloved Penny's early death to cancer. Richard's father had spent practically all his waking hours caring for his wife and young daughter Megan. When Megan had tragically died, following her mother to her own grave Aunt Mavis had been the one who he had turned to for help and comfort.

Sometimes garrulous and quick-tempered she was nonetheless a person with a kind heart and a passion for living.

She lived nearby in the next village and although it was unspoken between them he knew that she had been keeping a gentle eye on him these last few months. Twice a week she'd call in with: 'I was just passing,' when walking her two Golden Retrievers. Skilfully she'd enquire how he was and what he'd been doing with himself. She never questioned him about his loss, just listened when he wanted to talk and only gave her counsel if she felt he was asking for it. As of old he found her comforting and easy to be with. She exuded calmness and understanding. Gradually he had found himself telling her about his and Connie's ambitions, about the voyage, the storm and eventually the horror of Connie's death. His guard had come down bit by bit and, with it the tightness in his chest and throat had begun to ease as some of the stress began to leave him.

The one thing he couldn't tell her was about the relationship between Connie and Toby. Something in his pride stopped him in his tracks. Aunt Mavis therefore knew nothing about his worries and suspicions that Connie was possibly going to leave him for another man. Feeling a complete failure over losing your yacht and wife was one thing. If she had been going to 'jump ship' as it were, then this compounded his guilt. In that he hadn't taken enough care or paid enough attention to her needs. As if on cue he now espied Aunt Mavis marching up his drive, her two dogs' foggy breath steaming from their pink open mouths. Must be Friday he thought fondly, Auntie's visit time. He went through to the kitchen and pulled open the solid oak door.

'Hello I was just thinking of you, I wondered if you'd come today. Come in; leave your boots under the radiator. There are your old slippers ready for you. Hello Tess, Tango.' He greeted the two dogs that bounded in, feathery tails wagging, and smiles agape on their faces, 'I already have the coffee on.'

Mavis and the dogs followed Richard from the small outer hallway into the comforting warmth of the huge farmhouse-style kitchen. The dogs immediately went to the bowl that Richard kept just for them and lapped sloppily at the water, droplets covering the surrounding floor.

'Messy dogs,' said Mavis eying the wet flags, 'go and lie down.' They needed no further telling and promptly made their way over to the thick rug in front of the Aga. They flopped down with grunts of satisfaction, lay their heads on their paws and gazed at Mavis and Richard with their moist brown eyes. Soon their wet flanks were steaming with the newfound heat from the stove. They rolled over contentedly, fast asleep.

Richard didn't know it yet but today Mavis was going to make a suggestion. If he wasn't going to go back to work soon for whatever reason, or replace his boat with another, then maybe it was about time he filled his days a little more. She had thought about some voluntary work, either at home or abroad in some worthwhile project. Or why not take himself off to the Alps for the remainder of the ski season. Skiing was another passion of his and the fresh air and daily ski workout would improve his overall health. She didn't say that staying in a cosy ski chalet in a chic resort with other like-minded people would give him the social contact that he was still missing – mostly shut away by himself in his country home in Bishop's Waltham.

She knew about his invitations to friends' dinner parties, but they had been joint friends mostly and the overall situation was a little unreal. He needed new friends, and new places. He needed to meet people who knew nothing about his recent nightmare. She also thought it was time he began to ease up on the punishment he was inflicting on himself.

'You remember my old school friend Phoebe? Well, her daughter owns a ski chalet in Megève. I don't know if you've heard of Megève but apparently it's very pretty with typical French Savoire chalets, and very chic. Nice restaurants, bars and ski equipment shops. It's not too big, quite French and as not too many Brits go there it's not yet been turned into one of those ghastly spoilt resorts. The chalet is situated right in the middle of town, so it has wonderful easy access to the ski lifts and the ski runs. The skiing is supposedly superb with stacks of red runs and some even more challenging black ones scattered throughout the resort. The chalet itself is gorgeous and she has enough bedrooms for about twenty or so guests. The best bit is the food!

According to Phoebe who has stayed there on numerous occasions she always hires a top class cook and the food is – what's the modern expression nowadays? – to die for! Masses of it and hand-picked wines from all over the Savoire region.'

She enthused and then paused to take a sip of her coffee. They were sitting at the old scrubbed pine kitchen table, ceramic coffee cups in front of them. Richard was facing Mavis and regarded her fondly as she unravelled her little tale. He had to suppress himself from telling her that she sounded so like a travel brochure. He guessed what was coming and loved her too much to forestall her enthusiasm. On the table between them lay a brightly coloured bowl of Moroccan origin filled with golden chrysanthemums. Their earthy woody smell combined with the aroma of the fresh coffee and wet dog. He felt an intense moment of pleasure that surprised him. He smiled and raised his coffee mug to his lips, breathed in the vapour and took a sip, studying her over the rim.

'Go on.'

'Well I just thought, in passing of course that it might do you good. You know you're a bit too thin at the moment,' she continued, 'and guess what, she happens to have a room free for March and early April.'

She leaned back in her chair, cradling the warm mug between her hands.

Fancy that! 'Mmmm. Well I'll have to think about it.'

'Of course you will. Anyway the company is run on very casual, friendly lines. You can join in as much or as little as you want to. Being part of a chalet party also means that there is bound to be someone of your standard of skiing if you want company on the slopes. Or you can ski on your own of course,' she finished with a slight challenge in her voice.

Richard heard the challenge for what it was and again he smiled and gave a short laugh.

'You are an incorrigible old woman at times, and it's lucky for me that I realise that!' he paused and then continued, 'I must confess I hadn't thought about going skiing for a few years. I reckoned I'd be spending the next couple of winters at least in the Caribbean,' he added ruefully with a small sigh.

'I know love. I can only imagine how you must feel, but you should also know that things change; times move on. They have to, or we'd all end up bitter and twisted and hating everything and everyone in the world. One day, all of a sudden, you'll find that realization dawns; and when it does, you'll look around you and find yourself surprisingly in an entirely different world.'

She covered his cold hand with her own dry, warm one and squeezed it gently before continuing, 'I don't mean to either pry or preach, but don't hurt yourself too much lovey.'

Richard suddenly smiled a real smile and the effect lit up his handsome, thin face. 'OK, Margery Proops the second. As I said before you're a wily old bird and know too much sometimes. OK I promise I'll think about a ski trip.'

She laughed good-naturedly.

'Good. Then I'll leave the brochure that I just happen to have in my coat pocket and you can look at it when I've gone.'

She delved into the voluminous pocket of her heavy woollen coat and produced a slim folded brochure that she tossed onto the table in front of him. The front cover showed an idyllic snowy vista with long glistening ice crystals hanging from the gables of a picture-postcard chalet. In the distance a lone skier could be seen descending down a snowy slope.

'Right. Now I'd better be going. I need to go to Winchester this afternoon and although the snow has now disappeared the roads get icy in the late afternoon. Thank you for the coffee. Come on girls.'

Both dogs stood up on the rug and stretched lazily, then shook their bodies. Neither seemed in a hurry to leave the snug warm kitchen for the cold hard gravel of the drive outside. She called them to heel and they pushed in close to Mavis's side, tails now wagging in anticipation of another walk across the fields. There was a sudden burst of a cold draught as Richard opened the kitchen door and the dogs bounded through.

'I'll see you later next week,' she said, 'heel girls!' With that she was over the threshold and already following the two, noses down tails high, excited dogs.

Richard watched as they disappeared round the corner and then closed the door and went back into the kitchen. He picked up the two blue coffee cups from the pine table and placed them in the dishwasher.

Did he really want to go skiing? It would be great during the day, lots of energetic exercise to take his mind off things. But what about the evenings? He remembered other chalet party holidays that he'd taken; masses of good food and wine – that's a plus. Convivial chat – maybe. Silly games? He'd always enjoyed them before. For the first time he really thought about how he might appear in front of others. Was he really being a coward and a total pain in the arse? Should he stay here and feel sorry for himself or give himself a good shake and say, 'For God's sake, Mavis's right. You've got to move on and give yourself another chance!'

He picked up the colourful brochure and took it over to the better light at the window. Inside the front cover there was a typical snowy scene with two skiers laughing and posing outside a mountain restaurant. The sun was shining high overhead, the snow sparkled, and the skiers looked tanned, fit and healthy. And happy. He might just contemplate it. Connie had been gone for nearly three months now. She wouldn't have wanted him to wallow in self-pity.

***

March. A week had passed and with it a real change in the weather. There was no sign of any more snow, and the days were drier and even warmer. The coming of March boded well: spring flowers, lambs, and nesting birds. It was the customary time to throw out the old and welcome in the new. The grass verges and hedgerows showed signs of new growth: soft yellow primroses, fuzzy catkins and pussy willow, sticky buds and cowslips in the rolling meadowland beyond.

With the improvement in the weather Richard had also decided to improve himself. He'd visited the local hairdressers for a decent styled haircut. He'd finally realised that long hair didn't suit him. Or was it his age? Anyway, the long dark waves had disappeared along with the rather shaggy beard that had appeared almost overnight. His face stared back at him in the mirror. He definitely looked better. The haunted look was beginning to leave his eyes and he found himself smiling at silly things more readily. Terry Wogan on Radio 2 had him actually laughing out loud. His clothes needed an overhaul so, he found a men's shop with garments that appealed and bought himself half a dozen casual shirts and some well fitting jeans. With a couple of lightweight sweaters he felt that overall he had spruced himself up and no longer went around looking like some would-be vagrant. Even his twice a week cleaner noticed the change in Richard and enthusiastically swept through the house cleaning and polishing with a cheerful song as if to encourage him on.

Richard had decided not to go skiing. This year's winter had been so cold and he was quite frankly glad to see the back of the frigid snow and ice that had lain around for so long. He wasn't sure if he wanted more of the stuff voluntarily. He was sure Mavis was right. It would be good for both body and soul, but he had decided that he was better off on his own territory. He was beginning to feel a whole lot better in himself, stronger and not so angry.

Chapter 8

The garden had never looked so beautiful. After the snow disappeared a mild spring had heralded in a fantastically warm early summer and the country benefited with a rich bloom of flowers and luxurious hedge and tree growth. Richard spent the morning cutting the lawn and came to the conclusion that there was nothing so English as the smell of freshly mown grass. He cut the engine on the motor-mower and gratefully wiped his sweaty brow with his discarded cotton shirt. He surveyed the almost parallel green stripes with satisfaction and feeling pleased with himself wandered in from the garden for a pre-lunch beer. It was actually very hot and he washed his face and hands gratefully under the cold kitchen tap. He opened a bottle of beer, took a swig and decided to relax for a few minutes on the back terrace to enjoy the heady scent from the roses. Lunch today was going to be a simple salad with some smoked fish and fresh crusty local bread and he was already looking forward to it. He was on the point of going back outside when the shrill ring of the telephone checked him. With a little irritation at the interruption to his break he went over to the persistent ringing and picked up the receiver. The sun streamed in through the kitchen windows; shafts of light with dust motes were caught whirling in the slight breeze. Outside the nodding deep blue delphiniums contrasted with vivid reds, orange and pinks of potted begonias and geraniums.

'Hello?'

'Hello. Is that Richard? Richard Barker?' asked a hesitant and soft female voice at the other end.

Richard felt a slight prickle of apprehension. He felt sure he recognised the voice on the other end of the line and yet didn't want to.

'Speaking. Who's calling?'

There was a short pause and then she answered quietly.

'It's Miranda.'

There was a roar in his ears and he felt a slight quickening and thump in his chest. His legs felt weak as he leant against the wall in some shock. Miranda! How many years was it since he'd last seen his cousin Philip's wife? He did a quick mental calculation; he was now 49 and he'd last seen her when he was 35 and she was about 30. That was about 15 years ago! What a depressing thought. Where had the last 15 years gone? The years had simply flown when he had set up his business and started making real money. Miranda. She had been drop-dead gorgeous. Blond, tall and beautiful at thirty. She had had legs that went on forever and such huge fine grey-green eyes. He remembered a dusting of faint freckles on her cheekbones, which she'd hated, and fine silky hair on her arms. He had been completely besotted with her. Bowled over from the first time that they had met at a party. Unfortunately, he hadn't been too self-confident with beautiful women back then – he still wasn't a whole lot better and at first he had felt clumsy and inadequate in her company. But he was determined to overcome this and from then on he went to as many parties and functions as he could in order to bump into her. For the first time in his life he was seriously in love, he adored her. But because of his shyness he had kept most of his thoughts and feelings to himself.

With a little mental shake he brought his thoughts back to the present and replied with something banal. He squirmed. Damn! Did he really just say: 'long time no see?' He couldn't think of anything else to add as his mind was still racing, remembering his reactions to her before, so long ago.

'Yes it's been a long time, I can't remember quite how long,' she replied.

Richard doubted that. Miranda had had a fine methodical brain and there was no way that she couldn't recall past events. He wondered what she was doing calling him now. More importantly what did she want? He'd always loathed his cousin Philip, her husband and had never kept in touch with him. Cousins were far enough removed he thought, especially that slimy little toad.

He decided to take the initiative.

'Um, why are you ringing me now?'

He knew that she and Philip had separated shortly after he had married Connie. Aunt Mavis had informed him, but he'd never asked the reason why.

'It's to do with your father.'

'Dad? But he's been dead six years now. What about him?'

He was puzzled and couldn't see any connection between her and his late father William, familiarly known as Bill or Billy Barker.

'Well it's a long story but, someone's been trying to get in touch with him via the internet and eventually by using the family surname tracked him down. I don't quite know how or what but Philip had done some early research on the family.'

At the mention of Philip, Richard's lip gave a little involuntary curl. Philip! That little devious, deceiving creep. He glowered at his memory. He should have throttled him when they were at first school together. He was always trying to steal his lunch money or get his gang of bullies to rough him up on his way home. He didn't know what he was doing now and Richard didn't care, just so long as he didn't have to see him again.

Miranda continued. 'They managed to contact me and we've been corresponding for a week or two now. Trying to sort something out.'

Strangely enough for her she wasn't making sense to Richard. With some exasperation he said, 'Sort what out? Who wants to know about Dad?'

'An American. His name is Joe McCaffrey, and his granddaughter Sorrel.'

'Is that name for real?' He gave a short laugh.

'Yes. I'm afraid it is. She sounds an all American girl!' She gave a little laugh in reply. 'Anyway, her grandfather was a flier during World War II, and got shot down over France. Apparently, he never properly met your father but he has some property of his that had been in his custody for nearly 60 years. Now, he wants to return it to its rightful owner.'

'Now? After nearly 60 years? Well I'll be dammed!'

Richard thought back to when his father was still alive. He had been a private and quiet man in so many ways and most especially when it came to his part in the war. Like the majority of war veterans he'd hardly ever mentioned it and sadly Richard realised that now he'd never know what had really taken place during those dreadful years. Their talks had been too sporadic and painful to William Barker. All Richard knew for certain was that he'd been captured by the Germans in 1942 and had been interned for the rest of the war years until finally being released at the end of hostilities. He also knew that he'd been decorated with the Distinguished Service Medal for outstanding bravery. He must have been some sort of hero. But here too he was reluctant to talk too much about his past. He had dedicated the rest of his life to caring for his beloved wife Penny and his sickly little daughter Megan before she too had died prematurely. Richard had spent a lot of time away from his family as soon as he had reached his twenties. When he had finally found an occupation that he enjoyed he also soon realised that being an entrepreneur meant that you worked hard, long hours. During the time it took to build up his company he spent less and less time visiting his family and so the father and son relationship became more stretched and thin until eventually both found that they had little in common. Of course he bitterly regretted this now.

Now here was someone who had perhaps shared some of the ordeal during the internment. It was, if nothing else, certainly interesting. Maybe he would find out where his father had been sent after his capture and why he had been so reticent to talk about it after so long.

He came back to the present as he realised Miranda was still speaking.

'The granddaughter Sorrel is the one I am actually corresponding with. She says that her grandfather is really ill and frail and is not expected to live much longer. They've been putting his affairs in order and came across some old World War II artefacts and got interested about them. When they questioned him about them your father's name cropped up in the conversation.'

'Did she tell you what it was that belonged to Dad?'

'Yes, she did. A Bible.'

'A Bible! But, Dad was never religious. In fact I would even go so far as to say he was probably agnostic if not exactly an atheist,' Richard exclaimed with some surprise.

'Well that's all she said. Perhaps she knows more but wants to tell you herself. Anyway it's got his name written on the front inside cover. It also had some dates of when he was captured by the Germans, place names, that sort of thing,' she replied testily.

Dates of when the Germans captured him! That sort of thing! Didn't she realise the significance of any of this. Richard couldn't believe that she was being that insensitive. Or maybe he was overreacting; after all it was a long time since the two of them had actually spoken to each other.

'OK. Sorry. So what now? You said that she wants to tell me more herself. Do you have any idea what she might have in mind?'

'Yes. She has to come over to the UK for a business trip, so she is rather hoping to meet up with you and hand the Bible over to you then. I have her email address here so you can write to her. Have you got a pen and paper handy to take it down?'

There was a silence over the line when he had finished copying the message down. He wondered where Miranda was living now and if she ever saw her ex-husband.

It was Miranda who spoke first. 'Er, well I suppose that's all I can tell you. I'd better leave you to get on with whatever you were doing.'

All, thought Richard. We were close for two wonderful years and I thought you were perfect! You knew how I felt and despite my fumbling around I was about to ask you to marry me. Suddenly, super slime sod of a cousin Philip is sniffing around. The misery he caused! And lo and behold he produces this huge diamond, of God knows how many carats and he's popped the question! Done it before I have hardly drawn my breath to say 'I love you.' Talk about the rug pulled out from under my feet. And you say: 'That's all you can tell me?' Inwardly Richard fumed. He was surprised at himself for still having feelings like this. But, he couldn't let it go that easily. No, he couldn't help it; he overcame his pride and stiffly asked,

'What happened to wonder boy?'

This time there was a definite pause and he heard a hiss of indrawn breath. He knew he was being just the tiniest bit of a prick. He should have held his tongue. Oh Christ, sometimes he never learned.

'Philip wasn't quite so wonderful. We separated after a few years and I got a divorce. Let's say he never lived up to his promises. Oh except I got to keep the house and Mercedes.'

Richard whistled silently to himself. That house was worth a small fortune; he had always wondered how Philip could have managed to afford it unless it was doing something highly dodgy. 'I would like to say I'm sorry. I'm sorry for you but, he was a bastard all his life and I can't honestly say I feel sorry for him in the slightest. You knew how I felt about things.'

'Oh Richard! Please let's leave it there shall we? I know I made a mistake. Sometimes I thought that you and I,' she sighed and let her voice trail off before continuing, 'but then you met Connie and I'm sure you did love her,' she stopped.

This time it was Richard who took in a big breath.

Miranda was aghast, 'Oh Richard I am so sorry. That was utterly thoughtless of me. Please forget I said that!'

He could only imagine Miranda's embarrassment. Her eyes would be wide with concern and splashes of hectic colour would flush her freckled cheeks.

'It's OK,' he replied, 'I'm finally coming to terms with her death. Each week it gets easier and it's now more than six months since the accident. I'm a survivor.'

'I'm sure you are,' she breathed in relief. 'Well I really had better go. It was nice talking to you again.'

'Yes,' a pause then, 'you too.'

Richard replaced the telephone receiver and stood facing his newly cut lawn through the kitchen window, not seeing it. Why hadn't he confessed his love to her properly way back then? And why hadn't he fought Philip over Miranda? He knew that pride is a terrible thing and he had only himself to blame. He came to with a start. Miranda and Philip. Connie and Toby. Was this a repeat of history? What a stupid bugger he was at times. He let everything he treasured slip through his fingers. Was it because he didn't act quickly enough? He was so confident at work and making money and yet when it came to women he was utterly useless.

Chapter 9

The Lufthansa plane finally touched down with a slight bump and lurch at Hamburg Airport. Alien non-German passengers impatiently undid their seatbelts and stood to open the overhead lockers to retrieve their hand luggage. The native well-ordered Germans remained firmly seated with their lap belts fastened. They *waited* for their orders to disembark. Such is the German psyche.

Richard walked along a carpeted corridor following the signs for baggage retrieval, grateful to be free once more from the constrictions of air travel. He waited at the carousel and after identifying his leather holdall walked out through to the main concourse. Like most of today's modern airports, Hamburg was clean, well ordered, over-heated and sterile. He felt that he could be in any one of maybe a thousand identical airports in the world. He saw the same food-chain restaurants serving the usual fast food that he could only describe as over-priced, tasteless muck. Expensive boutiques stocked with strange clothes that ordinarily you would never dream of buying in your own hometown high street. He passed the countless electronic gadget shops with yet even later models of quite what he didn't know; shops selling perfume, alcohol, chocolates, caviar and Scottish smoked salmon! Each brightly coloured shop was almost a replica of every other shop in every other airport throughout the world. Richard turned away sighing in exasperation. He was trying to remember the last time he had entered a shop that looked different from all the others. Moreover one in which he actually bought something that he wanted, and something that was individual. He realised that he was over-tired and probably just jaded. He needed a strong coffee to perk him up and sought out a coffee shop, knowing that it would probably be one of a chain of course!

The espresso arrived, a tiny cup of steaming fragrant coffee. He enjoyed the aroma and took great pleasure in his first sip. He leant back in the erect stainless steel chair and stretched out his legs in front of him, scanning the constantly moving groups of people for a sight of the American girl. The strong coffee had hit the spot and already his head felt clearer. People moved all around him, singles, couples and small family groups. Everyone going somewhere, anxiously scanning the overhead illuminated notice boards for departure times and arrivals. The tannoy rang out, the female Germanic voice stridently clear and drowning out other nearby sounds. He listened for the announcement of the arrival of Sorrel's' flight from Washington.

After the unexpected phone call from Miranda he had wasted no time in contacting Sorrel McCaffrey. He had sat down at his laptop in his study, thought briefly about what he wanted to say and composed a short email introducing himself. He mentioned that Miranda had called him and put him in the picture. He hadn't expected an immediate reply due to the time difference but in fact, within hours he had received an enthusiastic email. It had taken no time to arrange a meeting. Sorrel was coming to London in a couple of weeks for business and she had thought that it would be just wonderful if they could get together in order for her to give him his father's Bible in person. She had given him the dates of her trip and as he was particularly intrigued by it all and nothing else loomed large in his social calendar agreed to meet her up in London before she was due to return home to the States.

Home he had soon found out was in Annapolis, Maryland right on the Chesapeake Bay. There she ran a successful art gallery, dedicated to exhibiting and selling the large number of local artists' works. With the many thousands that visited Annapolis each year, the turnover in local art was high and provided her with a comfortable income. Richard was interested in the gallery's location, especially as not only was Annapolis the home of the US Naval Academy, it was also one of the country's principal yachting centres. He'd been fascinated to hear her tales about the local inhabitants up and down the many rivers and creeks and, listening he'd felt a small pang as the Chesapeake had been one of the many selected areas that both he and Connie had wanted to visit after the Caribbean.

However, he soon found out that in Sorrel's company, you didn't dwell too long on feeling sorry for yourself. She was all get up and go, or as her 'buddies' might have said, 'pure dynamite.'

How often can a name conjure up an image of a person, and then when you finally meet that person the image is completely different? He only remembered Sorrel being the name of a horse in some forgotten childhood book or even as a food flavouring! This Sorrel he soon found out was anything but horsey. In fact to his slight annoyance she was the epitomy of the All American Girl. Loose-limbed and tanned, perfectly shaped white teeth (probably bleached he told himself), long reddish gold hair and a taut figure that obviously spent a lot of time in the gym. For the first time since Connie's death he found he could look at a girl objectively and appreciate what he saw. She was definitely not a classic beauty, but she had a certain attractiveness.

Despite his reticence caused by a feeling of betraying his loyalty to Connie he felt a sexual attraction as soon as they met and shook hands. Richard knew that she was single, thirty 'something', and had one or two current boyfriends of a fairly casual nature. He liked the fact that she laughed a lot, displaying her very neat dental work, and idly wondered if she laughed as much when she was taken to bed. He suddenly felt annoyed with himself; she was the complete antithesis of all that attracted him in a woman. She was noisy, talked too much and appeared far too good to be true. He soon had her marked down as a 'pushy' female from the States.

She had originally suggested meeting at her hotel in London as she could organise a convenient parking place for him. They could have dinner in the hotel restaurant, which apparently served better than most hotel restaurant food. Richard had agreed, not bothered either way. After all he only wanted to meet the girl, pick her brain and collect his father's Bible.

He waited with some irritation in the hotel foyer for Sorrel to arrive and idly studied the tourists as they walked through the hotel on their way to dinner or to a theatre somewhere. She was already ten minutes late. Typical. Bored with the tourists he turned his attention to the hotel itself. The foyer led through to a softly lit lounge. The tiled floor was covered with deep-pile dark blue Chinese rugs and the two suites of furniture in the room were of dark terracotta with matching curtain fabric. Stylish vases of gorgeous fresh flowers were placed in corners and alcoves; the walls hung with pictures depicting English scenes. It was cosy and intimate, especially for a London hotel.

Suddenly he was aware of a figure at his side and turned.

The woman was dressed in a knee-length, soft emerald green, clingy jersey dress that showed off her lithesome figure to perfection and mirrored the green flecks in her eyes. Her jewellery was simple and tasteful: diamond and white gold earrings and a thick gold necklet. Her rich gold hair was caught up in a loop affair and kept in place by a matching gold clasp at the base of her neck. She was not beautiful but the overall effect was stunning and suited her to perfection.

'Hi! The reception manager said I would find you here. You must be Richard William Barker. I'm Sorrel McCaffrey. How are you doing?'

He hated the American way of greeting. He always wanted to reply with, 'how am I doing what?'

He remembered his good manners, took her hand and introduced himself.

'Very well thank you, pleased to meet you.'

The restaurant was full and fairly noisy; and the clientele were not too self-absorbed or discrete to ignore their entrance. They were shown to a table and a waiter quickly took their orders for an aperitif and left them the menus to peruse. Richard and Sorrel faced each other with mutual interest over the crisp white and apricot tablecloth set with shining silver.

'So. First things first, let's order,' she said as she scanned the menu quickly.

'I'll have the foie gras, the sandre in beurre blanc followed by the lamb,' she said and noticed Richard staring at her with his mouth slightly open. She quickly grinned, shrugged her shoulders and explained, 'I'm starving!'

Richard smiled, liking her candour. At least she was natural. He carefully chose duck as his main course and the sommelier was happy to suggest suitable accompanying wines. He graciously suggested a glass of Monbazillac to go with the foie gras and a red Château for the meat. Mineral water would cleanse their palates in between courses.

The foie gras was perfect: lightly toasted and warmed, the wine liquid gold. The grilled fish melted in their mouths. The meat was succulent and you could have cut it with a fork.

Richard was surprised. He felt his earlier irritation lifting as he tucked into his meal. Perhaps the evening wouldn't be such a chore after all.

'Mmmm. I sure could get used to this. I never knew your British restaurants were so good.'

'Well, I have to say I am a bit surprised. Most hotel restaurants leave a lot to be desired. This duck is excellent. I'll have to remember it.'

'Well it sure beats a lot of our restaurants. We have a lot of swell eating places too, but nowadays far too many rely on pre-packaged food and menus that are the same. You know, burgers, French fries and coleslaw.'

Richard inwardly winced. He couldn't remember the last time he'd had a *good* British burger!

Throughout the meal the atmosphere between them had got better. Richard had eventually relaxed and lost some of his reserve. Despite Sorrel's easy random chatter he found that she was actually a good listener, and was a vivacious advocate for many ideas close to his own heart. He also learnt that she was a clever, witty girl with a mischievous streak. As they neared the end of their meal, Sorrel reached over to the empty chair next to her. She handed Richard a small brown-paper parcel. He glanced at it and knew instinctively that it was the Bible.

He held it in his hands and turned it over. He made no attempt to open it there and then. Instead he put it into his jacket pocket saying.

'It's waited nearly sixty years for me; it can wait another few hours. I'll open it when I get home and can study it better then.'

His hands slightly shook and his mouth betrayed the intense feeling he felt over handling the package. He wanted the privacy of his own home when he finally laid eyes on this war relic of his father's.

Sorrel nodded her agreement; she was acute enough to know how he felt.

After a moment's quiet contemplation Richard picked up their earlier conversation.

'My father, William Barker was usually known as Billy. I always knew him as Billy. Anyway, he was a regular in the Royal Navy before the start of the war, and so he was in it right from the very beginning.'

Sorrel showed some surprise at this. She had thought that most of the prison camp internees were either army soldiers or airmen and commented on this fact.

'Oh no. Dad was captured somewhere off France when his boat went down. Looking back he was very lucky when you consider the many thousands that died with their ships. Can you imagine being in a ship that is torpedoed and going down? It must have been horrendous. That's why most sailors couldn't swim. They wanted a quick death. Poor devils, I wouldn't have liked to have been a sailor during those times whichever side I was fighting on.'

His faraway thoughts were for his father and his lost friends. Poor Dad.

Sorrel took a slow sip of her wine and waited for him to come out of his reverie; her strange gold-green eyes studied him over the rim of her glass.

'Anyway, I think he helped scuttle his boat to avoid its capture and then was caught himself before he had a chance to get away. Unfortunately he was never one for disclosing much information about the war, or rather his part in it. When I was younger I didn't ask many questions and later well, I wasn't living at home then and when we did meet we talked about other things. It's something I regret now of course. Like you always do. Regret only seems to come with age and experience.'

Sorrel nodded as she listened to Richard. When he finally fell silent she mentioned her grandfather and his own part in the war. He had been a flier in the American forces and had been shot down. She was sure that he had been in the same camp as Richard's father some time during their internment.

She opened her handbag and took out some sheets of paper. She quickly scanned through the hand-written notes until she found what she was looking for.

'It says here, Grandpa was shot down near Hanover on February 24th 1944. Apparently he was liberated in April 1945 at Mooseburg by the 3rd Army, the 14th armoured division, the 99th artillery and the 395th infantry.'

She continued to look down and read from the thin spidery English.

'So, some time from February 1944 to April 1945 they must have been in the same place.'

'Must have,' he mused. Richard stirred his coffee with a small silver spoon and then absentmindedly put it back in the sugar. Sorrel followed his movements, her head propped to one side on her hand, an amused smile on her face.

'What? Oh sorry. I wasn't thinking, do you want some?' he said when he realised what he'd done and smiled at her. She shook her head at the offer of the sugar.

'I wish he'd told me more, and I really wish I'd taken more notice of what he did tell me,' Richard finished a little dejectedly.

Sorrel watched him for a moment before carefully choosing her words.

'You know the whole thing was shocking and slowly even more stories are coming to light. They must have suffered many hardships, some that they chose to forget, or block out. It doesn't mean that he didn't, well, want you to know, or that he didn't care for you. Maybe he simply wanted to forget. Like maybe he wanted time to heal and to live for today with his folks.'

'Yes. He certainly was a family man. When he was discharged out of the Navy after the war he found it very hard to find suitable employment. He had fairly nasty shrapnel wounds to his thigh and after his internment never found it easy to get around without some pain. The Navy medic had classed him as physically unfit so he was given a gratuity to live on. Money was of course very short and for a time he tried to supplement this with casual work. My Mum and sister were very special to him and he doted on them.'

Richard paused to pour the remainder of the wine into their glasses.

'Anyway, poor Mum died back in 1977 when she was only fifty-four years old. She and Dad had spent the rest of their lives caring for my sister who was always very sickly. He was fiercely opposed to her being looked after in a nursing home whilst he could care for her, and despite the hardships and lack of money he coped as well as he could. I did my bit once I was old enough to pay my own way, especially once I had finally stopped messing around with various jobs and settled down to build my own business. I found a nice bungalow for him that I had modernised so Dad could manage easily without any social service assistance, and offered to pay all the utility and maintenance bills. But, you know he was an obstinate and proud old bugger and old-fashioned when it came to being a father and provider for his female dependents. We had constant battles over money. Still, they're all gone now.'

He toyed with his wine glass and then tossing back his head finished the contents with a gulp.

Sorrel watched him and then tentatively reached and touched his hand lightly. She had only just met him, but somehow she knew him and just how he was feeling.

'I'm very sorry,' she said huskily. 'I really am. He must have been quite a guy. I felt the same when Grandpa passed away.' She withdrew her hand and picked up her coffee cup.

Richard shrugged and gave a short laugh.

'Oh yes, indeed he was. But, as I said he had other sides too. He couldn't stand other people trying to take him for a ride. By all accounts he was what we call a 'bit of a mucker' when he was younger. He was a lightweight champion boxer in the Navy and enjoyed a good scrap and a tot of Navy rum or two. I know he got moved during the war from one warship to another because of a bit of a fracas below decks. Yes, he must have been a character and wild with it. I always long suspected he was a rogue.'

The mood had suddenly changed and become lighter as Richard thought about a younger, fit and happy William Barker.

'Thank you for listening. Do you want anything else? More wine, coffee or have you had enough?'

She shook her head.

'No thanks; I shall have difficulty getting to sleep if I over indulge. But, dinner has been just so perfect. I'm so glad we finally got together!'

'It has been a pleasure but I think we had better get the bill now and let the staff get off to their beds. Most of them are yawning their heads off!'

He gestured to their waiter.

'I had better be making tracks home. It's a fairly long drive.'

Sorrel followed him outside for a breath of fresh air before going up to her hotel room.

Outside the English summer night was both warm and balmy. They stood outside the hotel on the pavement waiting for the garage boy to bring his car round. Not *sidewalk*, as Richard corrected Sorrel on her English with a laugh.

At this time of night there was far less noise, less traffic and the majority of the hordes of visitors were safely tucked up in their over-priced hotel beds.

'I just love cities at night and your River Thames with its Houses of Parliament and Big Ben is just so awesome! We have history back home but nothing compared to the centuries that you can study here.'

She had then mentioned the Civil war and Richard had found it hard to keep up with Sorrel's intense knowledge of the events. Instead he had listened avidly as she described the major battles with some detail. When she drew breath she looked at him with consternation as he had become very quiet.

'Oh my God I'm boring you. I know I talk too much, especially with people I've only just met,' she said appalled.

'No. No! You're not I promise. It's really interesting. I'm just ashamed that I know so little about your country and history. Oh of course we have numerous television programmes and films, but their portrayal of events are poor compared to your knowledge.'

He couldn't be sure but he would have sworn that she blushed in the lamplight. 'Oh that's Grandpa's fault. He just loved the old history and especially the battles. He had whole armies of lead soldiers and enacted all the fighting. He used to make me a General of one army and we used to play for hours. I guess I sort of picked it all up from him. When he passed away he left me all his books and soldiers and ancient maps. He knew I would be the one to get the greatest buzz from them, and he hoped that I would keep them and then pass them on to my children. Not that I've got any kids yet!' She paused and then continued, ' look is this your car?'

Sorrel turned to him and looked as if she was about to make a suggestion, then seemed to change her mind. Instead she held out her hand and said, 'Well goodbye Richard. Good luck with the Bible and your research. It's been great meeting you.'

Richard took the proffered hand. 'You too. Thanks for bringing it over here. Goodbye.'

***

Later as Richard was driving back along the almost deserted A3 he went over the evening's events in his mind. He was strangely pleased at how the evening had gone. Despite his early irritation with Sorrel and her bright chatter he had gradually relaxed as the night wore on. It was strange that he had felt he could chill out, especially in a stranger's company. Or was that why he could? Because she was a stranger and consequently knew little of him and his past? She surprised him too. She was obviously clever and educated, but underneath all her enthusiastic noise was she as nice as she appeared? Was she genuine? Was her smile just too perfect? However, it hadn't passed him by for a minute that she possessed an amazing body.

***

The fantastic weather was said to continue for the rest of that week and Richard made the most of it lounging in the garden and hiking on the Downs with Mavis's dogs for company.

A couple of days after his evening in London he checked his emails and found one waiting in the inbox from Sorrel. He read the little note and found his mood alternately changing from one of surprise to one of irritation.

Sorrel suggested that as she had a couple of days left could she come down and see him in Bishop's Waltham. She had a proposal to put to him. She had looked up the train timetable and could catch a train to Winchester and then take a taxi to Bishop's Waltham. What did he think? Of course if he were busy she'd understand.

Richard didn't know what to do. How dare she impose herself on him and suggest visiting his village and probably want a good look at his home. Bloody Americans! Have they no sense of propriety? And what was this proposal all about?

On the other hand he wasn't really doing anything special. It would please Mavis for him to start having new friends, so why not? He wasn't best pleased but it would help pass the time. Sorrel and her talking certainly knew how to do that.

With some reservations Richard picked up the phone and dialled her mobile number.

***

When Richard drove Sorrel down from Winchester to Bishop's Waltham she saw the countryside at its best. He'd picked her up in his Jaguar SK8 and the car purred along the leafy lanes. Sorrel had expressed her pleasure in his choice of car, exclaiming that she'd always wanted to travel in a Jaguar. She pronounced it *Jag-Waar*, with a slight drawl.

The countryside whipped by; overhead the trees blurred into a dizzy canopy of mixed greens sprinkled with gold. The fields looked lush and bursting with tall strands of glowing wheat and barley or stocked with sleek pasture cows. This year was a bumper time for pheasants and they laughed at the antics of a couple of colourful males that were so plump from their field thievery that they couldn't find the energy to fly off the road into the surrounding hedgerow. The fresh loamy smell from the woodlands filled their nostrils and Sorrel said that it felt like heaven after the exciting but hot fume-laden air of London.

Richard turned the car into his drive, the tyres crunching on the thick gravel. He pulled up in front of the house and switched off the engine before turning to Sorrel.

'Welcome to Barn Owl Cottage.'

Sorrel uncharacteristically said nothing for a minute, taking in the scene before her.

The house was set in its own grounds of about an acre and a half. An enormous solid oak door was set in the front of the house with a highly polished brass doorknocker in the shape of a large Barn owl. Over the door was a tile-hung porch covered with the most beautiful yellow and deep pink roses and honeysuckle. As a slight breeze lifted the tendrils of the trailing plants they could smell their heady and pervasive perfume. Set to the side of the house and stretching away behind, Sorrel could see mixed woodland of deciduous and a scattering of fir trees. The whole effect was charming.

'It looks bigger than my idea of an English cottage,' she stated as she opened her car door and climbed out. 'Wow. But it's beautiful! How long have you lived here?'

'Oh, for about 15 years now. I found it nearly derelict and gradually rebuilt and modernised it. I was so lucky as it had been on the market for ages. When the price eventually fell to my budget I snapped it up and I've been here ever since. I love it.'

'And your wife? She must have loved it too? No one could fail to love living here.'

Richard had told Sorrel the other night that Connie had died last year. He had touched briefly on the circumstances, the Atlantic sailing and the disaster that occurred. She had sat at the dinner table and listened without saying a word, instinctively knowing that he would be a bit touchy on the subject.

He answered her query with a slight sigh. 'Actually – er yes and no. Connie at first wanted to move nearer to the heart of things. She had always been a city girl and really hadn't any experience of living in the country. She missed her groups of friends, and things like the shopping centres and being able to choose to eat out in any restaurant that took her fancy. She gradually came to terms with living here, but she still hated having to drive in to work each day. I don't know, maybe once she'd retired she'd have found new things to interest her but I always knew that if I had suggested moving into town she'd have gone like a shot. We had some pretty spectacular rows about it.' He smiled in remembrance of them.

'Oh. So she didn't choose the house then?'

'No. I hadn't met Con when I first found the house.' He looked round him and then gesturing said, 'shall we go in?'

Taking her small overnight case in one hand he led the way through the front door. A smell of lavender and beeswax polish hit them as they entered from the covered porch way. There was a hallway of gleaming polished floorboards with scattered red and black woollen rugs.

Kneeling down Sorrel stroked the pile of the nearest one. 'This is beautiful. It is Turkish isn't it?'

Richard was impressed. 'Yes they are all from the areas of Cappadocia and Bergamon. They're about eighty years old. I started collecting them when I first visited Turkey about twenty years ago. Then you could pick up absolute bargains, now you have to be careful.'

He led Sorrel through to the sitting room and she gasped at the enormous fireplace at one end of the large room. 'That's awesome! I almost wish it were winter and we could sit by an enormous log fire and roast chestnuts and marshmallows,' she said.

He laughed at her enthusiastic girlishness. 'You like doing that too?'

She took in everything in the room with acute interest; when he showed her the study she halted in the doorway.

'Oh my God. Don't tell me you have a Logan!' she turned round to him with a picture of astonishment on her face.'

'Actually I have a pair,' he replied showing her the second tiger painting by the celebrated artist Helen Logan. It was in an alcove deeper within the room.

'Wow. You sure do have taste. How did you come by it?'

'Actually Helen is an old friend of mine; we went to school together and she now lives in a village called Alderbury near Salisbury. I especially love her wildlife paintings and bought these two last year. I also have a landscape of hers in the office.'

Sorrel whistled in surprise. Amazed by his unassuming manner she followed him around the rest of the house and he was quite adamant that she treat it like home. Eventually he led her upstairs to her bedroom. He had decided earlier that she could stay for the one night. He could manage to put up with her little annoyances and not let it bother him for that short time.

The room faced the back garden and had the most wonderful views over the light wooded area to the side of his land and across to the valley beyond. A couple of thoroughbred horses belonging to his immediate neighbour were grazing in their paddock, and in a far field they could hear bleating from a small flock of sheep. It was all so incredibly pastoral that Sorrel had to almost pinch herself to make sure she wasn't dreaming.

'Wow,' she said. 'That's an amazing view. It's actually what I have always thought English countryside should look like. I'm going to love my short visit here.' She stood grinning at Richard in pure pleasure.

He smiled back. 'We aim to please. Now, I thought we'd eat in tonight, as you might be a little tired. Is that OK?'

'Sure. I'm not at all tired, but I would love to stay in. It'll be fun. This place is just so beautiful.'

'Good. I have a simple meal in mind of lamb, new potatoes, vegetables and a side salad. I know you Americans don't get a lot of lamb on account of all that steak!' he joked. They both laughed and decided that a bottle of good red wine needed to be opened right away and to hell with the tea.

***

Despite Richard's earlier misgivings Sorrel's visit was a success. They spent the next morning visiting Salisbury Cathedral with its dreamy tall spire. As a special surprise he had rung up his artist friend Helen and she had cordially invited the two of them over for lunch. Sorrel was overjoyed to meet this wonderful, talented lady and spent a blissful couple of hours pouring over her newest work. She was particularly struck by a striking study of Salisbury cathedral rising up out of the early morning mist, terracotta roof tiles in the foreground. She decided that she had to have the picture for herself, either for her gallery or home, especially as she had now visited Salisbury.

They were a little early for Sorrel's train back up to London so they decided to while away the time in an old-fashioned cafe. While they waited for the tea to brew Sorrel went over the proposal that she had put to Richard the evening before.

Her grandfather had died a few weeks ago and, she had decided to visit one of the old German prison of war camps that was now open to visitors and served as a museum. This wasn't out of any ghoulish whim, but because she had loved and respected him and she wanted a better understanding over what that lost time had meant to her grandfather.

'Would you come with me?' she had asked. Her questioning gaze was open and friendly, with just a touch of hesitation. She realised that it might be a tall order for Richard.

When she had first met Richard she had instinctively recognised the hunger within him that had been eroding his normal zest for life. Apart from her own reasons for visiting she tentatively suggested that a short trip for Richard with his normal curiosity could possibly help overcome any lingering moroseness. Had his father suffered hardships and did he later live a happier life? She believed in respecting the past and yet making the most of what was in front of you. Strangely enough Richard found himself interested in her idea. He had looked though his Times Atlas when he had first received the Bible. He'd poured over the pages covering both Germany and Poland recognising some famous place names. Richard had an idea that some of the old names had changed and had checked them out on his fast broadband computer connection to the Internet. With further exploration he had soon found a long list of past prisoner of war camps. The names conjured up old war films, Mooseburg, Heydekrug, Nuremberg, Gross Tychow, Lamsdorf, and Thorn. An uncontrolled shiver had run down his spine at the time. Which of these camps had Billy and Joe been in at the same time? Richard knew that his father had been in many camps and was moved around a lot. He also knew that the same applied to Sorrel's grandfather Joe, but as he had spent a far shorter time being incarcerated there were fewer holes in his history. In February 1944 he had been aircrew of a B-17 plane and flying his 6th mission over Germany when he was shot down. He spent the remaining fourteen months as a POW, in numerous camps and suffered many hardships. Billy's Bible must have been acquired during this time. His name and address was inscribed in it but it had returned with Joe to Maryland when he was liberated in 1945.

Only when he fell ill did he then decide to try and trace Billy.

Eventually with Sorrel's patience using the Internet she found a site at Root Web.com and a connection was finally made. Thanks to her the Bible was returned to the Barker family *nearly sixty* years later.

When Richard had first unwrapped his father's old Bible, the first thing he saw was his father's name and address on the inside cover. He went on to read that the Ecumenical Commission had issued it for the Chaplaincy Service of POW in Geneva. So Billy had been given the Bible while he was at Stalag XXA Gepruft 42, near Thorn in Poland, but according to what Sorrel had told him, Joe had had the Bible in his possession on his release at Mooseburg.

There was one curious inscription within the Bible that totally confused Richard. '*Blew up on 31st August, adrift for 3 days in an open boat, picked up & taken prisoner 3rd September 1941.*This was definitely not his father. Billy had been captured in January 1942. So, the Bible had changed hands at least three times in its life during the war. Richard wondered; how many people had sought solace in its covers during those horrendous days?

***

Now four weeks later Richard was sitting at Hamburg airport awaiting Sorrel's arrival from Washington with mixed feelings. He wasn't quite sure if he really wanted to be here in Germany where his father had obviously had a ghastly time. Neither was he sure that he was ready to get involved in something with Sorrel. She was OK he supposed. Not quite as 'in your face' as she had first appeared during their initial meeting in London. Perhaps he just liked his own company at the moment. Or was it something to do with their age difference? He was forty-nine and she thirtyish, quite a gap in ages and probably in tastes.

The American Boeing arrived thirty-five minutes early and Sorrel was standing laughing before him, her luggage at her feet. She looked good, not as if she had just flown nearly three thousand miles across the Atlantic.

Her face was lightly tanned, and he could see a few new freckles on her cheeks and nose. Her simple pale green dress was of a cut that emphasised her shapely curves and ended a few inches above her knees. Thin tapered feet thrust into tan sandals with kitten heels put her almost eye to eye with Richard.

'Richard. Hi!' she said with a deep smile and he was enveloped in a cloud of Davidoff's Cool Water 'Woman' Eau de Cologne as she kissed him

He stood back slightly thrown off balance by her directness. 'Sorrel you look very well. Now I know I made the right decision in coming to Germany. I can put up with lousy German food and wine if you look as good every day!'

'That's a scandalous thing to say! Surely Germany has some decent restaurants?' She laughed back at the unexpected compliment.

'Well all I can remember from my last visit some years back was masses of wurst or sausage, sauerkraut, tough black bread, lousy lager and even worse sweet, crappy wine. But, perhaps this time things will be different.'

'Ah. And I thought you were a good European.'

He gave her a look that could have meant anything and picked up her luggage to join his on the trolley. Lightly taking her arm he guided her outside to where their hire car was parked under the canopy, shielded from the hot morning sun.

After stowing their baggage in the boot he adjusted his seat, checked the mirror and then fastened his seat belt.

'All ready?' he asked.

'Mmmm.'

'Hope you're good at map reading.' He tossed a map onto her lap and started the engine of their hired BMW. 'Now, where's the exit for the autobahn?'

***

Two hours later they turned off the motorway with its amazingly heart-stopping fast traffic and traced the map along more minor roads. They followed a fast flowing river, the hot sun shining down onto the lush green banks either side. They were looking for a shady spot to have their picnic lunch of ham, cheese and bread rolls. The river would cool their water. Richard spied a small gravelly turning off the road. He slowly drove the car down the track and eventually came to the riverbank. Picking a clump of tall willow trees for shade he parked the car under them and they both thankfully climbed out of the car. It was nice to be able to stretch their legs and to be away from the dizzyingly hectic traffic.

The air was still and heavy with pollen, the drone of bees in the background soporific. Heavily scented wild flowers lined the riverbanks and the greenish water chuckled over the stones in the shallows.

Sorrel had soon kicked off her shoes and wandered down to the river's edge. She tested the water tentatively with her toes. It was cool and refreshing. She laughed with pure joy as she waded up to her knees and Richard watched with a happy smile on his face. She didn't seem to care that she might ruin her dress with stain from the river mud. She acted like a kid on holiday and he liked her for it. At this moment she was fun and easy to be with; maybe this whole journey wouldn't be as hard as he thought it would be.

He squatted down onto the grass and unwrapped their lunch. 'If you don't come now there won't be any left,' he jokingly called out to her. She scampered back towards him, bringing the bottled water with her and sat down next to him. He reached over to take the glass she was offering to him and as he did so his hand inadvertently brushed along her calf. It felt soft and cool from her dip in the river. He hurriedly withdrew his hand, muttering an embarrassed, 'sorry'.

He couldn't read her eyes through her sunglasses.

***

Sorrel walked across the hotel bedroom carpet towards the window. She was dressed in a damp, white bath towel as she'd just taken a hot shower. She grasped the heavy brocade curtains and drew them back to display an early morning sky of evil looking dark grey clouds. The torrential rain rolled down the windowpane in thick fat globules.

Damn, she thought. Depressing weather could have an influential negative affect on Richard's mood. Sorrel noticed that the temperature was noticeably lower too and shivered as she looked out.

If she didn't make a fuss maybe she could keep the atmosphere light. Today was going to be hard enough visiting the old camp. She so wanted to help. She truly liked Richard. She didn't know what it was, but he had an almost shy, boyish attitude towards her. She knew compared to him she was noisy and probably came over as brash. She couldn't help it. Until she knew a person better she always put up a bit of a show, a shield almost.

Sighing she turned away from the dreary window scene and walked back towards the bed. With a sudden determination she smiled to herself, dropped her towel and began to decide on what would be best to wear that day.

***

Much to Richard's disgust they had to breakfast on German cold meats and cheeses washed down with only passable coffee. Sorrel had laughed at Richard's discomfort as he struggled with the smoky tasting sausage and whispered that they would find a nice pastry shop in the village for elevenses.

Soon, they were slowly driving back along the country road towards their destination. The rain had now turned to a thin slow drizzle and their car tyres shushed along the wet tarmac. Either side of the road were thick woods, mainly of dark forbidding-looking fir trees, interspersed with belts of deciduous woodland. The air was redolent with the smell of sodden resin and the sharp acrid tang of animal lairs.

The road turned a sharp bend and immediately they noticed the half-hidden rusty barbed wire and old fence posts that stretched away over the slight hill. They fell silent and Richard turned off the car's radio that had been playing softly in the background.

'We must be near by now,' he said quietly.

They past a wooden road sign written in German, and carried on along the empty road until they came to the museum, once a prisoner of war camp. Richard parked the car in the neatly fenced and rubbish free car park and they both got out.

There was no mistaking the entrance. He looked up at the arched entrance and the inscription above him.

He suddenly felt terrified. In the grey morning the bleakness was all there. All around him, threatening to weigh him down. He turned to Sorrel and grasped her hand. To her his skin felt stone cold and his face was bloodless with sudden shock as he gasped.

'In there, or somewhere just like there, my father and thousands of other men spent years of their lives. Over three years Dad spent! Three lousy years! What must it have been like for him? And why? Why did they allow any of this to happen?'

He turned without waiting for an answer and again stared up at the gate. It loomed above them, a quiet sentinel of horror and despair.

BOOK 2

Chapter 10

The espresso machine slurped and gulped away in the corner, filling the kitchen with the deep aroma of Jamaican Blue Mountain.
Richard finished the last of his fried egg. Just like his father before him he carefully ensured that no trace of the rich yellow yolk remained; the plate was squeaky clean. Giving a small sigh of pleasure he pushed the plate away from him. Bacon and eggs were *always* welcome. Another leisurely cup of coffee and then he'd tidy up before this morning's task.

Richard had returned from Germany only a couple of days ago. He and Sorrel had said goodbye at their respective departure gates at Hamburg airport. Their parting had been brief, bittersweet. Neither being quite sure of one another, nor did they wish to make a scene out of something that had perhaps only been an illusion. They had become friends; there was no doubt about that and genuinely liked each other. They found each other's company amusing and were at ease with one another. Richard could laugh freely and she uplifted his spirits. During their German visit when Richard had found himself in a dark, sombre mood Sorrel had only to make some remark that released the hidden juvenile in him. But, that wasn't the only thing he found captivating about her. She was exciting, overtly sexy and completely without any affectations. How wrong he had been in his assessment of her when they had first met.
But, and there always seemed to be a but as far as Richard and women were concerned, there was one minor problem. He was 49 years old and she could only have been in her mid thirties. The last thing he wanted was to frighten her off by acting the ageing lothario. This didn't help matters when, for the first time since Connie's death he found himself highly sexually attracted. Altogether Richard found himself in somewhat of a dilemma.
So, at Hamburg Airport they had simply hugged and kissed in a restrained fraternal way. Promises were made to meet again when they had both settled back home and sorted through the back load of work that would have accumulated in their absence. Altogether they had

had an interesting time. Apart from the reason for travelling to Germany, they found in each other a kindred spirit. Long night hours had been whiled away whilst they explored each other's world. They discovered similar tastes in food, wine and music; and were mad keen on exploring different countries, sailing and skiing. Relaxed, over a second bottle of Chianti Reserve they listened without interruption as each took their turn over some anecdote or other. For once, both were on the other's wavelength. Sorrel would have simply said that she knew where he was coming from. Richard was beginning to enjoy her quirky sense of humour and obvious love of life. She emanated a personality that had at first seemed *too* nice to be true. The longer he spent in her company, the more he realised that she actually was a very special person who cared for other people, frequently putting their own needs before her own.

There was something he had to do first however. The visit to the German POW camp had unearthed in Richard an urgent need to understand more about his father. He already had a sketchy, pieced together history of his father's war that he remembered from long ago. Things were now hopefully about to change. In Richard's possession was an old chest that contained a wealth of information. When he had initially inherited the chest, he had only given the contents a brief cursory glance. Connie had taken one look at the scruffy, battered old trunk and had firmly relegated it to the attic. There, unlooked at and unremembered it had stayed. Now, he had the compunction to study his father's old relics without any feelings of guilt and certainly with more regard to the past.

Richard entered his study and crossed over to where he had left the sturdy, scarred chest on the carpeted floor. Earlier this morning he had remembered its whereabouts up in the loft where it had been dumped and laid soon after his father's death. Old picture frames, discarded hideous wedding gifts and Connie's golf clubs had been moved aside to locate it. Eying the golf clubs ruefully he recalled the few times he had escorted Connie around the local golf course at Leckhampton. He had decidedly hated it. It took far too much time, ruined what could have been an exhilerating, energetic walk and worse, it appeared from scrutiny of other club members that you had to wear the most sissy, ghastly clothes imaginable. He had voiced his own opinions loudly and rudely; give him deck shoes and good honest oilskins any time. Connie hadn't bothered to try and persuade him otherwise. She had known him only too well.

Anyway it hardly mattered now. Here was the chest. Richard painstakingly lugged it downstairs to check over its contents more thoroughly in comfortable surroundings.

Squatting down on the black and red Turkish rug, Richard worked at the metal clasp. It was stiff and rusty from disuse and the friable metal would surely break up into pieces. Undone, he heaved the lid back and leaned over the box. Old smells wafted up to him and pervaded his nose as he removed his father's treasures one item at a time. He thought he could recognise the slight tang of salt, a sweet tobacco, stale sweat, a whiff of camphor – mothballs – and the musty mildew of ageing cloth. He imagined himself back in the dimly-lit bedroom of his parents' long ago, where his mother lay dying of the revolting cancer that would soon cruelly claim her body. He sorrowfully remembered all this and more. Passed down through decades of dust and past forgotten dreams.

He lifted out a handful of letters; light paper of compacted small writing, crammed into the 26 lines allotted during wartime. He recognised his father's hand as he pulled the faded, now pink ribbon from the bundle. A couple of hand-drawn Christmas cards fell into his lap. Turning them over he recognised sketches of a Christmas scene with a sailor and a young girl, a lone star and the lovers walking hand in hand. All drawn surprisingly well from the hand of Billy and clearly showing a young man in love and missing home.

Richard read each letter twice through and then with a curious sense of deja vu turned to the other bundle that revealed his mother's handwriting. He found her own writing was neater and yet somehow more childish in its carefully executed style. With a sense of wonder he realised that each letter was interspersed with short simple poems. As he slowly read through he recognised that only she could have written them.

Richard allowed his mind to wander as he thought about their lives. The young girl at home cherished by her family and yet waiting for her own love to return to her. And of a vital young man in the prime of his life wasted and languishing in a POW camp. What a waste of young lives. Richard returned his attention to the chest and picked up a soft cloth that was wrapped around a light thin object. Carefully he unravelled the yellowing cloth and inside he found a simple hand-carved wooden musical instrument. Its slender shape was of one piece and punctuated along its length were small holes at equal distance apart. It was some sort of recorder or suchlike. There was a name roughly scratched on the underside; it looked like Nathaniel. This must have belonged to his father's friend, the young Jewish boy Billy mentioned in his letters. He reached for the bundle and sorted through them until he found the one he wanted. Yes, see here, Nat. They had been together for a long time in the camp. Together they had escaped and then been caught. There were no graphic details but he said that Nat had then died and it wasn't difficult to imagine how. Everyone knew later on. The world had soon learned what had happened to 4.6 million Jews. The sad little instrument must have been a poignant reminder to Billy. He must have thought a lot of Nathaniel to keep it all those years.

So why was a German silver belt-buckle included amongst these precious items of letters and love poems? Was it a keepsake from an amiable, kind guard? He knew that Billy had met some kindly Germans, not all had been in love with the Nazi idealism of that time. It must be something like that. If only his father had been more forthcoming.

Richard next found letters from the Admiralty and the one from the King. These he remembered he had seen before, along with Billy's medal. The medal still sat snugly in its little presentation box, the metal now slightly dulled with time. A fleeting thought passed through Richard's mind as he realised he had no son of his own to hand it on to.

'Dad, Dad! Show us your medal. The one you won in the war!' he'd once said when he was about ten years old and badly wanted to show off in front of his friends from school. Eventually his father had grudgingly shown them the medal, but had steadfastly refused to be drawn into conversation either then or later about his wartime experiences. The little Richard knew, he had got from his mother, and she didn't tell him everything, that he was sure of. Eventually after years of trying and then being refused Richard had given up asking. It had simply been too much like hard work.

Delving deeper Richard found the usual quota of ration books that every family still seemed to have tucked away somewhere at the back of an old sideboard or stuffed in along with old grainy photographs of long forgotten relatives. Billy's Naval Allotment book and letter followed next. The stark badly typewritten letter stood out boldly. It seemed that the Admiralty had been ultra-quick in stopping Billy's pay when he had gone missing. Richard gave a cynical snort, strange how some things never change as far as bureaucracy is concerned. He had now reached the bottom of the chest and Richard thought it was almost empty; but he suddenly realised that there were two slim books lying hidden under an old Navy jacket. He lifted the books into the light and opened the stiff cover of the largest, the navy blue one.

He suddenly was transported back in time, studying old photos of his father. Moreover, with a start he realised a dark-haired father. He stared at Billy, as a handsome young Naval rating. The album was a treasure trove of wartime photos taken of shots from around the Mediterranean. The lead-in date began in 1939, when Billy was a stoker on HMS *Warspite*. *Warspite* was one of the most famous of all battleships, a glorious old lady that had been around since the First World War. Aboard her he had seen action in Malta, when Admiral Sir Dudley Pound was the 1st Sea Lord. In Gibraltar, there was a record of The Royals March Past, sight-seeing in Tangiers, Spanish Morocco, Nice, and Cannes. There were graphic photos of the ill-fated Jose Lois Diez from Franco's war, when she had gone aground attempting to get away. Billy had written about the dead that were still on board and, how they had to remove the victims by lashing them up in their hammocks. The caption underneath the photograph of the ship read: 'Saluted and submitted to the deep. Farewell to the Brave.' How sad and how very stirring. War seemed such a futile thing.

Turning the stiff, black page Richard found himself staring at a second time in Gibraltar. There were football matches with Billy's mates playing, and everything was recorded against HMS *Barham* and Home V Med Fleet. They had drawn 2–2 and they 'wos robbed!

Alexandria and Cairo were next in line. Richard studied fantastic pictures of real clarity in black and white, photos of camels and feluccas, pyramids and fellaheen. Billy obviously hadn't thought much of his time there; he said it stank too much but they had a good time poking fun at the locals in their strange headdress and getting as good back.

An amazing photo showed the record of the first of the Air Mail Boats. Richard hadn't realised just what an amazing venture it had been, especially during those times, of a small aeroplane laying on top of a larger one. A pig aback liner in fact.

Scattered throughout the album were numerous photos of Billy and his mates standing posed for the camera. The captions said it all. ' 'The Sprogs cackle the fat.' They did indeed.

Richard was stunned. This was such a marvellous collection of wartime photographs that he was simply staggered as he slowly turned the pages and studied them one by one. Why had he never seen these before? He felt saddened that they had lain so long forgotten in the chest. He closed the album, and then reached over for the smaller one.

***

1939–1941

William (Billy) Barker stoker second class, was twenty-one years old when he was first assigned to the Queen Elizabeth-Class battleship; HMS *Warspite*. As he stood under her bow and allowed his gaze to travel along the side of her hull he was overcome with awe. At over six hundred and forty-four feet in length and weighing 33,410 tons she appeared and *was* massive.

But, the 'Jacks' who served aboard her had no time to be awestruck; there was a war to be fought and Billy had to knuckle down almost immediately. He soon had integrated with the others. This most glamorous lady of the Royal Navy became his home and he was justifiably proud to be part of her company. The whole crew rated her the best among the other battleships and honour and competitiveness was a top priority.

At top pursuit speed she could go at a cracking pace of twenty-four knots, and then when on patrol or an endurance voyage she was cruised down to preserve her precious tons of oil and coal.

She wasn't a new ship by a long shot, having been commissioned on 8th March 1915. By 1937 she had been fully modernised with a retrofitted aircraft hangar and radical changes made to both her armament and propulsion systems. Warspite' spotter aircraft could be catapulted off her deck at 75mph, whilst her torpedo crews below destroyed enemy vessels with their well-known 'tinfish.' She was formidable and had a glorious tour in the Norwegian campaign. She attacked and sank the German U-boat U-64 by dispatching her Fairey Swordfish bi-plane and later destroyed the *Erich Koellner* and the *Erich Giese*. Together with other British destroyers *Warspite* was victorious in eliminating all of the eight German destroyers trapped in Ofotfjord near Narvik. Such was her glorious role and of course her glamour rubbed off onto her crews. She wasn't only a majestic battleship, she was the best!

Full with the cockiness of youth and recent battle successes Billy came home to Portsmouth where he immediately got stoned. It was inevitable that he became involved in a brawl in a Portsmouth pub as soon as his feet touched home territory. The Pompey pub owner was irate over his smashed plate-glass and destroyed bar stools; he wasn't slow in calling for a Naval shore patrol. Billy was thrown into the brig to cool off not knowing that this time, he had overdone it. It was the last fight of one too many. Brawls over women were meat to him; he was a stroppy mucker ashore. Onboard was a different kettle of fish. He was diligent and used his initiative. The powers above shuffled their bits of paper around; he was fast becoming a real pain in the neck. Better that he was removed and reassigned. So, William Barker stoker 2nd-class was 'handpicked' for service in the Motor Torpedo Boats. Once he was sober and cleaned up, Billy was given his new orders. He was shocked. Taken from his beloved Warspite with its ship's complement of over one thousand men. He was going to join a skimpy seventy-feet-long wooden boat with a crew of at most, two officers and eight ratings! Were they all stark raving mad? He couldn't believe that any of the stories he had read or heard about the MTB's 'Glory Boys' warranted as much recognition as those aboard a battleship! Moaning and groaning, with a great deal of colourful language he packed his kit bag ready for his new boat.

Billy had some shore leave owing to him but was at a bit of a loss on what to do with it. As an orphan he had no mother or father to visit and his only immediate relative was an older brother Bert who lived in

Guildford. Their difference in ages hadn't made them the best of companions when they were young lads and Bert's attitude didn't help matters. Their mother, who'd died when a direct hit had killed both his parents outright at the war's beginning, had allowed herself to indulge Billy from the time he was born. Always short of money, she had nevertheless gone out of her way to ensure that Billy hadn't wanted for anything if she could help it. Not that she preferred Billy to Bert. It was just that he was eight years younger and had the most appealing way when he wanted something. Bert was just plain jealous and always landed Billy a clout for nothing if he could get away with it. The upshot of it was Bert became a nasty bully and as Billy grew older he saw him for what he was. A thoroughly disagreeable person. He certainly wasn't going to waste any of his precious leave or money on visiting his bad tempered brother. As far as Billy was concerned the only good thing to come out of it was that he had to learn how to defend himself against his older sibling. There was hardly a day when he lived at home when he hadn't a black eye or a yellow bruise or two on his body. Fast on his feet and quick with his hands he soon picked up the art of fisticuffs. Once he had joined the Navy the PT instructor had quickly seen his potential and had trained Billy up to become a junior boxer. Billy had loved the challenge and took to the sport readily, soon becoming something of a local champ.

Right now he had a little time on his hands and very little money. He decided that if he could hitch a lift over to the Isle of Wight then he would pay a visit to the boat builder who was putting the finishing touches to his new posting: Motor Torpedo Boat number 47.

The day was fair but blustery. Billy had blagged his way onto a small launch that zigzagged its way out of Portsmouth harbour over the Solent towards Cowes on the Isle of Wight. Billy looked around him in interest at the different types of craft that plied these waters. Always a busy stretch, the outbreak of war had increased the numbers of boats both large and small and the harbour was choppy with their comings and goings. Asking directions he soon found the boat builder he was looking for and his MTB. Along the quayside was a row of black painted bollards. He found one that wasn't covered with seagull lime and perched himself on top while he took out a crumpled packet of Senior Service. He lit one and inhaled, the acrid smoke disappearing on the breeze. He gazed across the quayside and screwed his blue eyes up against the bright morning sun, his dark brown hair lightly ruffling where it had escaped from under his cap.

She looked bloody small on the quayside compared with what he had been used to, he thought to himself. But, he knew (after asking a few questions around the mess hall) that with her four thousand and fifty horsepower engines she could gain a top speed of 39 knots. So, no slouch, she'd be very fast. She'd have to be; she was only made of wood! He also watched with interest as the mechanics wrestled with the forward and aft guns. Although Billy was a stoker, he was also a crack shot with a machine-gun. If he had the chance he'd enjoy letting a few rounds rip into the enemy. He pulled out his crumpled packet of cigarettes again and it was then that he became aware that he was no longer alone on the quayside.

'Well, what do you think of her?' asked the stranger in a well-educated voice. He was dressed in civvies, a pair of grey flannels and a tweed jacket and tie.

Billy turned sideways to the young stranger instantly liking his open friendly face despite his cultured accent. He found himself responding rather more enthusiastically than he would have thought 24 hours ago. 'Marvellous. That's my boat you're looking at.'

The newcomer chuckled, a low rich timbre to his voice. 'Ahem. No, I beg to correct you, but she's not actually. She's *my* boat. Allow me, I'm the skipper. Lieutenant Chalmers. And you are?' he grinned at Billy and thrust out a hand.

Billy nearly fell off his perch as he took the proffered hand and stood up all at once. Surprised he returned the introduction, 'William Barker stoker 2nd class Sir. Soon to be part of the ship's company, Sir.' 'Ah Barker yes.' He replied taking a keener look at Billy. 'Well it's good that we've met. As she's to be my new command I need to get acquainted with the crew. Is that a pub over there? Do you think we might get a pint of their best before lunch?'

Surprised by this unusual officer Billy replied, 'We can certainly try Sir.'

***

His shore leave over, Billy was walking on his way for his first briefing and official rundown on his new MTB posting. His boots rang out as he briskly marched along the metalled road.

The heavy bombing on the two cities of Southampton and Portsmouth was second only to London. Adding this devastation to the fact that parts of the areas were little more than run-down slums that should have been demolished years ago, made for a highly undesirable region.

Billy made his way down narrow streets behind the crowd of warehouses to the distant dockside. He passed a few green squares set aside for food allotments, their produce struggling to grow in the soil and accumulation of dust and rubble from the bombing. The windows of the shabby houses were covered with sticky tape to prevent the glass shattering when the enemy dropped their bombs; likewise the public buses.

He noticed recent chalk marks on the roads and walls; innocent games from local children. Poor little sods, he thought; so not all of them have been sent to safety in the country. Most of the children in Southampton and Portsmouth had been put on trains and dispatched to safe houses in places like Bournemouth or Dunstable. Some evidently had not. He wondered what the townie children thought when they were let loose in the country. What did they think when they were sent on nature walks to collect rose hips in their satchels, in order to make nourishing rose hip syrup!

A faint breeze from the river brought with it the now familiar smells of destruction. The gag of raw sewage, acrid burnt timber, and the occasional whiff of escaped gas. There was a fine covering of dust over every surface. Where once buildings had stood, bomb rubble lay everywhere. Billy supposed that eventually the broken pipes would be mended and the houses would be rebuilt. But, stopping and looking around at all the desolation, it would take a long, long time before this place looked good.

He had already met the rest of the crew in addition to his skipper Lieutenant Chalmers, who was in actual fact younger than himself and on his first command. The other crew included the second officer; engineer Bates, the sturdy reliable Cox, two leading torpedo men, torpedo gunner's mate, and the gunners. It was a right mixed bunch and all of them very young. When Billy had first seen MTB 47 she had been surrounded by a miscellany of fishing craft. At first glance she had resembled a flat iron, a dark grey shapeless hull of little beauty. Now, he saw that she had been given a coat of paint and the carpenters and painters had finished the accommodation below. The living spaces for both officers and men were in the fore part. The crew were to occupy one compartment that opened into a tiny galley, whilst the captain and his navigator, a sub-lieutenant, RNVR occupied the other. They were to sleep in folding bunks. Going to be bloody cosy, Billy thought as he had nosed his way around below decks.

At just 70-feet long, the MTB carried two eighteen-inch torpedo tubes, depth charges, and anti-aircraft armaments. She was the smallest of the Royal Navy men-of-war. He had read somewhere that it was possible, by a combination of circumstances, for one of these 70-feet long hornets to disable and perhaps even sink a 35,000-ton battleship. Surely it was unthinkable. But, given the chance he was itching to give it a try. After all, the Germans had killed both his parents.

At the lecture the crew were told that the hull was built of double diagonal laminated mahogany with calico sandwiched in between the layers. These layers were held together by glue and up to 400,000 screws and copper rivets, plus a mile or so of wire. The boat builder had put in big Merlin engines that were capable of up to 40 knots. There were also two smaller ones for manoeuvrability in berths and harbours. The lecturer, an experienced torpedo gunner's mate didn't mention MTBs' endearing little habit of the transom suddenly becoming very loose, when the trip home then became a toss-up between going fast and getting in before sinking or a slow motor home to try and stop the transom becoming completely lost. Imagine losing the whole of the back of your ship! Either way it was a gamble. Hopefully this crew would never have to find out for themselves.

It soon quickly dawned on the crew that MTB 47 had to become operational as soon as possible. The crew were new to each other and a series of mock battles were to be organised with other MTBs immediately. "All good stuff", the men thought. They'd soon be back in the war proper, shouting 'Come on you bastards! Let's be having you!'

The 'Glory Boys' found that they were due to receive special tinned rations, officially called 'comforts.' They quickly discovered that 'comforts' were indeed needed.

***

It was only barely morning as Billy and his colleagues climbed into the wooden dinghy in the harbour. The wet seaweed on the uncovered wall and ladder had a sharp tang that mingled with the tarry smell of the piled warps on the quay. There was a sharp nip to the early air and they pulled their jackets round them closely.

MTB 47 was swinging at anchor, her deck rising and falling with the swell and with a slight pitch and roll of her bows. The crew came alongside and were soon scurrying around, handing up supplies and storing everything securely away below decks. Loose mooring lines and fenders were tidily stowed in lockers.

The skipper and his coxswain were on the bridge. A thick soft rubber pad underneath their feet, to absorb some of the shock as the boat struck each successive wave when at sea.

Lieutenant Chalmers studied the harbour, getting his bearings in the dim light. A pair of binoculars was slung round his neck; he raised these to his eyes when he wanted to identify something more clearly. His legs were ready braced for their departure.

'Start engines Cox.'

'Aye, aye Sir.'

A cough and a savage roar as the engines were started. Whilst they warmed up, the order to weigh anchor was given. A smell of high-octane fuel permeated the air together with a damp vapour mist. The steady pulsating rumble accumulated turning to a thunder as the throttles were opened to full.

The sudden increase in power raised the bows, and the crew became aware of the unfamiliar noises from the hull and inboard. These creaks and groans were added to the slap of water against the hull.

'Full ahead. All engines.'

The bows rose several feet as the MTB shot forward, the water shooting over her in sheets as they bounced from one wave-top to the next. Boots clattered on the wet grating as the crew raced to find handholds, their knees bent to absorb the fierce jolts. The screen was already soaked and those on the bridge had to keep constantly dabbing and wiping their faces with old neck towels.

'Ease down to 15 knots. Alter course, steer north by east.'

The boat turned gracefully, its stern rising and spewing foam, the spray shining on her hull. The incredible din from the engine room moderated and dropped abruptly to a soft purring note. The crew on deck all looked at each other and grinned. By God, but she was fast! All the crew were youthful, none older than 25 years and most were under 21. Despite this, in 1941 they were all highly experienced sailors and each loved the exhilaration of a fast craft.

They ran through their checklist on equipment; six pound forward and twin Oerlikon aft guns, the machine-guns and the torpedo tubes, depth charges, ammunition magazines, belts of ammunition. They practised to load, fire, and load over and over again until they got it right.

When completely satisfied with the performance of both crew and boat, Chalmers gave the order to head for their home port.

They turned their bows towards the skyline of Portsmouth as the dusk began to fall on the purply pink evening sky.

Thick Spam sandwiches and mugs of hot kye were handed round to everyone. Billy munched on a sandwich, ravenous from the sea air and the recent strenuous activity. His dark eyes keenly looked around him. He had thoroughly enjoyed the day and was now looking forward to going ashore for a few bevies. But, right now hot kye would do. Hot cocoa made from grated unsweetened chocolate, sugar and condensed milk; the mainstay for every MTB crew.

Gosport loomed ahead as the dusk darkened and Billy could make out the tower on Haslar Naval Hospital.

'Strange how Jerry hasn't hit Haslar yet,' he commented to Ginger, one of the torpedo men.

'Arr. There's a rumour going round that the Luftwaffe use it as a bloody navigation aid. They aim for the tower as they're coming in, before they drop their loads.' He nodded towards the high tower with his chin. He stood there leaning against the guardrail, a six feet-six giant from the West Country with startling red hair and eyebrows. Billy regarded him with interest. He looked like he'd be useful if it came to a hand fight at any time. More to the point he looked like he was solid enough to put Billy through a brick wall. Better stay on the right side of him he thought. He knew which side his bread was buttered.

'More kye lads?' They both looked round as they were joined by a gunner known as Tubby; a chubby-faced 20 year old with a perpetual smile. He held up a flask in query and Billy and Ginger nodded keenly. The temperatures were falling and the hot thick sweet drink was warm and satisfying after a gruelling day's exercise. Together they held out their mugs as Tubby uncorked the flask and poured out the steaming aromatic chocolate.

'Soon be back now,' he nodded towards the fast approaching shoreline, 'there's a bit of a do at the local tonight. Skip says with a bit of luck we'll be back in time and not miss it. Last time loads of girls turned up. Loads of girls.' He gave a grin as he imparted this little morsel of news to them.

The others at the rail all turned to Tubby eagerly. Girls! They'd spent the last week working all hours getting their MTB ready for the sea. There had been no free time to speak of; all the crew had fallen into their bunks as soon as they had finished their chores and then supper. They had been absolutely cream-crackered! A few hours shore leave with the added attraction of girls sounded like heaven. A good run ashore was long overdue for these young men with healthy appetites.

Tubby loved being the harbinger of good tidings. He moved on down to the bows of the boat, stopping to refill mugs and give the good news to the other hands.

***

Billy, Tubby and Ginger were joined by Bates that night as they made their way through Haslar Creek and headed for the 'Star and Garter' in Portsmouth, a pub very popular and much frequented by sailors down the years.

'Cor brass monkeys tonight,' said Tubby shivering, hands in pockets and shoulders hunched against the cold wind, 'glad we've finally made it.'

They swung open the partly glazed door to the pub bar inside. A cacophony of noise, heat and thick acrid tobacco smoke hit them as they stepped across the threshold to mingle with the smells of beer, sweat and cheap perfume.

'Phew,' muttered someone.

The place was heaving with uniformed sailors jostling for a place at the bar. Space was at a premium and all the tables were taken by groups of Jacks and girls dressed up for the evening. Everyone appeared to be having a good time, determined to forget the war and its hardships for a few hours at least. The girls were wearing their prettiest dresses, some lucky enough to have a thin smear of priceless lipstick across their laughing mouths. They wanted to be able to enjoy being young again, to cast off the heavy yoke of responsibility and to feel free of burden for just a short time.

The ceiling was stained a filthy dark ochre by the years of cigarette and pipe smoke. In the corner a pianist was belting out favourite tunes on an old upright piano. A few sailors lounged against it, joining in with a broken chorus and much ribald laughter when they got it wrong. The smoke soon stung their eyes and Billy had to shout above the din to give his order for their pints. Once they had their filled glasses he and his mates pushed their way over to a small space along the wall and helped prop it up. The noise was deafening.

Billy took a sip of his beer and cast his eyes over the other customers. They were mostly sailors and a few men in civvies. All the girls appeared to be attached. The four of them had got here too late.

Tobacco smoke hung in a pall above their heads; he didn't see any reason why not to add to it and fetched out his packet of smokes.

Suddenly the door opened, scattering the smoke, and four girls walked in. Heads turned to see who it was, and lascivious eyes followed their procession over to the bar with interest. Of course they had no trouble finding space whatsoever. A few Jacks brazenly stood in their way with a friendly suggestive, 'fancy a good time love?' or 'hi gorgeous, you looking for me?' which the girls laughingly brushed aside. Three of the girls were much of the same age, knowing and confident in their surroundings. They happily chatted together at the bar and joked with the barman as they ordered their gins and orange. The fourth girl that made up their quartet was younger and she hung back before shyly presenting her coin for a half of cider.

She hardly looked more than a schoolgirl, fifteen at most, Billy thought. Just what the devil is she doing in here?

She stood there, slightly to one side of her friends, clutching her cheap handbag in one hand and her glass in another, looking horribly out of place.

Her build was small and slight, only about five feet three inches tall. Her hair was shoulder-length mid-blonde and hung around her thin waif-like face. Billy couldn't see her too clearly in the dim fuggy light, but he could make out enough detail to note that from where he stood she looked pretty in an elfin way that interested him.

'Cor, take a shufti at those bints! Let's go and chat 'em up before someone else beats us to it,' said Bates, half-finished pint in hand and poised to cross over to the bar area.

'Jesus, they're coming over here anyway. Er, shall we make a bit more space for them?' answered Ginger speaking out of the corner of his mouth. For all his size he looked horribly terrified as if the thought of four strange girls was more menacing than Hitler and all his bombs put together. He hurriedly smoothed down his hair and quickly smiled a nervous welcome grin as the first girl reached them. Tubby came to the rescue and good-naturedly made introductions to stop Ginger collapsing on the pub floor with terror.

First there was Mavis; tall and slim with short brown bobbed hair and a freckly face. She had a loud raucous laugh. Next came giggly Betty, almost as tall but more curvy in body, and blessed with generous breasts, dark curly long hair and a wide scarlet mouth. Edith had a cheeky grin and mischievous knowing eyes that flashed from one Jack to another as she rapidly took in their attributes. Lastly, there was little shy Penny.

Betty, Mavis and Edith were soon laughing away with the boys and happily accepted another round of gins and orange. They flirted outrageously, and the air was soon ripe with wicked innuendo. Penny was still on her first drink and sipped it slowly as she took in all that was going on around her. Although she smiled a lot, her slightly worried eyes mirrored her discomfort in the company of these older girls and sailors.

Billy found himself with an empty glass and made to push through the crowd over to the bar for a refill. As he brushed past Penny he caught her eye and putting his mouth to her ear asked if she was ready for another. She nodded her assent and followed his progress as he fought his way over and then back with their two new drinks.

They clinked glasses together and stood a little off to one side away from the others so they could make themselves heard above the din.

'No, I don't go in pubs very often,' she said in reply to Billy's question. He could have kicked himself. He was right; she probably shouldn't even be in here at all.

'But, today's Mavis's 20th birthday and she wanted to celebrate it here. Mavis is my older sister and she asked me to tag along. She thinks that I stay at home with Mum and Dad too much and I should go out more to enjoy myself.'

'Oh, a bossy older sister eh?'

Penny smiled as she nodded, 'something like that.'

'And are you enjoying yourself?' he asked.

'I think so.'

'So does she boss you around much at home?'

'She's not too bad. Except when she wants to go out of an evening after tea and tries to get out of her share of the washing and drying up.'

'Well I can't blame her for that. My older brother and me used to fight all the time over who was going to wash and whose turn it was to wipe. He usually disappeared to the lavatory for ten minutes and hid until it was all done.' They both laughed.

He continued, 'So if you don't go out much what interests you?'

Penny looked down into her glass as she considered his question before replying.

'Well I don't think pubs are really my cup of tea. They're a bit too noisy and smoky for my liking. I much prefer just being out in the country. When I have time to myself I like to walk for miles and explore places. There's so much to see that you don't realise is right under your nose. I suppose you could say I never grew out of nature rambles from schooldays. I could tell you where all the local badgers live and mother otters and their cubs. I also love bird watching.'

Bird watching! Badgers and otters! Billy was a city boy from Southampton and couldn't remember the last time he'd gone into the country, let alone for a nature walk. He did recall the occasional family trip out on the bus when he was a lad. They had picnicked together by a slow meandering river Hamble that eventually ran down to the Solent. The memories of a cricket or rounders match came back to him. He could almost smell the grass of the bumpy overgrown field and hear the sound of the unknown wheeling birds overhead. His mother had whacked him when he tore the seat out of his pants as he caught them on a ragged nail on a fence post. She'd been furious, after all money didn't grow on trees. Bert, his brother had sniggered behind her back.

No, cows and horses with their smelly pancakes were somewhat of a mystery to him, but he'd always enjoyed those outings. He'd come home filthy and tired, but somehow revitalised from all the fresh air and his surroundings. He was sorry that his mother had now departed and he would no longer spend any time in her company on country outings or otherwise. He missed the closeness they had had together, and how they relaxed in each other's company. He was interested in what Penny had to say about her life and hobbies and an hour passed before they realised it.

'Perhaps if you like you could show me. You know the village where you live and we could go for a walk together. I don't know nothing about birds or wild animals, but I'm always willing to learn something new,' Billy asked. 'I could catch a bus over and we could take some sandwiches. Make a real outing of it.'

Penny looked surprised, as if she didn't really believe him. Most of the village boys she knew would have made fun of her. They weren't interested in country walks or bird watching. Half a cider and then a quick half hour behind the bicycle sheds more like.

'Well maybe.' She looked doubtful before continuing, 'I suppose I could show you round. Our village is very pretty. It's also very old what with the remains of the Bishop's Palace and stables. Do you know it dates back to the 11th Century? Fancy that! And some of the old Queens and Kings have stayed there in the past. You know Queen Elizabeth and such. But, are you sure you won't be bored?'

'No, no I know I won't be,' he said hastily. Suddenly going into the country with Penny seemed the most terrific thing to do. Her shyness and her certain naivety bowled him over. She was different somehow. He'd cast an eye over her older sister and friends with their obvious charms; they were slightly brassy and a bit common if you like. Penny's different-ness intrigued him. So what if he knew nothing about birds and maybe didn't even want to. He wanted to see *her* again. Besides, leaning against the pub wall and studying her face close up she was appealing. She had a funny little elfin face, half hidden by a cloud of shiny blonde hair. Her eyes were wide-spaced and the colour of cornflowers – did he but know it – and her mouth was a little too wide. But, when she smiled her whole face lit up, he found her enchanting. Strangely pretty, unusually quirky, but quietly serene with it. She possessed a maturity that went way beyond her sixteen years.

She looked anxiously at him as if she thought that he was teasing her before she said. 'All right then. On your next time off. You can telephone the local coal merchant down the road and they can let me know when you've got a bit of time off duty.'

Somehow Billy felt delighted that he had fixed a date with this slightly odd girl. Over the next few weeks he soon found out that Penny was indeed vastly different to the countless other girls he usually took out or spent endless hours chatting up. For a start she appeared shy and quiet. His other girlfriends had been more noisy and pushy. She had a bit of class.

However, when Billy first ventured out to her village of Bishop's Waltham in Hampshire he soon realised that on her own territory she was much more confidant.

Her parents, Maggie and Maurice Clarke owned a small farm on the outskirts of the village. When the hostilities had broken out they had quickly learned that the country needed them and their food production. Food convoys were often prevented from reaching British shores and local farms had to increase their crop yield. 'Dig for Britain' was the saying and together with already established farmland, every household garden had forsaken rose beds and border flowers for rows of anything edible.

Of course Penny's parents had a head start. They had a field of free-range hens, a large duck pond with its inhabitants, and their other acres were covered with fruit and vegetable crops. They had been granted permission to keep the family cow for milk and cheese and occasionally when there was a birthday to celebrate, Penny's Mum Maggie would make a forbidden pint or two of cream on the quiet.

Billy was amazed at the choice of food grown on the small farm; some fruit he had almost forgotten about! Strawberries and cream in June! He hoped he would still be around then. The thought of them made his mouth water. At least they didn't have to rely entirely on Spam, powdered egg and a thousand and one ways of using turnips with government issued recipes.

At sixteen, Penny was officially too young to sign on for employment to help the war effort. However, by helping her parents around the house and farm she had a full time job that they all considered she did more than her bit by. Her sister Mavis was having none of that. Work on a boring farm in a small unexciting village where nothing important happened. Oh no. There was more to life than that for Mavis. Especially when she had heard that munitions factory girls could earn double the wages of the land girls. Not that there was an ammunition factory near by but, there was employment to be had in the cities working on assembling parts of their fighter planes. Mavis and her friends were determined to enjoy themselves war or no war. Sweating on the land was definitely not on their agenda.

Every clothing coupon was hoarded until they had enough to go into the town and splash out on something worthwhile. It was months since they had had new stockings, lipstick, powder or scent. A sudden rumour of a new supply in town had them joining the queue and waiting for hours outside in barely contained anticipation. New scarlet lipstick and, *real silk stockings* – not a pencil drawn line down the back of their legs as usual. It all annoyed Penny who thought it a bit silly. Why waste valuable hours queuing for a bit of face powder that only made you look like one of those Chinese dolls. Her sister had always been a bit empty headed, but despite that she still loved her. Penny got on with her chores: collecting the eggs, feeding the fowl, hoeing out weeds and picking the fruit and vegetables at harvest time. So what if people thought her a bit strange and boring, she liked what she was doing and beside, the simplicity of it made her happy. Then there was the housework that she took over from her mother. The washing, turning the mangle in the outhouse and pegging out the huge pile of laundry to flap away in the breeze like sails out at sea. She learnt how to cook and sew, and unravel old jumpers to reclaim the wool to re-knit into new garments. Socks and mittens for soldiers and sailors. She held up a finished scarf and imagined it on Billy as he went out on one of his night-time sorties. Yes, she was happy and content, uncomplicated and despite her youth, dependable.

Billy was confused. Ever since he was fourteen and had found cigarettes, beer and had an uncontrollable reflex action in his loins, he'd chased a certain type of girl. He liked them best easygoing and carefree, ready to join him at the drop of a hat for a night of fun and no commitment. As soon as he got some shore leave, he'd gather up a few friends and they'd go out on the razz looking for a party or a pub where the girls were ready and willing. With his smile and handsome looks the girls liked what they saw and most fell for his easygoing charm. He loved a spicy life and lots of variety. A girl in every port had seemed the perfect ideal to him. That was until he met Penny. She was a normal girl with a good sense of humour and liked a healthy outdoor life. She wasn't the type you normally met on a pub-crawl or danced the night away with at the Palais.

True to her word she loved long walks along the chalky cliff tops of Portsdown or through the bluebell woods and cornfields. He was fascinated that she knew so much about the wild world about them, pointing out and making him see things right under his nose. She kept him entertained for hours in ways that a few months ago he would have laughed at with scorn and derision.

He couldn't quite believe himself when he gave up the chance to go with Tubby and two sexy little Wrens for a wicked night together on their next short pass. Instead he found himself helping Penny make good the hencoop. The ramshackle old door needed re-hanging and some of the wood replacing to stop the foxes getting to them on their nightly raids.

After a satisfying morning Maggie had shooed them out of her way with an oiled bag containing egg sandwiches and a flask of weak tea. They had trekked over the marshlands to watch the late summer waterfowl gathered on the sparkling waters. On their way the air had been alive with birds wheeling, diving and calling, curlews, skylarks, swallows, dunnock and songbird. On the water they'd found heron, jewel-coloured kingfishers and grey geese. The weather was perfect: clear blue skies, a few cotton wool clouds drifting high overhead on a slight cooling breeze. The air was a mix of many smells: tangy salty marshes, warm loamy wood, softly perfumed grasses, here and there an acrid foxhole or two.

Billy and Penny lay side by side on the springy grass gazing up at the wide horizon. They felt relaxed and sleepy under the hot sun and soon Penny was fast asleep. Billy chewed a stalk of grass and watched her while she slept. She was curled on her side, her slight breasts rising and falling with her breath. He had no desire to be anywhere else but here with this girl. He suddenly sat up. With a jolt he realised that for the first time in his life he was in love. Billy the mucker, the joker, love 'em and leave 'em, in love!

This was a complete turn up for the books. He wondered what Tubby and Ginge would say. There were bound to be plenty of filthy jokes and endless leg pulling. Better to keep quiet for the moment, at least until he was sure himself. And what of Penny? How was he going to find out for himself how she felt about him? The whole thing scared the living daylights out of him. What if she was put off, didn't want a relationship other than a casual boyfriend? Jesus.

Chapter 11

Autumn 1941

The clack clack of the signal lamp pierced the still, black, moonless night. MTB 47 was sending a signal to the other MTBs that together made up their flotilla. Within a minute or so they had the returned messages giving both the acknowledge and affirmative.

The MTBs steadily moved ahead, further out into the open water of the English Channel. They were on yet another night mission; their eighth in succession, and the tiredness and tension was taking its heavy toll. Over the past months they had faced many enemy ships and gunboats. Each time they had portrayed fresh bravado alongside sheer, gut tearing fear as they had returned the enemy's fire.

'Alter course, steer north by east, revolutions 20 knots. Inform the W/T to inform the flotilla,' said the Captain. 'Prepare immediate gun action.' Chalmers looked tired and tense as he stood up on the bridge, his binoculars seemingly glued to his eyes. The past few months of constant action, immense risk and the subsequent loss of four crewmen had added years to his boyish face.

The waiting crew burst into life. Feet were heard to clatter down the short ladder leading from the bridge and along the deck. Covers were removed from the guns, and the men peered ahead into the darkness. They waited, listening and shifting their weight in restless anticipation for the whereabouts of the enemy. The deck guns were swung from quarter to quarter waiting for action. Suddenly, there was a brilliant white flare in the dark sky followed by red flashes. Fierce explosions hit the air with a whumph, followed by rapid machine gunfire. Soon, they could see star shells drifting overhead.

Thrum, thrum! They could now hear the heavy diesel engines of enemy boats.

'Keep your head down!' was the order shouted along the decks and repeated man by man.

MTB 47 roared into life, as the Cox spun the wheel and the boat responded by surging forward. The crew felt the sudden increase of wind and sea in their faces, as the ragged spray was torn back from the boat's bows. The wooden boat began to shake and rattle. A familiar wildness began to build in the men on deck as the boat gathered speed. The most unholy din deafened those below decks in the engine room.

The sea suddenly erupted behind them on their starboard side. Fire seemed to leap from the sea as one of their flotilla was hit and burst into flames. There was a concerted groan from those of the crew of MTB 47 who had noticed it and had to stand helplessly by as the fuel that had spilled from the stricken vessel blazed like molten metal lighting up the sea surface. Men, their comrades, were burning and dying back there.

'Open fire!' commanded the Captain in grim response as he witnessed the tragic scene expanding on his right hand side. His bridge shook violently as the six pounder cracked out and was joined by the deafening machine guns on either side. Meanwhile in retaliation the remaining MTBs raced from the shadows with every gun firing to join MTB 47 as they took on the German boats.

The fire from the dying MTB lit up the sea around them and they could now make out three enemy boats well on the starboard side. They had been sitting silently; waiting in ambush using the old ruse of lying near a navigational buoy. The radar would have only shown them up as one blip – that is if they had had radar.

Their combined cannon shells tore into the hulls of the enemy; a fraction of a pause and then one boat exploded in a huge flash. 'Must be a mine carrying ship,' muttered the Cox half to himself. The Captain heard and nodded grimly. Before he could reply the sky was suddenly full of lethal pieces raining down upon the crew, on the decks and into the surrounding sea. Spray shot up alongside their own hull as the fragments from the destroyed ship landed in the sea.

'On helmets everyone.'

The air was soon full of thick choking smoke from the burning wreckage and then immediately joined by tracer balls that swept down relentlessly on the MTB flotilla. The accuracy of the gunners became threatened as they fought to dodge the trace and wipe the tears that streamed down their faces. A man suddenly shrieked in pain as bullets and shells ripped past the bridge and deck guns.

The MTBs own tracer shells rippled along the enemy hulls and bridges causing their own mayhem.

'Depth charges,' said the skipper as he wiped his stinging eyes with a sodden neck cloth.

The crew got to work and there was a sudden clang as the depth charges were lobbed across the nearest enemy's bows. The charge went under the German hull and there followed an almighty explosion as it made contact. The enemy hull appeared to leap from the water, lifting her bows high until they were pointing to the skies. The depth charges and the internal blast had dealt her a mortal blow and she was breaking up. Slowly, she went down under the frothing waves, hissing and groaning, leaving her men to flounder in the sea.

Chalmers gave the order to come across broadsides of the last enemy E boat and then, 'Stand by torpedoes. Fire!'

The torpedoes leapt from their tubes, the front end lifting slightly as the metal fish increased their speed. They struck their target and immediately she exploded with a piercing flash. A solid wall of flame shot up the side of the stricken vessel. The sudden new light picked out tiny details with a shocking starkness and clarity as the ship gleamed in the fire from the explosion below decks.

Billy could smell the stink of cordite and blistering paintwork and something else. He noticed the upturned floating bodies in the water and hurriedly turned away, to retch over the side.

He'd never get used to it. Never in a million years. Whether it was enemy or friend. Part of the Coastal Defences job was to probe and jab at enemy supply lines and their own defences. It meant never giving them time to rest or to increase them. Sometimes they got caught out themselves and their losses were high. Then, they would stagger home, dejected and saddened by all that they'd witnessed and done. They were often called the Navy's Infantry and it was frequently said that the Coastal Forces took all the hard cases and others rejected by other branches of the Navy. Whatever the truth, they fought hard and tough often against unmitigating odds with sheer bravado and guts.

'Got the bastard, thank Jesus Christ!' said Ginger standing next to him at the boat's side. He had a smear of blood down his left cheek where a bullet had grazed him. Billy silently wiped his mouth on his sleeve, the acid and bile lingering hot in his throat.

A signal was given from the bridge and the now smaller flotilla regrouped. By now there were no longer any men floundering in the water. Those that had been were long gone; burnt by the burning oil or mangled by the ships' screws. Grim-faced and exhausted the men of the little flotilla turned their boats and headed for home.

The gunners sat by their weapons, their tired weary eyes straining into the night. Although homeward-bound they still had to maintain a good lookout. Casualties all too often occurred on the home leg. They roared through the darkness, a furrow of their wake pale behind them in the starlight. The thick glutinous kye was passed round the men, accompanied by thick Spam sandwiches. The hands welcomed the sustenance and wolfed it down dry parched throats lustily.

After a motor ride of an hour the flotilla hove to and the crew were posted around the deck. They listened with their engines off for the whereabouts of other enemy boats. The machine gunners silently swung their barrels in wide arcs, while the torpedo men checked over their remaining metal fish.

Billy's boat had one serious casualty. The young crewman was carried down from the open deck by Billy and Ginger and gently laid on to a bunk. Below decks the lighting was dim and the cabin walls were running wet from a leak in the decking.

They found Tubby hurriedly ripping open wads of lint ready to place in the injured boy's groin to staunch the flow of blood. The boy's face was gleaming with sweat in the dim light as he quietly moaned for his mother.

Billy joined Tubby to give him a hand, noticing the boy's critical condition. Tubby met Billy's eyes and gave a barely perceptible shake of his head. He shifted the position of the pressure bandage in the boy's groin and as he renewed the dressing Billy could see the boy's blood pumping out of him. There was nothing they could do to stop the flow and by the time they got home it would be too late for the surgeon. The young sailor stopped moaning and slipped into blissful unconsciousness. His face was deathly pale in the light and they knew that he hadn't long to live.

A shadow passed over them and looking up they realised that the skipper had joined them below.

'What chance?' He asked the question softly.

Tubby shook his head in resignation.

Chalmers let his gaze rest on the boy for a minute. He had only been with them for two months. Compassion showed in his face and the realisation of the futility of the first aid. Only a few minutes and he would be another victim, another statistic of the war. Another letter he would have to write to a mother, leaving her grieving along with thousands of others. Nineteen years old. No life. What a waste. He sighed and straightened up, passing a hand over his red-rimmed eyes.

'Do your best. As you always do,' he added and turned to go back out onto the deck. One fatality on board his boat and the entire crew of another MTB. Plus of course the enemy's dead. You couldn't forget the enemy. They also had mothers waiting feverishly back home for the latest news of their sons.

Chalmers stomped back onto the bridge and gave the order to increase speed. Sod the rationing of fuel. The sooner they got home the better, he thought. We've had enough shit thrown at us for one night.

He thought of home. He thought of his fiancée Fiona. Of her pretty smiling face, her soft breasts and her welcoming arms. Yes he longed to get home. Safe and stress free.

The boat surged forward throwing up great arcs of frothy water from the bows, soaking both the Cox and captain up on the bridge. The captain ignored it. It was just one of the irritations that went with the job.

The reflections of the stars swayed and danced in the broad wave that gracefully curved back from the bows as the MTB slowed in the home approach. A dark line appeared on the port bow; soon dawn would find them safely back in harbour.

A dockhand caught the heaving line flung ashore by Billy. 'Where've you been mate?' he asked as he took a turn around the bollard.

Billy thought for a moment. Of all the past night's activities. The fatalities and the horror of it all. Who could understand?

'Sitting in the front row of the stalls, chum.'

Chapter 12

The crew could hardly believe it. Thirty-six hours shore leave!

Billy couldn't get washed and changed quickly enough. He legged it to the dock gates and hailed a passing Land Rover. With his silver soft tongue Billy hurriedly thought up a convincing enough story about needing to get home to a sick relative. With some relief he managed to persuade the Naval occupants to give him a lift as far as the railway station. From there he could easily catch a train with his Naval rail pass for the rest of the way to Bishop's Waltham. He was delighted that he didn't have to be back until twenty hundred hours on Sunday evening. That gave him and Penny two days and an evening together. It was almost a weekend. Time enough to relax and unwind. The thought of spending so much time with Penny excited him more than he would have at first thought possible.

He had hurriedly packed a few essentials into his kit bag: razor, smokes, fresh underwear, and socks. He'd also picked up a few goodies that he had managed to cajole out of Carole from the mess. He'd scored well this time; tea, half a pound of butter, a piece of ham, a little sugar, a small piece of bacon and for Pen's Dad a small bottle of Navy rum. Penny's parents always made him feel welcome and even more so once they had learned that he had lost both parents not that long ago in the bombing. Hopefully, Maggie and Maurice would be right pleased to see him and his gifts and would forgive him for dropping in at short notice.

The train pulled into the country village station with much wheezing and hissing of steam. Billy climbed down from the sooty carriage and let the door slam shut behind him. The cold wind whistled around the roof rafters and he shivered slightly in his uniform jacket pulling his collar up around his ears. He looked around him in recognition and again felt the same warm comforting feeling he always got when he visited here.

He didn't know just what it was but whenever he came here he felt as if he was coming home to peace and quiet and a little normality.

Somehow being in the country helped him to forget the horrors of the past six hectic months since joining the Coastal Forces. Sortie after sortie. Long cold hours spent cruising up and down the south coast, or lying in wait, silently in the dark listening for the enemy. Staying in the submarine pens of Dover. Those spooky cavernous dark holes where the black water sucked and gurgled against the hull. They had spent weeks of patrolling, searching for scattered convoys, rounding them up and escorting them to safety. The repeated attacks. Constant work on the boat after seeing action: oiling the guns, repairing the hull after being strafed with bullets, rebuilding the bridge deck after a hit, refilling the cracks and splinters, reloading the ammunition, depth charges. The list was endless and the crew totally exhausted.

Of course not all the crew were original. There had been seven injured and of these five had been fatal. Billy constantly counted his chickens and although he didn't believe or know how to believe in God, he felt something powerful was surely looking down upon him.

The stationmaster blew his whistle and cheerily waved at the engine driver leaning out of his cab window. The train gathered speed as it moved on along the shiny metal tracks and out of the station. Billy nodded politely to the stationmaster, hitched his kitbag onto his shoulder and pushed his way through the little white wooden gate and turned onto the path leading to Lower Lane. He passed the duck ponds, swelled with the recent rains and noticed the large resident flocks of waterfowl. Although he couldn't name them all he recognised (thanks to Penny) mallard ducks, coots, moorhens and a family of swans. The parents – he had been informed – were made up of a pen and cob and their three growing cygnets from last summer. A few months ago he wouldn't have looked twice but Penny was painstaking in her rural education for him and now he smiled to himself as he remembered her gentle lessons. There was no harm in it anyway.

Now the pond life was busy diving and whistling amongst the waterweed and seemed to appreciate the weak early morning sunshine. It had been cold last night and around the water edge the grasses and reeds were still spiked with a glistening frost.

Billy whistled a popular tune he'd recently heard and stepped out the half-mile or so to Hoe Cottage down the country road. The lane was sheltered from the wind and the air felt warmer and soft against his face. His boots crunched through the thin ice on a puddle and a robin sang shrilly from a holly bush still covered in red berries. Under the willows he could see some tiny white flowers nestling in the grass. He hadn't a clue as to what they might be but he knew Penny would soon put him right. He picked her a small posy as a present. The white petals stood out starkly against the deep green of the stem and leaves. Small, white and pretty, just like Penny he thought with a smile playing around his mouth. She would be so surprised to see him and overjoyed that he had thirty-six hours shore leave.

Looking back, he realised with a sudden jolt that they had been together for over six months courting. And what's more he'd not looked at another girl during that time spent together. Well, not seriously anyway. In his heart he knew Penny was special. He only had to look at her and he felt different. She made him feel slightly dizzy and his mouth would go dry. He always felt like he wanted to look after her and protect her.

Over the past few months, the desire of going out with the lads on pub crawls around Gosport and Portsmouth, or chasing after the girls had gone out of the window. Now he wanted to behave more seriously, more adult and caring. Foremost he wanted to look good and shine in her eyes. He had even fleetingly thought about asking her to wear his ring to show her and the others how serious he was. The thing was he was scared to. Scared that she'd not accept him; maybe he wasn't even good enough for her. After all she was a farmer's daughter and he was just a simple sailor. But he could try to improve his lot, get promotion and once the war was over, well who knew what that would bring?

Feeling happy and eager he let his heels ring out smartly on the metalled road. He passed the postman and a horse-drawn dray carrying large milk churns and a fat dairy man. They both wished him a cheery morning and once again he drew in the fresh, clean air and the unhurried pace of life here in the country. For once he felt at peace, safe, warm, unafraid and whole.

Penny's home stood back from the road. The front garden would normally have been filled with cottage garden flowers and plants during peacetime. Now the flowerbeds were dormant, waiting for the planting of saladings in the forthcoming spring. Flowers were a luxury no one could afford these days. Behind the house the acres were filled with the much valued vegetables and fruits needed to help feed the country.

Billy opened the little white picket fence gate and started up the front path to the door. He suddenly had an idea and on impulse changed direction and went around the side of the house leaving his kit bag on the front grass.

Somehow he had known just where to find her. There she was in front of him grappling with a huge white sheet, pegs stuffed in her mouth as she endeavoured to anchor it to the washing line.

'Here let me,' he said taking it from her arms and skilfully slinging the wet item over the line.

'Billy!' she squealed in delight. He reached down and placing his hands on her waist swung her up and around.

'What are you doing here?' she asked breathlessly when he eventually put her back down on the grass.

'I have a 36 hour pass. Sorry love, I couldn't let you know in advance. It was suddenly sprung upon us.'

'That's all right. A 36-hour pass! Oh Billy I'm just so glad you're here.'

She buried her head against his chest and hugged him close breathing in his familiar smell of Navy serge, tobacco and a slight salty tang.

'We'd better let your Mum and Dad know I'm here. And see if I'm welcome to a bed,' he smiled down at her and draped an arm around her shoulders giving her a squeeze.

'They won't mind a bit. They love having you here, especially Dad as he gets a bit fed up with just girls in the house. He even complains that the chickens are all female except for the cockerel! Besides having no sons doing their bit for the war effort irks him a bit so he enjoys having you around and listening to your heroics.'

'Oh I don't know about that.'

She laughed and almost skipped along at his side as they walked back to the house.

'Mum, Dad guess who's here?' she called as they opened the back door.

A warm delicious smell of baking hit them as they entered the little lobby before the kitchen.

Maggie Clarke wiped her floury hands on her apron, as she turned from her pastry, with a surprised smile of welcome on her face.

'Well, Billy my dear you're a surprise. It's nice to see you. How come you're here?'

'Hello Mrs C. It's nice to see you and to be here. I've got a 36-hour pass and don't have to be back in Gosport until eight o'clock tomorrow evening. So, I wanted to surprise Penny and well, here I am. Er, is it convenient? Please say if it's not.'

'Lord yes. You know you're perfectly welcome anytime. Anytime. And I expect you'll be wanting a bed for tonight? Well, it's no trouble. Penny can sleep in with her sister and you can have Penny's bed,' she replied.

'Uh oh. I hope Mavis doesn't mind.' He knew Penny's waspish sister and how difficult she could sometimes be.

'Now don't you bother about her. She's been a right little madam just lately. Getting too big for her boots is our Mavis. Ever since she started working at Vickers. Thinks she is above us all here. Well she needs to be kept in check and to remember that she's just a chit of a girl and she's still living at home. Whilst she's still under our roof she'll do as she's told,' Maggie said with a frown of annoyance passing over her kindly face.

'Well if you're sure. If there is any trouble I can always ask at The Crown for a room.'

'What and waste good money giving it to that rogue of a landlord? You will not. No, certainly not, Maurice and I are very happy to have you here. Now how about a nice cuppa? Penny love, be a good girl and put the kettle on.'

Penny looked at Billy and smiled a complete look of contentment, Billy grinned back in response. Maggie pretended not to notice the look that passed between them. Much as they liked Billy, Penny was still only sixteen. Mind you with this war on, who was to know what would happen next? She sighed to herself. Young love, who was she to interfere?

'Oh, I forgot. I've left my kitbag outside. I've got something for you. I'll just get it.' He retraced his footsteps out the back of the house.

'Oh ma. Thank you for letting Billy stay. You don't know how much it means to him.'

'I do. I know he still regrets his parents passing away and he misses his mother especially, even if he doesn't say so. Besides I have a lot of time for that young man. He's conscientious and treats you well. Not forgetting the rotten job he has to put up with. No, your Dad and I wouldn't dream of him staying elsewhere.'

They heard the back door opening and Billy re-entered the kitchen carrying a heavy looking kitbag and the posy of snowdrops. He upended his bag over the kitchen table and Maggie and Penny both squealed in delight at the cascade of goodies spread before them.

'Ooh tea, butter and look at this bacon and ham. Your Dad's going to love that rum. Chocolate too! Billy you spoil us something rotten.' Together they cooed over the spoils on the scrubbed pine.

'That's the idea Mrs C,' he grinned at her, 'can I put this somewhere out of the way?'

'Penny take Billy up to your room and show him where to put his stuff. I'll just put these in water. Oh thank you Billy they're lovely and our favourite.'

She shooed them both out of the kitchen and returned to her pie making. The ham would go nicely with the two rabbits that she'd got from old Ted. Ham and rabbit pie. What a treat! Damn Hitler for trying to starve us out. We'll show him. Stewed apples for afters with a spot of jam. A proper feast they'd have. It would be nice to have something to celebrate for a change.

***

Penny led Billy outside when it was time for her to feed the chickens and collect the newly laid eggs. They found nineteen brown eggs and carefully laid them in the empty feed basket before putting them in the pantry.

'Fresh eggs for breakfast and some left over to sell,' she said, 'we're luckier than most. We can have eggs whenever we want and fresh fruit, saladings and vegetables. Old Ted regularly gives us a rabbit or pheasant, and we have plenty of fresh milk from Bluebell.'

He remembered the last summer during strawberry time. Maggie had made a little cream for the family on the quiet and, even now he could still taste the delicious strawberries and cream they'd had for tea along with a cake. Cor! There was nothing like a real good English tea. His own Mum had been a dab hand at baking, thick slabs of rich fruitcake, rhubarb crumble and custard, and apple pies. The food they got back in their mess was probably enough for the demanding role they played but not what you'd call good home cooking.

That was one of the problems with the war; everything was in such short supply. Most things had to be bought with ration coupons and, even then after you had spent ages in a queue there was no guarantee that you would be able to get just what you wanted. There was very little variation in the diet and the quality of the goods was often very dubious.

However, supper that night was a different matter with Billy's exotic additions to the family's meal and voted a rip roaring success.

***

It was getting late as Penny and Billy walked back from the Crown that night. They had only had one drink, as this was 'blank week' for Billy. It could have been 'bleak week' as far as he was concerned in so much as 'blank' meant pay day was far off.

The pale winter sun had long gone to bed and there was a raw coldness in the air. The sky was very clear and the stars shone with a sharp silver brittleness. The hedges and ditches were already edged with a keen hoar frost and nothing moved to rustle the dead leaves at their feet. They walked swiftly to keep their bodies warm and the only sound was their footsteps as they crunched along on the dry road.

'Going to be a sharp frost tonight,' said Billy his hot breath forming great whirls in front of him.

Penny shivered involuntarily in her check woollen coat, her hands deep in her pockets.

Billy looked down at her. 'Cold? Here,' he said and put his arm around her and tucked her nearest hand into his own pocket, 'better?'

'Mmm. Much better now,' she replied sighing and snuggling closer into the comfort of his arms.

'Not far to go now, we'll soon be home. I hope your Mum and Dad have kept the fire going.'

The lane stretched ahead in complete darkness. The blackout was effective; no light shone from any of the nearby houses. It should have been eerie but somehow the blackness was comforting all around them.

Penny's house loomed up ahead of them and soon they were feeling their way along the path round to the back door. The kitchen stood warm and welcoming after the freezing cold outside. They thankfully pulled off their heavy coats and outdoor shoes and stood in their stockinged feet before the kitchen range. The warmth was heavenly after being outside. Billy put his arms around Penny and pulled her closer. She closed her eyes in anticipation and met his lips as he bent his head down towards her. The simple kiss was sweet and they drew apart with lips parted and their eyes shining. Neither said a word. This time the kiss went deeper and longer until they remembered where they were and drew apart breathless, their hands trembling.

'I think we'd better go through to the other room,' Billy said a little shakily.

Penny nodded in agreement. Her face was quite pink and rosy from both the outside cold and Billy's kisses. Taking his hand she led the way down the hall.

Maggie was sitting in her chair to the right of the fireplace. There was a log fire burning brightly and the whole room was filled with the pleasant smell of wood smoke. She had been quietly knitting; reading glasses perched on her nose as she counted the rows of the intricate pattern she was making. Maurice was semi-dozing, his newspaper half draped across his knees and half on the floor. Nell the collie was of course hogging the hearthrug. She thumped her tail in welcome but made no effort to move from her prime spot in front of the fire. The whole scene was warm and cosy. The furniture was old and well-worn but comfortable and homely. An eighteenth century Grandfather clock happily ticked away in its oak case in the corner while the fire threw out flickering shapes and shadows around the walls. It was a room that made you feel relaxed and happy to be in.

Billy sighed to himself in contentment. If only the others could see him now. They'd surely envy him this girl, with her warm comfortable house and friendly family. He realised that he'd never felt happier. If only it weren't for Hitler and the war, life would be just about perfect.

They settled themselves on the carpet in front of the fire and made a fuss of Nell. She nuzzled them eagerly and then rolled over onto her back so they could tickle her stomach more easily.

Maggie enquired as to whether they had had a nice walk to the pub and who had been there. After a few minutes of small conversation, she rolled up her knitting and put it behind her chair in a large brightly coloured bag. She stood up and addressed Penny's father as he struggled to pretend to still be asleep. It was so warm in here and not so upstairs. He knew only too well what was coming.

'Come on Maurice. Time's getting on and you may as well sleep in your own bed as down here.' He gave a slight groan of protest but stopped as she gave him a look. Stiffly he stood up and stretched himself. With choruses of 'good night' all round and 'don't forget the fireguard' and 'don't be too late to bed', Maggie and Maurice departed up the stairs.

Billy smiled at Penny who giggled in reply as they drew closer together on Nell's hearthrug. Another five minutes or so alone together wouldn't hurt.

***

Sunday was another bright and frosty, cold day. Again the promise of wintry sunshine would melt the frost and thaw the ice on the duck pond.

Nell needed a good long walk as she was in danger of getting too idle in front of the fire. So, after the lunch things had been washed and put away Billy and Penny had grabbed her lead and set off over the fields and woods. Nell was tireless and they had walked a good three miles or more before they had decided to turn for home. The countryside was deep in the depths of a cold winter and they saw very few other people out walking. Cars of course were hardly ever seen due to the petrol rationing.

They walked back through the grounds of pretty St Peter's church in the village centre. The grounds were typical with fallen and leaning old tombstones covered with lichens and ivy. The yew tree stood in a corner and loomed dark and pagan against the pale blue winter sky. A blackbird hopped hopefully amongst the debris of leaves and moss at its base in search of food. A pigeon cooed mournfully from the church roof. They paused before the stone cenotaph and read the names of the dead that had fallen during the last Great War. The names were local to the village and Penny pointed out this name and that and who they had been in relation to the living. They decided there had been too many. The stone was sobering, especially to Billy who too had lost many friends in the last few years. They left the churchyard and it's sleeping inhabitants and headed back down Hoe Lane.

The house was quiet when they got back. They had the place to themselves as Maggie and Maurice were visiting Maggie's sister who lived in the next village of Swanmore. Earlier they had both gone off puffing their way along the lane on their ancient bicycles. They had said not to expect them back for tea and they were to help themselves to fresh bread and a bit of that ham from the pantry. A piece of seed cake was in the tin for them too.

The bright afternoon light had given way to the twilight of a winter's evening and soon the full darkness would descend on them as black as Jack's Hat.

The sitting-room fire had got very low. Billy added a couple of good sized logs and a small handful of precious coal to get it burning brightly while Penny made them a cup of welcoming tea. Nell was flaked out on her usual hearthrug.

They sat on the rug, either side of the dog, drinking their tea. They didn't say a word. Billy's pending 8 o'clock curfew was looming mournfully over them.

The warmth of the fire made Penny drowsy and she yawned before she placed a chair cushion on the floor and laid her head on it. Billy watched her for a minute.

'You're very pretty lying there, half asleep.'

She opened her eyes and smiled. 'I'm not really asleep. I was just thinking that I didn't want you to go back.'

They gazed at each other, a stillness suddenly descending between them.

Billy moved nearer to her and took her face in both hands. He kissed her gently. She wound her arms around his neck and kissed him back eagerly. She no longer felt like a 16 year old to him. He kissed her again, gently and tenderly and then turned to bury his face and breathe in the clean scented profusion of her hair. His hands felt beneath the soft wool of her sweater and blouse the slenderness of her young body. His own heart thumped like a drum imprisoned in his chest, and every nerve in his body jangled with his need of her. His strong fingers trembled as he made short work of all the tiny buttons of her blouse as she lay there. She didn't attempt to stop him. He kissed her mouth, her neck, and her tiny creamy breasts. Her response was shy and sweet and accepting. 'You're so beautiful.'

As she kissed him back he knew that she had been simply waiting for him.

***

It was later. A charged disturbance now lay between them. He thought she was the most exciting, provoking, beautiful girl he had ever met. A girl who seemed completely unaware of how attractive she was. She stirred in his arms and sat up. Her clothes were in complete disarray, but her face was serene and smiling.

'We'd better tidy up before Mum and Dad get home.'

In response Billy leaned forward and kissed her. They had loved twice. Once with unseemly haste and the other with less urgency. Time between to kiss and whisper endearments before passion overwhelmed them and they had fused into a whole. Afterwards they had clung together, neither willing to part. The wonder of it had shown in her face.

'I love you,' she had whispered, her lips close to his ear.

'I love you too.' His hands had shaken with the realization of the beauty which had taken place between them.

Now, he had to think about leaving her and travelling back to his base. Back to night-time sorties and their horrors. What if he was killed and didn't come back? He'd never know a real life with a woman. There would be no time for a home, or loving or children.

'I don't want to leave you, but, I have to. This damn war. But, my dear, I'm deadly serious. I want you to be my girl. Maybe even wear my ring and later…'

'Ssssh!' she placed a finger on his lips, 'I know you have a job to do. We all have our role to play in this horrible war. But, I'll be here and I'll always be your girl. You must know that. You are my first and last lover.'

Billy could only gaze at her in wonder. This girl of 16 was more of a woman than most of the others he'd known. Sometimes she seemed much older and wiser than he gave her credit for.

The sound of the back door being opened and the sudden cold draught that followed stopped them further. They guiltily sprang apart and Penny smoothed down her skirt and wild unruly hair. Billy sat in a chair and called the dog over to pet with assumed nonchalance.

'Brrr. It's a bit parky out there. Think we need a cuppa,' said Maggie as she poked her head around the door. 'What have you two been up to? Did you have a nice walk?'

'I'll get it Mum,' said Penny and hurried out of the door to the kitchen.

'Think a drop of that rum won't go amiss. Billy lad, will you join me in a tot?' asked Maurice holding up the bottle that Billy had brought him.

'I won't, thank you. I have to be going to catch my train back to Gosport way.'

He would have loved a drink. Especially after all that had happened this afternoon. The rum, however, was a gift. Shorts were non-existent in the local pubs and Billy got more than his fair share on board.

Penny saw him to the door. Maggie was searching for his coat and muffler until Maurice told her to 'stop fussing woman and let them say goodbye to each other proper like.' She caught his knowing eye and getting the message withdrew to the warm sitting room.

Billy and Penny stood stiffly as they gazed in silence at each other.

Finally she couldn't bear it any longer. 'Have a good journey back and a safe trip tonight, wherever you're going.'

She pressed her face against his chest, her voice muffled. Billy had his arms tightly held around her. He breathed in the smell of her hair, woody from the afternoon log fire. He'd remember it later, when he was cold and alone on the deck of his boat, somewhere on the dark English Channel.

'I can't say what we'll be doing tonight, but I will take care. Anyway as I've said before I lead a charmed life. I'll try and telephone you on Thursday. I think we're due for a spot of maintenance work then in the shipyard. Can you get to the coal merchants to take a call?'

They stepped out into the dark garden, shutting the door firmly behind them. No chink of light was allowed to show. Some people had even been fined recently for these small breaches of the rules.

Together they walked to the gate and Billy hoisted his kit bag onto his shoulder; a lot lighter than when he had first arrived. The cold night air enveloped them in a cocoon of misty fog.

Penny felt a sudden panic. There was a deep sadness and an intense feeling of being left all alone and bereft. 'Oh Billy! Please take care. I couldn't bear it if anything happened to you.'

A lump was building in her throat making it hard for her to swallow. She knew that if he stayed much longer she would break down and cry her heart out. She never wanted him to see her selfish, foolish tears. Billy laughed. 'Me love? Oh nothing's going to happen to me! I know that something powerful is looking after this Jack! I'll speak to you Thursday. Go on, go in, don't catch cold.'

He placed his hat jauntily on his head, gave her a kiss and a last squeeze around the waist and was away. He didn't stop and look back; after all it was bad luck. Penny watched her first love until he was swallowed up by the dark night.

Chapter 13

It was a filthy night; just right for feeling wretchedly, miserably seasick. MTB 47 was punching her way west in the teeth of a rapidly rising south-westerly gale. No sailor likes a gale; those in a small 70-feet wooden boat hate them.

The seas were huge as she plunged her nose into an advancing wave. Masses of solid sheets of water poured over her sending sheets of spray up onto the bridge.

It was as black as Jacks hat, and not a light showed. The entire southern coast of England was under a complete blackout. Not a chink of light was shown anywhere.

'Flash on the 'orizon on the port bow Sir,' said the Cox gruffly.

There was a sudden fiery trail as a rocket cleft the air, way over to the coast of France.

They continued on their course, pushing their way towards that other coast. Hostile shells continued to fall. There was a violent explosion and a bright flame of detonation as they found their target, the funnel of a small coastal steamer.

Billy was below in the engine room. The noise and smell here was overpowering adding to the discomfort of the lousy weather.

Billy and a second stoker were assisting the engineer, making up the 'black gang' on board. The engineer was an ex garage mechanic and no doubt would go back to fixing cars once peace was declared. For now he was coaxing the best out of the hard-working engine. On a previous sortie, an exploding shell from a German destroyer had damaged the shaft to the starboard screw. It had been fixed as best he could but it was nowhere near as good as it had once been.

Billy felt really sick and tired. The gale hadn't been foreseen and they were all taken by surprise. The last two weeks had been spent in company as ' a combat flotilla on special ops.' MTB 47 plus five other MTBs had been carrying out attacks on enemy supply ships. They had been issued with extra mines that they carried on deck, additional drums of fuel, and torpedoes and magazines for the rapid-fire

147

armament. Their whole position had been extremely dangerous and stressful.

Luckily, the wind was now starting to ease down, 44 knots of wind dropping to 36 knots and then 24 knots. The waves began to fall but the long swell would continue for a good while longer.

Tonight for once they were on their own. A clandestine operation. They were to head towards the French coast and at a prearranged location were to run a spy ashore. It was dangerous at the best of times, but doubly dangerous with this weather hampering events. They needed the seas to calm down before launching the rubber boat to carry their passenger in to the beach.

Billy and his run-ashore oppos knew there was going to be trouble that night when he had overheard the number one saying, 'there's a bit of a flap on Sir.' Trouble that was, for them on board. Whenever they received poop from Group – that is official word from on high, they knew that the shit was about to fly!

So, now they were about fifteen miles out from Cap Gris Nez where they knew the enemy had a battery of shore guns lined up. The wind and sea continued to die down and MTB 47 slowly headed nearer towards the coast. They altered course to avoid the sand spit of Ridge and headed for the buoy that was two miles off France, easing down to a mere 3 knots at the final approach to the buoy. Numerous ships had come to grief along this stretch of coastline. The enemy liked nothing better than to hug the buoys and prey on unsuspecting allied craft.

Billy was sent up on deck to give a hand with the launching of the rubber boat. He paused and grabbed a lungful of fresh air before crabbing his way along the deck towards the launch team. They had a winch prepared and soon the boat was being lowered over the side. The spy was squashed in the tiny galley, keeping well out of the way until he was called for disembarking. Suddenly, the night erupted with exploding shells flinging up great columns of water all around them. There were overhead star shells that lit up the sky followed by sharp bangs and cascading spray.

The covers were hurriedly ripped off the gun muzzles; hatches and doors were slammed shut. The gun operators were jammed into their harnesses and behind their gun-shields.

'Hard a – starboard,' yelled the Captain. 'All guns open fire!'

The MTB slewed around, the gun crew hammering violently their return fire. Their faces showed their tension in their red-rimmed eyes. They were now toughened hands; no one older than 24 years but, they readjusted their gun sights like older men; now as experienced as the old timers. Toughened hands that once held office pens, pushed a baker's bicycle or served in grocer's shops gossiping with the housewives, their customers.

Splinters appeared in the hull as a shell ripped through the flag locker and then exploded above the side deck. More bullets and cannon shells followed it.

'German E Boat Sir!' yelled number one.

'Yes, and accompanying fire from on land I see,' he replied grimly, nodding towards the near coast. 'I don't see how we can now make the drop.'

The German E boat was much bigger than the MTB. With her camouflage paint of blue and grey and black stripes she looked huge and menacing. She had three Daimler-Benz diesel engines and could easily outrun them with her own 42 knots. Her weaponry was also superior, boasting powerful 30 and 37 millimetre cannon and four torpedoes.

'Looks like we're going to have our work cut out. On helmets everyone!' he yelled from the open bridge.

The cannon and machine-gun fire continued, crashing into and around the boat. Small flames, smoke and wood splinters filled the air.

'Helm on the wheel.'

'Stand by torpedoes.'

There was another crash and rattle of gunfire. Tracer cut across the pale dawn.

The crew could feel the deck kick slightly, and saw the brief splash beyond the bows as: 'Torpedoes running, Sir!'

The MTB curtsied round. She fought with her rudders and screws to get clear of the danger from the enemy boat. Tearing the water apart she emerged from behind a wall of smoke.

Billy was thrown roughly against a baulwark. Righting himself he saw that the front gunner was hanging lifeless by his harness straps. He staggered along the side to the gun and eased the dead sailor out and gently down onto the deck. A quick feeling of remorse flickered across his face as he looked down at his now dead friend before he took his seat behind the vacant gun. There was no one else to take the dead sailor's place.

'Come and play you bastards,' he muttered to himself softly.

Bright green balls of tracer shot across the boat; they all ducked instinctively down. They could hear the distant crump, crump, crump from the shore battery getting nearer. They were at the mercy of the enemy from both sides. They said that a single year in the Coastal Forces made you a professional. Billy let rip with the gun, swivelling round in a wide arc. Well, he was a professional all right!

There was an enormous bang as a shell exploded half a cable from the MTB. The next second Billy was being lifted from his position. He half-turned and watched as the wheelhouse and the whole bridge deck burst upwards and outwards. With a groan of despair he saw bodies being flung around like bundles of ragged scarecrows. He stumbled painfully to his feet, brushing off broken woodwork and glass, and took in the chaotic scene before him.

The entire bridge party of skipper, number one and coxswain were lying on the lower deck. Christ! What carnage!

Keeping low he scurried over to the skipper. 'You OK, Sir?' he asked. The skipper was looking dazed and blinked at Billy crouching before him. Blood oozed from a wound on his forehead and trickled into his eyes. He was half lying amidst the chaos. Small flames flickered around him.

'Yes, near thing though. Slight wound on my head,' he gingerly touched at the 3-inch gash above his eyes and was breathing heavily. The wound showed as a thin white slash in the light from the deck fire.

Billy looked around him. The cox was lying facedown a few feet away. Billy turned him over gently looking for a wound. He suddenly realised with a start that he was dead but unmarked, killed outright by the blast. He groaned to himself. Oh no, not Coxie. He was as tough as old boots. If Billy had had to place a bet on anyone he would have wagered a week's wages on Coxie seeing the war out. He had been a good all rounder. Hard on discipline but scrupulously fair on all the lads. They'd all miss him and his smelly pipe on the bridge deck. And what about his wife Nancy? She was just expecting their first child. Coxie had been as pleased as punch when he had let slip that he was going to be a Dad. Now the child would never know its father and poor Nancy would be distraught. Guiltily, Billy felt relieved that he wasn't the commanding officer with the unenviable task of letting wives and mothers know when their husbands or sons had been killed in action. It was happening all too often. He knew that relatives feared the envelope that would bring them the dreaded news. He laid Coxie gently back down on the wet deck and moved away from him. His attention was now turned to Number One. Billy didn't need to examine him too closely. The Number One was lying half-propped against the boat's side, pinioned by a sheet plate embedded in his chest. Billy didn't need to look twice to check he was dead.

'Poor bugger,' he said to himself. He had been some sort of scientist, a botanist or such in Civvy Street before the war. The last person you'd expect to find on board a warship. All he'd ever wanted was to see the war out and rejoin his beloved companions at the University where he had been studying for a Doctorate. He had been a gentle soul. Intent on getting the job done in order to carry on the life he had led before he'd joined up. Billy and the rest of the lads had never really understood him but they had respected his quiet courage and despite a few unkind jests had got on with him pretty well.

What about the others on the main deck? Stumbling forward he soon came across Tubby. Or what had been Tubby. His face was torn away. Ginger was lying nearby and dying fast. His left arm was missing and he had a massive wound to his groin. His blood was all over the deck and mingled with the seawater. Billy recognised the familiar smell of iron and his mouth filled with water brash as he swallowed hard to stop himself vomiting.

The thrum, thrum of the heavy German diesels brought him out of his sickened trance. The enemy, without mercy had raked them, and they had to retaliate fast. He raced back to the gun he had been manning before the blast. Fire and reload. Fire and reload. The gun shimmered with heat. He found he was seized by a frantic haste to avenge his mates' deaths. All his mates' deaths. He didn't know how long he stayed there until he was suddenly aware of the figure that appeared at his side; the skipper had staggered down the deck to find him.

'It's no good Barker. We're the only ones left. They're all dead. I've been below,' he stopped and swayed slightly on his feet. Billy put out a hand to steady him. The skipper looked ashen faced in the flickering light from the surrounding burning debris. He continued in a hoarse voice.

'The rudder has been badly hit and we've sustained a bloody great hole in the port side. We've been going round and round in an ever decreasing circle and getting hammered from the shore guns.' He suddenly pitched forward and collapsed unconscious at Billy's feet.

Billy was momentarily speechless and stood there stock-still. What the hell was he supposed to do? He couldn't let the boat fall into enemy hands!

That was the last thing the skipper would want. But, he'd just heard that everyone else was dead, and the skipper didn't look too useful at the moment either. He released his hold on the gun and bent over the skipper, checking that he was still breathing. He could discern slow, shallow breaths. The head wound appeared to have almost stopped bleeding and only a slow trickle was falling onto his already sea-drenched duffle coat. He eased the neck scarf out from around his skipper's neck and tied it around the wound. Picking the lieutenant up under his arms he dragged him under the gunwale. Here they would at least get some protection from the enemy.

Billy paused with his head to one side; the guns had quietened down from both German sides. They are probably waiting to see if anyone has survived and then they'll blow us out of the water he thought.

Well we'll see about that. He had an idea.

The rubber tender was unbelievably still attached on its winch and half lowered over the side of the MTB. Miraculously it looked as if three of its four tubes were still intact and inflated. If only he could get the skipper into it and out of harms way they might be able to slip away into the night before the dawn. A slim chance he knew but the alternative was too horrible to think about. He thought about his dead friends. They would all be up for it, every last one of them including Number One.

Keeping his head down he slithered across the deck back to where the skipper lay. He shook him slightly in order to try and bring him round. The captain groaned and clutched his forehead with a shaking hand.

'Sir, Sir! It's me Barker. If you can listen to me, I may be able to get us out of this.'

'Don't think so,' he gasped, 'the rudders pretty much knackered, we can't get away.'

'No Sir! I mean the rubber duck. It's still intact. If we can get you in it Sir, we may be able to sneak away in the smoke and dark before Jerry sees us.'

'It's worth a try,' he paused while he fought for breath and steadied his trembling hands, 'but, I can hardly see, so I don't know what I can do to help you.'

It was true. By now he had a huge contusion over his right eye, which was completely swollen and closed shut. His left eye wasn't much better but at least it was intact and apparently undamaged.

'No Sir. Just you leave it to me. I can do it. Here let's get you over to the side and in place.'

He placed his arms around the skipper's chest and half carried, half lugged him alongside to where the rubber dinghy was attached to the winch.

'Think you can manage to climb over and scramble down if I help you Sir?' he asked when he had got his breath back.

His skipper nodded assent. His face was shining a deathly pallor in the light from the small fire from the bridge superstructure. Billy took a quick look around him. There was no sign of the enemy, and the smoke from the fires was putting up a good screen. Taking a deep breath he put one arm around his skipper and heaved him up onto the side of the boat.

'It's just a short drop Sir. Can you slither over and I'll hang onto you and then let you go when you're in position. You'll have a soft landing on the rubber floor.'

Without waiting for an answer from Chalmers, Billy grasped him by his duffle coat and pushed him over the side. With a little surprised squeak Chalmers fell the short distance and bounced from the side of the dinghy onto the rubber floor below. He lay there, not moving. Billy softly swore to himself. He had no time to go and check on Chalmers' condition. He'd have to leave him for a time whilst he got on with his plans. There was very little time left as it was; dawn couldn't be that far off. Even in the depths of winter the sun could rise and expose them.

Scrabbling back onto the foredeck Billy opened the door into the cramped sleeping quarters. He slipped past the tiny galley and down through the companionway into the engine room. Below he found a grisly mess. He had to ignore the remains of the engineer and the other stoker while he decided which action would be the best to take. The engine room was already partly flooded with its own lethal high-octane fuel and the fumes were overpowering. He negotiated his way back to the crew's quarters and moving aside fallen chairs and a table he located the flare locker. Its wooden door had been blown off and he could see the flares tucked away in their metal boxes inside.

Backtracking to the sleeping quarters Billy threw aside the crew's personal belongings until he found a canvas bag and then he tore back with it to the flare locker. Quickly he upended the boxes, tipped their contents into the bag and then he dragged this outside. His first thought had been to let off a flare in the engine room but on seeing the mess in there with the escaped fuel he quickly decided that that wasn't a good idea at all. He and skip would go up with it!

Instead he found a heavy claw hammer back down in the engine room and edged round to find the big seawater inlet hoses for the engines. He grimly raised the hammer and with all his might brought it down upon the valves of the hoses. Two, three blows and the valves were smashed. The hoses became detached and seawater poured in to the engine room. Time to go he thought. At least with the boat scuttled the Germans wouldn't be able to take her as a prize. With a silent prayer he raced back up the stairway, grabbed the canvas bag and legged it to the side of the boat. He peered down over the side making sure that the rubber dinghy was still there, and saw that Chalmers was still lying unconscious in the bottom. Next he needed his knife, which luckily he found within seconds. He sliced through the webbing strap of the hoist and the boat dropped the last few feet into the water. Billy got astride the boat's side rail and was about to jump down when there was a sudden flash and a shot rang out. Cursing soundly he clutched his thigh in agony as a white-hot stab of pain raced down his leg and he toppled off over the side and fell heavily in the rubber boat.

In frustration and desperation he scrabbled around looking for his knife to cut the painter to which the dinghy was still attached to the MTB. The pain in his leg was coming in waves that made him feel sick and dizzy and disorientated. He couldn't find the knife. Tears of pain and anger ran down his face until he realised that he had in fact put his knife back in his pocket after all. With trembling hands he reached over and grasped the end of the sodden rope and began to feverishly saw away at it.

'Part you bastard,' he swore between his teeth. Freedom and escape lay seconds within their reach. At last the rope fell away from the doomed MTB and they began to float into open water.

Billy lay back gasping with pain and exertion, the blood seeping through his torn trousers mingling freely with the seawater in the bottom of their boat.

The captain suddenly gave a groan of pain and Billy turned his attention back to him at the same time as a sudden beam of white light dazzled them.

'He! Sie dort stehen bleiben-handehoch!' (Oi! You there. Stop! Hands up!)

The unscathed German E-boat had come round the stern of their sinking MTB and was now slowly motoring up to them. A huge white searchlight down on them from its bows. The taste of defeat was in Billy's mouth.

God Almighty; it's the Bloody Hun! he said softly to himself.

Chapter 14

Four days had elapsed since the attack and the scuttling of Billy's boat. Now he found himself locked in a miserable barn together with some other forlorn captured British waiting to be sent to Germany. The outside temperature was freezing cold; the puddles in the rutted track heavily rimmed with ice. Despite the hardships of their temporary accommodation the men were thankful for the last few bales of hay left remaining from the cattle's' winter feed. At least it was dry and above freezing inside the barn.

Billy's injuries had been superficially treated on the German E-boat that had picked them up after MTB 47 had sunk. He had taken a thighful of shrapnel that had badly lacerated his skin and muscle and, he'd lived through agonies of hell for the first 48 hours. Apart from his own injuries and his capture by the Germans he had his skipper to worry about. Chalmers had eventually regained consciousness and Kapitan Witschell of the E-boat was decent enough to ensure that he was given the appropriate medical treatment for a head injury.

On their arrival in France, Chalmers and Billy were separated. Apart from the necessity of finding a hospital bed and doctor for Billy's skipper, Chalmers was an officer and Billy presumed he would be treated differently. He did not expect to see him again.

The last couple of days had held sheer terror for Billy. It was the first time he'd ever set foot on foreign soil and he had agonised as to whether he was going to be shot or not. The other prisoners had heard rumours of an SS Totenkopt (Death's Head) Regiment in the area and as a matter of course they did not take military prisoners. Billy and the others in detention had sat in sick dread waiting to be lined up against the farmhouse wall and mown down by their machine guns. Their mood was of the deepest depression and even the more jovial among their small band eventually gave up trying to jolly the others along. However, there was a stay of execution. They had been assigned to a small group of older guards who were to escort them to Germany. These guards, many of whom had their own old war wounds, were only too thankful to have escaped from the German invasion of Russia in 1941 and to have been assigned less arduous and safer duties like escorting prisoners to detention camps.

Some of these soldiers proved to be not too bad and one or two were even likeable. They too missed their own families and homes and longed for the war to be over. Those that spoke some English each had a story to tell and as Billy worked hard cadging smokes off them and keeping an eye open for any food going spare he tried to build up some sort of rapport with a middle-aged father of two children from Cologne. However, it was hard work and there was always a certain amount of distrust on both sides and besides, he was only too aware that if he was too friendly with the enemy then he could be branded as a collaborator, even if he did share out his cadged cigarettes.

Early the next morning it was time to move out. With much shouting and gesturing they were made to line up outside. Next, despite their protests they were searched; an altogether very unpleasant experience.

By now it had started to snow and there was again a lot of shouting and pointing of guns. They were ordered to remain in their lines and that they were to march to the nearest railway station. Despite the enforced rest in the barn, Billy was in poor shape and had been given no medication for pain relief. Everyone had been given inadequate rations for the last three days and it was having the worst effect on those who were wounded. Billy wondered how far he would in fact be able walk let alone march. A fresh-faced lad with a Suffolk accent found him an old yard broom that would do as a makeshift crutch. Billy propped it under his armpit and after thanking him, joined the others lined up outside in the biting wind.

Off they set. They walked along a sandy track that passed through a lightly wooded area. As they had little or no kit they thankfully had little weight to carry, and because of the bitter cold, any extra clothing they did have, they wore. As they trudged along the tracks they soon developed blisters through their thin socks, and their inadequate boots froze against their bloody, swollen sore feet. They talked little amongst themselves, saving their energy for the hard slog. Billy estimated that they had probably walked about 21 miles when they came upon a mean-looking dilapidated farm. The yard was full of weeds and the farmhouse was derelict and abandoned. The window glass was non-existent and the front door lay broken on the ground. It had clearly been the site of some past battle and the inhabitants had either all been killed or had fled in fear long ago. They all silently noted the dubious dark streaks that covered one of the walls in what had been the kitchen. There remained a rickety long pine table that ran the length of the room and five wooden chairs. The sink had a broken tap that issued no water and was full of smashed beer bottles. Along the windowsills and on the floor were the evidence of resident mice and other vermin. Everything was covered in a thick layer of dust; the house hadn't been visited for years, not even by local courting couples or inquisitive children.

The men were exhausted. They were wet with perspiration inside their jackets, – yet their feet and hands were completely numb with the cold. The guards moodily indicated that they were to sit against the far wall where there were no windows or doors. Two of the guards were told to watch over them by the surly sergeant in charge. When his back was turned they quickly grabbed two of the old chairs for their use and sat with their Mauser rifles at the ready.

Billy lowered himself to the hard floor with a sigh. He leaned his head back against the mouldering wall and expressed a shudder of relief that they had finally stopped for the night. His whole leg throbbed and his feet were a bloody mess. The other prisoners weren't much better, and the older guards were suffering too. The sergeant came back into the room and barked out an order in German to one of the guards who had a smattering of English. Two of the prisoners were detailed to rake out the old range and get a fire going using the old wooden window shutters as firewood.

Billy longed for a cuppa, a smoke and some hot food. But, he knew that rations that night would again be meagre, as they hadn't picked up many extra supplies along the way. A few potatoes had been scavenged from desperate-looking peasants, a few kilos of bread and some strong tasting sausage. Everyone was famished and bolted the food down, along with icy-water drawn from the well in the courtyard. All too soon they had finished and they had to bunk down for the night as best they could on the hard and cold floor. The miserable night passed slowly, broken only by the groans and sighs from sore, weary and hungry men.

Next morning, the snow had stopped falling and the clear sky promised sunshine. The men were forced outside for their latrine requirements. A guard stood sentry while they crouched behind a broken wall of a former pigsty. This was no time or place for modesty.

Again they drew the icy water from the well and washed their faces and hands as best they could from a broken pail. Breakfast was a few crusts of the remaining leftover bread from the night before. They wolfed it down quickly as they were being shouted at to line up in threes. All too soon they found themselves once again dejectedly stumbling out on to the road. This time they moved more slowly, each step more painful than the last.

As the day wore on some of the guards became more and more impatient, as the prisoners became a lot slower. One or two took pleasure in kicking the stragglers up the backside accompanied by a vicious swipe from their rifle. Billy was determined to keep up and not to become easy prey. He didn't trust a couple of mean looking Bavarians not to take advantage of their power and to shoot those that lagged behind. Mostly the guards were fair, albeit with short tempers but they too had lost family and friends, killed and wounded. War is war and each country involved was continuously sloughing off its sons and would continue to do so until peace was called.

Most of the guards couldn't speak English and vice versa and so their frustration was taken out on the prisoners with their shouted and rudely gesticulated orders. The few English words they had picked up were trotted out with glee and used over and over again: 'for you the war is over' and 'England was Kaput!' They truly believed London would soon be in their hands. Billy and his companions soon learned not to join in with any argument and plodded on keeping their faces glumly turned to the ground.

As the weak winter sun began to set over the surrounding hills, the sorry group of prisoners of war and their guards found themselves in open deserted countryside. It was all too apparent that to stumble on in the dark would be a futile exercise and so the Germans gestured that they should enter into a small field. A guard detail was posted around the outside, poised ready to shoot anyone foolish enough to try to escape their clutches.

'That's a bloody laugh,' muttered one of the prisoners next to Billy; a thin man with lank mousy hair, 'none of us has the 'effing energy to think let alone walk further today.'

They all dropped down behind the hedge to rest. As the night drew on it got colder; sleep was only to be had in snatches, everyone would awake stiff, cold and cramped. They only had the clothes they were captured in. They had been given no warm drinks and perishing little to eat. The night seemed endless and when they were forced to move out in the cruel grey of the early morning nobody could hold back their protests with much loud moaning and swearing. The grim faced guards resorted to shouting a little louder and working up a sweat with their rifle butts.

Billy noticed that one or two of the men had cut down their boots in order to ease their feet; but judging from their bloody tattered socks they were still suffering. A guard told them in halting, guttural English that today they would get their rations. Or tomorrow. It soon dawned on Billy and his mates that they were being forced on with false promises.

By mid-morning they had arrived at a small French village. They noticed the curtains twitching behind the wooden shutters and eventually a few women risked coming out to greet the prisoners with a drink of water, or if they were really lucky a bit of bread or a strong tasting French cigarette. Billy thanked a pretty young-looking woman who shyly handed him a hunk of fresh crusty bread and a tin cup of water. He gulped the water down before handing the cup back to her so she could refill it for his companion. The bread tasted delicious. He couldn't remember bread tasting so good before in his life, and he swallowed half of it in two enormous bites whilst he saved the rest in his pocket for later that day. An older woman had a packet of cigarettes and eventually Billy managed to catch her eye and smiled as she offered him the last remaining cigarette. He inhaled deeply and he felt the satisfaction as the tobacco reached his lungs. The luxury of it all was immense. Next to him his companion hadn't been so lucky as all too soon the cigarettes had run out and he pointedly glanced at Billy as he puffed away in bliss. Billy reluctantly withdrew the cigarette from his mouth and handed it over to him. His companion thanked him and Billy watched, as he took down a deep lungful of tobacco. Together they both sighed in contentment and passed the smoke back and forth between them until it became too hot to hold and regretfully they had to throw the butt away.

They passed through no more villages that day and the occasional person usually scurried away as soon as they saw the pitiful band approaching their way or stood and watched from a safe distance. As evening approached a deep chill fell upon them and it was with relief that they came to an empty barn on the edge of a field. The Sergeant was barking at them to turn into the gateway from the road and enter the barn for the night. Inside there was a fair covering of musty hay upon the earth floor and a neat line of straw bales against two of the walls. Billy and the others soon had rearranged the straw to make improvised bedding and the comfort to be had compared with the last night had one or two of them attempting to crack a few jokes to uplift their spirits. The Germans had obviously bullied the villagers on their passage through that day as supper that night was two or three boiled potatoes in their jackets with some turnip and a bit of hard cheese. Not much, but a feast compared to that of the previous days.

The night was a more restful one only broken by the soft moans from those fretting from their sore feet and recent wounds.

However, by early morning all the prisoners were in bad shape. They soon realised that they had all picked up body lice and most had diarrhoea.

Billy had never felt more wretched. His body felt as if it was on fire, especially in the warmer moist parts of his armpit and groin where the body lice collected. His thigh was still stiff and painful; his feet were a constant source of abject horror and now to cap it all he had the misery and embarrassment of cramping guts and bloody stools.

They picked and stumbled their way along the road with many necessary halts and dashes into the side undergrowth. The only bright side to their ailments was that their guards were suffering nearly as much as themselves. They too scratched and swore and hastily made their own way off into the shrubs at frequent intervals.

At last they came upon a railway embankment and judging by the sudden change in the attitude of their captors they took this to mean that they were nearing their transportation. The guards became more aggressive as they rounded the corner and saw an engine at the head of a row of cattle trucks. They were prodded and shouted at and it soon became apparent that this was indeed their intended mode of transport as they were herded into the trucks.

'Lovely scran,' said Billy later as he stuffed his mouth ravenously. The ration promises had finally been kept and the sorry band were wolfing down hot cooked soup made with potatoes, some stringy meat and green vegetables, accompanied by a hunk of bread and some ersatz coffee. The coffee was the first hot drink they had had in days. A chubby dark haired Londoner replied with a straight face. 'Yeah, makes yer almost like them!' This was followed by snorts of derisive laughter and rich language. One or two took the mickey, as always in a deplorable situation someone in a group will try to make light of their plight and endeavour to boost morale.

'All we need now are some smokes, some girls and we'll be in heaven.' The group settled down in the truck. For the first time since they had all been thrown together they were speaking to each other. The comparative better food and the halt to their enforced march had helped them tremendously. They knew not where they were being taken or how long it would take them to get there, but they all believed that the Geneva Convention rules on prisoners of war would be enforced and they would be at least safe and treated accordingly.

The journey towards Germany was very slow and took nearly a week, often due to the havoc created by their own British bombing of German towns and cities. They found themselves confused as to exactly where they were being taken as peering out of the enclosed cattle trucks gave them only limited vision to the towns that they passed through. As far as Billy could make out their journey took them by Brunswick, Magdeburg, Hanover and Tarmstedt; but he was not at all certain never having been to Germany before and he'd never really studied his old school atlas. They were told that they were going to a prisoner of war camp; a Marlag or Marinelager; a camp for naval servicemen.

The train shunted into the sidings and they were ordered from their stinking truck. First they were to be processed through the transit camp or Dulag. Here they were required to give their name, rank and serial number according to the Geneva Convention.

The office soldier who interviewed Billy was short and fat. His piggy little eyes disappeared into rounded unhealthy cheeks and his thick jowls hung over his collar that was unfastened, presumably to enable him to breath. He grunted at Billy's entrance and left him standing while he shuffled his papers and then asked Billy for his details. He spoke good English with a heavy thick Bavarian accent. Finally he laid down his pen, lit a cigarette and blew smoke across to where Billy stood on the thin brown linoleum floor. The room was overheated and uncomfortably hot. The revolting fat German had a line of perspiration round his collar and he smelt of stale sweat and cooking fat. Billy barely suppressed a shudder.

'So. You are coming from England?' he asked. 'How are things in England?'

Billy looked at him blankly. Was he seriously expected to answer him?

'You are not liking the bombing, I hear?' Fatso chuckled to himself and leaned back in his chair, which creaked under his weight in protest.

Billy thought of Penny and her family, the hardships that ordinary innocent people had to put up with. The death and destruction all around in the larger cities, caused by German attacks.

'People get used to it. Especially now we're bombing German towns,' he answered, a defiant glint in his eyes. He lifted his head higher, his aches and pains and his bloody guts almost forgotten.

'Ach so! That I am knowing. British bombing German towns. Killing many innocent women and children.' His lower jowls quivered in anger and his face flushed a mottled floridness.

This is a dangerous conversation, Billy thought in sudden awareness, for Christ's sake hold your tongue, he told himself.

'All Germans know you British are finished. Kaput! You have no food. Rommel has beaten your army at Benghazi. Our glorious U-boats are fast sinking your ships. Soon the war will be over. This is good for you. You can go home.' He smirked a self-satisfied smile, his heavy podgy hands folded across his considerable girth.

'Now that the Americans are with us, we'll soon be winning the war, not Germany,' Billy retaliated quietly.

The German rose from his desk, his face mottling purple. His mouth quivered with rage. He came out from behind and around his desk and hit Billy once, his hand hard across his face.

Billy fell back shaking with shock. He could have killed the German there and then with his bare hands. Through his white anger he knew though that if he raised one finger the German would have him shot.

Billy wheeled about and walked back out into the corridor outside where armed guards stood over the other prisoners waiting to be processed. They all looked with shock at the livid mark on his face and it was enough. No one questioned him.

***

Billy was first sent to Poland. He didn't know it at the time but he was to see many different POW camps during his incarceration for the rest of the war. Like many other younger men in his position he found life completely intolerable. Many had joined up to help protect their country and fight for what they believed in. They had anticipated some action with maybe a medal or two, perhaps even ultimately death – but never ever capture. On arrival at a POW camp the procedure was always the same denigrating process: a thorough search, a delousing, a shaven head, being given an inmate number and then being photographed like a criminal. The prisoners then began the struggle for the petty necessities of life as a prisoner of war. So far during Billy's career he had had an equal measure of fear and excitement. He had enjoyed the Navy life: the uniform, the routine boat drills and dramatic briefings with the other crew. Time had been from moment to moment, day-by-day and stretching onto infinity. Life had held a bizarre mix of peril and banality. This now would all change.

Chapter 15

Billy soon found that life in camp was hard but it could be borne with stoicism. The surrounding squalor that the prisoners lived in was horrendous and all attempts were made to keep themselves clean and healthy. The one thing that couldn't be ignored however, was hunger. No matter how the men tried to keep themselves busy or their spirits up, if there wasn't enough food to keep body and soul together then many would perish by ill health or simply put: starvation.

The camp commandant was an Oberstleutnant; a Lieutenant Colonel named Müller. His uniform had the stiffest of collars that fitted snugly against his thick, squat neck. His skin was the colour of waxy parchment and he had deep fleshy creases around his pale blue eyes. With his fat cheeks and thick lips he was almost a caricature of Nature imitating art. Billy remembered his last altercation with that other solid German officer and the similarity between the two sobered him somewhat. It's like having met real life Tweedledee and Tweedledum he thought to himself. In normal circumstances it would have been funny.

This commandant faced the line-up during the early morning roll call with a permanent look of disgust on his face. Billy knew that certain officers would not hesitate to overexert their power so he was mindful to toe the line until he knew the ropes at least.

He was marginally thankful to be over the gruelling rail journey that had brought him here and he recalled the hardships and deprivation that they had all suffered before they reached their final destination.

First, they had had their boots removed to ensure that no one could escape and make a run for it. They were then herded and encouraged with rifle butts into one cattle truck with their guards in another. Their journey was a slow monotonous struggle of constant stopping and starting. This became a total nightmare as they were given very little food; the rations had soon run out – and as cargo, prisoners were definitely a low priority on the German agenda.

Consequently, everyone was permanently tired and hungry and all were still suffering from various ailments including diarrhoea.

The train had no heating and Billy's feet were completely numb without his boots. Every few miles it seemed they were jolted awake whilst the train was shunted around. The engine was decoupled and then re-coupled to the rest of the train with a stop-hiss, and everyone was again jerked violently awake. Soon, Billy was red-eyed and ravenously hungry like all the rest and would willingly have sold his soul for a hot drink.

Bishop's Walton and his Penny seemed a million years away and he endured everything by simply concentrating on his time spent with her. He would have given everything to see and hold her for five minutes once again.

The train had pulled into a siding; there was no station to speak of. Suddenly, the doors were thrown open followed by the customary shouting from the German guards. It hadn't taken Billy and the others long to become used to their behaviour. Some of the men muttered sullenly, but a blow from a rifle butt across thin shins or shoulders had them up and moving down and out onto the cinder- track. They were marshalled into ragged lines by harsh German voices and received more blows from the Mauser rifles.

Most of the prisoners were at least thankful that the nightmare journey was at last over. They moved into the lines with dreams of a hot meal, a drink, and a warm bed creeping into their tired and dispirited minds.

Their boots were retrieved and dumped into a pile in front of them. Line by line the men were shoved forward to select a pair that would hopefully fit them. Billy stood waiting, hoping and praying that it wouldn't be only the smaller sizes that were left when it came to his turn.

Booted up they were marched out, trudging along a road that led through a thick forest of pine and fir trees. The scents around them were thick and heavy with resin and after the squalid foetid cattle trucks Billy sniffed appreciatively. The light was dimpy and a flurry of light snow began to fall, making their boots scrunch on the road surface. The air turned damp penetrating through their layers of clothing and the thin soles of their boots. Billy sighed to himself. Another route march. Everyone was silent. No jokes, no whispers. It was going to be another long cold walk. Poland in February was bitterly cold.

The forest thinned to more deciduous trees, and tiny white flowers were bravely poking their heads here and there in tight small clumps on the ground. Snowdrops! Their tiny fragile white pureness seemed out of place to Billy.

The column turned the corner in the road and abruptly heavy wooden gates loomed up in front of them out of the thick gloom. They could see tall wooden towers either side with guards leaning over their guns watching the arrivals below. A command was shouted, four soldiers rushed over from a brightly lit guardhouse and together they unlocked and pushed the gates open. The procession filed through reluctantly into the forecourt and the gates were clanged shut behind them with a finality that went through each captured man with a sharp stab of pain in their throat or heart. Piercing white searchlights in the towers were suddenly switched on and shone down onto the prisoners. They stood there imprisoned within their white cage of light.

Again they heard guttural harsh voices shouting commands, followed by heavy boots scraping over the compound and the accompanying sound of rifle-bolts being worked back.

Is this it? thought Billy, his throat and mouth dry and constricted, unable to swallow. Have we been brought all this way just to be shot now?

***

The camp commandant slowly moved from the open doorway of his office, drawing on his thick leather gloves as he did so. He paused on the top step, as a guard shut the door after him and quietly and briefly surveyed the scene in front of him. He brushed at the falling snow on his overcoat and then strode down the two steps onto the compound ground. He had turned out reluctantly from his cosy snug well-furnished office to inspect his latest group of charges. His contempt towards them was only too apparent by the thin sneer on his face. He turned to another younger officer that had appeared by his side and gave him a short brusque order. The officer drew himself up smartly and saluted his commander before replying. Satisfied with his response, he nodded and returned the salute before turning on his heel and heading back into his office. The pool of golden light from the opened door spoke of a warm interior before swiftly closing and leaving the prisoners standing outside shivering in their fear and anticipation.

Billy stole a look around him. He could see the terrible glint of barbed wire coiled across the top of the chain-link fence. The sight stilled his breath for a moment. What was going to happen to him? He felt like he was in some horror story. A burning sensation of bile rose in his throat and he swallowed hard. Despite the bitter cold he was soaked in sweat and his legs were shaking. All around him his companions of the past few weeks stood and stared. They were shocked, terrified and unbelieving that this could be happening to them.

The second officer was moving amongst the guards that were lined up in front of them; their rifles menacingly trained on the group. Billy's attention was switched to him as he issued orders to the guards.

Soon, Billy was following a soldier down badly concreted paths and past shadowy huts, the high fences all around. He was led into another smaller compound and into hut number eleven. Inside he found wooden bunks of two or three tiers, set close together with barely four feet between them. The floor was more broken cement. The windows were small and a lot of the glass was either cracked or broken. The holes were stuffed with whatever had come to hand; rags, paper or straw. In the centre of the hut was an unlit blackened stove. Billy could see no mattresses or blankets. Inside it was marginally warmer than outside and certainly almost as bleak.

With much shouting Billy and his travel companions were made to understand that this was to be their hut, their billet. One tall fellow who could speak a smattering of German asked haltingly if there was any food for them. This caused some consternation among the guards who had escorted them to the hut.

'I think what they're saying, is that there's no food to be had until tomorrow!' he translated and looking around him in dismay at his fellow prisoners.

'Tomorrow!' was the chorus.

'The last three fucking days we've sodden well lived on next to nothing, now we have to wait another bloody day. And there's no guarantee about that,' growled another.

In deep misery Billy found himself a vacant top bunk and wearily climbed into it. Tomorrow. What would happen to them tomorrow? Oh Pen, if you could see me now. Your happy go lucky Jack. He lay and stared at the cracked grimy ceiling above him. With a deep sigh of despair and hunger pangs he eventually fell into a deep and exhausted sleep.

***

The following day, Billy had a good look around him. He wanted to see first hand what type of place he had been forced to enter. The camp was of course entirely surrounded by the tangle of vicious wire. In addition there were regular patrols of foot guards, deep trenches and sentry boxes, all placed strategically around the camp. The sentry boxes were on stilts and were manned by bored and cold looking guards armed with machine-guns and searchlights. Escape was going to be no easy matter then.

He hurriedly turned to other more immediate matters. Billy found that the latrines were ghastly. He looked in horror at the rows of seats placed over a reeking cesspit. There was no partition between them for any privacy and toilet paper was usually non-existent. As the majority of the prisoners had chronic diarrhoea they were subjected to embarrassment every time they hurried over to the foul smelling hut and dropped their trousers. The newcomers soon came to look forward to the pelican books sent to the inmates by the Red Cross although these were mostly used before they could be read. When the cesspits were full, they were pumped out and spread over the fields as manure.

Billy's feet had hardly improved over the last few days and were constantly sore. The problem of his ill-fitting boots was solved though as the Germans took all their boots and shoes away and they were replaced with ill-fitting rough shaped peasant wooden clogs. Everyone now shuffled around the camp and, it was like watching men old before their time.

It soon became obvious to Billy and the others that everything in the camp had a value and was subject to bartering. With the extreme cold, every piece of clothing that came their way was seized upon and worn. The roll call in the morning produced a raggle-taggle gathering of men dressed in overcoats, scarves, gloves and balaclavas. Some of the prisoners who'd spent some time in the camp made offers to the newcomers of priceless items like toothbrushes, razors and most worthwhile, advice. They soon knew who to trust and who not, who had a sadistic streak and who among the guards were basically fair.

The prisoners all had different ways and means of coping with their incarceration. Billy realised that the majority of the old-lags had erected some sort of mental barrier against the inevitable sense of depression.

Outside news that filtered in was pooled and hurriedly spread through the camp. The latest war news was avidly gathered from Billy and his mates. Their valuable news would be discussed, dissected and complained over. Those that had been incarcerated for some time were very eager for news about the RAF large-scale raids on Berlin, Mannheim and the Ruhr. They were shocked to learn about the huge numbers of German air raids on the tiny island of Malta and her brave inhabitants. Lastly, although further afield and with news being in shorter supply they were keen to hear about the Americans and the part that they were playing in the Pacific.

Billy noticed that men that were captured together, more often than not kept together in their own huts. Although it wasn't their real 'family', there soon formed a certain band of togetherness. On the other hand many men acted and spoke as if they were in some sort of dream and would do nothing to claim attention to themselves. They would sit listlessly about on their own and, seemingly with almost shut down emotions, remain withdrawn and aloof from the rest of the camp. Others would refuse to take part in any organised camp activities such as playing cards, singsongs or a sport like cricket or football. Billy thought he understood them. Perhaps they felt that by not joining in, their stay was not permanent. It would give them the small comfort of a temporary illusion. After all they shouldn't be there, so soon they would be free.

Meanwhile, Billy himself was finding life under the Germans hard and he frequently found himself clenching his fists and jaw in anger. But, he remembered the arrogant German officer at the Dulag and kept his mouth shut. He soon realised that not only was the camp life hard but it was also extremely tedious and mind-numbingly boring. Not everyone was at all friendly or even honest and, the scroungers lived by their wits. Camp economy was based on cigarettes and racketeers and, some prisoners dealt with the Germans. Billy was unsure that this was the correct principle, as he felt uncomfortable around the guards. He had always understood the simple logic that power corrupts and because of this he didn't want to fall into temptation. However, he was not averse to hard bartering amongst his own peers.

Gradually, they noticed that the weather was slowly changing. Through the first few weeks the snow lay around the camp in deep drifts. Lying under a full moon, the thick snow had sparkled in the moonlight giving the camp a strangely pretty but sinister impression. The snow had now melted and pools of rutted mud and sickly pale yellow grass lay between the huts and compound concrete paths. The warmer weather soon brought its own problems however. Almost everyone suffered from fleas. In the spring the beds were stripped and washed along with their clothes. The wet linen was laid out in the sunshine to help get rid of the body lice. One of the worst garments to offend were the heavy winter trousers as lice collected in the waistband. As Billy and everyone else stripped off to enjoy the sunshine angry red weals were apparent around their waists. Billy was warned not to scratch his skin too much as, if he broke the skin it could become infected by the excreta left by the lice. With little or no medication and their low resistance due to their poor diet, the men truly suffered. However body lice were not their main enemy.

The Germans were menacing and wielded their authority with a long steel rod. At 5am every day the prisoners were made to get up and stand in line for a roll call. The counting took time and was made even longer if some prisoners decided to shuffle around just to confuse and irritate the guards. This was all very well in the warmer weather but in the winter it made for a very long cold wait before they had some food or a hot drink. The long wait was also excruciating for those with bad diarrhoea.

So, Billy had to learn patience. He had to settle down and deal with hunger, dirt, lice, boredom and tedium, day after day. He began to dread looking at the same thin faces and listening to the same conversation. The food was mostly vile and only enough to keep them alive. There was nothing to look forward to with swede soup, potatoes, a meagre bread ration, the occasional piece of cheese or sausage, ersatz (acorn) coffee and jam. Nothing fresh ever legally entered their diet and their elderly and middle-aged guards fared only a little better with the addition of a bit of grey, gristly meat.

Billy discovered early on that according to the Geneva Convention everyone was entitled to a Red Cross parcel and he eagerly looked forward to receiving his. However, he found it hard to accept that not many actually reached the prisoners of war; and of those that did frequently found them to be violated. The boxes were opened and their contents scattered throughout the box. The recipient usually found an unsalvageable sticky mess of sugar, honey, jam, chocolate, coffee and tea.

Billy began to have wild and distorted dreams that conjured up vivid images of food, home and Penny. He found that he was ashamed to admit even to himself that although Penny was consistently on his mind she came a poor second to thoughts of luscious food.

With spring and summer came some relief from the everyday boredom. Small working parties of men were sent out to help repair roads and bridges or clear waste ground. Although he was technically still unfit, Billy worked hard to get accepted and assigned to a group that were regularly sent outside. Here, so long as they were careful they could sometimes make contact with Poles who were friendly enough to help them in their plight. Despite their own poverty and hardships, the Polish people could sometimes spare them the odd loaf or a few eggs that they then hid under their coats away from the prying eyes of their guards. Once Billy returned to his hut in the evening his companions would surround him as he always shared the food out. Billy found that the eggs tasted like heaven. The men gathered round the smoky cooking stove in their hut and watched as the eggs were cracked into a black pan. Soon their mouths were watering almost painfully as they stood and took in the aromas of the sizzling eggs.

When Billy was given his egg he would eat the white part first. Slowly morsel by morsel. The yolk was left until last and then eaten in one mouthful; the tin plate scraped and licked clean. Not one speck was allowed to remain uneaten. Billy would find himself repeating this ritual for the rest of his life every time he had an egg.

The days passed relentlessly slowly in the camp. Outside, Germany's war machine carried on its own relentless onslaught against the allies.

***

Billy's hut was told to get down to the 'Barbers shop' on camp for a haircut and shave. The haircut was basically a cut of 'all off' to keep the lice down! They were all told to dress in their uniforms to have their photos taken. As if by magic, extra boots and uniform jackets appeared for the photo shoot. The cynics among them soon had the measure of the Germans.

'Gerrie wants it for propaganda. They're going to send our mug shots back to Blighty and show the folks back home how well they're treating us.'

Everyone felt cheated and soured by the blatantness of it all. The new boots and jackets would be returned to the stores and they would be back to their threadbare rags and clogs. Billy felt outraged; Penny would get a copy. But, he somehow took comfort in the fact that at least she need never know the truth of how much they were all suffering.

Eventually, letters began to arrive from home. Billy waited at the back; a throb beating feverishly in his head while names were called out for the lucky recipients. He had been allowed to send heavily censored postcards to Penny with the barest of messages on the back. Sometimes he had composed a simple verse when he had felt too despairing of his true surroundings. Better she didn't know the truth of the conditions here he thought. Right now he was desperate to hear from her. He wanted to hear all about the clean and simple life that she led back home. Life in camp was so monotonous and boring and conditions were incredibly hard. Billy would spend hours lying on his hard bunk going over and over the time they had spent together, what they had said and done. He had to concentrate to visualise her sweet face and he worried that over the time he might be unable to recall her features with clarity.

He realised with a start that his name was being called. His heart began to beat wildly. At last a letter had arrived especially for him! He pushed his way through the throng of men hovering anxiously around the camp 'postman.' An opened envelope was handed over to him; others glanced momentarily in envy before turning their attention back to the postman. Billy read the writing on the outside savouring the moment. He knew it was from her. He could imagine her as she had sat down to write her letter; quiet concentration on her face as she had wondered what to tell him. Clutching the letter he hurried over to his hut and made his way to the sanctity of his bunk.

He smoothed the pages of the letter out on his blanket. He knew that the censor had already read it but it didn't matter. She had written this just for *him*. Slowly he read the blue lines penned in her large open-handed style. He learnt that she had been so relieved when after contacting the Admiralty they had finally told her where he was. She went on to tell him that although he would be incarcerated for the remainder of the war she was so glad that he was safe. She felt guilty, selfish and confused that she was glad he wouldn't be exposed to any immediate danger on the sea although there were still thousands of their boys out there fighting the enemy. Billy understood her confusion and the greater relief she felt for his safety. She wore her heart on her sleeve and his chest felt tight as he took in all that she told him. The rest of the letter she had deliberately kept light hearted. He could picture her going about her everyday business, collecting the eggs and helping her Dad, Maurice with the vegetable and fruit allotment. She had learnt to knit and so far had made a dozen scarves! Maggie was now teaching her the more difficult task of knitting gloves and socks and she was glad to do her bit for the war effort. The thought of Penny concentrating with knitting needles made Billy laugh out loud to himself. She was such a funny little thing and very dear to him. All too soon he came to the final paragraph of her letter and here she told him that she had been under the weather for a couple of months after he had been reported missing but, she was now feeling a lot better.

Concern for Penny clouded Billy's mind. To him she was his anchor back home. The one positive thing he could focus on. As an orphan he had no one else close enough to write to or to care for. All his thoughts were channelled to her and of course her immediate welfare concerned him. He hoped that her illness was nothing serious and reread the last paragraph again. He then reread the whole of her letter through another two times and then neatly folded it and tucked it back in its envelope. No, she had been ill because she had been worried about him he told himself. He felt better and whistled softly as he went back outside into the compound to find his mates. He would read her letter again just before lights out.

Lines that she had written flashed through his mind as he walked across the compound:

Keep smiling, in spite of the grief and the pain:
We all know the sunshine follows the rain.
 and
One day we'll be together, so
Our love and trust forever keep,
Within our hearts sweet memories sleep.

As the week progressed he found that thoughts for Pen unsettled him. What if he could escape and make it back home? There had been numerous escapes and attempted escapes. A few must have succeeded in reaching home. Not all recaptured prisoners were returned here though, so the actual numbers were difficult to ascertain. The thought preyed on his mind during the day. He could possibly get away when he went out on a work party. He lay on his bunk, a plan already formulating in his mind.

He had heard from the others that many escapees had been successful by changing places with a work party member. As he was already a party member he was halfway there. His possessions were few and he could easily carry them on his person. Best of all, the road they were presently working on required the wearing of boots and these were given to the workers each day. The next few days he saved and scrounged as many cigarettes as possible. These would be vital for bribing the others of the work party to cover his initial escape.

The perfect moment came one morning as they made their way to the workplace; he couldn't believe how easy it was to silently slip away. At a tight bend in the road there was a derelict hut with a sagging half-open door, which he had decided, would make a good temporary hiding place. As usual, this morning the working party was strung out along the road, with guards positioned fore and aft of the long crocodile. As the group approached the bend Billy made sure that he was on the nearside of the road's edge. Once he was level with the hut none of the guards noticed as he took advantage of their blind spot and quickly nipped into the open doorway. He made his way to the back of the murky hut, keeping well out of the early morning light. His working party continued tramping past. Billy's heart thumped painfully in his chest as he waited for the shout and the sound of a rifle bolt sliding home. The boots sounded unnaturally loud as they thudded past and then gradually faded in the distance. Billy's heart slowed down to a more normal speed and he wiped the sweat that glistened on his face. He breathed a little more easily and cautiously moved over to one of the grimy windows that looked out onto the road. About ten minutes had past since he'd slipped away. Everything was silent. The road was empty both ways. Taking a deep breath he quickly made a dash into the thick forest that loomed behind the hut. As he entered the deep gloom he felt as if the deep penetrating trees were swallowing him up.

At first, the elation of his newfound freedom after months of being bored and depressed kept him going at a relentless pace. His intention was to walk as far as possible from the camp during the day and first night and then, to find a place to hole up in and sleep when the following morning came. Billy had a few meagre food supplies, hard bread, a couple of cooked potatoes and a scrag end of some gristly greyish meat. He saw no one that first day and night as he travelled through the thick forest. He hadn't been prepared for the vastness of it and was beginning to wonder if he would ever find his way out or would be forever doomed to wander. Getting lost and starving to death had never entered into his equation when planning to make a run for it. He stood up feeling rested after he had managed a bit of fitful sleep in the middle of a thick group of bushes. His spirits were still high and he instinctively knew that he had to maintain them so to be able to carry on. He pressed on doggedly following his stars whenever he found a break in the tree canopy overhead.

On the third day all his food had run out and finding water clean enough to drink was becoming very difficult. By now the forest had sufficiently thinned and on the outskirts he had espied one or two remote farms. So far he had given them a wide berth, as he was afraid that their dogs would alert their owners' to his presence and give him away. However, his thirst was raging and he had to get some water fast. He waited in the shadow of the trees until night fell. When he judged that it would surely be safe enough, he slipped out and crouching low, edged over to the perimeter of the farm. Satisfied that the coast appeared clear and all was still quiet he carefully climbed over the fence into the peaceful farmyard. The pump stood etched in the soft moonlight as the clouds scudded across the sky. The cool water tasted better than the best bitter back home in The Anchor! Billy had filled the wooden pail and tipped his head back as he'd gulped the fresh sweet water down. He spilled the water down his front in his haste to slake his thirst and had to pause momentarily to get his breath back. Again he raised the pail to drink and, as he did so the yard was flooded with light as the farmhouse door was opened. He was caught in a pool of golden light with the pail halfway to his mouth. An exclamation of surprise and then a shouted question from the doorway filled Billy with horror as he realised that he had been rumbled. He dropped the bucket of water and decided to run. Farmers after all have shotguns and Billy was unarmed. He tore across the yard making a beeline for the fence and tumbled over it. A ridiculous idea passed through his head as he sailed through the air that his PT instructor would be pleased with his vaulting prowess. He stumbled as he landed and ignoring the furious shouting coming from the farmhouse door he again took to his feet and dashed for the cover of the woods.

His heart was pumping hard in his chest and his breath was coming in short gasps. He had to get far away from here as soon as possible as he didn't know whether the farmer would report him or not. He walked that night as far as his feet would manage and his exhaustion was made more desperate by his starvation. In the early morning he knew that if he was to continue on his way then he had to have some food. He followed a thin path that took him out from the woods onto a dusty lane. Ahead there was a sleepy hamlet of three or four houses. Smoke was rising from one of the chimneys and in his extreme need he knew that he would have to risk spying out the houses in the hope of finding some vegetables in the gardens or some eggs if there were hens. Anything would do.

It was still very early and the morning light was still dim enough to give him some cover if he kept close to the hedgerow. He skirted along the road, keeping well in and noting that there was no escape into the surrounding fields. It was a very dangerous risk to take. At first all went well and he made it to the first house that appeared to have a well-kept vegetable garden. Suddenly, he was looking ahead of him. A German patrol motorbike and car had appeared from around the corner. He froze; maybe if he stood still they'd pass and they wouldn't see him in the dull light. He felt a cold sweat break out on his back. Too late they'd seen him; he saw their guns dully glinting as the weak sun appeared. In mute supplication he held his arms up and stood still as the Germans came to a halt beside him.

A senior NCO stepped out of the car and shouted an order as the rifle butt blow caught the back of his head. Billy pitched forward wordlessly into a dark oblivion.

***

Strange sounds and lights flashed through the dark recesses of Billy's mind. Somewhere hidden deeply, Billy was trying to block out the unfamiliar and slip away back into the safe velvety black. Heavy and thick, he pushed away these irritations until he realised that subconsciously a red hammer was beating in his temple. Nausea rose as his senses became more heightened until, nearing full consciousness bile rose in his throat and he rolled over and retched horribly.

He felt a thud in his back – just below the kidneys – and spasms of white-hot pain shot up his spine. He couldn't help groaning as the blow was joined by another and then followed by a guttural voice,

'Get up British pig!'

Again he groaned as, slowly and painfully he opened his eyes. He didn't recognise the cell in which he was lying. As his eyesight adjusted to the gloom he recognised one of the two German guards that stood either side of him. One was a middle-aged man and a stranger. He recognised the younger one though. His mouth felt dry and he could barely swallow. This man, the younger of the two, had an unhealthy liking for maltreating prisoners. He grinned down at Billy, one side of his mouth raised in a calculated sneer. He drew back his booted foot just as the cell door opened and an officer walked in. The officer took in the scene at once. The prostrate prisoner, his head caked in blood and the grinning guards.

The officer barked out some orders in German and the grins vanished, to be replaced by stony-blank faces. They hurriedly stood to attention and saluted their officer. When he had finished his reprimand they bent down and hauled Billy to his feet. The officer gave another command and they obeyed by dragging Billy over to a metal bench covered by a ratty blanket. Unceremoniously, they dumped him onto the bench and then without a word they followed their officer out of the cell and clanged the door shut behind them. Billy heard the bolt being shot home as he was locked in.

Solitary confinement for three weeks. Twenty-one days with nothing but bread and water. Billy felt his eyes prickle with tears of frustration, despair and humiliation. He then felt a wave of anger rush over him. Sod them! He'd not let them get the better of him. He had a girl waiting for him back home. He had to stay well to see her again. Three weeks solitary; so what? Look on the bright side. That's three weeks rest from the gruelling heavy roadwork. A cell to himself. He didn't have to listen to the others snoring and farting and yammering away all day and most of the night. He was free of the overcrowded huts with their dirt and fleas. Yes, he'd look on the bright side. After all it could have been much worse.

Chapter 16

Slowly, intolerably slowly, the months and then the years for Billy passed in prison. For some unaccountable reason he was moved from camp to camp. Each time this happened he was thrown into a panic, as he was given no explanation for the moves. He thought every journey might be his last as armed guards ordered him into yet another truck or cattle wagon.

New found friends were lost and the loneliness and confusion added to his latest overall depression. His new POW camp was in Germany. When he was being transferred from Poland to Germany, Billy had passed through a transit camp, which had previously been a Jewish extermination camp. He and the others with him had slept in tiered bunks, and the lavatory was a particular horror; a pole placed over a foetid pit, which had once been cleaned out by the previous inmates' bare hands. Their guards on this occasion were ex soldiers who had been badly wounded at the eastern front and Billy found them all to be quite decent. Perhaps their own recent dramas had led them to be grateful to be relieved of the terror of their own battles. Indeed they seemed as shocked as Billy and his companions with the transit camp conditions. With the coming of the new morning and before they were ready to move out, Billy had watched a melancholy procession of Russians carrying corpses to a lime-pit and unceremoniously tipping the bodies in. He had shuddered in fascinated horror as he dragged his eyes away from the shocking scene before him.

Now he had entered his latest POW camp. He found the usual wired enclosure with wooden lookout towers and searchlights, armed guards with machine-guns, wooden huts set in a grid pattern, three-tiered bunks, a central inadequate stove, and ancillary buildings. These usually comprised a delousing hut, a fuel and vegetable store, a hospital, a recreation area and grim punishment barracks.

But, it was all grim Billy thought.

His first impression was of a very depressing and run-down camp. The latrines were near to his own hut; and beyond was an open exercise space for the prisoners and for the Germans with their counting and haranguing. Each hut had thirty bunks apiece with a small stove and a couple of rickety tables. Billy always endeavoured to obtain a top bunk. Even though this would mean a ten-feet descent at night in total darkness to the latrines and a repeat journey back. Being on top gave you at least some feeling of privacy and space from the others below. The food was distributed to the hut in bulk and divided up but there was never enough to go round. Loaves of bread were shared out between as many as twelve men, and the potatoes served up were little more than grey liquid mush. Everyone was painfully thin and Billy soon found to his cost that rapid movement could cause a blackout. The winters had been very cold and they were all weak from malnutrition. Most possessed only the clothes they stood in and the fuel given to them for the stove was insufficient. They had either to burn some of their beds or they had to find an alternative fuel.

Billy had a thought. He always kept his eye open for the main chance, and he and a couple of others decided that they would 'rescue' some of the coal from the fuel dump near the main entrance. It was simply that or they would freeze. Each night Billy and the others would black their faces and don whatever dark clothing they could obtain and then they crept stealthily out of their hut. Carefully like silent huge bats, they silently traversed the length of the camp keeping to the shadows. Once they reached the high fence they burrowed their way through the wire into the fuel compound. They each carried a small bag made from old sacks that had once contained their potato ration; these they filled and then returned to their hut by the same route. They judged that the fuel dump was large enough and their stolen booty was small enough to go unnoticed. Even so, the risk that Billy and the others took was huge and the punishment if they had been caught would have been instant death by firing squad. Despite this, the adrenalin and excitement it created in these young men together with the benefits of a warm hut made them feel it was well worth it.

Billy continued to receive letters sporadically and looked forward to Penny's latest news and sometimes a verse or two of a poem that she had written whilst daydreaming in the hay meadow back home. The poetry was a complete surprise to Billy as it was to Penny. She had never ever written as much as a line before he was sent away and yet somehow his incarceration had inspired her to write. At first Billy was rather baffled. Why would she write lines like this to him? After a while, and once he had taken the time to sit down and reread it he understood and suddenly felt important. His girl, his Penny was writing something special just for him and it made him feel wonderful and more especially not forgotten.

"Within my lonely little room,
Beside the fire to light the gloom,
I seem to picture your dear face,
Through the flames and in the space.
Each loved and well remembered day
Brings back those memories far away.

I miss you so; it makes me sad
To think of all the joys we had.
And now we're far apart, although
One day we'll be together, so
Our love and trust forever keep.
Within our hearts sweet memories sleep.

Christmas! Christmas was nearly upon them once more and although Billy couldn't match Penny's artistic talents, he endeavoured to make a special card for her showing his constant love and devotion. He even made a self-conscious attempt to add a verse of his own to make it seem extra special for her.

From Christmas 1942 onwards each POW had been receiving a Red Cross parcel that now was more or less 'intact' since complaints from the prisoners' had eventually reached the right ears. Each inmate had excitedly opened their box that revealed to them the wonderful and almost forgotten contents: jam, bully beef, cheese, tea, cocoa, Canadian butter, pickled eggs, cigarettes, curry powder and condensed milk.

Billy and a couple of mates in his hut had spent the last few weeks illicitly distilling a brew from potatoes for the Christmas season. Their brew did produce the required effect of inebriation, but the taste was incredibly foul!

As the party happily devoured their parcel contents and got rapidly soused, their talk inevitably turned to the more interesting subject of women and sex.

They already had a favourite pastime in their hut of playing a game of whom they were going to 'have as tonight's girl' and each tried to outdo each other.

'I'm going to take that Betty Grable home tonight after a slap up fish and chip supper,' crowed one Bristol lad happily.

'Nah Myrna Loy is a much better bet, a right little goer!'

'Viv Leigh's got a smashing pert bottom.'

'Marlene Dietrich's deep foreign voice just does something gooey to me.'

And so on. Each had their favourite dream that rapidly got out of hand with the more grog they drunk. As they lay on their beds and fantasized, hands caressed their own bodies and dreamily they felt the firm flesh of their dream-girl. She in turn was both passionate or timid according to whatever their whim and, their bodies responded with a climatic rush of semen, peace and guilt.

The camp had an entertainment committee; they would put on shows for the whole camp's well-being and morale. Usually, a large majority of the cast would be 'ladies', who performed a hilarious song and dance routine for an hour or two. Their costumes and wigs were outrageously improvised, and the show would culminate in a raucous singsong despite the complaints from their surly guards. The musically talented among Billy's mates would be press-ganged into putting on concerts and even an operetta recital was periodically staged. Billy regrettably had no stage talent – or so he said – and kept himself well out of the way when the theatre touts came looking for new hands. He was however, willing to help out backstage using his own methods. When the theatre cast needed a particular item Billy would be one of the first to use his initiative by skill, theft or bribery from their captors. His input did as much to improve the camp's morale as the actual entertainment and he felt pride in being able to help.

It was after the New Year in 1944. Christmas had come and gone and life in camp was one day much the same as the rest. Billy and his hut mates were hungry for War news. They listened attentively to anything that was garnered from men on the outside working parties, or from new prisoners that were brought in fresh from capture. A few entrepreneurs had secret crystal sets that occasionally picked up an 'underground' transmitter They had just learnt about the previous autumn Russian Offensive, and the Soviet retake of Roslavl and Smolensk. The Germans had made a last major offensive on the Russian front at Kursk, which marked the beginnings of a series of massive offensives that would eventually take the Soviets to Berlin and Vienna. The Allies had invaded and liberated Sicily in July and the British X111 Corps had crossed to the toe of Italy in September. The Allied landings at Salerno led to the September Battle of Salerno and the signing of the Italian armistice, whilst the Germans led a daring rescue of Mussolini from the mountains of Gran Sasso. In mid November the Aerial Battle of Berlin had begun and there was a seesawing of wiles between the Soviets and Germany on the Eastern Front. When the British Navy sank the notorious German battle-cruiser Scharnhorst on December 26th at the Battle of the North Cape, Billy's heart had soared and he fervently wished that he'd been there to see it, to play his own part in it. The 38,000 ton Scharnhorst had inflicted much damage on the British fleet and together with the other battle-cruiser Gneisenau they had sunk a total of: a British aircraft carrier, two destroyers, an armed merchant cruiser and 22 Allied merchant ships. Her loss was a severe blow to the German High Command and a welcome victory to Britain. Meanwhile up in the skies there was a major offensive battle going on. Billy and the others hadn't yet heard, but February 20th 1944 was the 'Big Week.' A bomber offensive had begun on German fighter and ball bearing factories, and the air attack was to continue until March 24th and 25th when the RAF made their last major raids during the aerial Battle of Berlin.

***

Today was a fine one, and many prisoners had taken the opportunity to strip off their beds and give their rank smelling covers a thorough airing in the mid-morning sunshine. Somewhere a blackbird sweetly sang in a small bush nearby and Billy thought that if you closed your eyes and ears to the everyday sound of the camp you could almost imagine yourself back home lazing in the back garden of a country pub. What he and the other lads would give for a pint or two of the best bitter! However, as Billy opened his eyes the scene was the same as ever; the dismal long huts and the poorly made pathways of hurriedly mixed concrete. He had decided to spend his free time that morning loitering in the vicinity of the vegetable store. Always an opportunist, he was looking for the wherewithal to purloin anything of 'edible value' that might come his way if he persisted in keeping a good watch on the comings and goings of that weeks' deliveries to the camp. A sudden commotion at the outer gates caught his attention. The heavy gates swung open on their huge well-oiled hinges to admit an army truck that continued through to the inner commandant area. After a moment's interest Billy turned his nonchalant attention back to the vegetable store. Much to his disgust, when the guard came out and locked the door behind him he vulgarly gestured to Billy to 'move off' in no uncertain terms. Billy shrugged and shuffled off to look for further opportunities.

It was now late afternoon; the shadows touched the concrete paths in long dark streaks and reached deep into the living huts. There was a slight draught as the door to Billy's hut was opened and admitted a small, slight-framed lad of about nineteen or twenty. His hair was dark and almost curly; his fine-boned face gave him an almost girlish look and his hands were slim with long tapering fingers. He was engagingly handsome. However, he was in a badly bedraggled state. He was unwashed, uncombed, a large blue-purple bruise covered the right side of his neck and he looked as if he hadn't slept for a week. Billy caught the look on his face as he glanced nervously round the hut and at its occupants, who had all stopped what they were doing to gaze in interest at the newcomer. The silence was tangible as they stared. The boy seemed scared and, had an almost haunted and lost expression on his face. He stumbled forward into the hut and would have fallen if Billy hadn't quickly reached out and caught his shoulder. He looked at Billy in a daze and muttered something inaudible in response. Billy nodded and listened with the others while their hut officer accepted terse orders from the guard that had accompanied the boy to their hut. They soon learned that he was to join them as they had a vacant billet. The bunk below Billy was empty. The previous occupant had stumbled in exhaustion and fallen under an approaching lorry whilst out on a working party. He had been brought back to camp in a broken sorry state but died of his injuries. He left behind a wife and two children, one of which he had never seen.

The hut officer, a tall lean man with pale washed out red hair and freckles beckoned Billy over to where he stood with the boy. He removed his empty pipe from his mouth as he said,

'Barker. You've got a spare bunk beneath you. This here is Jacobs, Nat Jacobs. Show him his billet and the ropes will you? He was brought in earlier today. They have no room in the RAF hut, so he will stay with us for now.' His words came out in a quick, clipped staccato voice that brooked no nonsense.

Billy nodded his assent.

'Aye, aye Sir.' He turned to the boy and beckoned him with: 'Follow me, down here.' He led him down the tightly packed hut to where his own bunk lay.

'You can have the middle one.' Billy indicated the spare bed before continuing, 'it's not much I know. We'll pay a visit to the 'stores' later and see if the Red Cross have been good enough to send us some more blankets. God knows we could do with some more; the majority of us sleep in most of our clothes, as our own blankets are so threadbare now. But, the Red Cross have been lucky lately, in getting a lot more of their parcels through to us. This last week we have had a consignment of ciggies, some clothing and it's bacon and beans for tea tonight! You'll soon find that you live for Red Cross days. So, this is your bunk and I'm on the top one, with Taff on the bottom. He's alright, except when he's talking in his sleep and his feet do whiff a bit especially after he's been playing football for our inter hut matches. Good goal scorer though. Could have played for Pompey a few of the lads reckon. When he does mutter and shout you have to give him a sharp poke or he wakes up half the hut and you'll know soon enough that it's all your own friggin' fault. Right. Ready? I'll show you where the latrines and wash basins are, you've certainly got a treat in store there!'

Nat limped after Billy. He hadn't uttered a word so far. His brown eyes were heavily fringed with thick dark lashes and they nervously darted around his surroundings. Billy was pleased to have something different to do and happily prattled on to the boy as he showed him around the camp. They paused at the recreational area and Billy went through the normal drill of the day. He started with the early morning roll call at 5am and then hut inspection. He explained the importance of tidy beds as the fastidious German Under Officer would throw a wobbly at the smallest of excuses and cause them to forfeit dinner that day.

Slowly, Billy took Nat round and eventually found after some gentle probing that Nat didn't smoke. He made a mental note of this fact and felt sure that he could use it to his own advantage before someone else did.

It was now after the evening meal. Some men sat around playing cards and smoking a cigarette or two. A few others were having a nostalgic singsong and some quietly read or composed a letter home to some loved one before lying on their beds and losing themselves in their thoughts.

Nat was gradually beginning to relax in Billy's company and he even managed a slight smile when Billy made a joke of him talking too much.

Billy eventually asked him what news he had from back home and, how he came to be here in Germany.

The evening was warm with a gentle wind blowing in the trees beyond the perimeter fence. They were sitting just the two of them, on the hut step and they could hear the low voices of the card players inside as they griped and joked over their game of poker. Somewhere an owl screeched overhead and its mate answered in reply far off in the dark woods. The singers came to the end of their noisy number and someone enthusiastically shouted for a refrain. The group leader picked up the opening words to the first verse and they lustily began again.

Nat leant back against the door jam and stared ahead of him into the darkening gloom away from the spilled light from the hut. His eyes looked slightly out of focus as he turned his thoughts into himself and remembered home. Billy waited patiently and listened as he began to tell his story.

Chapter 17

Nat Jacobs was only 20 years of age. He and his friends had volunteered to fight for their country as soon as they reached their 18th birthday. He said that like many young men he had been hoping for a glamorous role to play in the war, but deep down he knew that he was only kidding himself and he would only qualify for something suitable to his rather modest academic achievements. He and his intake group had suffered impatiently the long weeks and months of training and, had waited with even more impatience for the 'magic door' to open. They thought naively that they had concealed their eagerness with assumed nonchalance. Nat had at first been desperate to train to be a pilot. After a few days, he realised that he wasn't good enough and was more or less content to settle for wireless officer training. He had been stationed at RAF Honington. During the course of his service, the raids had eventually blurred and merged into each other as he was now flying two to three missions a week. He softly recounted the tiredness he and the others had felt, which rapidly led to confusion and then the awful numbness from losing their friends. Those that failed to return from a raid had all traces of them removed from the camp. To those left behind they had 'bought it' and Nat had lost many friends that way. However, there was simply no time to mourn because, as time moved on the raids had steadily become even more hazardous. They were often hit by enemy flak. Nat told Billy that he remembered attacking Hamburg, Duisberg and Wilhemshaven day in and day out.

He paused to take in a deep breath of the soft evening air before he continued.

On his last sortie the crew had been five in number and they had only been together for about three weeks. There was the pilot Wilf, the bomb aimer Douglas, the front gunner George, rear gunner Bob and himself as the wireless operator. This time their targets were to be German factories. Somewhere near Hamburg they were hit by flak.

'I remember the glowing shrapnel that had hit the underneath of the floor of the plane,' he said. 'There were coloured stars from the bursting flak and trace from the anti-aircraft guns. The searchlights were catching us in their beams. The gunners were in their turrets and I was crouching on the floor,' he paused.

'We dropped our bomb and the searchlights continued to play their beams over us. Wilf the pilot was always thinking about his crew, and he checked over the intercom that we were all alright back there. Everyone answered him and said that they were all fine. The tension in the plane could be felt and the relief was noticeable in everyone's voices. Suddenly, there was white tracer; two white flickering points of light. A German plane had us in his sights!' Again he stopped and rubbed at his forehead with his right hand.

'Wilf threw the plane into a roll to starboard, and Bob the rear gunner fired a short burst at the Jerry plane as it shot past us. We were now right off our given course and were flying lower at about six or so thousand feet. Again the bastard – a fighter Messerschmitt it was, came straight at us. I know I remember thinking how horribly close it was, and then I felt a dull blow to my thigh.'

He gestured to his leg where his trousers had a large tear in them. Dark stains shrouded the gaping star-like hole and a grubby bandage showed beneath.

'I suddenly realised that our engines had changed pitch and that it was sounding a bit strange. I unplugged my oxygen mask and managed to half walk, half crawl forward. Eventually I found Wilf slumped over the controls. It was then that I noticed that the starboard engine was burning brightly with a huge deep flame. In the flickering light I could see that the rest of the crew were all dead.' His voice had become lower and quieter until he finally stopped and stared down at the ground by his feet. He took a deep shuddering sigh.

'All dead. All my friends were gone in one blow. I think self-automation took over as I found a parachute and put it on. I remember clipping it to my harness and crawling towards the back of the plane. I remembered that from emergency drill we had to locate the escape hatch.'

Billy looked at Nat with a puzzled look on his face.

'It's a flimsy partition in the floor near the rear-gun turret,' he continued as Billy nodded in understanding.

'I kicked the panel out and sat on the edge of the hole. I was shit scared I can tell you. The plane was still flying straight on autopilot. I could feel the air whooshing and sucking, pulling at my legs. I had only done a couple of practice jumps from a hangar and within the company of a long line of other airmen. Crikey, this time I was on my own and it was really happening. I could hardly believe it.' He looked across shakily at Billy as he remembered. A thin line of sweat had appeared on his top lip.

'By now the fire was spreading and the plane was in real danger of exploding and blowing me up with it. So I knew that it was now or never and I jumped. I counted slowly from one to seven and felt the sharp tug on my shoulders as the 'chute opened. I was slowly drifting down and I had the weird thought of how peaceful it suddenly was up there.' He shook himself slightly at the memory of it all.

'Suddenly, without warning I hit the ground! It was pitch dark after all. My knees and hips took the blow and the wind was knocked out of me. I fell onto my side, took a mouthful of dirt and the last thing I remembered before I passed out was how incredibly sick I felt.' Once again he paused as he thought back to that dark night.

'Go on. What happened then?' asked Billy, fascinated. He had never jumped from a plane, nor could he imagine himself ever wanting to do so.

'Well, eventually I must have come to and found myself lying on the ground at the edge of a wood. I sat up slowly as I still felt a bit sick and giddy and looked around me. All was quiet so I released the harness buckle and stood up. My legs were still trembling from the scare of jumping and my stomach ached from the winding. My thigh was throbbing and it was then that I noticed that it felt wet. Looking down I realised that it was sticky with blood.' He ruefully rubbed his bandaged leg.

'I knew I couldn't stay there too long. So, I struggled to stand upright and nearly passed out again from the pain in my leg. I fell over, and then managed slowly to again stand and then make it over to the cover of the trees. That was jolly hard work I can tell you. I leant against a thick tree to get my breath back. It was then that I heard the dogs in the distance. I could make out pinpricks of torchlight and eventually cries and shouts as they got nearer.' Again he stopped and this time he looked Billy fully in the face. His dark handsome face had gone chalk-white and there was a sheen of sweat on it. He raised his hands from his lap and they shook as he made a gesture of frustration and helplessness.

'Now I knew I was in big trouble! I'd never before been in a foreign country let alone one we were at war with! I'd only ever seen Germans as goose-stepping monsters on cinema newsreels. Now they and their vicious growling dogs surrounded me. I tried to keep calm. After all I was in uniform and had my identity on me, so I wasn't a spy. But, I'd heard all the stories about the Nazi extermination camps and their purpose of mass murder by gassing. You see I am Jewish. My full name is Nathaniel Jacobs. It's not too difficult to guess my origins!' He managed a small rueful smile that didn't quite make it to his eyes, but it did change his face. In the gathering dusk and the soft light from their hut, his huge dark eyes and soft facial skin gave the clear impression of a beautiful girl. Billy shifted his weight uncomfortably on the rough wooden step and then hurriedly looked away. What the hell was he thinking of?

He cleared his throat before he gruffly said, 'go on.'

'Well as I said I was surrounded by Jerry. They prodded me with their guns and shouted at me. They made signs to show that I was to walk with them. I stumbled along with them until we came to a road where a couple of trucks were parked and they shoved me in the back of one of them. I lay there trembling with exhaustion and in absolute bloody pain. The truck set off, heavily grinding its gears and bumping along on the rough road until we thankfully stopped about a half hour later. Out they dragged me again, with even more loud shouting, and I realised that I had been brought to some sort of local HQ. My ID was taken off me and I stood and sweated in sheer panic until eventually I was taken indoors before an officer. The building was an old large house with a rather grand staircase and lots of rooms opening off the hallway. Anyway I was frog-marched into this inner office and there seated at a large polished desk was a German officer. I stood, how I managed I don't know as I couldn't stop my legs from shaking and I was in such pain. The German at first didn't say a word; he just took out a pink form from a drawer, unscrewed his fountain pen and then looked at me. I think I need some water.' Nat stopped and made a move to stand up. Billy put out a restraining hand, 'It's all right. You sit still. I can get it for you.'

He returned with two chipped enamel mugs. 'Bottoms up,' he said in a mock toast, 'what did he say to you?'

'He asked me what I was doing in Germany and where had I come from. I answered him with the information that we were told to give back home. You know, the usual name, rank and number. In front of him perched on his desk were my red and green ID discs. He picked them up and then said softly, so softly that I almost didn't hear him and nearly asked him to repeat his question: "Jacobs. Jewish name is it not?" I nodded a scared yes. By now I was fighting back the pain and almost in tears with fear and exhaustion. He continued to hold my discs in his hand and was casually swinging them back and forth in front of me. He then laid them down and said, "You are wounded?" Again, I nodded yes and he said he would get a doctor to take a look at me. He called out to the guard standing outside in the hallway and said something in German to him. The guard indicated that I was to follow him outside which I did. I was quite thankful to get out of his office. I followed the guard and eventually was led into another building that smelt like a hospital. You know smelling of Dettol and the like. It seemed like ages before a doctor arrived to see me and I could tell he didn't want to be bothered with the likes of me. He argued with the guard before he eventually gave in to his impatience and dressed my wound. He kept saying how busy he was, and that the wound wasn't that bad and would heal in a couple of weeks. After that I was taken out and put into a cell like room to myself. It was small and contained nothing but a bed, chair and bucket. It had a single light bulb and a small window but, thankfully it was warmer than outside and at least it looked clean. Later, I was given a meal of sorts, weak strange tasting coffee, a piece of cheese, sausage and some dark chewy bread. I really didn't know what was going to happen to me but I was thankful to have somewhere to lie down. Later that evening, the same German officer who had questioned me earlier came to my cell,' Nat stopped. His voice had faltered and he obviously didn't want to carry on. He stared out into the night.

Something made Billy look hard at Nat. He saw a look of bleakness on Nat's dark face. His eyes looked black and luminous, almost wet.

Nat gulped and continued, 'he said that he had gone to a lot of trouble getting the doctor to treat me and he then –.' He turned his face aside and shuddered, his shoulders heaving. Billy felt a sharp spasm of anger and pain for Nat. He tentatively put a hand on his shoulder; he was almost afraid to touch him. 'It's all right, you don't have to go on. I understand what you're trying to say,' he finished gruffly. Nat stared miserably into the distance, his face a study of shame and humiliation.

They sat in silence. Far off in the night they again heard the owl as it called once more to its mate. Near to the camp a dog fox barked. The sound was eerie to their ears. Billy waited patiently. He knew Nat needed time to recover himself. He had to restore his self-respect and dignity. Nat shuddered and then sat up straighter, wiping his mouth on his jacket sleeve.

'Thanks. Sorry.'

Billy stood up and reached out a hand to help Nat stand up.

'It's nearly time for lights out. Let's have a slow walk round and I'll have a last cigarette.'

Nat looked at his outstretched hand. He saw it for what it was. A hand reaching out to him in friendship. He gave a wan smile in return and grasping it with both his own hands, stood up.

***

The days past and life in camp carried on with its regular monotony.

Billy and Nat had become unusual friends. Unusual in that Nat was such a contrast from Billy. Billy got to know Nat well and he soon realised that they came from very different upbringings. Billy was an orphan and had got used to fending for himself during his working-class background of Southampton. Whereas Nat came from a traditional Jewish middle-class family of mother (his father was dead) and two older sisters, one of whom was married. He was very much the baby of the family and had no domestic skills whatsoever. He shamefacedly admitted that until he had come away and joined up he had let his mother do everything for him. He knew that he was a bit young for his age; although he had matured since the war, and as far as girls were concerned Billy could tell that Nat was very much still a virgin. Billy decided that that piece of information he had better keep to himself. He knew that certain members of the camp would like nothing better than to make Nat's life a misery if they got to know that he still had his Cherry.

So, as far as Billy could tell, Nat's mother and sisters had kept him soft by over spoiling and protecting him.

He feared that life in the internment camp was going to be extremely hard on his new friend.

Billy decided to make Nat his own project. By looking after him and guiding him, it gave Billy an added dimension and purpose to their long days. He hoped that Nat would eventually come out of his shell and take in interest in life around him.

A tentative bond began to grow between them. Nat learned to trust Billy and willingly accepted his advice on camp matters and politics. He had soon realised not to draw attention to himself amongst the guards, as a number of them needed little excuse to goad and torment the prisoners in their own boredom and frustration. Their hut mates were a mixed bunch. Some took little or no interest in the shy newcomer whereas a few of the louder occupants enjoyed teasing Nat to extremes. Billy watched events from the side. Ready to step in and support Nat if the need arose. However, as Nat settled in with a quiet and shy determination it soon became apparent to the others that he had no malice within him and his nature was normally of an open sunny disposition albeit with a trace of naivety.

He became popular when he displayed a natural talent for acting and singing and was soon in great demand for the Amateur dramatic productions. With his handsome, almost pretty face he was usually cast in the girl lead, but it made no matter to him, as he was pleased to be accepted into 'the family.'

Someone whittled him a penny whistle and he spent hours whiling away the time learning to play simple tunes. Within weeks he had mastered the musical instrument and was composing his own sweet melodies. He began to talk excitedly of when they would get home and the possibility of learning to play the flute, or maybe joining a real theatrical company.

He was very proud of his real family and always informed Billy what his gorgeous sisters were up to when he received mail from home. His latest letter from his mother enclosed a photograph of his mother and sisters. The happy smiling group were standing outside the canopied foyer of the Berkeley. They had been to celebrate his mother's birthday with a splendid meal complete with oysters and champagne! Nat reread the part about the meal and described the food and wine to Billy. Both men drooled at the idea of eating a sumptuous meal in an airy and pretty restaurant instead of the dreary food that they endured. But surprisingly neither resented the girls enjoying themselves on this occasion up in London. There was little enough of anything to be cheerful about during these times and everyone needed a treat sometimes. Billy studied Nat's photograph and noted the strong family likeness, the dark hair, eyes and slightly sallow complexion. The older sister was truly beautiful with thick lustrous curly hair and wonderful almost almond-shaped eyes. Her smile would have bewitched even the strongest of misogynists. He returned the picture to Nat who tucked it away with the letter into his pocket. Billy found himself telling Nat about his own Penny. How when he got home he wanted to marry her if she would have him. He described her life at home amongst her chickens and the other animals that they kept for milk and meat. He remembered her doughty parents and flighty, bossy sister and wondered what mischief she had been caught in lately. He reminisced about the Hampshire countryside with its rolling chalk downs and fields of wheat and corn, and the woods in May and June, knee-deep in thick scented clouds of bluebells. The walks across the meadows and marshlands with the high call of the skylark and curlew, the pretty swarms of brightly coloured butterflies of which he had no idea of their names and the sharp tang of the raw salty sea air on the breeze. Billy could picture it all and feel the warmth of the sun and the smell of Penny's skin as she lazed back sleepily in the lush soft spring grass. Their walks and cycle rides. Their excited talks of when peacetime would come and what the future would bring for them. Swimming and dancing, holding each other close under the slowly turning multifaceted ball at the Mecca dance. He could picture and remember it all, but it felt so long, long ago.

Slowly the months passed and the war continued outside the walls of the camp. Nat had almost forgotten that he was a Jew amongst Gentiles. The older guards were tolerant and the latest Camp Commandant was a decent German officer. The year passed slowly on.

Chapter 18

Nat now ate pork. He didn't like eating it. It wasn't Kosher and therefore it did not fulfil the requirements of Jewish religious laws. But, as Billy argued if he didn't eat the sausage and the scraggy meat given to them in their appalling rations then he would surely starve from malnutrition. And, what would his mother think of Billy for letting him die of starvation? He felt sure that in the circumstances she would understand. So, to keep the peace (and he knew in his heart that Billy was right) he ate everything that was given to them, and although he didn't admit it, it helped him to blend in better.

Later that summer saw a change in their Camp Commandant and a recycling of the guards. There was also a resurgence of the Waffen SS or armed SS in the area and these units worked outside the rules of the Geneva Convention.

In Billy's camp the British found themselves working alongside prisoners of war from the other Allied Nations and also with civilian slave labour from the regions of Soviet Russia and Poland. These prisoners were regarded as *Untermenschen* in Nazi ideology and, were targeted most harshly by their gaolers. They were often systematically worked and starved to death. The British POW's lives were much better in comparison and they still had their sporadic Red Cross parcels to augment their camp rations. As often as possible Billy and Nat found themselves sharing their German soup with their starving Russian neighbours as they couldn't bring themselves to condone their German gaolers evil deeds. However, the Gestapo and the SS put a stop to it once they realised what the British POWs were up to.

For Billy it was nearing the end of the afternoon after a long day working on the roads. As the gates swung shut on the little weary bunch of men, he reeled with tiredness and aching limbs. He felt little relief as he trudged across the dusty compound towards his hut. He longed for a deep hot bath to take away the aches and pains and knew that the meagre trickle of cold water from the shower would do nothing to dispel them. He flung his patched and worn boots under the bunk, pulled off his threadbare jacket and lay for a minute or two to recover from the day's hard graft. He had new blisters on top of old and his old wound throbbed like mad. He sighed thankfully as his body settled down into the hard bunk and closed his eyes. Within seconds he was in a deep, dreamless sleep.

An hour or so later Nat stumbled into the hut and without a word to the others made a beeline to the back where he shared the triple bunk with Billy. He limped as he made his way between the narrow corridors of bunks and his breath came in laboured sobs.

Billy had just about regained consciousness and was thinking of cleaning himself up before their evening meal when Nat lurched into view. Nat kept his head turned away from Billy as he struggled to take his coat off and it was only too apparent to Billy that he was in some pain.

'What's up with you?' he queried as he jumped down from the upper bunk and landed with a wince on the hard concrete floor below.

Nat made no answer and continued to remove his outer garments. Billy took hold of Nat's shoulder and spun him round out of the shadows. A livid purple bruise was beneath his left eye which was swollen and beginning to close. His top lip was cut and the blood had dripped down onto his collar and pullover.

'Bloody Hell! Who did this to you?' he asked in anger.

Nat could hardly talk as he was bent forward, his arms around his body hugging himself. Billy repeated his question as he guided Nat down onto the lower bunk. 'I said, who did this to you? Tell me and I'll sort them out!'

Nat's breath came in short gasps. 'You can't. It was the Germans.'

'Fucking hell. Your face is a right mess. What about your chest? Did they beat you as well?'

Nat took his time before answering. 'They hit me with a stick and then one or two put the boot in.' He closed his eyes in pain. His face was deathly pale beneath his dark hair.

'Bastard new officer knew I was Jewish and decided to have a little fun interrogating me. He knew I had been shot down, but he wanted an excuse to rough me up.'

'What a sod! If only I could get my hands on him,' Billy snarled, his face dark with fury and his fists clenched tight.

Nat's face suddenly crumpled in anguish and tears slid beneath his eyelids.

'That's not all. The worse thing is they destroyed my photograph of my family. I've got nothing now to remember them by,' he almost sobbed in anguish.

'What? Why?' demanded Billy although the sadism of some of the Germans was well known.

'The officer asked questions and when I refused to tell him nothing more than my name, rank and number he got really angry. Raging even. He had me searched and found my photograph of mother and my sisters. He then showed me what he considered his racial superiority and his utter contempt for Jews.' Nat paused and took in a painful gulp of air. Tears continued to roll down his face, ' he screwed the photograph up in my face and then rubbed it between his backside. He was using it like a piece of lavatory paper! All the time he was snarling and saying "Jude" and "Scheisse". Then, as if that wasn't enough he opened his trousers and pissed all over it! He was laughing now. I went completely mad and went to hit him. The other guards looking on held me down while he thumped me and then put his boot into my side. I think I've got a broken a rib or two.' He finished, grief, misery and distress in his voice. Billy realised that he was finding it difficult to talk out of his swollen mouth and he noted that he had at least a couple of teeth missing.

What to do? He'd report it at least to their hut leader and he'd get a protest off to the International Red Cross. But that would probably be a waste of time and nothing would get done.

'We'll report it,' Billy fumed.

'Waste of time,' Nat replied in between gasps. 'The German said that worse would happen if I attempted anything. He also mentioned that I would be transferred to a vile concentration camp in Poland. I don't have blond hair and blue eyes. I'm not the Aryan of Hitler's Valhalla.'

Billy was shocked and alarmed. Sporadic stories about the Nazi extermination camps had filtered through to the POW camps and they had all heard rumours of what went on in them. He could see Nat being sent off in a cattle truck to an extermination camp. He needed to do something; and do something fast. Anti-Semitism was more widespread in the camp now due to the new regime.

'We're getting out of here,' he said punching his fist against the bunk, 'the sooner the better.'

***

A group of French prisoners were toiling on the land. This day was slightly different as two of their number were making hard graft of the usual straightforward planting and tilling. Their clumsy hands were not used to the farming equipment and their backs ached from the long hours bent over or squatting in the field. The French were guardedly friendly and did their best to keep them in the midst, carefully, silently guiding them in instruction and covering up their amateurish agricultural efforts.

If only Penny could see me now, thought Billy, as he shook and then wiped the loose soil off a carrot before throwing it into the bottom of his sack. He wiped the sweat off his brow with the back of his hand; it was hot work and he was thirsty.

The guards lolled over by the dry-stone wall. Relaxed and at ease. They smoked their cigarettes at leisure, laughed and joked with one another, and teased Hans when he accidentally missed the bush he was aiming at and pissed over his rifle.

That night the guards locked the prisoners up in a barn on the edge of the field in which they had been working. It made sense to their gaolers to keep them out of the camp and near their place of work. They could make an early start at first light and get more vegetables dug up. Why waste valuable fuel transporting them to and fro?

The prisoners had had their evening rations and most were glad to settle down and have a smoke and a good nights rest before tomorrow. They had been locked in at night here before and it made a change of scene from the overcrowded POW camp. Moreover, Gilbert their leader, knew exactly which part of the brick barn wall was loose and how with a bit of cunning and effort a hole could be made by removing a few of the bricks.

The French themselves had played no part in trying to escape as they considered the surrounding German countryside too hostile for escapees, and besides, their families back home were being held hostage while they worked the land for their masters. They had seen at firsthand the reprisals handed out during the earlier years of the war.

However, they understood that Billy was desperate to get Nat out of camp and away, and that if he stayed, then sooner rather than later he would be either shot or sent to an extermination camp. After a lot of arguing in true French fashion and some considerable bartering for cigarettes and clothes, they had finally agreed that they would cover for them. As Billy said somewhat caustically to Nat later on, nothing is free in this world except maybe, disease.

The warm evening passed slowly for the two of them and night could not come too soon. The prisoners had three new Germans guarding them who spent their own night encamped by their truck. The pleasant temperatures meant that they were quite comfortable out of doors and they could enjoy the unusual freedom away from the confines of the POW camp and with no senior officer to bark orders at them. Billy and Nat could hear their voices as they jovially bickered over their game of poker. Stringent acrid smoke from their cigarettes drifted over to the barn on the night breeze and one fellow crowed loudly with undisguised pleasure as he scooped the pot in the middle. A chorus of groans followed and renewed bickering; two of the guards resented the other's long reign of luck. There was a chink of coins as they fell on the empty beer bottles on the grass. A mumbled voice, slurred with alcohol protested for a moment and then there was a silence. The warm night and the beer had got the better of them. The guards were relaxed around their campfire. They felt safe in their knowledge that the French had never attempted to escape. They drunkenly rolled themselves in their blankets to snore the night away.

Inside the barn the night was soft and dark and humid. The would-be escapees sweated with nervousness as they waited for the guards to settle down to sleep. From the grimy, small casement window Billy could see little moonlight. It boded well. Somewhere deep in the night an inevitable vixen barked and nearby an owl hooted. The almost eerie sounds raised the hairs on the back of Billy's neck. He would feel much better once they were moving. The guards were finally quiet, wrapped in their grey blankets, boots loosened for comfort, mouths agape and snoring to the world.

Gilbert had secreted a broken hoe into the barn, hidden under some rubble in the darkened recess at the back. He disturbed the rubble and produced the hoe, holding it proudly aloft. He hissed an order and two members of his group instantly made their way over to the window to keep watch. The others remained lying on the floor keeping well out of the way. He silently gestured to Billy and together they began to slowly scrape away at the old mortar around the softened bricks. The first brick took some time. It was a little tricky prising it out from the gritty wall. But, the second and subsequent ones came away in their hands more quickly.

'We only need a small hole to wriggle through. Then you can replace the bricks. With luck the Germans won't notice. The mortar can be mixed with the rubble already on the floor and this old sacking can be spread out to hide any scratch marks,' Billy whispered.

Gilbert grunted his agreement, his lethal breath enveloping Billy as he prised out another brick.

'Oui. I think that the 'ole is now beeg enuff.'

'Nat are you ready?' Billy whispered to the dark gloom where he knew Nat sat tensed and waiting.

A scraping on the floor indicated that Nat had heard him and was moving into position by the small hole. As he drew closer Billy noticed that he held his penny whistle in his hands. Nat had been most adamant about bringing it along with him. After his photograph had been destroyed he had nothing else personal left and his despondency had been pitiful. Billy understood how he had felt and was glad that he had found some small outlet in which to channel his grief.

Nat put the simple musical instrument away, tucking it down the front of his shirt. He checked the laces once again on his boots (one of the 'perks' for being on a working party), and then quietly squatted down next to the hole. He peered at Billy in the grey darkness.

'You go first,' he said.

Billy clasped Gilbert's hand and briefly touched him on the shoulder. They stared at each other for a moment.

'It ees good. Plees go wiv ze God,' said Gilbert his eyes and large teeth gleaming in the darkness.

'Thank you,' he replied. 'Are you sure you can cover for us?'

'Ah oui. Tomorrow they 'ave the bad 'eads and stomachs and will be 'appy to go to their beds. They weel not bother to count us, and pouf! if they do then they weell argue wiv themselves as to 'ow many we are. We weel just get on with our work and pretend to not, 'ow you say, comprend? Because none of we ever make the escape before they will be trés confused. Also, they weel none of them admit to being wrong as they would themselves be punished.'

The simplicity of Gilbert's explanation was not lost on Billy.

'Good. Thank you once again,' he replied. He raised a hand to the others sitting and lying quietly around the barn. He could not make out their features clearly, but he could feel the intensity of their interest in his and Nat's intended plan to escape. Smiles were exchanged between them.

Billy turned and after patting his pockets and making sure his jacket was buttoned up he got ready to lie down before the hole. Taking a deep breath he lowered himself down flat onto his stomach and began to wriggle and crawl through the tight gap. Bits of hard and crumbly mortar brushed against his face and for one awful moment he thought he had got his backside stuck. But no, with a pause and then another wriggle he managed to emerge onto the other side of the barn wall. The cooler air fanned his cheek as he lay for a moment listening to the grunts and farts from the guards over by their truck. All seemed quiet. He slowly got to his feet and then keeping his body crouched down low he crept over to a low wall that lay in shadow. He was perspiring heavily now, the sweat running down his face and into his eyes. Using his sleeve he wiped himself dry and after a minutes safety pause he then waved the all clear for Nat to follow.

Dithering Nat peered through the hole to the outside.

'Go. Go,' whispered Gilbert urgently, 'he 'as waved you to go.'

He knelt down and then pushed himself towards the hole. He too felt the loose rubble as it scraped over his face and cut into his cheek. He winced but didn't stop until his head emerged on the other side. He heard the faint screech of an owl as it called to its mate in the field beyond and he felt the caress of the fresh air on his bare face. With deliberate slowness he raised himself to his feet and followed Billy's path into the shadows. He was breathing heavily with nervousness and the exertion. His chest was still hurting from where he had been beaten by the German and the bruises were taking a while to disappear. Billy tapped him on the shoulder and pointed to where the guards lay curled up in their blankets. Their loud snores were audible in the still quiet night and their bodies were clearly outlined against the glowing embers of the campfire at their feet.

Billy again pointed, this time in the opposite direction away from the guards and along the low dry-stone wall. Nat nodded and together they turned and crept as quietly as possible keeping well to the cover from the shadow of the trees and wall. When they thought that they had gone far enough to be out of earshot they left the wall and loped across the field towards the dark safety of a wood.

'We've got to get as much distance between us and the Germans, just in case they do cotton on in the morning,' said Billy in between puffs.

'They'll eventually find out anyway when they do the next roll call at the camp. So we'll walk mostly at night when it's dark, keep well away from towns and lay up during the day to sleep for a few hours at a time. Remember, we might not be able to trust the road signs. I don't know if the Jerries have switched their signs around to confuse the enemy like we've done back home. We'll just have to hope they haven't and we can get by with a bit of luck by following the sun's direction. You know rising in the east and sinking in the west. It's the best we can do without a compass.'

Nat nodded, gasping for breath at his side. Bad diet over the months and years had done nothing for their fitness. Exhaustion would soon set in if they were not careful. They had hoarded and brought along a little food, but soon they would have to supplement it with whatever they could find and steal. Vegetables and fruit were to be found in the fields and a few lucky clutches of hens' eggs and of course poultry. Stealing other food was more risky as any observant *hausfrau* would soon miss it. She would dutifully inform the authorities all too quickly and a manhunt would commence as two and two were put together.

They skirted the edge of the wood and made good progress covering about three miles an hour for the four hours before it got too light to move freely in safety. They had found potatoes and carrots growing in a field and pulled up handfuls for their breakfast, brushing off the soil as best they could. Water was more difficult to find. They had looked at dubious duck ponds and ditches half filled with muddy water and had ruled them out. They didn't want to get a foul stomach ache and diarrhoea. Once or twice they had come across a gravelly stream and had drunk as much as their stomachs could hold of the cleaner water. The best find of all was when they came upon two full milk churns waiting to be picked up and taken into town. By cover of a hedgerow they had dragged one over to the side of the road and had removed the metal cover. They hadn't tasted fresh milk for a long time and for a moment the warm bovine smell and the glistening full cream nestling on top had caused them a moment's pause. Not for long however. Using the churn's cover as a shallow dish they had filled and refilled it until both their thirst and hunger had been satisfied.

'Fresh milk! I can't remember when I last tasted some.'

The milk fat lay unfamiliarly heavy in their stomachs and for the first time in years Billy slept on a full belly.

Their journey wasn't easy. After the fifth day Nat, never in the best of health, developed a nasty bout of dysentery. Nothing eaten or drunk stayed where it should, inside him. Twelve hours later and he was in a considerably weakened state and Billy began to fear for his life. His skin showed signs of dehydration, thin and wrinkled and his eyes had taken on an unhealthy yellow tinge to them. For the first time Billy began to have doubts about whether they would make it. He wouldn't leave him as he was committed to getting him to safety. For Billy he was another reason for living. He had given him a purpose. The other reason was Penny. He knew she was as safe as could be back home. Her letters spoke of her devotion, but she had never demanded anything of him. Her love was like a child's; unconditional. Once she had got over her bout of illness as he recalled in the summer of 1942 she had kept him up to date with all her news. This was so important to him as she was the only one who was allowed to write – the Germans being strict in allowing only one correspondent per prisoner. With Nat it was different and his feelings for him were simple. Billy had neither mother nor father. He had an older brother, but the difference in their ages meant that they had never been close. Plus the fact that Billy had never liked or trusted him, thinking him a devious little shit. When his brother, Maurice had moved away to Gloucestershire, he had never kept in touch, and now the ties were even more tenuous. With Penny so far away and in the bosom of her protective family, Billy needed someone. Someone to talk to, to be with, to protect even. Nathaniel was young, immature even and most definitely naïve. He had a simple, easy going nature and a wonderful smile that lit up his whole face. But, left alone he could hardly look after himself. Billy had taken on the role of older brother, father, protector and friend. In the present circumstances Nat had become his raison d'etre, whilst Penny was safely tucked away back in the home country.

Nat was no better and Billy was becoming quite desperate in deciding what was best for him. He could only think that he had to find him a continuous supply of fresh drinking water and somewhere safe and comfortable in which to lie up and let him rest and recover. He hadn't come across a river that promised clean water and so, despite all their previous agreements Billy decided to take the chance of entering a small village in the depths of that night and finding a village pump.

He left Nat shivering with fever, and lying under a hedge in a dry ditch half covered by nettles and bracken. Billy had wrapped Nat in his jacket and had then set out in his shirtsleeves as soon as he judged it was dark and quiet enough. As he softly trod along the rutted track leading to the village he kept a wary look around him. It may appear quiet but, you never knew who might be interested enough to look out of their window even at this late hour he thought to himself. Soon he was approaching the first of the cottages and turning the bend; he realised that the village was bigger than he had first thought. Keeping to the shadows he crept from darkened doorway to doorway. Suddenly, without warning a door opened further up the street, the light spilling onto the roadway as a small party of four of five tipsy German soldiers noisily left the premises. The music coming from inside the building carried up the street to where Billy had frozen to the spot and it sounded like a bar or café. The band of soldiers were weaving their way towards where Billy stood petrified under the canopy of a doorway. He didn't know what to do. He hadn't time to turn and run for cover back down from where he had come and if he stayed where he was they would surely see him as they drew level. In panic he broke out into a cold sweat. He drew back as far as he could into the shadow of the canopy praying that they were all too busy laughing at some joke or other when he suddenly felt a hand grasp his arm. Billy nearly had a heart attack as turning startled, he realised that the door behind him had opened a crack and he was being pulled inside the house. A voice hissed in warning, telling him in softly accented English to keep quiet and quickly come inside. Billy needed no second telling and silently slipped inside the darkened house as the door was pushed shut behind him. He stood inside a hallway, his heart thudding in his chest, feeling dizzy and sick with the near brush with the enemy. Enemy? What was he thinking? Here he was deep inside Germany and inside a German house. Who was his saviour? He turned towards the figure next to him and began to speak.

'Sssh. Follow me inside here,' and again he let himself be led, this time into another room further away from the front of the house.

A sudden flare of a match startled Billy and he hurriedly turned towards the small light in alarm and then blinked in surprise.

She had lit an oil lamp and the amber bowl was soon aglow and casting pools of warm light across the room. She crossed to the other side of the room and bending down she then lit a couple of white church candles that were standing in little saucers in the hearth of a small fireplace. She then turned towards Billy hesitantly, a touch of fear lurking in her eyes.

'You're a girl!' he said in some confusion.

She allowed herself a small smile.

'What did you expect?'

'Well. I dunno, I –.' Billy for once was at a loss for words. 'Are you German? Why did you save me from those soldiers?'

She shrugged. 'Why not? And yes I am German. I happened to glance out of the window and saw you coming along the road and I saw the soldiers. By your movements I knew you had to be an escapee and I have heard rumours, so, –' again she shrugged her shoulders and spread her hands.

'Well Miss I am very thankful you did. I can't tell you how panicked I was when I saw them coming along the road.' Billy let out a great sigh of relief.

'You will have to be very quiet. Everyone is very suspicious here. I will get into serious trouble if you are found in my house.' She looked extremely worried and seemed to be having doubts as to whether it was a good idea to have let Billy inside in the first place.

'Don't worry I shall be as quiet as a mouse. Do you live here alone?'

A hint of wariness was in her voice as she replied, 'No. I live here with my baby daughter.' She paused and then continued hoarsely, ' you won't hurt us will you?' Her look was one of sudden fear and confusion, as if she had just realised what she had done. In letting a complete stranger inside her house during wartime and an enemy to boot.

Billy looked shocked at the idea.

'Good God no! What do you think I would do to you? You've just saved my life and besides I'd never hurt a woman.'

'It's just that you hear so many things,' she finished lamely rubbing her hand against her leg.

'Yes. I understand. So do we. A lot of it is propaganda, you know to spread disinformation.'

'Are you hungry and thirsty?' She suddenly looked brighter, 'I can give you some food to take on your way.'

Billy suddenly remembered why he was here. Nat! He had left him back down the lane in a ditch. What about his condition?

He raised his troubled eyes to the girl. She was moderately pretty. She stood at about medium height with a small neat figure. Her hair was cut short in a bob and her thick fringe was just above her grey eyes. She had a wide generous mouth with naturally red lips and in normal times looked like she would have been fun to be with.

'I have to tell you I'm not alone. I have a sick friend hidden just down the road. He needs some water and medicine very badly Miss.'

She stared at Billy in consternation. She understood exactly what he had just said and the implication in it.

Billy continued, 'I don't even know your name.'

'My name is Elsa.'

'Well I'm very pleased to meet you Elsa. My name is William, but I am usually known as Billy.'

'Billy. That is nice. And your friend?'

Misunderstanding Billy said that his name was Nat. He didn't elaborate further thinking that she might well realise that Nathaniel was Jewish.

'No, not his name, I mean where is he, and could you get some water to him?'

'Well yes, but I think he needs a bit more looking after. Somewhere a bit more comfortable than the ditch I left him in. I wonder, I hate to have to saddle you with my problem, but do you have an outhouse or shed where we might hide for a day or so. Only just until he's a bit better of course. I promise we'll be no trouble and we'll be gone as soon as he's able to walk.' Billy looked at her with hope as he pleaded their case. Elsa didn't immediately answer him. A small frown covered her brow.

'Someone might see you as you bring him back here,' she said clearly not at all happy with the idea.

Billy sighed in resignation and slightly nodded his head.

'All right. I understand you're not keen. Well if I could have some water and a bit of food maybe. I'll try and keep Nat warm and comfortable until he's recovered and we can be on our way.'

'Yes of course. I have a flask somewhere or I could let you have a water bottle? I also have plenty of fresh bread and cheese,' she looked relieved.

'Thank you that'd be marvellous. By the way your English is perfect, apart from the strange accent. Is it American?' Billy queried.

'No it is Canadian,' she replied and then let out a deep sigh that almost ended in a sob. 'My husband and I were living in Toronto in Canada. We had emigrated there and loved it. The local people were very welcoming and friendly, we had a very sweet, and cosy little house. We both had good jobs there working as schoolteachers in the local high school. Dieter was the assistant headmaster. At the beginning of the war, well just before, we had returned here, as Dieter's father was taken ill with a bad heart attack. He died shortly after and we stayed to help his mother arrange the funeral and give her some comfort and support. Suddenly we realised that the war was very real and we were unfortunately stuck here. We ourselves had no quarrel with Poland or any of the other annexed countries that Hitler was taking over in the name of the *Third Reich*. Dieter was forced into joining the German army, although he said he had no wish to fight and our home was now abroad. He tried to get out of it and he was told that if he persisted in being a traitor to the *Glorious Fatherland* then he would never see any of his family again. Indeed we would all be put into labour camps and God knows there are enough of them. Do you know almost every town had one now? Worse still any criticism of the state is an offence, and many offences are punishable by death. Dieter has only come here once on a short leave in all this time. He doesn't know about his baby daughter and I wonder if he will ever see her.'

Her voice trailed away into a whisper and Billy could see the glistening of her tears beneath her thick dark eyelashes. Her obvious misery showed in her face and in the way her thin arms were held hugging her body for comfort. Billy felt awkward and clumsy and didn't know how to respond. A silence hung in the air between them.

She lifted her face to Billy and the light from the lamp caught the sparkle of her unshed tears. Bitterness entered her voice as she said,

'Damn the war! Damn Hitler. Go and get your friend. If he is as bad as you say he is then he needs to be better taken care of. There is a way around the back of the cottages. I shall show you. Come, follow me.'

With a fierce proudness she led Billy to the back of the house and showed him the path that led around the back gardens and into the rutted lane.

'We are the fifth cottage along. Don't make a mistake and go to the wrong one. As I told you no one else here will give you any help and would call out the special police. Go with care.'

Billy slipped back out of the backdoor and across the small garden. A washing line was hung across the lawn and a line of nappies hung limply in the warm still air. Billy left the garden and ran along the lane back towards where he had left Nat.

* * *

Getting Nat back to Elsa's house had taken almost all of Billy's strength. Although Nat was of a small build, Billy himself had suffered during his years of incarceration and had very little spare energy. The camp conditions, poor diet, little medicine, arduous work and both physical and mental abuse all took its toll. He had also never really recovered from the injury he had suffered when his Motor Torpedo Boat was shot up back in 1942. Now exhausted he lay slumped on the bottom stair of Elsa's house. Somehow between them they had carried the almost unconscious Nat up the steep staircase and onto the single bed in the spare bedroom. They had both been terrified that the noise of their feet would waken the next-door occupants, or that Nat would cry out in sudden pain. But, they had managed it quietly and just now Elsa was finishing giving Nat a mug of warm milk laced with a spoonful of honey.

Billy felt exhausted. He was drained both mentally and physically. He longed for a good night's sleep and would have given almost anything for a soft bed with a pillow.

The door closed softly above him and he looked up to see Elsa coming down the stairs.

'Everything all right?' he asked quietly.

'Yes. He is sleeping now. We shall have a hot drink for ourselves, and a sandwich for you. Then I shall show you where I keep the spare blankets. You had better sleep in with Nat in case he wakes and wants something. It is better if you are there to keep him quiet.'

She was now quietly in control of herself and the situation. Billy felt relief flooding through him. He leant his head back against the wall behind him and closed his eyes to hide the sudden threat of tears. It was going to be all right.

***

They had been staying with Elsa for two days now. Nat's diarrhoea had finally stopped and he was able to keep down fluids and the soupy meals that Elsa prepared for him. He spent most of the day and all night asleep recovering his strength and for this Billy was grateful. Elsa hadn't made any comment on his dark, obvious Jewish looks and if his presence wasn't there then the subject would never be raised.

Billy was curious about the village in which Elsa was staying and to whom the cottages belonged. He wasn't sure as to how many questions he could ask her without seeming too nosey and took care not to be under her feet especially when she was nursing her baby.

During one of their conversations she told him that the cottage belonged to an uncle of her husband's and he and his wife lived in Hamburg. They had owned many properties including a factory before the war, but bombing had destroyed almost half of them. Subsequently they detested the British and her allies. Elsa said that they did not visit the village at all so there was no danger of them suddenly appearing on the doorstep to collect their rent. Billy shuddered at the thought. As to the rest of the village inhabitants, they were a mixed bunch of farm labourers and artisans such as tilers, smiths and a baker or two. Simple folk who liked a quiet life but, who would rise to the occasion if they thought there were enemies of their country in their midst. Elsa clearly felt awkward when Billy discussed anything personal to her. Although she had agreed to assist Billy and Nat for a few days, she had made it only too clear that she would be much relieved when they felt that the time was right to leave. Billy was embarrassed because he had no money to give Elsa for their keep. She responded by saying bitterly that the Nazi state paid women a generous allowance to stay at home and have babies, so she had no need of his money.

Nat was visibly improving. So much so that Billy had decided that one more day's rest and the following night they would leave Elsa and her little cottage and baby Monika.

The day was just beginning as a rosy sun had climbed above the little coppice that lay beyond the garden of the cottage. Elsa had bathed and fed her baby and put her into her pram to lie and doze under the shade of the apple tree. Her chubby little face was flushed pink and she contentedly sucked her thumb as she slumbered beneath her soft, white cotton blanket.

Elsa was hanging out freshly laundered nappies and bed linen, happy to have mundane chores that took her mind off the war and the present danger that she had unwittingly placed both herself and her daughter in. A sudden knocking at her front door left her momentarily poised with a handful of wet towel and peg in hand. Slowly, she replaced the linen back into the clothesbasket and unconsciously ran a hand through her short hair before walking resolutely through the house. Again there was a knock and as Billy peered down at her from the upper floor landing she held a finger to her lips for silence. They had agreed what to do in advance if any officials came asking leading questions. Billy had been quite unshaken when he had sworn on his honour that he would give both himself and Nat up and state that they had forced Elsa to hide them.

She waved a hand motioning him to get back into the bedroom and when all was clear she opened the heavy oak front door.

Billy could hear nothing except a brief murmuring and then a soft thud as the door was pushed closed and footsteps walking down the two steps and away down the road. He didn't know if Elsa had left the house with the caller or if she had come back inside and shut the door. Unclear he decided that either way she would soon climb the stairs when she needed to. He made himself comfortable in the armchair next to Nat's bed and idly thumbed through an old pre-war magazine. When an hour had passed and there was still no sign of Elsa he decided that he would go in search of her. Maybe she had a heavy job that needed doing by a man?

Quietly, he slowly crept down the stairs – missing the second to bottom as it creaked loudly. There was no sign of her in either the small sitting room or in the neat, freshly cleaned kitchen. A beaker of ersatz coffee was still sitting on the kitchen range. Billy lifted the lid and although it was still fairly warm he knew it wasn't freshly brewed. He poised before the open kitchen door that led out into the back garden and saw that she was sitting on the old unpainted wooden bench next to Monika's pram. Even from the distance from where Billy stood he could see that she was as white as a sheet and looked very shocked. He couldn't go out to her, nor could he call out to get her attention. Completely immobile he stood by the door wondering what he should do. Monika's sudden crying caught Elsa's attention. With almost catatonic-like movements she stooped over the pram and lifted her baby daughter. As she cuddled Monika to her breast and raised her ashen face, Billy had a sudden bleak premonition. Very softly, he called her name.

Trance-like she turned to where he stood half hidden in the doorway and as Monika's cries became more insistent she held the baby tighter to her. She didn't see him.

'Elsa!' he hissed, 'come in.'

Slowly she focused on Billy, recognition dawning in her eyes. She looked down at the baby bawling now in full flood, its little hands clenched in tight fists, its tiny face screwed up with pain.

She started and released her tight hold on the infant, concerned now, cajoling and murmuring. The baby's cries subsided to deep sobs and Elsa hoisted her over her shoulder, patting her gently on her back. She looked at Billy hollow-eyed and then slowly walked towards him.

***

Later, Billy was to recall that as soon as he saw her face he knew. He knew that Dieter would never see the beautiful daughter that had been lovingly made between them. Little Monika would never feel his strong arms as he lifted her over a tall fence, or pushed her high upon her swing in the garden, or brushed away her tears as she cut her knee or chased off uncouth young men when she was still feeling her way towards young womanhood. The truth was Dieter would never come home. He would forever lie somewhere on the Eastern front, buried beneath the tangle and detritus of war.

The rest of the day was spent in a blur of making cups of tea and coffee. Cajoling Monika and keeping Nat informed of events. Elsa hardly said a word. Dry-eyed all day she attended to her baby and then refused Billy's offer of help with the simple evening meal. After the meal Billy was in a quandary as to what he should do. He had planned that he and Nat would leave that night as soon as the village was dead asleep. But, looking at Elsa and how quietly she had reacted he feared of what she might do later on, especially if he wasn't there. Tacitly, he and Nat decided that they would stay another day and see how she was after a night's sleep.

Now Monika was in the land of nod, tucked up in her cot with her favourite soft toy clasped in her podgy little hand. Nat too was taking advantage of another night in a comfortable bed and had drifted off. Elsa had retired to her room and Billy was playing a quiet game of clock patience to while away an hour or two. The house was unnaturally silent except for the loud tick from the Swiss clock that sat over the heavy sideboard in the sitting room. He couldn't decide whether it was an annoying sound or a comforting one. He sighed as he thought of Elsa and Dieter. Who was it that said that the dead are forever young? He folded his cards and reshuffled them. He couldn't make them work for him. Three times he had drawn a blank. He might as well call it a day and have an early night as well. He lay the cards back down on the table, stood up and then turned down the wick on the oil lamp before leaving the room. Softly he mounted the stairs and paused outside Elsa's bedroom door. He could hear no noise from within; hopefully she had fallen asleep. He turned to continue down the corridor towards the room he shared with Nat.

Her door suddenly opened and Elsa stood on the threshold. She had obviously been getting ready for her own bed as she was wearing a fine white lawn nightgown. Her feet stood bare on the beige coloured carpet. At first she didn't say a word, just stood and gazed at Billy. Billy's heart went out to her. She opened her mouth to say something and suddenly her face crumpled. Huge fat tears slid down her cheeks as she struggled to speak. Instead she shook her head slowly from side to side in her grief. Something inside Billy snapped as he took a step towards her and enfolded her in his arms. She lowered her head to his chest and stood there silently crying, huge convulsions shaking her body.

Slowly, she recovered and her tears became less. She gently withdrew Billy's arms from around her and stepped back into her bedroom. She held out a hand to him and without thinking he took it.

'Please close the door,' she said, 'please stay. I have been so lonely. For almost a year I have always known that Dieter would never return. I don't know how I knew but I just had this feeling deep inside. But it has been so awful. No one to talk to here. Treated with suspicion in this hateful parochial little village, as they believe I am a foreigner and possibly guessing what Dieter's feelings were towards wars. It has been quite dreadful. But the worst has been the loneliness. Please stay. I need you to stay.'

She walked over to her bed, pulled back the eiderdown and sheet and got in. She then shuffled over to the side of the bed against the wall. She lay on her back and held out her arms to Billy. Her eyes implored him.

'Please sleep with me. Here in this space. Dieter always slept on this side. He said I would be safe against the wall. Safe from bogeymen.' She tried to attempt a laugh. It came out brittle and falsely bright. 'Please I just want you to hold me. I'm not asking you to make love to me. Just to hold and comfort me. Make believe that my Dieter is here with me for one last time. Through just this one last night before you go. Is that much too much to ask Billy?' Her voice was hoarse as she whispered his name.

The blood roared in Billy's ears as he contemplated the pretty woman lying in front of him. *Penny, Elsa, Billy, Dieter. Penny, Elsa, Billy, Dieter.*

Billy went back to the open door and quietly closed it. He then walked over to her bed and sat on the side. He removed his boots, socks and then his shirt. Elsa closed her eyes as she felt the bed move under his weight. She felt the warmth of his body as it lay down the length of hers. The hardness of it. The masculine musky smell of it. Murmuring a little cry she turned towards him and his arms encircled her tightly.

Chapter 19

Billy and Nat were fitfully resting in a disused coalhouse near a railway line. They had spent most of the latter part of the day dozing and taking turns keeping watch. The coalhouse had seen better days and judging from the state of repair of the other surrounding buildings had been the target of an aerial attack. Whole parts of the railway track lay mangled for a distance of about 100 yards around them. It would be a while before the Germans would be able to clear the debris and resume transport and troop movements in these parts. Good old RAF, Billy and Nat agreed. Time we gave them a taste of their own hell.

They had left Elsa six nights ago and had both been grieved to leave her to cope alone with her sadness. She had been very good to them and had made sure that they had plenty of extra food to take with them on their journey. Not that she had that much to spare herself. But, she had insisted on boiling up all her eggs and potatoes, and giving them hunks of black bread and smelly cheese. An old WW1 Army water bottle had been found and rinsed out. Mercifully it didn't leak so it too was filled, ready to accompany them on their way. The parting had been tense. Both Billy and Elsa had found it difficult to say much in front of Nat and Nat himself could sense that there was more left unsaid. He had thanked Elsa for all her kindness and had deliberately been the first to leave the safety of the little cottage garden leaving Billy and Elsa to make their goodbyes in private. Now they had left her far behind and were once again learning to live by their wits. So far they had been lucky and this time food had been easier to obtain but again finding palatable water remained a problem. Today they hadn't had a drink since they had left an old abandoned farmhouse with a usable well. The day had been very hot and they had long ago finished off all the water in their bottle. Nat always seemed to suffer far worse than Billy and had begun to lag long before Billy wanted to call a halt to the night's trek. He still suffered from the injuries to his chest and had developed a hacking cough that he found difficult to control. The little weight he had put on at Elsa's house had once again dropped off and Billy doubted that he would find the strength to continue following the sun's journey as it settled in the west every night. Right now they were in a filthy dirty coalhouse with not a drop of water to be found in the vicinity. The water tower had been completely obliterated in the bombing.

'I'll have to go and have a scout round,' Billy said as he peered out from the sooty grimy window of the coalhouse. 'There must be a well or pump in that hamlet further on down the line. You stay here at the back in the dark. You should be well hidden in case anyone comes snooping around. Keep a good look out and if you do see anyone you can get out the back way through here.' He nodded his head towards a sagging door that was hanging off its hinges. The archway looked safe enough and there was a tangled scrubby copse behind. Woody enough in which to lie and hide up in for a few hours at least.

Billy slipped out from the coalhouse and made his way along the edge of the railway track. As soon as he left the bombsite he found that the way was typical: large heavy wooden sleepers, a well-used metal track and cinders strewn along the path. Billy kept to the sleepers as the cinders made too much of a noise as his boots crunched through them. The going was relatively easy and he made good progress towards the hamlet. As he got nearer, the trees thinned away and he saw that if he continued down the track he could be seen silhouetted on the incline. So, making a swift decision he changed his course and headed towards a wall that lined a freshly ploughed field. He vaulted over the wall, landing badly, swore under his breath at his stupidity and then once again headed off in the hamlet's direction.

He judged that he was going northwards for want of something better to think about. Surely even a small village such as this would have some sort of square with a pump? He kept going. The road was clear and the surface surprisingly good. He had to tread softly to stop his boots ringing out on the metalled surface. The first buildings were all completely shrouded in darkness and undoubtedly private houses. There was no sign of a well or pump. He continued on his way keeping well into the overhanging shrubs and trees that lined the road. He nipped down an alley that led to the back and drew a blank. Nothing. Once again he retraced his footsteps, treading lightly as he remembered from his childhood that alleys always have an echoing, almost ringing effect with loud footsteps. Further on down the road he came across a building that was much larger than the others. It had a fence all round it. Worth a look over though. He could smell a sweet perfume of flowers he thought vaguely. A rose bush brushed against him as he grasped the top of the fence and hauled himself up and over, silently cursing to himself as he felt his trouser catch on a wicked thorn. Taking care not to make a sound he freed the torn cloth and continued over the wall into the yard on the other side, this time his landing was better. The yard was big and dark shadows loomed around him. There had to be water somewhere here. Catching his breath after his climbing, he flitted from the fence and over to the building. He then edged along the wall until he had reached the corner and took a peek beyond. What a sight! There standing tall and proud stood a black iron hand pump.

Nothing had ever looked quite so beautiful he thought. He took a good look round him as he removed the strap that held the water bottle from around his neck. He waited a while, and then when he was certain that all was clear, he moved cautiously over to the pump and placed the neck of the bottle under the lip. With his right hand he grasped the handle and pulled it down. The handle moved and as it did so it squeaked in protest. Billy stopped. The noise had sounded so loud in the quiet of the village. Damn! Far too loud. He moved with more caution and once again took the handle and this time pulled it down more slowly. Much better. He repeated the movement. Down, up, down up. The fresh water gushed out into his bottle spilling out from the neck and spurting onto Billy's trousers. He put his mouth to the flow and drank greedily at the cool waterspout.

It was from an upstairs window that the blond boy looked down with keen interest at the scene in the yard below him.

Billy slaked his own thirst and filled the water bottle. He carefully stoppered it and replaced the strap around his neck. He retraced his footsteps and once again climbed back over the fence and started heading back down the road that eventually led towards the railway track and to their hideout.

In excitement the boy let himself out of his house by the front door and left it on the latch. His house was in darkness and both his parents had long ago retired for bed. The boy had been illicitly reading under the bedclothes with a torch that he had been recently given. By sheer luck, he had heard the telltale squeak from the pump.

He knew an easier way over the tall fence and had Billy in his keen sights as he made his way back towards where Nat lay in wait. Quietly, like a cat stalking a mouse he followed Billy. The last house before the railway line belonged to a friend of the boy. The low squat building loomed up in the moonlight and the blond boy softly called through the ground floor bedroom window belonging to his friend Heindrich. Within seconds another boy of about the same age, 14 years or so, pushed aside the curtains and peered out at his friend. His bedraggled fringe was in his eyes and he had obviously been fast asleep.

'Yes. What is it? What do you want?' he asked timorously. His friend was the more daring of the two.

With barely controlled excitement, the first boy whispered what he had seen in his yard. He egged Heindrich to join him and find out what the stranger was up to. It must be illegal or he wouldn't be creeping about in the dead of night. Heindrich needed no excuse. He threw a pyjama-clad leg over his windowsill and hurriedly scrambled down to join his friend in the lane. Together they swiftly ran down the village road in the direction Billy had taken. By now the moon was scudding in and out behind low clouds. In between the periods of darkness the boys espied Billy as he moved along the wall lining the field before joining the railway track.

With unconcealed excitement Heindrich said. 'He is going towards the old depot site. I wonder what he is doing there? There is nothing left of the old buildings.'

Keeping well back and out of sight, the boys doggedly followed him, putting to good practice all that they had been taught. They were well used to orienteering and had spent hours following laid trails. One might have thought that they were just keen boy scouts. Unfortunately for Billy and Nat however, they were not.

They were the Hitler Youth. More commonly known by British soldiers as little sods. They were not like regular soldiers working for their wages. These were boys full of zeal, Nazi spirit, and ideology and almost swooning in readiness to lay down their lives for Hitler and the Glorious Third Reich. They were dangerous in their patriotism.

Unaware Billy carried on, now keen to get back to Nat and give him some water. He also was looking forward to his own rest. The boys followed at a respectable distance, their shadows mingling with the moon-dappled trees overhead.

Within fifteen minutes Billy had reached where Nat was hidden. He softly called his name before he entered the building and he was rewarded by an answering call of 'all clear.'

'I've got some water. It was a bit of a hike to a small village and lucky that I took the right direction,' Billy said as he hunkered down in front of him unslinging the water bottle from around his neck.

'Drink all you want. I can always go back for more. The village is as quiet as the grave.'

Nat took a long pull at the bottle and broke into a cough. Even in the moonlight Billy could see that his face was mottled with the exertion of coughing and a slight sweat shone on his forehead.

'Do you feel alright?' he asked in concern.

'Yes, not too bad. Just a bit tired with this cough. It still hurts my ribs.'

'Well you don't look it,' said Billy grumpily. 'Is there any food left?'

'Just a couple of eggs and a crust.'

'We'll need to have a scout for food later on then. Right now I could do with some kip.'

Billy removed his jacket and bunched it up into a makeshift pillow. He loosened his bootlaces and stretched out on the filthy floor. Something was digging into his side. He shifted position and then in exasperation from his tiredness sat up and removed the offending article from his pocket. A bright object fell from the scrap of soft material that it had been wrapped in. Billy picked it up and gave it an almost reverent brush with his fingers. It was a gift from Elsa. A silver belt buckle that had belonged to her husband. She had given it to Billy on the day that they had left her, murmuring that Dieter would have wanted him to have it for bringing her comfort that last night. He sighed to himself, before rewrapping it up and pushing it further back down into his pocket. He lay back down and looked up through the destroyed roof rafters to the stars above.

'Not exactly The Ritz is it?' he grumbled good-naturedly before he fell asleep.

Nat smiled at his recumbent body, silent in slumber. He owed everything to Billy. From their first meeting in the camp, his protection and friendship, and now their attempt to escape to either a neutral country or better still England. England! He dreamed of his comfortable home with his over protective mother and his beautiful older sisters. How they would be surprised and full of joy if, no, *when*, he walked in the front door! His mother would cry and put on the kettle. She'd make a special meal just for his homecoming. He knew she'd have something especially hidden away for the occasion. They'd all make a fuss of him and Billy would be made into a hero. He carried on dreaming and with a slight smile still on his face eventually joined Billy in sleeping.

Outside the boys had crept up unnoticed and, had watched and listened to the muted but audible voices with deep interest.

'English! They're English! Do you think they are spies that have parachuted down?' asked Heindrich thrilled.

'Maybe. Or perhaps they are escaped prisoners,' replied the blond boy. 'We must get back to the village and get assistance with this.'

They both sneaked some way back up the railway track and then paused to take stock of the situation.

'It would be better if you go back to the village and get help. I will stay here and keep watch on these two felons.'

Heindrich agreed, nodding earnestly and was soon on his way, speeding as fast as his legs in his pyjamas would take him.

The blond boy stayed concealed behind a thick tree trunk lying half across the track. It had probably been brought down by the enemy bombing and made good cover. The irony of it was lost on the boy as he crouched hidden. He felt certain that the two mystery men were going to stay put for a while. The one with the cough had sounded weak and ill. Time seemed to drag as he waited with unaccustomed patience. Unknowingly Billy and Nat slept on, hardly feeling the uncomfortable ground beneath them.

A faint noise came from the direction of the village. The blond boy stood up and dusted his clothes down, smoothing out the rumples in his Hitler Youth shirt. Without realising he had stood to attention as the vehicle drew nearer. With luck Heindrich had brought the local

Gestapo. He imagined the admiration he would get from them for his vigilance and public spirit. He might even be given an award! How proud his parents would be if he *and* Heindrich too of course, were to be decorated with a medal! That would make the others in the village sit up and take notice. Too often they went around pretending the war wasn't their concern, just complained under their breaths because of the shortages everyone had to suffer. Well, he was made of sterner stuff. He stood for the Country and their glorious leader. *Heil Hitler!*

The vehicle rumbled closer, and then stopped some way back down from the track. The engine was cut and the night was again quiet. The blond boy stepped out from the shadows and waved an arm to indicate his position. Soldiers jumped down from the back of the stationary truck, their arms full of torches and rifles; two had dogs straining at the leash. A tall man who was obviously the officer in charge approached him and the blond boy gave him a stiff Nazi salute. The officer responded with a short curt wave of his arm and quietly asked him where the suspects were. The blond boy proudly pointed to the building and watched in satisfaction as the *Ordnungspolizei* trotted over to the ruined coal shed. Heindrich had jumped down from the rear of the truck and excitedly joined the blond boy. Together they followed at a respectful distance, eager and inflamed with the events. They were keen to see the two men who were obviously spies or felons being caught and taken away for punishment.

The soft balmy night air was suddenly filled with the sound of furious barking and shouts. The Germans had found their quarry, still curled up innocently asleep. Boots and guns kicked and prodded them into action, while the dogs bit deep.

Chapter 20

The rain was torrential. It poured down with the strength and force of a monsoon hitting the corrugated roofs of the huts with such energy that it rebounded upwards before falling in sheets to the ground below. The noise was deafening.

The prisoners were thrown out of the back of the truck and rolled in the thick mud in front of the punishment block. The whole contingent of prisoners had been forced to line up in their usual places as if during a routine role call or *appell*. They stood miserably in their ragged lines, soaked through and rapidly becoming chilled. They resented yet another disruption and futile order from their gaolers. Quiet mutterings could be heard in protest. As Billy and Nathaniel were unceremoniously dumped out into the compound their fellow prisoners stopped their moaning of dissent. A hush descended over the camp broken only by the relentless falling rain.

A duty guard opened the door to the Commandant's office and the tall thin senior German officer stood posed in the doorway surveying the scene before him. As if by sorcery the rain suddenly ceased and the officer smiled a little smile of satisfaction. Huge swollen drops of rain fell from the hut roofs and ran in little rivulets to fill the muddy puddles that lay between the concrete paths.

Billy and Nathaniel were covered in cuts and horrible bruises. Nathaniel's right eye was a pulpy mess and Billy could hardly stand; his old shrapnel wound to his thigh was excruciatingly painful.

The camp commandant barked an order in German and two guards whammed their rifle butts into Billy's leg and Nathaniel's unprotected shoulders. Their *schadenfreude* or malicious joy clearly showed in their faces as they snapped to obey their commandant. Billy and Nathaniel were then ordered to stand up and face him. Billy shook the blood specks from his eyes and slowly stood as tall and straight as he could manage. The effort it took him was enormous and he stood there trembling with shock and endeavouring to stop himself swaying and passing out. Dizzy with nausea, Nathaniel found that he could not move. He scrabbled around in the mud, an agonising cry of pain escaping from his lips as a guard once again whacked him in his lower back. His shirt was torn and filthy with his blood and the dirt from the ground.

Again the commandant spoke; this time more softly and because of the softness it seemed to those who could hear him with added malice. As he finished speaking he then turned on his heel and walked back to his dry office, fastidiously avoiding the worst of the mud.

Two more guards joined the original pair and for a moment stood looking down at Nathaniel as he lay on his side in the mud. In accordance and with unaccountable fury, they lifted their weapons and, using them as clubs brought them down upon him. Blow after blow rained down upon his body accompanied by an almost mesmerised chant of: "Jude, Jude".

Billy shouted in fury and outrage at their barbaric behaviour. His anger turned to despair as he tried to intervene but his leg prevented him from moving quickly. He howled in rage as he rolled helplessly on the sodden ground in front of the outrageous scene taking place before him. The guards ignored him. Nathaniel screamed in agony and anguish as he tried to protect himself with his bare hands and then, he screamed no more.

Billy could only look on and shake with horror, shock and disbelief at the battered and broken body of his friend. Slowly Nathaniel's blood seeped from his split skin. His face was unrecognisable. He was a friend no more. Billy gagged and closed his eyes with revulsion. He couldn't believe what he had just witnessed. He heard a low moaning without realising that the keening was coming from himself. He rocked to and fro, tears rolling unchecked down his face.

The hush that had descended on the camp suddenly broke. First there was a scared whisper, then a murmur that grew to a furious roar from all the witnesses who stood before the spectacle. That was murder! The extra guards, who had been stationed around the perimeter of the assembled men, hoisted their guns to their shoulders, their actions only too apparent. If there was trouble they wouldn't hesitate to shoot to dispel any riotous behaviour. There was a great deal of shouting and pushing as the irate prisoners were pushed and clobbered back into their lines. Gradually, an uneasy stillness descended on the gathered tense crowd. The Oberfeldwebel took charge, giving his curt orders left and right.

Billy had remained where he was and the guards ignored him. They picked up the body of Nathaniel and dragged it away. His boots left shallow trails in the bloodied mud from around where he had laid. Left in his place was his little penny whistle that had fallen from his pocket. Unnoticed Billy stretched over and picked it up, wiping it clean from the muck and blood that covered it. For a moment he looked at it almost reverently before tucking it safely inside his own torn, filthy shirt.

Two fresh guards returned to where Billy had fallen to the ground and cruelly dragged him to his feet. He was informed that he was not to be shot – yet – solitary confinement was his immediate punishment. The guards stood either side of him, not touching him. One looked at him with assumed curiosity, 'Why are you so concerned? He was only a Jew jah?' Billy could make no answer.

A movement among the crowd of onlookers broke the tension. A prison chaplain stepped away from the appalled men and with single-mindedness walked over to Billy. With resolution he deliberately ignored the agitated guards as he did so.

Holding out his right hand he said, 'take this. It may help you in your solitary. May God comfort you and watch over you.' Billy was speechless in his wretchedness. He looked at the chaplain and then down at his outstretched hand. In it he held a Bible. The chaplain held Billy's distressed gaze and thrust the Bible into Billy's hands. Billy clung on to it like a man clinging onto dear life. Saying nothing, seeing nothing. His eyes were clouded as the guards led him away.

The rain began to fall again. Beyond, on the other side of the cruel fence the trees wept bitter tears.

**

The bright light beat down onto Billy's bare head. He squinted in the unaccustomed daylight and held his arm in front of his eyes to protect them. He was thin, pale and extremely haggard. His once thick dark hair was now completely white.

He shuffled with lacklustre eyes out into the area in front of the punishment block, limping badly, his face still scabby from the blows meted out to him three weeks ago.

Billy had read the Bible from cover to cover. But, apart from enjoying it as an interesting read and doodling on its pages with a stub of pencil he was no nearer; in fact he was even further away from believing in God. He felt empty, bitter, guilty and full of remorse. It was his fault that Nat was dead. It had been his idea to escape. He had gone to the village for water and led the police back to their hideout – crude as it was. He simply hadn't thought and planned it through enough.

Maybe Nat had never been in any real danger at the camp. It might all have been bluff in the beginning. What had God done to help either of them? He had found no comfort at all. During his confinement he had agonised over Nat's death and now he was no nearer to coming to terms with it. And what about his other mates? The crew on his motor torpedo boat all shot up or drowned in the English Channel. Friends at home, when Portsmouth and Southampton was bombed incessantly. What was the point of it all? Let God tell him or show him by some sign what it was all for. At the moment there seemed no point in living.

On his release he had been taken past the other cells. As he passed the third barred door on his left he glanced in and noticed another shadowy figure in solitary. Moving quickly sideways he chucked the Bible through the bars at him.

'Yours mate. Maybe you'll find some comfort in it, but it didn't help me in any way.'

He entered his old hut, ignoring the looks of pity and heartfelt enquiries from the others. He brusquely replied that he just wanted to lie down in peace. He was all right but didn't feel like celebrating his release right now.

He reached his bunk, noticing that the one below was still unoccupied. Without removing his clothes he clambered up and lay down with his eyes wide open staring at the ceiling. He knew every crack and mildew stain by heart. He felt sick with self-loathing and desperately lonely. If only he could speak to Penny. The thought of her warm, slight body, smelling so clean and fresh filled his heart with anguish. He must write to her, this very day. He would tell her everything. About how low he felt. How life wasn't worth living. He couldn't take anymore. He turned over onto his side, drew his legs up and closed his eyes.

***

'Letter for Barker.'

The messenger with the bad attack of face pimples tossed an envelope to Billy who was waiting in the group clustered around, hoping for a letter from home. Billy grabbed it and scuttled away to the seclusion of his bunk. He had a new bunkmate below in Nat's place and hadn't yet got to grips with accepting him. It wasn't his fault; Billy found he was friendly enough, but Billy was still leery about letting himself get too close to anyone after Nat.

With shaking hands he opened Penny's letter.

'My dearest Billy,' he read.

He read it through quickly and then started again, more slowly this time right from the beginning. When he had finished he put the letter down; he couldn't believe what he had just read. How could she have kept all this from him for so long? All this time since he'd been captured? He felt deceived and his heart thumped hard in his chest.

Chapter 21

The early morning sky was the palest of eggshell blue, shot through with streaks of mauve-pink as the tiny stars faded in the gathering light. The weather had been good for the past three weeks and together with some war news that had filtered into the camp had done marvels for the men's' moral.

It was late September 1944 and the allied forces had had some recent good luck. In northwest Europe the Canadian offensive had closed the pocket at Falaise, which in turn forced 50,000 Germans to surrender. There had been allied landings in Provence, a Paris uprising and later French and US troops had actually entered that beleaguered city. Their own British troops had taken Brussels and Amiens and the hazy rumours concerning Italy whispered of yet more victorious landings and the taking of prominent towns and cities. The news had excited the camp inmates and fuelled talk about what had to be the eventual capitulation of the Germans. Everybody walked with an added swing to their step and a more general light-heartedness had filled the place of the usual boredom. Even the latest chilling edict issued by the German High Command to all prisoners of war hadn't quite depleted them of their newly found cheerfulness. They had been ordered to stand for yet another roll call and an officer had read them the following in his strident English:

Sondermeldung To all Prisoners of War!

Germany is determined to safeguard her homeland, and especially her war industry and provisional centres for the fighting fronts. Therefore it has become necessary to create strictly forbidden zones, called death zones, in which all unauthorised trespassers will be immediately shot on sight.

Escaping prisoners of war, entering such death zones, will certainly lose their lives. They are therefore in constant danger of being mistaken for enemy agents or sabotage groups.

In plain English: Stay in the camp where you will be safe! Breaking out of it is now a damned dangerous act. All police and military guards have been given the strictest orders to shoot on sight all suspected persons. Escaping from a prison of war camp has ceased to be a sport!

The edict was issued on Saturday 23rd September 1944.

Now, would-be escapees would have to think twice about the subsequent consequences if they were recaptured. Something had certainly rattled the cages of the German High Command.

Billy had visited the wash hut. He had freshly shaved himself with a new blade that someone had swapped him for a few eggs that he had pilfered from the guards' stores. Clean and smooth-faced he felt like a new man. Finishing his wash he straightened up and frowned at himself in the single cracked and spotted mirror above the stained and leaky basin. Only his eyes still held the brilliant and vital blue of his youth. His skin was the colour of dull pastry, his face was thin, gaunt even. He could only mourn the passing of his head of thick black hair for the close cropped cap now of pure white. Since his capture in February 1942 the months and years had severely aged him. Sadly he no longer looked like a young man in his early twenties. He sighed to himself as he rinsed the blade of dark stubble.

He suddenly smiled to himself and the transformation was instantaneous. He had turned his thoughts to Penny and of the gigantic bombshell that she had dropped in her last letter to him.

In the letter he had sent to her, he had thought; bugger the censors, and had proceeded to pour out his heart to her. He took great care not to mention the mundane things about the camp and the squalor that they all endured; or the harsh and sometimes brutal treatment endorsed by some of the Germans. He had simply told her about his friend Nat and that he had been killed. He gave no details about how. He briefly explained that they had been on the run and had spent some time hiding out before eventual recapture. Instead he told her how it had been his fault for not planning the whole thing properly. After all he had been the senior, and had far more experience. There should have been no need for Nat to die and for him to live. Billy explained how bad he felt and that all the blame was his and lay firmly on his shoulders. Because of this, he should have been the one to suffer, and he couldn't come to terms with that. Was he being punished for his friendship in some way? He said that he had wanted to die himself and the only thing that stopped him was the thought of her.

'My dearest Billy,' her letter had begun.

'Your latest letter fills me with so much pain and sadness. Your friend Nathaniel must have been a very special person for you to go to so much care and trouble. You had put both yourselves at risk by attempting to escape and, although I am truly sorry about your friend, I am so relieved that you have now been recaught and are back inside. Yes, back inside and safe! You are alive and you are not being shot at from some other ship or being bombed. I know I sound so selfish but I have to be. You see you are no use to me dead and forgotten in some foreign country. I need you to come home to me. I didn't tell you before this, about how much I cared, not in so many words because I wanted you to want me for myself. Not because you felt you had to. I'm not very good at explaining myself am I? I need you. We need you. Yes we. I'm afraid I wasn't very truthful when I told you that I was ill when you were first captured back in Feb 1942. I wasn't exactly ill at all, but I was unwell when I found that I was expecting your baby. At first I was so afraid, of lots of things. Afraid that you would be so angry and not want anything to do with us. About what my Mum and Dad were going to say. And then I was scared because I know nothing of babies and, how on earth was I going to bring it up? For a little while I couldn't tell anyone. I felt almost ashamed. Oh, I know that it happens to dozens of girls, especially now during the war when everyone is flying around and nobody knows what tomorrow is going to bring. But, some people are so horrible to unmarried mothers and they go out of their way to make them feel even more embarrassed. Why? I don't know. Surely if you love someone it should be just natural shouldn't it? And accidents happen.

Anyway, by the time I had stopped being sick and I had started to put on a bit of weight my Mum sat me down one morning when we were on our own, Dad having taken the oldest hens to sell at market. Straightaway she said she knew. She had guessed. Something about the way I looked, different, like you see. She explained that she had been waiting for the right time to talk to me. I was so relieved when I realised that both her and Dad weren't going to send me away to some horrible home where my baby would be taken away from me. She said it was all right with them and that it would be nobody else's business but our own. They knew it was yours of course.

So my dearest, darling Billy you have a beautiful daughter named Megan. She has your dark hair and blue eyes and when she smiles and laughs she looks just like you. I tell her about her father every day and show her your photograph; the one you gave me of you in your best uniform looking so smart. Already she calls you Daddy. I hope this is not too much of a shock for you. Please tell me you are not cross. It was a beautiful mistake and now I'm so glad it happened. You must see that you are missed and needed so much. Please, please, please, do not try to escape again. I couldn't bear you to be killed. The war must end soon, we keep hearing rumours and we're all keeping our fingers crossed. Just think of yourself coming home to where you belong. We'll have such a party to celebrate.

Billy put the letter down. He hadn't been able to read anymore, as his eyes had misted over and the huge lump at the back of his throat was causing him trouble. Penny, his darling girl had borne him a daughter. He had a daughter! She must be nearly two years old. What did she look like? What does she say? He imagined Penny and a tiny little tot walking in the garden of their cottage. They would visit the chickens and gather any newly laid eggs. Lots of walks down the country lanes, picking bunches of wild flowers to brighten the home. Calling in at the village post office to pick up a parcel and chat to the neighbours. They'd admire his little daughter and chuck her under the chin. He could just see her little hands, imagine her face, listening to all that was going on around her. His head reeled with a sudden joy and knowledge. He felt a release of all the built-up anger and sorrow that had been within him. He could almost swear he felt it flowing out of him. Now, he had a real reason to live. A double reason. He had a gorgeous girl who loved him beyond all else and, most amazing of all a daughter, they were waiting for him to come back home.

He gave a sudden whoop of joy and jumped down from his bunk. His immediate hut mates jumped and looked at him in surprise. For far too long he had been downcast and depressed. Some days he had hardly communicated with them at all, instead he had been terse and withdrawn. They had tried but they all had their own lives to live, and their spirits to keep up.

'I'm a father! I have a beautiful daughter!' he yelled excitedly.

They all looked at each other and smiled. Good family news was always welcome and shared by all.

The hut wisecrack replied, 'can't be right Barker. Firstly, your ugly mug couldn't produce anything reasonably attractive let alone beautiful. Secondly, you've been in here too long. What was it, an immaculate conception then? Or the milkman's?'

This bought guffaws of good-natured laughter; but the joker had a point. Billy had been a prisoner for over two years.

Billy explained and somehow, someone produced a flagon of some foul, evil home brew to belatedly wet the infant's head and toast the new father. Sometimes just when you thought life was completely pointless and you simply existed to get by, something wonderful like this happened. For Billy it felt like his life was maybe just beginning. All right. So he knew he had to stay put and wait for the end of the war but, if he had learned nothing else in the camps, he knew that by now he had oodles of patience.

Chapter 22

You could almost feel the pulse of the tension and anxiety throughout the prison camp. It was now 1945. Rumours were running rife. The favourite gossip was that the Allies were fast closing in and that the prisoners of war were going to be marched elsewhere. The Russians were nearing Berlin and the Allies were making a hard push from the west.

The senior camp men among them advised everyone to regularly tramp around the camp, in order to get their bodies in some kind of fitness state and most importantly, become used to walking again. Simply put, when they were to be evacuated they needed to be fit to be able to walk. For some men at the end of their tether, the last dregs of their physical capability would be drained if this were to happen; they wouldn't be capable of long marches.

A few grumbled at the advice and looked around them unsure at what was best to do. They were scared because of the total uncertainty with all the rumours flying around the camp.

As for Billy he was buoyant with expectation. He had heard for himself the distant rumble of artillery and had rushed to inform his hut officer. His mates gathered around on tenterhooks and with some alarm. In the middle of all this the Germans unloaded a long overdue consignment of Red Cross parcels and distributed them around the camp.

'If it comes to it, it's best to take everything you can wear or carry,' was his own advice to those who would listen.

Billy had two sets of underwear and woollen socks. He had an old Navy coat, ratty, patched but warm and he had managed to 'rescue' a pair of almost new American army boots from the camp stores.

The evacuation order came that week.

Billy had collected his 'treasures' together and laid them at the end of his ramshackle bunk in hut 19. There wasn't a lot to account for over three year's incarceration at the hands of the sometimes-brutal Germans but to him they represented his life and more importantly his soul. He thought about the refugees that had filed past the gates of his camp. Old people, women with children, babes in arms, the injured, burned, terrified, deranged, all fleeing from the horrors. The Christians among them, struggling to believe and reconcile their beliefs with Nazi cold-blooded excesses and mass murder.

He considered his pitiful little pile: his Christmas cards from Penny, her heavily censored letters and her simple but evocative poetry, the hand-made playing cards, two unsmoked cigarettes, a German soldier's –Dieter's – belt buckle and Nathaniel's penny whistle. Nathaniel. Billy shook his head in regret and fought back the familiar choking feeling in his throat whenever he thought about him. He thrust his dark thoughts aside and continued picking over his possessions. He would take as many clothes as he could carry. He had nothing heavy; he'd given his Bible away, hopefully to someone who would put it to better use than he. He gathered the articles up and tied them into a bundle with his faded and well-darned pullover, and slung it over his shoulder. He straightened his back, lifted his head and stood as erect as his gammy leg allowed. I'll march out of here *proudly* he thought. Together with his comrades they formed into ranks and smartly marched up to the gates. The weak and sick were supported by their stronger colleagues, their spirits rising. They were leaving this God-forsaken place. They didn't know where they were going but, surely nowhere else could be as bad as here.

***

Billy was assigned to the first evacuation column that consisted of around a thousand POWs. For some unexplained reason they set off shortly before dark. Billy reflected on the last time he'd passed through the gates after his unsuccessful escape attempt and his following weeks in the 'cooler', cut-off from the outside world with just the Bible for company. He grimaced at the thought, never again. The cooler had been a dark, dingy wooden box-type room with the only detail being a foetid metal bucket for toilet purposes. It contained no bed, not even a mattress. For sustenance Billy was given one piece of bread and one cup of water daily. It had been barely sufficient to survive on but somehow he and others before had managed it. With Penny's begging letter about not attempting to escape, and Hitler's edict stating re-caught prisoners would be shot he seriously doubted whether he would have seen the 'cooler' again anyway.

Together they marched past the Stalag camp gates, a defiantly displayed Nazi flag flying from a lookout tower. The ground crunched beneath their feet; once again Billy realised he was trudging through a bitterly cold frost. The temperature rapidly dropped as they continued on their way and soon they felt the tiredness setting in. They were all feeling the impact of having had to survive for years on a poor diet with scarce healthcare. They were allowed to halt for a few minutes rest every hour or so and eventually after eight hours slog they reached a village. The bedraggled column collapsed into the barns and outhouses allotted to them for shelter. The phrases, 'shagged out and knackered' filled the dusty air of the buildings. Side by side and grouped close together for warmth they slept in the hay; hundreds upon hundreds of spent prisoners. Fires were verboten and they were given no food. After covering about twenty or so miles, in sub-zero temperatures, they were all physically and mentally exhausted. The night air echoed with the sound of men who coughed and grumbled in their cold and discomfort.

On the second day, the column assembled. They were told to be ready to retreat from the advancing line of allied artillery. The men were a sorry looking bunch. Most were suffering from dehydration and to quench their thirst, attempted to gather handfuls of snow that had fallen overnight. A German NCO was sent on ahead to find the 'Burgermeister' in the next small town. He gingerly set off on his bicycle to warn the inhabitants of the pending arrival of the column that evening and to endeavour to scrounge enough potatoes or turnips for food and water to drink.

During the march Billy kept his eyes straight ahead. Like everyone he was desperately hungry, thirsty and tired but at least something was happening. He day-dreamed of Penny and his daughter and how soon he might be able to see them. He also thought that he had heard fighter planes in the sky off to the north. They had to be the Allies.

The column struggled on. Soon, Billy became all too aware that he had developed blisters on the soles of his toes and feet. The blisters broke down; they soon began to bleed and then froze. Billy was terrified that if he removed his boots, he would never get them back on again. He had to grimly try and push the pain to the back of his mind and get on with the march.

Because of their numbers, the men could find nowhere to wash and so, after a few days their bodies smelt rank. It seemed their smell was so bad that even the local dogs slunk away in disgust. Body lice, always a problem, were once again rife. Everyone soon became infested whilst sleeping in close confines together in the hay barns along the way.

Many of the weakest men soon became ill and their numbers became decimated by overnight deaths. Sadly it became almost commonplace to wake the next morning only to find that your neighbour had died quietly in his sleep.

Billy suddenly felt very weak and vulnerable and questioned himself. Would he survive this seemingly pointless, starving route march? Where on earth were they going? Many of the men couldn't keep up and surely risked being shot. Some had had enough and slipped away during the night to take their own chances. A lucky few with a currency of hoarded cigarettes and watches managed to hire a farmer along with his horse and cart and have a lift for part of that day.

Any crops in the fields adjoining the roads along where they walked were fair game to the prisoners. A few root vegetables were available in the frozen landscape accompanied with the rifle butts of their guards. Most were so desperate that when they came upon a ditch half-filled with water they rushed it, only to be beaten by the guards who feared that they were trying to escape. Such was the confusion between both prisoner and guard.

More and more people became sick as the column struggled on: dysentery, pneumonia, frostbite, pleurisy, and exhaustion. Billy was suffering along with everyone else. Not only were his feet torn from the blisters but also his old thigh wound dragged him down. Before long he realised he was lagging behind, and was forced to join the others who were slow or sick at the back of the column. He limped along, now terrified that he would be forced to stop because of his condition. Ironically enough some of their German guards appeared to be in little better condition than they were themselves. Some of them had also been injured in the long war and now had to cope with almost the same hardships. Gradually the group became separated from the main column and despairing they saw the distance between them grow. Again, they heard distant planes high in the sky, only this time they were nearer.

It was at this moment in time when Billy and his immediate colleagues were feeling really low in spirits that one of the German guards appeared with a horse and cart. Billy and those that were really at the end of their tether thankfully scrambled up onto the flat cart bed and collapsed exhausted. They arranged themselves as comfortably as they could around the confines of the cart, as it was already carrying a cargo of three fuel drums on board.

***

Meanwhile unbeknown to the POWs the American Army had completely surrounded them. Also unknown to them, was the fact that the SS troops who had commanded this area were stubbornly refusing to surrender to the Americans. The fighter planes were heard quite plainly now. Billy and the others, who were not asleep, looked around to see if they could spot them and identify which side they belonged to.

The Germans guarding Billy and the others on the cart were unusually friendly. They shared their rations with them, bread, hard-boiled eggs and a flask of ersatz coffee. The unseen planes continued to drone overhead.

Towards mid-afternoon they entered another village and slowly the weary horse trundled its load into the little square. But, instead of neat and pretty flower boxes and tubs waiting for their spring flowers to come forth, the square was lined incongruously with four SS tanks. The tired horse was blowing with the day's effort and came to a standstill, its head drooping with fatigue; flanks heaving and covered with a thick lather. Groups of SS stood around watching as the accompanying German guards were ordered to offload the fuel drums by a SS officer. It appeared that the SS had been waiting for their fuel.

Billy was watching all this with interest and not a little apprehension – he knew of the SS and their reputation, when he had an unexpected premonition. Their guards had known that the SS were to meet them here, and with the fuel.

He went cold all over and shivered. The hairs were prickling and standing up on the back of his neck.

The reports heard in the camp had been true! The Allies, the Americans and Russians were all somewhere in the vicinity! Suppose that there was a risk that allied fighter planes would attack the fuel tanks? The fuel was obviously destined for the SS tanks and it was vital to them. Subsequently the bastards had thought of using Billy and his ill colleagues as 'human shields.'

'Everyone, off now!' he shouted to the bemusement of those lying on the wagon floor. In desperation he pushed and prodded at the inert bodies that lay around the floor of the cart. Against mutterings and heavy complaints, he eventually managed to persuade every last man off the cart but only when he had managed to get the message through that they were possibly in great danger. A few still grumbled, but the majority had listened and had taken in the severity of the situation. The lift on the cart had benefited them to the extent that they had caught up with the main party and now began to stumble along behind them. The fuel tanks were left in the square along with the SS and their tanks. Billy and his friends had served their purpose. The fuel had been brought to the village unscathed...

Suddenly, there was a terrific explosion behind them. Billy swiftly turned in time to see a handful of Typhoon bombers as they swooped over the village they had just departed from. The fighter-bombers had found the target they had been looking for, the tanks and their masters. The road behind them was bathed in a rising fireball of orange and billowing thick black smoke. They had escaped by minutes. They all stopped and stared. Some in excitement as they recognised the allied planes, others in fear because of reprisals; the cart group realised the significance of the too near target. A few shook their heads in disbelief, and then thanked Billy for his quick thinking. Most however, were still too exhausted and numb to acknowledge anything other than that they were once again on their feet and at the tail end of the departing column.

As evening approached they staggered into yet another village and found whatever clean empty outhouses could accommodate them for sleeping. The weather had turned warmer, almost spring-like and in the distance they could clearly hear the heavy crump, crump of guns.

In the morning it was strangely and almost eerily quiet. Billy struggled to his feet and pushed open the barn door. He was dying for a pee and as he walked over to a nearby hedge he could see a faint mist rising from the wide river beyond. He stood and gazed around him as he lazily watered the vegetation. The guards, clustered in a small glade of trees saw Billy but just stared. He was surprised that they didn't shout or command him to get back with the others; so used was he to their ways. Finished, he slowly sauntered back to the others and re-entered the barn.

'I don't know what's up with Jerry but our guards are cowering down in that clump of trees. They didn't seem too bothered when I appeared. None of them bawled at me to get back inside,' he told the others who were now groggily waking up for the start of yet another hard day. Those nearest turned towards the open door where the early morning was beginning to stream in. Dust motes speckled thickly, caught in the shaft of sunlight.

A sudden burst of firing had them up on their feet fast enough. A Typhoon plane roared past, swooping low over the trees, followed by a short burst of machine gun fire.

'That's the Yanks,' shouted someone excitedly.

'The Yanks are here!'

By now everyone had scrambled to their feet. All their wounds and sickness were forgotten in the excitement. Was it finally going to happen? Liberation from the Germans?

As a group they all rushed over to the open doorway, jostling and pushing in their eagerness to reach the open air. Those nearest gaped open-mouthed as a jeep came round the corner and skidded to a stop outside. Its cargo of GIs all piled out with their firearms ready. As if watching in slow motion an American tank rolled into view and they stood mesmerised by its gun turret gleaming in the morning mist and sun. It was a Sherman; all nineteen feet of it, complete with its five guns and five crew. Relief at last! Spell-bound they watched as their own familiar German guards crept out of their hiding place, chittering with terror, their hands held high as they surrendered to the Americans. Billy and his companions cheered with delight and threw whatever they could get their hands on into the air.

'Hurrah!'

***

Things moved fast for Billy and his companions from then on. The men gathered around the Americans excitedly asking for news from home and what was happening in the area. The Americans were shocked at the pitiful state of the POWs and couldn't get over the sight of these thin, gaunt and pale men dressed in layered tattered clothing nor the staggering effect that they were having on them. The animated POWs were screaming, crying and laughing over and over again as they mobbed the GIs with hugs and kisses.

As soon as the Americans' could organise it, Billy and his friends were whisked off to a field camp where their injuries and illnesses were dealt with. Billy found himself once again being deloused and stripped of his ratty clothing. He simply marvelled at himself as he stood staring down in admiration at his new clean clothing. A fleet of lorries arrived and they were informed that they were to be taken to the ruined and devastated Nuremberg from where they would be held until transport could take them all home. They were each given a small pack that on inspection contained a full day's rations. It was hard to take in all that was going on around them. For so long they had been used to receiving a sometimes near-starvation diet and of being prisoners to a group of people that held them in contempt and mostly didn't care. These new kindnesses were in such excess, they didn't know now whether to laugh or cry.

Billy was avid for real news. He wanted to know just what had really happened during the last few months.

After all, back in the camp all the news that they had received was subject to much rumour and speculation. The bombed cities, the fighting among the armies scattered around the globe, the death and suffering of many thousands hadn't really touched them, or only faintly. They had been cut-off from the outside and incarcerated in a barbed-wire enclave for so long. Only after D-Day did events in the outer World become more significant. Billy was like a sponge as he mopped up the information he begged from the Allied soldiers. He soon learned with much sadness that there had been no easy victory.

The Allies had had to fight for key points. Each bridge had to be blown, each river crossed and ferociously fought over. Expectations among the Allies had alternately risen and then faded. When the

Russians had finally got through he learned that there had been total confusion. Like his own camp, other camps were evacuated and the POWs had marched through Germany facing horrendous weather, the fury of the local Germans, and the possibility of their own Allied bombs creating havoc among them. Some prisoners had escaped the columns as they thought that they might be better off to go it alone and wait to be found and rescued. The SS systematically cleared the camps of any stragglers that were left behind.

By January 1945 the Red Army had stumbled upon the biggest Nazi extermination camp, Auschwitz-Birkenau. Here the Nazis had attempted unsuccessfully to conceal all trace of their hideous mass murder.

By now Germany was one huge battlefield. Roads were constantly being bombed and strafed and this helped to explain why the Red Cross supplies hadn't been getting through to the camps.

In March, the US Ninth Armoured Division had made a mad dash over the bridge at Remagen. They had had ten desperate minutes before the Germans had planned to blow it up. This crucial timing made it possible by Sunday 25th March for the Remagen bridgehead to expand to a thirty-mile front, ten miles deep.

Billy's mind reeled as he learned more of the events that had occurred whilst he was behind barbed wire. It was hard to grasp what was happening outside, whilst inside there had been a strange, almost preserved air of frozen tranquillity despite the rumours and even leading up to the time of the signs and noises of the fast approaching armies.

Quickly, Billy found that the US forces came heavily fortified with tanks, GIs and gum. As they had sped into the village from where he was eventually rescued he remembered how they had overcome the German resistance.

Their faces streaked with sweat and dust they had sought out the SS men making a last desperate stand in the trees. When the firing from the SS had stopped, Billy had known that he was indeed at last a free man. It was still hard to believe at times. He kept himself sane by having one thought on his mind. That was to get home to his darling girl Penny. He would be able to hold her and breathe in the smell of her. And to meet at last his little daughter Megan.

There was so much lost during the last few years. So much that could never be spoken. And yet some stories would be told, for their hilarity and humanity.

It was General Patton's army who had liberated them. Billy was unabashed when the General had climbed down from his jeep, pausing to talk to some of the injured and then walking over to where Billy had sat, propped up against an old wall of a cowshed. Old 'blood and guts' had commiserated with Billy over his own long tedious war and had then moved on with his Staff Officer. Another US officer wearing a freshly laundered uniform with sharp creases had approached Billy with an air of outrage and hostility. Looking him up and down he demanded of Billy,

'Don't you ever salute a superior officer, buddy?'

Billy had stayed where he was. Foot-sore, weary and still in pain. He was a first-class stoker in rags. He remembered his Captain and his mates lost on MTB 47 in the English Channel and of those friends who'd perished during their intolerable incarceration on German held land. He had had enough. He looked at the officer with cold blue eyes and said.

'Don't you?'

The officer took a step back, non-plussed. He spluttered, unsure of himself and finally without quite realising it he saluted Billy. Billy pondered on whether to give him a piece of his mind or not and decided that the little prick really wasn't worth it. He heaved himself to his feet and then casually sauntered over to cadge a cigarette off one of the well-supplied GIs.

***

Going home. What a ring that simple saying had to it. Going home. He shivered in delight as he remembered all those two words meant to him.

Billy looked down on the sunlit hills, which were passing beneath the wings of his Dakota aircraft. He saw a green land bathed in a soft spring afternoon sunshine. Thankfully, it was a short flight. Only as far as Brussels in Belgium. Thankfully, because he realises that he hates being up here in the air. Somehow he is both excited and terrified at coming home. Since his capture in February 1942, England had seemed so distant in his imagination. During the long boring years spent as a prisoner, he has known every emotion from terror to joy, despair to hope. Now, with the aircraft engine throttling back for landing, the lost years were slowly being misted over.

Surreptitiously, he wipes away the lone tear that threatens to roll unchecked down his cheek as he remembers. With clarity, he recalls the heroisms, the hilarity, the tragedies, the mirth, the leaders and the losers. The acts of brutality and the acts of altruistic kindness. The companionship and the solidarity of his brothers.

He is shown with the others, to a hotel. To an actual hotel. He is escorted courteously to a bedroom containing a real bed with crisp white sheets and blankets, not one, but two! They are served a meal at a table. Sitting down and being waited on by a pert, saucy young waitress in a snowy white apron over her dress. He tries hard not to stare openly at her breasts as she approaches with their dinner-plates, nor at her long slim uncovered legs and her neat little bottom. So long has it been. He sits at the table and regretfully, instead lets his eyes slide away to the gaily coloured table-cloth of bright yellow and blue checks and to gaze with child-like wonder at the vase of scented spring flowers; their colour vivid against the remembered greyness of the past years.

He trembles as he chokes back the sudden rising in his throat of a thousand suppressed laughs. He feels like he is holding back an unchecked pressure gauge that threatens to bubble over.

They are given presents in a cotton bag. Good things like; soap, socks, a flannel, hair cream, toothpaste and brush, handkerchiefs, and bars of chocolate. Best of all, there are dozens of free smiles all around them. All the time. Unconditional smiles, given away all for free.

He wallows unashamedly in a deep, hot bath that leaves him shrivelled and white like an old weathered leaf. He sinks down into the bed that smells of linen that has dried and aired outside in the sunlight and sleeps the night away in the luxury of uninterrupted slumber.

In the morning, after a breakfast of grilled tomatoes and mushrooms and seemingly unlimited toast they are driven to the railway station. There is much gawping and finger pointing as they pass through the streets of Ostend. There, they find the ship is waiting to take them across the Channel and with much waving goodbye at the quayside, the ship slowly slips the harbour and steams her way towards English soil, her wake a frothy white V spreading far behind them.

The White cliffs sparkle as the sunlight catches them and each man lining the rail is choked with emotion as he finally realises that; now, the war is really and truly over.

Chapter 23

Billy and Penny were married in the Norman parish church of St Peter's in Bishop's Waltham. Penny's parents, Maggie and Maurice, her sister Mavis and fiancé John were thrilled as the happy pair stood slightly stiffly posed for a few photographs beneath the church's fine archway. The photographer was a friend of Maurice's and had promised to supply the family with a modest album of the wedding. Photographs were still expensive and difficult to obtain so, Maurice was delighted when he realised that he would be able to present his younger daughter with such a lovely record of her day.

Penny was as radiant as all young brides should be. She had worn her mother's wedding dress that had been carefully stored away in a linen press between new cotton sheets. Together, she and Maggie had lifted the sheath of fine white silk from the chest and shaken away the creases and folds. A faint smell of camphor mothballs had arisen from the fabric which would soon disappear when the frock was left to air in the breeze. Another carefully wrapped bundle produced a frothy train of lace and a tiny veil pinned to a half circlet of crushed silk flowers.

'Those flowers look like they'll not recover enough for wearing,' eyed Maggie in some consternation.

'Oh, it's all right. I'm happy enough to wear fresh ones in my hair. We can pick enough wild flowers to match those of my posy,' Penny replied with a delighted smile on her face as she held the beautiful silk up against her.

'It looks like it's going to be a little too large. I was always larger boned than you. Never mind, with a few nips and tucks and maybe an added dart or two and it'll look right as rain!' Maggie smiled in return at her daughter. Penny had blossomed since Billy's return and looked almost beautiful and certainly rosier than she had ever been. She still kept her mid-blonde hair long and it clung in soft clouds around her face. Since the birth of her daughter Megan, she had acquired a serene more mature air about her, yet still managed to retain her almost elfish look.

Now, standing outside the church in the sunshine, the bells peeling merrily, Maggie could only give her thanks to God that he had seen fit to return Billy safe and sound to her daughter. She gazed fondly at the solemn Billy, who was still thin and somewhat drained from his long ordeal. Standing next to Penny, he looked slightly awkward in his unaccustomed new suit of clothes and highly polished shoes. Just then, he glanced down at his new wife and she caught the familiar grin pass between them. For one moment she glimpsed the old irrepressible Billy; happy and full of life. She knew they would be happy together and it gave her a deep warm glow.

'Come on now, let's have a photograph of the whole family,' said the keen photographer as he organised the little group to stand in strategic positions around the bride and groom.

'Say cheese! Lovely. Now let's have one with all the friends and hangers on.'

There was a lot of good-natured laughter and joking amongst the guests as they jostled for position. One or two more and they were done.

The family had a final round of good luck handshakes and thank yous to the vicar and organist and soon they would go back to the cottage for the wedding breakfast. As it was such lovely weather, Maggie had planned the meal outside under the apple trees and everyone was looking forward to it. Earlier that week local friends had appeared with hoarded treasures of bottled fruit, hams, chickens, rabbit pies, pickles, trifles, cheeses and a little cream, a bottle or two of homemade wine and a whole keg of beer from a local brewery. Everyone wanted to contribute to the occasion. The mood within the Clarke family was as happy as when they had celebrated VE day back on May 8th.

Maggie looked around at all the wedding guests as they stood happily chatting together in twos and threes in the warm sun. They had all donned their best clothes; the prettiest dresses and freshly pressed suits; all especially kept and chosen for a memorable event such as this. The girls who had managed to save a pair of silk stockings wore them for just such an occasion and those who hadn't, painted a thin pencil line down the back of their legs for pretence. A wedding was always a jolly time and the Clarke family were well liked in the village. Penny was a delight and the villagers had accepted Billy. They all knew a little about his time spent in German POW camps and moreover, as he had reappeared as soon as he was able to, and lay claim to Penny and his little unknown daughter, he had fast earned their respect. Respect. What a fine word. Even Billy's long estranged brother Bert had managed to turn up for the big day, treating Billy with a kind of newfound consideration. The way he enthusiastically shook Billy's hand perhaps showed that the war changed everyone in some way.

Maggie looked down at the little girl who stood beside her, her hand held tightly in her own. She had big blue, wide eyes and a mop of dark unruly curly hair. She was dressed in a cotton frock of pale pink with a full skirt that she loved to giddily twirl around in. Her skinny brown legs were encased in little white ankle socks with a hint of lace around the tops and her feet, in new black shiny shoes, of which she was immensely proud.

Just now, she couldn't take her eyes off Billy, her dada. She utterly adored him from the very first time he had limped into the cottage and been welcomed home by an ecstatic Clarke family. Billy had been made much of and when they all realised that he was still suffering from his war injuries they made sure that he was given the comfy warm chair by the fireplace. Megan had watched all this with big round eyes and had then toddled over, clasped his knee and looked up fully into his face. As soon as she was satisfied she had solemnly said, 'You're mine. You're my Dada,' and then promptly scrambled up onto his knee. She continued to study him intently for a moment, her pretty little face serious. When it seemed that she was happy with the situation she smiled and then popped a thumb in her mouth. Sighing deeply, she then leant back against him, and in a short minute or two, fell fast asleep much to the amazement and amusement of the others.

'Well,' said Maurice with a short laugh, 'looks like she's got you sorted out fast. You'll soon know your place. That girl is going to have you completely wrapped around her little finger in next to no time!' The others looked on with delight at the little scene.

Billy was a little perplexed and yet, at the same time pleased. He had absolutely no experience of children at all. This serious little girl had claimed him above all others. As the days and weeks passed in her company, he found that when he spoke to her she listened and appeared to understand everything he said. Her mother stood by and watched with interest. She was both relieved and delighted. Her enchanting daughter was both grave and funny at the same time. She usually took her time in sorting out who was worthy of her attention, and not everyone met her criteria. Her scrutiny and acceptance of Billy obviously meant he was worth the trouble.

As for Penny herself, she had been uncharacteristically in a dither when she knew Billy's arrival was imminent. Normally calm and serene, she was both anxious and nervous about meeting with him after such a long absence. She had been prepared for changes; her parents had quietly recalled the first World War to her, when battle weary, injured and shell-shocked men had come back and then had had the hard task of settling back into normal peacetime life. Of course, they said, Billy's case was different in some ways, but he would still find it strange at first. Sensibly they advised her to be ready for possibly a somewhat different Billy than the one she remembered.

He had finally arrived on the train in Bishop's Waltham, and Penny and Maurice were there to meet him with the van to fetch him home. Yes, she had been primed, but she still suffered a jolt when he emerged hesitantly in the carriage doorway. His hair once thick and black was now prematurely pure white. His facial features were the same, but so thin and pale. Where once his blue eyes had sparkled with mischief, she now noticed an anxious and haunted look in them. She held herself stiffly in check for fear that she would gasp out loud in outrage at all the hurt he had suffered. A great tenderness spread over her as he limped down the step towards where she stood waiting, hardly daring to breathe. There was a questioning look now in his eyes, and she didn't realise that she gave a small shriek of delight as she bounded forward to take him in her arms. Enfolding his thin body tenderly to her breast she held onto him tightly. Billy had buried his face in her long hair, deeply breathing in its unfamiliar fragrance. Indeed, almost everything about her was unfamiliar and yet not so. Her smell; she'd nicked her sister's hoarded bottle of scent for the occasion, her body was no longer so childish as she'd filled out with more rounded curves since the birth of Megan. Only her face was familiar, marginally older but she still retained the same calm exterior, with a hint of mischief lurking behind her eyes.

He luxuriated in their embrace. He felt his legs and arms trembling, still so unused to the human feel of comfort, love and tenderness all around him. His throat constricted and he fought to contain his pent up emotions. For so long he had faced terror and abject misery together with the many other thousands of men like him. So many of his past friends and mates would never feel the comforting arm of a mother, or the beautiful safe embrace of a lover. They would lie forever, lost and buried in the dank ground of some foreign soil or in the chill of the deep ocean.

For the moment he could and would live in the present, and for this he was immensely happy.

***

For the following few weeks Penny and her family were careful in their treatment of Billy. Although they couldn't know anything of his past nightmare, and he took care not to tell them too much about the grim conditions and times he'd had when away, they were considerate and patient with him without going to extremes. Somehow, deep down, an unspoken understanding grew up between them and they realised that the healing process would take a long time. As time went on and the warm summer days drifted past Billy learned once more to relax and feel safe at home. Slowly, they watched as Billy found his feet and enjoyed his new freedom.

He was of course, still officially in the British Navy. His leave was now up and he had made arrangements to report back at headquarters. He was sent to the Royal Navy Hospital at Haslar in Hampshire, for a full medical examination by the doctor surgeon. The surgeon, who examined him, had a kind face and gentle manner. He was in his mid-forties and he studied the young man who stood before him with some compassion. He had witnessed too many surgical horrors during the years of the war and now, he desperately longed for a quiet country practice or some backwater hospital, perhaps hidden down in the West Country. He saw in Billy's eyes, the trouble and shock that still lingered and lurked at the back in his mind. He had quickly assessed that Billy was unfit for any more Naval service, both mentally and physically. He needed peace and quiet to fully recuperate. With some gentleness he questioned Billy about his personal life and Billy grudgingly found himself telling the doctor about Penny and his newfound daughter.

'Well, that's marvellous my dear boy!' he had exclaimed upon hearing this.

He quickly surmised Billy would convalesce far quicker with a loving and pretty wife and daughter than in some starchy, strict nursing home. Happily, he signed the papers which declared Billy medically unfit and which would lead to his discharge and most importantly, a gratuity. Billy felt both relieved and bewildered. He had been a full-time Jack ever since 1939, before the war had even started. With the Navy, which had then been all the family he knew, he had travelled to Egypt, Italy, Greece, Malta and Gibraltar. He had spent time both in big ships and later in the small MTBs. It had been such a familiar part of his bachelor life there would naturally be a certain regret that it was to be no more. On the other hand, he had lost so many friends. He didn't want to put Penny in the unenviable position of being separated from him again. Now, they had the opportunity of being together, this time for always. He could maybe get a job locally. He realised that he wouldn't be able to do anything too strenuous, as his gammy leg wouldn't allow him to but at least with a job and money coming in it would help supplement his Navy gratuity. His mind raced, as he understood the full implications of being together; worries and old fears lifted from around his heart. He had a wife and daughter who needed him, and he was going to be able to stay and protect and honour and love them, above all else. Nothing else mattered.

***

For once everything seemed to be working out for Billy and Penny. Money was always a great consideration, and although Billy knew Maurice and Maggie wouldn't let them starve, a job and small gratuity would help enormously. Besides Billy had his pride, and that included supporting his own dependents. When he had first gone missing, Penny had spent weeks of irritation and concern, firstly over his whereabouts and then how to sort out his Naval pay for him as he had placed this in her hands. After Billy's last weekend with Penny, just before his final assignment, Billy had assigned his Naval salary over to Penny. This way he had explained, she could save his pay for him; for the future, whatever that would be.

The first thing she knew about him missing was when the Admiralty had sent her a badly typed terse message on 5th February 1942. It read:

Madam,

I regret to have to inform you that in consequence of William Barker (handwritten) having been reported as missing, his Allotment in your favour ceases after payment on (crossed out)

I have accordingly to request that you will return the Navy Allotment Order Book to this Department as soon as practicable in the enclosed envelope.

I am, Madam,
Your obedient Servant,

(A handwritten signature followed)
Director of Navy Accounts
Admiralty
Bath

Penny was dumbfounded at the contained message and ham-fisted manner in which she was informed. The Admiralty had lost no time between Billy's disappearance and in sending her this letter either. Less than three weeks had elapsed. In order to keep her mind off the unmentionable; Penny set about finding out more information. With her first enquiries, a well-meaning Wren advised her to contact the British Red Cross, giving them Billy's details. They sent her a form, which she filled in and returned to the Red Cross HQ in London. In due course they informed her that they would do their best to help trace any whereabouts of Billy.

With sheer joy she read their letter in March notifying her of Billy's capture and of his being held prisoner in Poland. Shortly after, his name along with many other POWs was mentioned in The Times. Her relief was overwhelming. Now, at least she could write to him and offer him some comfort from home. She could let him know that he was in their thoughts at the very least. She wrote as regularly as she could, rightly suspecting that he would receive only a portion of the standard sized letters she sent.

***

Billy kept in touch with a couple of old mates that he found had made it through to the end of the war. He was gratified to learn that his old Captain from the ill-fated MTB, Chalmers, had indeed survived. He too had been a POW in Germany and in October 1945 he received the Distinguished Service Cross or DSC for short. At least one other member of the old team had made it! On 12th October, Billy too received a letter from the Admiralty. With calmness he read,

Sir,

I am commanded by My Lords Commissioners of the Admiralty to inform you that they have learned with great pleasure that, on the advice of the First Lord, the King has been graciously pleased to award you the Distinguished Service Medal for gallantry, coolness and resource while remaining behind with the Commanding Officer to ensure the destruction of H.M.M.T.B. 47 after she had been heavily damaged and stopped off the enemy coast in an action with enemy forces on the night of 17th/18th January, 1942.

This award was published in the London Gazette Supplement of 9th October 1945.

I am, Sir,
Your obedient Servant,

(Signed) T.S. PROOPS.

Stoker First Class William Barker, D.S.M.

He finished the letter and turned to the other white page of type, embossed with the Royal Coat of Arms and read BUCKINGHAM PALACE across the top. He continued down the page,

I greatly regret that I am unable to give you personally the award, which you have so well earned.

I now send it to you with my congratulations and my best wishes for your future happiness.

(Signed) George R.I

He turned the medal over in his hands. Mixed emotions were fast coursing through him.

Penny read his face and leaned over and gently squeezed his arm. 'Well done Billy. You deserved it.'

'No more than thousands of others,' he replied gruffly. 'I am proud to receive this. But most of all, I'll keep this in memory of all my friends and mates who never came home. Perhaps they deserve it more.'

He put the medal back in its little box, nestling on the satin material and tissue paper. He found an old sea-trunk of his and placed the little box inside it. There it remained, along with Penny's letters and poems, his handmade Christmas cards to her, Dieter's silver belt-buckle and Nat's penny whistle.

Megan blossomed and grew into a pretty child with an engaging nature. She was forever the darling of her father. Penny was happy and contented, caring for her daughter and husband. Billy became more at home in strange company and enjoyed an evening's pint or two down at the local. He had finally lost the haunted look in his eyes and, although quieter than before the war he regained some of his earlier joy in living. He worked happily alongside Penny's father, growing to love the surrounding countryside with its ever-changing seasons. The old dog Nell, had died a year back and they replaced her with an energetic Border collie named Joey that was surely wicked by nature. Joey kept Billy fully occupied, forever wanting a wild chase across the fields and through the bluebell woods hoping to flush out a wild pheasant or hare. Billy loved these times best of all; when together as a family they traipsed along a river, throwing a stick for the dog and Megan laughing in delight at his antics. The little family was devoted to one another, first and foremost. They needed no one else; together they could look forward. Forward to a post-war Britain and peace.

Chapter 24

The Present

As Richard opened the cheap, thin cardboard cover he soon realised with pleasure that the album contained wedding photographs of his mother and father. How his father had changed. During his time on HMS *Warspite*, the photos had told a story of a young physically fit, dark-haired young man in his prime. Tanned and lean, often propped up against the ship's bulwark, friends gathered around him. He'd enjoyed a drink, a smoke, the occasional fistfight and especially time spent ogling the girls.

His wedding photos were completely different. Although he smiled in each picture, the man standing there was thin and gaunt, and wearing a suit that hung onto rather than fitted him. The most startling feature was his hair. After his time spent in the camps he had emerged completely white-haired. And yet, he was no old man. It was only a few years later. His mother was slight and pretty; her expressionable face alive with a deep smile of complete happiness. In her arms she held a little girl with dark curly hair and solemn blue eyes that were definitely her father's. It could only have been his older sister Megan.

Funny little Megan. She had died far too young. Richard knew that Billy had mourned her deeply and had never got over her premature death. Her going had been a very sad and long phase that left a void in his life especially after Penny's death.

He turned the pages of the album and smiled at the expressions on his grandparents' faces. For him they had always been there, especially his grandmother. She had been swift to wipe away a tear when he had fallen and cut himself. A quick consoling hug when he'd lost the obstacle race at infant school. A short, sharp, quick whack on the backside when he was caught nicking fairy cakes straight out of the hot oven. He never did know whether it was for the stealing or because he was stupid enough to nearly burn himself. There were other mysterious faces that he hadn't a clue as to who they were.

Local friends of the family? It didn't matter now, as they were all long gone. Even the cottage in Bishop's Waltham where they had farmed the surrounding land. It had all been sold and the land parcelled off.

It was a small book that spoke of smiles and remembered pleasures. It had a pleasant richness of its own.

Richard allowed himself a small sigh. His father had found a love during the war. She had waited faithfully and patiently for him to return to her, as she had promised. As did so many other wartime couples. Their love had been deep, there was no doubt about that; his sister Megan had been the proof. He was sure that they had loved him too. But, he was born much later. Born in peacetime, when everything was different and more stable, without the fear of anything being permanent or long lasting. The true sense of urgency threatened them no longer. It was more benign, planned.

He replaced the items into the chest. He understood much more now. He could imagine how his father had felt. As he'd left the battleship life with its company of many hundreds of crew and then been thrust into a life that was much hairier aboard the small and infinitely more fragile motor torpedo boat. The death of his mates onboard and then the long incarceration in the POW camps, with their own uncertainties and special terrors. He couldn't possibly know all that the old man had put up with and suffered and he had struggled to understand in the past. But, now he thought he could at last feel sympathy for an old sailor's reticence to the telling of his own war stories and why he was so dedicated to his mother and sister. They had *needed* him so much more than Richard had himself. He had always been so much more independent. The image of Connie passed through his mind and how she had died. For the first time in years he felt really close to his father. Sorrel had been right, visiting and then going through his father's things had been therapeutic. He crossed over to his desk that was placed in front of the window and almost reverently picked up Billy's Bible that was lying there. It was amazing. A few months ago he had had no idea of its existence let alone that it had been kept in the States for almost 60 years. Now after meeting up with Sorrel and crossing over to Germany he had unearthed a wealth of past history that he had never dreamt of. The Bible had brought it all together. It made him feel good and whole again.

Book 3

Chapter 25

He fastened the clasp on the old sea-trunk and stood up, stretching the stiffness from his cramped legs. Time had flown and he hadn't realised how long he'd been crouching on the carpet. More coffee would be good, he thought as he moved towards the kitchen. Still thinking about the morning's discoveries he refilled the espresso machine reservoir automatically and then waited for the familiar smell to fill his nostrils. The view from the kitchen window was particularly beautiful this morning but Richard gazed at it with unseeing eyes, lost in thought.

The peeling of the front-door bell startled him out of his reverie. He hadn't heard a car drive up or the scrunch of footsteps over the gravel. He retraced his footsteps back into the hall and glanced at his reflection in the mirror on the wall above a small oak occasional table. He looked well; much fitter and healthier than he had been a few months ago and hardly looked his age. He was thankful in so much that he had come to terms with Connie's death and was able to see a life ahead of him.

Glancing through the small panel of glass in the front door he could see a woman standing with her back to him as she looked at the garden. Long hair hung around her shoulders in pretty soft curls; he'd always had a weakness for long hair. He threw open the door and almost gasped in shock as he confronted the woman who turned to greet him with a smile upon her face.

'Richard!' was all she said.

'My God! I didn't expect –! What are you doing here?' He gulped back in astonishment. He hadn't seen his cousin's ex-wife Miranda for years but he had recognised her immediately.

'I know, a bit of a shock after all this time isn't it? Are you going to invite me in or shall we stay out here?'

'Yes of course.'

He stepped aside as she crossed over the threshold and on into the hall. He closed the door behind them and turned to her with a question on his lips. She forestalled him as she walked further into the house and exclaimed, 'This is beautiful. I have often wondered about where you lived. You certainly have good taste.' Miranda looked around her with interest. She stood in front of an evocative landscape that could only have been executed from local composition.

'How long have you lived here now?'

Richard told her and then with some impatience as he couldn't abide small talk he continued brusquely.

'But, tell me. Why the sudden interest? When we spoke on the phone a month ago over my father's Bible you gave no indication that you might pleasure me with a visit.'

Miranda gave him a dazzling smile. So far, so good. Knowing him of old she knew that the brusqueness was an attempt to cover his sudden confusion. She hadn't been at all certain of a warm welcome; it had been a long time since they had seen each other and then they had parted not exactly on the best of terms. Neither had Miranda felt confident enough to go to Connie's memorial service. Now that Richard had actually invited her in to his home and was talking to her was all to the good. Of course it could just be his impeccable manners that she remembered from old but just the same she had to ensure that she used this to her advantage.

'Dear Richard you haven't changed a bit. I would have recognised you anywhere. Which way shall I go, through here?'

As she was already heading in the direction of the kitchen Richard nodded in agreement. He had to be civil but he'd see her out as soon as possible.

'Yes, through here.'

He gestured her into the room. Sunlight spilled in through the open back door. The contented murmur of honeybees from the nearby herb garden instilled a peaceful, serene scene outside compared to the tense awkwardness inside.

'Would you like a drink? A cup of coffee or would you prefer tea?'

It was too early to offer wine and he certainly didn't feel that friendly.

'Oh coffee please darling, yours smells delicious. What a fabulous kitchen, a cooks dream. And that view, heaven.'

She walked over to the door and let her gaze take in the garden and linger on the fields and wood beyond. The garden was still in full heady bloom; the flowerbeds crammed.

'Mmmm. So gorgeous it's almost chocolate box perfect.'

She sighed as she turned back to watch Richard.

Whilst she had been exclaiming over his garden he had busied himself with the coffee paraphernalia. To himself he had asked the question. Why are you here Miranda? And he hadn't come up with an answer. Although they hadn't had anything to do with each other since her marriage, he still could remember how she rarely did anything without an ulterior motive. Secondly, she had always been able to twist him round her little finger without seemingly trying to. All in all it boded no good for him. ,Don't be ridiculous, he told himself. That was when you were still an impressionable twenty something year old. Being nearly fifty meant that you should at least be able to keep one female under control. The little devil in him said, 'are you sure?' With clumsy hands he spilt the coffee as he was pouring it from the machine. Damm her. He was doing all right up until now. He hurriedly reached over for the cloth and wiped away the mess.

He remembered exactly how she took her coffee but he wasn't giving her that satisfaction. She would probably read something in it knowing Miranda.

'How do you take your coffee? White with sugar?'

Miranda hung her handbag over the back of a chair and then perched herself down at the table.

'Ple-ase!' she stressed the word with a faint frown, 'black and without thank you.'

She placed her manicured hands onto the scrubbed tabletop, palms down and tapped one long fingernail absentmindedly. Surreptitiously, she watched as Richard finished pouring the dark brew into their cups. He looked good. Much better than she had anticipated and still lean and fit.

Richard elected to remain standing and leant against the black granite worktop, the splendid garden view behind him. He raised his cup to his lips and took a large mouthful of coffee. The scalding liquid invaded his mouth and he winced as he burnt his tongue. God that hurt! Her sudden appearance and nearness had startled and unnerved him. She had always had this compelling hold over him. When they were younger his infatuation had been so great that it had threatened to take over his whole life. It nearly had. When she had married his cousin, Richard had been devastated. For ages he had hated her and what she had done to him. He also had hated himself for being what in his eyes he thought was so weak. Now, her sudden appearance was a total shock. He made himself a promise. If there was one thing he was certain of, *she* was not going to get under his skin again in *any* way possible.

'So. You still haven't answered my question,' he looked at her with a cold glance.

Miranda appeared unfazed. She lifted her grey-green eyes to him and opened them wide. Her gaze was frank and open as she candidly replied.

'I'm sorry. I know I should have contacted you first. But, I was simply passing near by.'

Richard's short snort of disbelief momentarily put her off balance. She coloured slightly and hesitated a second before she continued.

'It's true. I had been staying with a friend, down in Wickham. I knew Bishop's Waltham was only about ten minutes drive away and so, I couldn't resist looking you up.

She finished, flushed and embarrassed as Richard continued to study her. She knew he was having trouble with her sudden unexpected arrival.

As the pause widened Richard looked closer at the woman across the room from him.

The years had been kind to Miranda. From where he stood her face was remarkably unlined; her beautiful eyes still sparklingly clear. Her hair, still as he remembered. Long, thick and lustrous and almost the same colour of deep golden honey. He noted the vain absence of any telling grey and deduced that she must follow the current trend of having her hair fashionably coloured and streaked to suit herself. Her figure was almost as luscious as when she was his. Tall, slim and full-breasted and probably only one size larger, if at all. She was dressed only in a simple white linen dress that emphasised her figure, with light filigree jewellery for adornment. The dress she wore just to the level of her knees and as she crossed her legs Richard noticed that her calves had not lost any of their muscle tone and her ankles remained as slim as a girl's.

Richard idly wondered if she was still as enthusiastic in bed as he recalled, then collected himself before his daydreaming took over. For God's sake. The last thing he wanted was to give her the wrong idea and more importantly he didn't want her to have any sway over him.

Think about the way she treated you instead, he told himself. In a flood he remembered how smitten he'd been and how cruelly she had cast him aside.

'OK. So you found me,' he shrugged as if he couldn't care less and waited for her answer.

'I was also fascinated over the matter of your father's Bible. It was such an interesting story and such a coincidence that I made the first contact with the American family. I was intrigued to find out if you had bothered to follow it up. I also wanted to make sure that you were alright,' she finished softly with a shy smile.

Despite his good intentions, Richard let himself unwind a little. No possible harm could come of telling her what he'd done and later discovered. She might even know something herself as Billy had always had a glad eye for a pretty face, and Richard knew that he had liked Miranda.

The coffee was finished and Richard asked her if she would like another. He joined her at the table with freshly refilled cups and a plate of biscuits.

'Mmm. These are very good. Not shop bought shortbread I'm sure.'

He noticed her lips as she wiped the rich crumbs away from the corner of her mouth.

'My Aunt Mavis makes them. She is always popping in with biscuits and cakes, and the odd fruit pie or two. I think she's afraid that now I'm on my own I'm going to starve.'

He gave a short mirthless laugh before carrying on.

'She doesn't understand about the modern man and how we're quite capable of cooking reasonable half decent meals. Also more to the point, that some of us actually enjoy it. But, there you go. She is of a different era.'

'I know what you mean. Most of that age group grew up running around after their husband and children. The majority didn't have real careers; they didn't feel they needed anything other than bringing up their family. That was their whole life. Not that there's anything fundamentally wrong with that. It's just that nowadays what with most women working and bringing up a family often the husband has to play his part in the domestic role. Family life now has a totally different meaning. Your Auntie Mavis. Wasn't she on your mother's side of the family?'

'Yes. My Mum's sister. She's a good old stick really, just a bit bossy. One thing though, she'd never let you down.'

As he finished speaking and reached for another sip of coffee he felt himself grow hot under his collar as he realised what he had said. The implication was plainly there. Her silence made him take a quick glance at her face. She had the grace to look as guilty as hell. Good. He let the silence grow as he took another biscuit and bit into its rich buttery flavour. Then after considering he had made his point he continued.

'Anyway, the Bible. Yes, in answer to your query I did indeed contact the American flier. Well, his granddaughter really, as he wasn't at all well and the Internet just wasn't part of his everyday life. She filled me in with his side of things. It really is an amazing story.'

And then, Richard suddenly found himself telling Miranda about his trip to Germany and the subsequent visit to the POW camp and museum. He described the city of Hamburg, with its proud places of new buildings, bridges, canals and the old Rathaus. Then how he had turned south and driven through the scattered villages and fields, along straight roads with poplar trees swaying overhead in perfect aisles. A stark memorial stone set back in the grass before the prison perimeter fence; its inscription read but already dull inside his mind as he contemplated the edifice before him. A second sign directed visitors to a museum and exhibition centre. It was isolated, desolate, and silent. There had been few other visitors that day; who indeed visited it and why? Could they still learn lessons there? He recalled the feeling he had had of being watched by silent men in ragged clothing hung over fleshless bodies. He could hear the shrill orders and the rattle of shots, and feel the presence of ghosts who had starved and died, exhausted from their pitiless ordeal.

Miranda had listened in silence and then had shivered as his telling came to an end.

Absentmindedly he finished his coffee and then he had recalled what he had been able to piece together with the American's story. Of what might have happened to Billy during those lost years and of what he knew with certainty.

Miranda had sat engrossed throughout. Hardly interrupting him, only to ask a question or two. When he had come to a halt she then amazed him. Billy had had lots of secrets stored away in his cupboard. Richard sat up open-mouthed as he listened to her. She had known about Nat and how Billy had tried to get him away to safety. Lots of little things were explained, filled in and embellished. Most of which Richard had only been able to guess at so far.

'How on earth do you know all this? Dad never told me as much. It was always an effort to get him talking about the war at all.'

For some strange reason Richard didn't feel any resentment in her knowing. He was coming to realise that Billy had had hidden depths and if he had trusted Miranda then who was he to question his judgement.

'I don't know. We just clicked and liked each other I suppose. Perhaps it was because I was a woman and I didn't pose any sort of threat.'

'Well he certainly liked women.'

Richard let his thoughts drift over to the chest. Perhaps she had even seen the contents before him? She certainly knew of their existence. He wasn't going to ask her; his pride wouldn't allow him that much. Instead as he sat there, he listened calmly to what she had to say and was thankful that Billy had at least told her something of the past.

'I don't suppose for one minute that either of us know the whole story. It's probably just the tip of the iceberg; sad and yet fascinating at the same time. From the receiving of the Bible and tracing the story through the war. I wonder how often this sort of thing had happened and how many men tried to escape, and how many actually managed it. But, to have got all those letters written between your parents is wonderful. A very special treasure.'

She fell silent for a moment and then went on as a sudden thought occurred to her.

'You know the silver belt buckle – the German one. It wasn't a memento from any of the camps or the guards, nor loot grabbed when they were rescued and being transported out. It was a present from a German girl. When Billy and Nat were on the run, Nat was very ill.

She took them in and looked after them until Nat was able to travel again. Something happened whilst they were staying with her. I think I remember Billy saying her husband had been killed. Anyway, she was grateful to Billy for his compassion. Your father had seemed a bit embarrassed and sad about it.'

Nothing more was known about this tale and once again Richard was struck by how the old boy could still surprise him even after death.

The morning had flown, the sun at its highest point in the still blue sky. Richard felt the beginnings of the telltale grumbling indicating it was lunchtime. It came as no surprise to him that he found himself inviting Miranda to stay for lunch. He had resigned himself to her company for that day and, after her explanations he considered that she posed no threat to his newfound peace. Long ago she had always been an amiable companion, lively and witty when it had suited her. Besides, she was still good to look at and he was a red-blooded male. More to the point Aunt Mavis kept telling him he needed more company around him as he was in strong danger of becoming quite antisocial. At least he was taking her advice for once.

Miranda was both pleased and pleasantly surprised by his sudden invitation. She smiled at him and said, 'that would be lovely. But why don't I take you out to lunch? You must have a favourite pub around here? It's so gorgeous in this part of Hampshire and who knows when the weather will break. Please let me buy lunch. Call it a celebration of meeting up again if you like?'

She gave him such a beguiling look that he found he couldn't say no.

Two minutes later they had locked up and strolled along the lane in the direction of *The Sea Horse*.

Rounding the corner they came upon the whitewashed and black beamed public house. The car park was nearly full so they knew it would be heaving both inside and out. Richard opened the door leading to the lounge bar and stood aside for Miranda to enter. Heads turned as the regulars took in the newcomers and then let their eyes linger on Miranda with interest. Richard nodded to the few that he knew by sight. Taking her by the arm he steered Miranda further into the cool room in the direction of the bar. Nosey locals were one thing. Bring a strange woman in with you and the tongues would soon wag Richard thought sourly. He gave Aunt Mavis until tomorrow afternoon and then she'd be round.

'What will you have?'

'Oh a glass of white wine please. But remember I'm paying.'

'OK if you insist. But let me get the drinks and you pay for the food.'

He grabbed the lunchtime menu off the bar and offered it to her. She made her choice quickly, settling for a crisp oriental salad with Thai fishcakes in a sweet chilli sauce. Richard settled for kipper pate and locally made crusty bread.

As it was so beautifully warm outside and they were less likely to be overheard Richard carried their drinks out onto the stone terrace. Miranda found a recently vacated table partially in the shade of an old lilac tree and they claimed their seats.

'This is fab. What a perfect day and such a sweet little pub. Cheers.'

She raised her glass to chink against Richard's and then took a sip of her Semillon. Their eyes met across their glasses.

'Cheers.'

He decided small talk was the safest bet.

'We have quite a few good pubs in the area. Some serve great food but like everywhere else these days you have to shop around. Mind you it's good fun trying. This beer's a local brew and has quite a kick.'

She glanced at the nutty brown bitter in his pint glass.

'Is this the type of pub where regulars have their own favourite glass kept for them?'

'It probably is but I'm not one of them – yet. I think it takes about thirty years!'

They laughed and again clinked their glasses together.

Miranda leaned back in her canvas-backed chair and looked around her. The pub's garden was a pleasing mix of old and new. There were plenty of herbs and flowers nearby that attracted the insects. They all seemed to be popular at playing host to the drowsy, humming bee chant of midsummer.

'The flowers are so wonderful. I'll say it again, you're very lucky to live in such a lovely part of England, you know.'

'I do know. Apart from the ghastly wet winters this part of the UK is nearly perfect. Oh and the Government of course.'

'Ugh politics! Spare me. Are you so concerned though?'

'Well I hate too many petty rules and regulations, I like to make my own decisions and mistakes.' He fell silent.

Miranda stared.

'Do you intend to do anything about it?'

He thought for a moment and then sighed.

'Oh I donate to various charities. Write a few letters to my MP and to the local newspaper. I know I'm as bad the rest, I don't do enough but I'm not the type to get more heavily involved in politics. Perhaps most politicians start out with good intentions but, the bureaucracy seems to overwhelm them in time and then they're too busy fighting to keep their jobs and keep their party in power. I've always thought that all local government should be independent of any party.'

'That's an interesting idea.'

'But this is only my personal opinion of course. I'm sure there are thousands out there who think the complete opposite from the way I do. I just get frustrated at times. Perhaps that was why I thought it was a good idea to go off to sea for a while.' He gave Miranda a thin smile in explanation, 'anyway let's talk about something else. After all, politics is always a taboo subject any time.'

They naturally fell silent as the landlady brought their food out to them. She was a large lady with a round smiling face. She beamed with pleasure at Richard; he was obviously a favourite with her. She placed the laden plates down onto the old heavily lichened garden table in front of them.

'Here you are my loves. One Thai fishcakes – are these for you darling? And one kipper pate. I thought they'd be for you my love. I've also done you a plate of sauté potatoes to go with your salad, Richard, as I know you love them. You're looking well. And you my love, just visiting this part are you?' She turned an enquiring smile to Miranda, who nearly choked in amusement at her transparent downright nosiness.

'Yes just passing through. It's such a pretty place,' she spread her paper serviette onto her lap.

'Is that so? Passing through eh. Well you just enjoy your meal and maybe we'll be seeing you again. Like a refill?'

'Mmmm. Just an orange juice please. I do have to drive back later. I have to work tomorrow.'

'Oh what a shame not to stay. Right. Well I'll bring you your drinks out in a jiffy.'

Her curiosity satisfied she bustled back indoors with their empty glasses.

Miranda burst into a fit of the giggles and Richard joined her, laughing heartily.

He picked up a piece of crusty wholemeal bread and spread it thinly with butter saying with a straight face,

'Well. That will be all round the snug in a trice. "Richard has a lady visitor. Oh no she won't be staying, has to get back to work. Has an important job. Oh not too sure, something big in the city no doubt." She's terrible! You could see how her mind was working. I'm afraid nothing stays a secret in this village for long.'

'I'm sorry.' Then, ' Does it matter?'

'What. No. No.' He shook his head as he ate a piece of bread thickly covered with pâté.

'Perhaps we should have made something up. Given her something to really think about. Or do you want to keep your good reputation intact?' Miranda teased.

'How do you know I do have a good reputation? After all I'm single now. Connie's gone; although I hate the way she died and will always regret it, I no longer feel so, well, mortified. Don't get me wrong. It's just that I realise that the ones left behind have to pick up the pieces and carry on living.'

He gazed at Miranda as he finished what he had been explaining. She returned his gaze, her eyes steady and warm.

'I'm so glad. I, well I hated the thought of your being so despondent. I wanted so many times to come and see you. I didn't know what type of reception I'd get. Or how you were coping on your own. In the end, I have to confess I contacted your Aunt Mavis a couple of weeks ago. I'm sorry if you think I interfered. She was a bit cool towards me at first but eventually she said that you were much better and learning to put your grief aside. I'm sorry if you think I shouldn't have.'

Miranda laid a hand on his arm.

'I truly hope you don't mind. We've not spoken properly for so long. It's been too long. I thought it was about time that we made up. Can you ever forgive me?'

Richard studied her. The familiar face that he had adored all those years ago. Her gaze at him was open and appealing. A slight worried frown was between her eyes as she waited for his answer. His heart did a funny flip as he hesitated, then he picked up her hand lying on his arm and turned it over so that her wrist met his lips.

'Thank you. Yes it is about time. It has been far too long. And yes, I do forgive you, it shouldn't matter anymore, what's done is done. Let's forget it.'

Her look of relief was so apparent, plainly written all over her face. She didn't reply. Her response was a radiant smile that lit up her face before reaching her misted eyes.

Chapter 26

Much later, the air still heavy with the drone of worker bees, Richard and Miranda left their shaded table and strolled the short distance along the lane back to the house. They were relaxed and satiated by the good food, alcohol, and sleepy warm weather. High overhead, in the late afternoon sunshine, birds took wing, swooping and darting in their quest for airborne insects.

If Richard were true to himself he would confess that Miranda still confused him madly. He was perfectly happy that they had made up their differences and could be friends once again. But, herein there lay a bit of a quandary. He wasn't sure if it was just the wine, Miranda having relented and steadily downing two more glasses, or if he was imagining it. Whatever the reason, she was in a good mood, very animated and decidedly flirtatious.

He was daydreaming to himself, only half-listening as she merrily prattled on about some funny story that had happened to her recently. She finished with a peel of laughter and a fit of giggles, as she teetered slightly in her high heels. Her laughter was infectious. Richard joined in and obligingly put out an arm to support her in case she tripped. Smiling up at him she accepted his concern and happily snuggled into his shoulder. Not surprisingly Richard enjoyed the feel of a warm and vital woman once again on his arm. He knew not where it all might end but, why not just enjoy the moment and forget about his usual caution? If he wasn't careful he was in grave danger of becoming paranoid over her.

The long afternoon shadows were falling on the house as they rounded the drive and Richard fished in his jeans pocket for the front-door key. He was somewhat hampered by Miranda clinging to his side, when he heard the growl of an engine and the crunch of tyres on the gravel behind them.

'Oh. Oh. Are you expecting company?' giggled Miranda.

Richard looked up at the sound and with his arm still supporting her, spun round to see who was calling. He didn't recognise the shiny, new BMW but he did know the driver behind the wheel. With a cold spurt of anger, he glared at Toby through the windscreen. It must have been about eight months since he'd last seen him during Connie's memorial service. He remembered it had been a cold, wet and windy day. The sad farewell service over, they had stood outside in the porch where they had exchanged only a few terse polite words. The cold had seeped through their thick winter coats and into their bones but their looks and words to each other had chilled them even more so. They had neither shaken each other's frozen hand nor shown any small gesture of friendship then, nor had they spoken since.

Despite not particularly wanting to see Toby, Richard was naturally curious as to why he should suddenly appear now. Another blast from the past, with no preliminary warning he thought. This was certainly turning into a day for surprises.

Gently disentangling himself from Miranda, Richard waited while Toby climbed from the gleaming car. He stood stiffly, his hands on his hips, a dark scowl on his face. Forgetting Miranda he growled a greeting.

'Toby. What do you want?'

Toby glanced first from Richard to Miranda and then back to Richard. For a moment he seemed uncertain of himself. He took a moment to ignore Richard's question, and reached back inside his car to remove a slim folder of papers from the passenger seat. He then raised his head and coolly surveyed Richard before replying,

'Ah Richard. I was in the neighbourhood visiting a client and Tom needed to give you some company papers to sign and thought I could do both jobs while I was just passing through.'

Despite all that had happened between them, Richard had never changed his company's accountants. Their firm had always done a particularly good job for him and he didn't see why their personal animosity should get in the way. He normally saw the senior partner Tom, so Toby's arrival could possibly have its own hidden agenda tacked on.

'Funny you're the second person who's come out with that line today. Well now you're here you'd better come in. Will this take long?'

During this little altercation, Miranda, now completely sober and in control of herself, had watched the two of them with a slight rise of her eyebrows. The interest showed in her face as she had watched the body language and antagonism between them. Richard however had forgotten she was still there.

'Ahem,' she said in mock indignation. She was blowed if she was going to be ignored any longer.

Richard gave a slight start.

'Oh sorry Miranda. Miranda, this is Toby Ellis. He works at my company's accountants. Toby this is Miranda Barker.'

Toby did a double take as he looked first at Miranda and then back at Richard. He was speechless for a moment and then finally he said in a raspy voice,

'Miranda Barker? I'm – pleased to meet you.'

He stood gazing at Miranda; his face had at first gone quite pale and then reddened as the blood had rushed back. Richard watched, not understanding Toby's behaviour. He was never usually this quiet with a pretty woman in front of him.

Miranda thrust out a hand and Toby took it absent-mindedly, limply, before dropping his own. Puzzled Richard repeated that they should go indoors, and indicated the sitting room off to the right. Silently they followed him as he strode ahead to open the French windows overlooking the garden. The late sunshine and the perfume from the roses rushed in to greet them.

Toby shot a dark look at Richard's back. Cross, piqued and just a little curious, Miranda flopped down onto a comfortable settee and removed her red high-heeled sandals.

'Ouch. Oh! That's better. I don't know why I wore them today. It's heaven to get them off,' she rubbed her toes; her toenails were painted with clear varnish so they shone glossy on the carpet.

'Shall I make some tea whilst you two talk business?'

Neither responded, so without waiting for an answer she got to her feet. Richard flinched as he realised she had asked him a question and he was acting rudely towards her.

'What? Oh sorry Miranda. Yes please.'

Richard let her go. She'd find the tea in a stainless steel canister on the black granite worktop soon enough. There was no need to explain his kitchen layout to her. He really wanted to get rid of Toby ASAP.

Toby hadn't sat down. He had stood in the room that he remembered well. Nothing had changed since he was here last. The furniture and fabrics had the classic Connie stamp upon them. Rich colours, fine materials, good living. Connie. He slowly inhaled. His chest felt like it had a rigid band around it. The pain still hurt.

He stood and glared at Richard in sudden accusation. Stony-faced and pale despite his expensive tan.

'Miranda *Barker*?'

He asked in a low incredulous voice.

The bolt suddenly shot home. Richard was highly amused. He wouldn't let it show though. He could play this for a little while longer and enjoy himself. He wasn't a cruel person but he still thought Toby deserved it.

'Yes. Why ever not?'

Toby gave him such a look of intense hatred that Richard suddenly wondered if he was in danger of being thumped. He took the chance and ignored Toby's outrage.

'Well Toby. Are you going to get your pen out so I can sign whatever it is you want me to sign for Tom? Or do you have another reason for coming?'

'I did have. I don't know whether I can be bothered, or more to the point, do you deserve it after this? How could you?'

He indicated with a jerk of his head in the direction of the kitchen.

'Listen Toby I don't know what you're on about, on either account. So quickly get to the point.'

'You're a cold hearted bloody liar,' spat Toby. His face was changing alternately from red to white with suppressed anger.

'For Christ's sake keep your voice down. I don't want Miranda to hear what's none of her business,' hissed Richard.

'No I'm sure you don't. We don't want to upset that cosy little scene do we,' he growled back,

'All the times I've thought and worried about you, and whether I should come and see you. Put you out of your misery. And all the time you didn't need it. Don't waste much time do you? You hypocritical bastard.' He bunched his hands into fists in front of him.

Things were getting out of hand. This was too much for Richard; Toby had overstepped the mark in his house.

'I repeat. Get to the point or I'll bloody well throw you out,' Richard thrust his face towards Toby and spoke between clenched teeth

'How do you like your tea Toby? White, with or without sugar?' asked Miranda from the open doorway.

Toby whirled round and flushed as he observed Miranda watching him with a questioning smile on her face. If she'd heard anything then she was giving no sign of it.

'Oh white please and no sugar thanks.'

'Fine. Richard's I know from old of course.'

She smiled at them both and then returned back in the direction of the kitchen.

'Very pretty. You always were a jammy bugger. But in less than a year! I'd have thought that you would have had some scruples – poor Connie.' His voice broke and he turned hurriedly away, but not before Richard had seen the look of pure abject misery in his face.

Richard quickly decided enough was enough. He had better put him out of his misery before it finally went too far. He had had his cheap pennyworth of revenge and Toby's wretchedness was pitiful. He was obviously still mourning Connie's death far more than Richard had ever realised. For once, Toby was suffering the consequences of his numerous flirtations. Incredulously, he must have actually been in love with her. Softly he said,

'Toby. I think you've got it all wrong. Miranda Barker is my cousin's wife. Or ex-wife to be exact. Her surname Barker is by another marriage. She is nothing to me, not like you imagine. Only as an old, almost forgotten friend. Today is the first time we've seen each other for years and years.'

Toby raised his head. Unshed tears shone in his eyes as he took in what Richard was explaining to him.

'Do you understand?' Richard asked gently.

Toby nodded, 'I thought –.'

Blindly, he staggered over to a chair and slumped himself down in it. He held his head in his hands.

'Yes I know what you thought. I'm sorry.'

He felt cheap now and he paused before continuing.

'I didn't realise that you still really cared. I was being thoughtless and, oh I don't know, being somewhat cruel. I suppose I was still feeling jealous, spiteful. Think what you like. I'm not very proud of myself.'

He turned his back on Toby and looked bleakly out of the open doorway onto the garden. For once the view did nothing to make him feel good.

Toby looked up.

'I'm sorry too. Sorry about everything. I should have come before. But, well it was all still too raw and painful.'

He stopped as Miranda re-entered the room carrying a tea tray. Richard turned back as he sensed her entrance and rushed over to take the tray from her hands and put it onto a low oak table. He was glad to do something to help break the tension that was in the room.

'Here we are. Sorry to be so long. I couldn't find a milk jug. Richard, I've taken the liberty of adding a few of your lovely yummy shortbread biscuits. Toby, do try one. Richard's Auntie makes them apparently and they are divine. Fattening, I'm sure with all that butter, but so scrummy.'

Her entrance created a welcome diversion and both men breathed deeply at the return to normality. They were relieved to do as they were told and both helped themselves to a cup of tea and a biscuit.

Richard crossed over to a seat by the window and sat down, his long legs stretched out in from of him. A small silence enfolded as each contemplated the others in the hot room. The grandfather clock's tick sounded unnaturally loud and outside the bees hummed like a wire vibrating on the wind. The rose bushes swayed as a light breeze caught and dryly rustled through them.

Toby was the first to break the silence.

'Actually, I really do have something important to tell you Richard. It concerns Connie.'

He stopped and glanced first in Miranda's direction and then across to Richard. An enquiring look was on his face as if he was unsure whether to carry on in her presence or not.

Richard was quick to understand his dilemma. He had also had enough of secrets and squabbles for today.

'It's all right Toby. Miranda and I go way back. I'm sure that anything you tell me will not embarrass her nor will it need to go further than these four walls.'

Miranda looked across at Richard. 'Are you sure. I don't mind going out into the garden if you need a bit of privacy. Really I don't.'

'No. No it's OK. Go ahead Toby. No more secrets.'

Richard nodded his head at Toby to continue. He took a deep breath and then held Richard's gaze as he went on.

'Well. It's to do with the night Connie drowned. If you remember the ship diverted her course to come and rescue us. You had to scuttle your yacht to prevent her being a hazard to other shipping.'

Miranda quickly sat up. She was all ears and eyes. She had never heard the full story of course, about Connie's awful drowning. What was he about to reveal now?

He continued. 'You came down into the boat's saloon and we told you that it was already on its way.'

'Yes. You had used the SSB radio and made an SOS call.' Richard said tightly, remembering how annoyed he'd been with Toby at the time. He still thought that her life had been put at risk more by attempting to make that horrendous climb up the scramble net than by the storm itself. That would have eventually blown itself out.

'Well it wasn't me who actually made that call. I didn't know how to, I didn't even properly know how the set worked. Connie made the decision to do it. We did actually have a bit of a disagreement over it. I wasn't totally convinced we were that much in real danger. Anyway, she had had enough. She insisted that she should make the call. In the end it was her decision alone. Once it was done I had to go along with it.'

Toby finished flatly and sat back spent in his armchair.

A dreadful, shocked hush followed.

There was a full minute as each digested what he had just said.

From what Miranda had gleaned from Richard she sensed that Connie liked having her own way and would have hated to have been thwarted in any way. Even so she wasn't close enough to Richard to really appreciate all that Toby had told them.

Richard of course was dumbstruck. Connie had made the call! That meant she had taken the decision on her own. She had radioed for help, ignoring Toby's pleas to check with Richard. He knew her well. He could imagine how she had disregarded Toby. She had then had to climb the rope ladder and scramble net and sadly she had been thrown into the sea. It had all been her own initiative. Her responsibility and therefore the cause of her own death! Not Toby. Not Richard, her skipper and husband as he'd always believed. Richard felt his face grow white with a dull throbbing in his ears.

'Are you alright?'

He slowly looked up to find Miranda hovering anxiously over him. He blinked up at her. Then he felt as if a tremendous weight had been lifted from his chest. It wasn't entirely his fault. The last remaining vestiges of guilt slipped away leaving him reeling, light-headed and giddy with relief.

His breath returned to normality, Richard turned his gaze towards Toby.

'I don't know what to say except thank you. You don't know how much that helps to lay the ghost to rest. Thank you for having the decency to come and let me know.'

Toby suddenly stood up. He felt awkward and realised that Richard needed time to reflect upon what he'd told him. He'd done his bit and felt his own small relief. For the first time since the accident he and Richard shook hands. They could now at least be pleasant and civil to one another once again, even if their relationship remained distant. He made his goodbyes and walked out onto the gravel drive. He climbed into his shiny car and put on his black sunglasses. Richard could see his own reflection mirrored in the convex lenses.

'Be in touch.'

The wheels spun on the gravel heading towards the tarmac road. The heavy sun was now sinking fast behind the distant hills melding into a fat orb of molten gold. Wispy clouds trailed across its lower arc.

In silence Richard and Miranda looked at each other. She laid her hand upon his chest, giving him a deep smile.

'I think we both need a stiff drink, don't you?'

Taking him gently by the arm she led him back into the house, kicking the door shut behind them. In the shadowed hallway she slowly turned and then put her arms around him. Richard laid his head upon her shoulder; a shudder went through him as he returned her embrace. It had been a long time since he had held Miranda in his arms and it felt good. They stayed motionless while he brought his emotions back under control. Miranda lifted her head and gazed into Richard's eyes.

'Richard?'

Without thinking he suddenly found himself drawn into a deep kiss.

Chapter 27

He was drowning. Being pulled down against his will, into the blackness, he couldn't fight against the softness, the wetness, his arms were too weak, his legs were heavy and trapped, he had no fight left. Somewhere deep in his brain something clicked. The reflex to breathe; he opened his eyes and his mouth and took in deep sweet breaths. He was in control once more. He took another shuddering breath and this time he opened his eyes. He gasped and sat up, dragging the sweat-drenched sheets from around his legs. He thrust his legs over the side of the bed, trembling with both fear and relief. It had been a bad dream, a nightmare. Probably brought on by the recent events and past memories.

First Miranda and then Toby showing up, and then everything spilling out, thick and fast until he was shaken with each new revelation. He staggered over to his bathroom and splashed his hot sticky face with clean cold water. The coolness helped calm his chasing, overactive brain.

He'd never get back to sleep now he thought, as he dried his face with a thick towel. He retraced his steps back into his bedroom and reached for the cotton dressing gown hanging on the back of the bedroom door. His bare feet made no sound as he padded down the stairs to the kitchen. The lights cast a comforting pool under the wall cupboards as he went from kettle to tea mug. Tea, that best of all much revered drink.

What a weekend! He studied his reflection in the kitchen window. He scowled at the tousled hair, twenty-four hour stubble, and etched lines running across his brow. At this rate he'd soon age to ninety. He peered out through the glass to the garden beyond. No curtains covered these windows, as he had no immediate neighbours except for the pub a couple of hundred metres down the lane. Already he could discern the grey-pearly light seeping through the trees at the bottom of the lawn. It looked like rain. God knows they needed it. It had been a long dry summer and the water table was very low. The nearby rivers were either now dry or barely flowing. The Ministry's call to 'build, build, and build' more new houses was seriously threatening the already over-burdened local facilities. So much for their wisdom

Richard thought sourly. What prats! Taking his tea he sat down at the kitchen table. There was no point in going back to bed. He'd never sleep and besides the sweaty bed was no longer inviting.

Toby's visit had been timely if truth were known in more ways than one.

As for Miranda! Her visit was a little more delicate and he still felt a certain shock as he recalled that evening.

At the end of their kiss both had looked at each other with some surprise.

'About that drink?' they had said together, and then laughed to cover their embarrassment.

'Gin and tonic would be good.'

Miranda made her way over to the sofa and sat down curling her legs under her. She waited while Richard fetched their drinks. He poured himself a pretty hefty measure, and made Miranda's less so – she still had a journey to make home and time was getting on. A generous slice of lime, tonic and a handful of crushed ice. As he returned to the sitting room Miranda could hear the ice as it cracked and tinkled in the drinks. They briefly chinked their glasses together.

'Cheers.'

'Cheers.'

Eventually. They both knew they would have to speak.

'Are you pleased about what Toby said?'

'Yes. A huge weight has been lifted.' He made no mention about his wife's flirtation with Toby. That matter was entirely private. Besides, he had nothing concrete to go on, just a gut feeling. It either had (and that really would have been difficult on the yacht), or it would have led to more later on. Now, it no longer mattered. It was academic.

'Great. Then we'll drink to us.'

'Us?' Had he missed something? Surely it was just a kiss. Wasn't it?

'Yes. We're finally together again. I'm so glad. You don't know what it means to me. I've wanted to for years. Almost as soon as I'd married Philip in fact.'

'Whoa. Steady on! It was just a kiss Miranda.'

'Yes I know. Just, you know.' She shrugged prettily and again he felt his heart give a little lurch as she smiled at him.

However, Richard was shocked to hear her talking about her marriage to Philip like that and more than a little curious. He'd never cared for his loathsome cousin ever since their schooldays together. Miranda's confession raised his interest.

She placed her empty glass on the coffee table and seated herself more comfortably; her legs curled to one side and her head against the back cushions.

'Only women can sit like that,' reflected Richard. 'It must be something to do with flexible hips. It would kill me.'

Miranda laughed and uncurled her legs to the other side of her, moving closer to Richard as she did so.

Richard grabbed their glasses and hurriedly stood up.

'Another G and T, or do you think you've had enough for today? We did drink quite a bit at the pub earlier on.'

'Another I think. Make it a small measure. I don't want to fall asleep.'

'Righto.'

The evening dusk had given away to dim moonlight. Few stars yet shone, and from the open kitchen doorway Richard could see the gathering clouds above the hills. He sniffed the air. It already felt fresher; perhaps it will rain tonight.

With refilled glasses he returned to Miranda and sat down on the sofa. He was conscious of how her thigh felt, firm and warm through her thin summer dress, against his own. The room was bathed in a soft light from a lamp that glowed on the other side of the room.

Should he heed the sudden warning bells that rang inside his head?

Miranda took a large gulp and downed half her drink before putting her glass down. She turned to him, letting herself press hard against him as she leaned in closer. He noticed her slightly flushed cheeks, still with a trace of the old freckles across her nose. Her eyes were shining with a half dreamy look in them. She smiled in invitation and he felt his eyes drawn to her parted moist lips. Something deep inside him said No! in protest but too late. Her arms were around his neck and then her hand was on his thigh. Her tongue enquiringly tasted his. Skilfully, she explored his mouth, his eyelids, his throat. Her hand moved from his thigh to his groin and he felt himself quickly stiffen in response. It had been so long.

Like a magnet his hands were drawn to her. Her full breasts were soft and pliant. He almost gasped in shock when he discovered that she wore no knickers, and was wet between her legs. Her clothes pushed aside, she swiftly climbed astride his lap and sank down. Richard groaned. This shouldn't be happening. She was seducing him despite all his earlier good intentions.

She moved above him talking softly then her murmuring changed to more urgent commands.

'Bite me on the neck. Hit me. Yes hit me! Hard!' she screamed. Her eyes were wide and staring hard into his, a tear escaped from them.

Something snapped inside him as he came to his senses. This was all wrong! Something was not quite right. This wasn't him.

'I can't. Stop. Stop right now!' Richard sat rigid. His upper body was stiff and unyielding. His lower body, flaccid and unresponsive as all previous lust melted away. He pushed her away from him, all manner of feelings rising up inside him. Disgust, shock, revulsion, repulsion. The sooner he got rid of her the better.

Miranda tumbled onto the floor. She lay on her side, skirt up, her bottom exposed. Richard hurriedly straightened his own clothing and angrily stood up, moving over to switch on more lamps. He had had enough of the subtle, romantic lighting.

He was furious with both himself and with her. Annoyed that he had all too easily succumbed to her non-too subtle seduction, and angry and confused that she had encouraged him to physically abuse her. What did she think he had become? He'd never hurt a woman, either during sex or in anger. He had always been entirely straight; any depraved cheapness had never turned him on. Could she of all people not remember that? Most chillingly of all, what had changed her to act like that?

Miranda remained where she was on the carpet. Eventually, as Richard's anger had calmed down he realised that she was crying softly. His initial response was to ignore her and let her cry. Her silent tears ran unchecked onto the carpet where she lay. Richard's anger had subsided; everyone was different he supposed, who was he to judge? He knelt to pull her skirt back down over her legs, to make her decent once again, when he suddenly stopped what he was doing. For the first time in the better light he was aware of the ugly red scars and particular crisscross stripes covering her buttocks and lower back. Without a word, he drew aside the material to get a better look and quickly ascertained that these were no accidental scars, neither were they recent. The most hideous bore the distinct imprint of – an iron?

With a sudden chill and a feeling of foreboding he turned Miranda over onto her back.

'What the hell happened to you?' he demanded angrily.

As Miranda's tears turned to sobs and she covered her face with her hands he could only look on helplessly.

He persisted. 'Was it an accident? Was it?' eventually it dawned on him, 'it wasn't, was it?'

Her cries were painful and Richard found himself filled with pity as he gathered her up in his arms, to try to soothe away her obvious anguish. After what seemed an age, her crying began to subside. Her body shuddered as she took a deep gulp and then hung her head shamefacedly. Richard kept her cradled in his arms as she recovered herself. Underneath his fingers, despite the warm evening her skin felt chilled.

'So. Are you going to tell me?' he eventually asked.

Wordlessly she nodded and Richard then listened to one of the most horrendous and saddest story he'd ever experienced first hand.

He knew that his cousin Philip was a bully. Not only was he a bully but he'd also developed a nasty, mean character that had turned him into a man of complete revulsion. His bullying had become so great, in that he had to have complete power over those near him. This power also meant complete control.

To him, Miranda had been a trophy wife. Not too clever but, beautiful and amusing. She loved being adored and placed on a pedestal. With some gloating pride Philip had been happy to parade her around on his arm. The opulent diamond ring and wedding band on her finger warning off all those who knew him well. Gradually, his schizophrenic nature began to take over, clouding all judgement. At first, it was simple things that he imagined. Miranda had too many admirers he reckoned. She went out too often whilst he was away at the office; and whom did she see and meet? In a fit of mad jealousy one day he took away her car keys. From now on, he said, any shopping she did, he would accompany her. She didn't need anyone else after all. Compliant and a little afraid Miranda went along with his wishes. He began to give the orders for what clothes he thought she should buy and wear, discounting her own preferences and likes. He demanded that they ate only what he liked best.

Slowly, Miranda's freedom was being eaten away. Now, each morning before Philip left for work, he gave her a list of what jobs he considered needed doing around the house. Household chores, which any woman in those days would perform as a simple matter of course. On his arrival home, he expected that a drink be ready and waiting for him. Nothing very wrong or unusual in that you might say. But, as he went from room to room, sipping his cocktail, he would inspect her chores and usually, he would find fault in everything she had done that day. He would then insist that she redo it in front of him. He then developed a sadistic little ritual, in which he stripped her of all her clothes, beat her and then forced her on her hands and knees to get down and scrub the already spotless kitchen floor. Things began to get steadily worse. As he became more and more embroiled in his own cruel sickness, he devised more ways of humiliating and crushing her. If there were no more jobs to be done in the house, he thought nothing of throwing the contents of the coffee jug around the walls and then making her clean up or redecorate. He had special locks fitted, to keep her safe from intruders. He pocketed the keys and she became a virtual prisoner in her own house.

And, all the time he would take great delight in beating her. He forced her to watch filthy pornographic films that he bought from undisclosed sources. Films made abroad and, portraying sex in every form, with violence and bestiality being commonplace. This became the norm in their house. Over time, Miranda in sheer blind terror and exhaustion could no longer discern between what was normal and what was not. Philip had succeeded in totally corrupting her.

The final atrocity came when he blamed her for a slight burn mark on a favourite shirt of his. He blew his top and snatching the iron from her grasp he thrust the hot plate onto her uncovered skin. For Miranda, although horrendous and devastating at the time, this proved to be an ironic break. The burn was ghastly and painful and, with no immediate medical treatment turned horribly septic. Miranda became ill and luckily somewhere in Philip's deranged brain, he realised that she needed a doctor and despite his sick mind he still thought that he loved her. With the schizophrenic workings of his mind, in a clear period of crystal clarity he also knew that if she died he would be held responsible.

Miranda had then spent a year in hospital recuperating from her burns and nervous breakdown. The rest had passed in a blur; divorce proceedings and a settlement, Philip being sent away for his own mental treatment. She neither knew nor cared where he was now. As soon as she was able to she had sold the house and had moved.

Since then, her relationships with men had been strained. No, that wasn't totally true she said. Relationships with men were awful and almost non-existent. She couldn't ever forget the beatings that Philip inflicted on her, especially as he was incapable of performing without some form of ill treatment. For some reason she had blamed part of this on herself, and in some weird way had begun to expect the same of all men.

Richard found himself asking the question; but, why me? Their relationship had been long dead.

She had replied that that was easy. She and Richard had had a steady relationship. Everything had been *nice* and simple together. She thought that if she could go back, then everything would return to being safe and normal again. She said that she needed a thorough cleansing. Having sex with Richard should have been just that; she had hoped to overcome her shame.

Somehow however, in her mind Philip still overruled everything.

As Richard listened to the whole sorry tale he felt shocked and saddened. His loathsome cousin Philip had corrupted and ruined a lovely girl. Perhaps Miranda would never be able to have another normal relationship with a man again. Richard felt both compassion and a responsibility towards Miranda. The compassion was understandable. The responsibility was something else. Not only had she been married to a member of his family she was his past love. Perhaps, if he had been able to prove his own love to her by commitment earlier and married her himself she would have been spared all this. But, had she ever truly loved him anyway? Richard's mind whirled in confusion. She certainly wasn't in love with him now; for her a relationship with Richard would have purely been a chance at a solution to her problems.

She shifted her weight, as she lay supported against Richard and then sat up straight. Richard reached out and smoothed her wet hair away from her face. She looked a mess; dark runnels of mascara streaked across her face.

'I'm so sorry. I never imagined anything like this. I'm sure nobody did.'

'Billy did,' she said after a pause.

'He did? How come, did you tell him?'

'No. He sort of guessed. He was pretty shrewd your Dad and we'd always got along. Anyway, he asked me some time later. That was before I sold the house. He helped me with all that. I made him promise not to tell anyone, I was too ashamed.'

'Why? It wasn't your fault.'

'No. I know that. But well. Anyway, he'd known all wasn't OK from almost the beginning of our marriage. You see his own brother had been a bit of a pig and a bully in his own right. I told him some of what had happened, not all of course as I said before I felt too ashamed. I thought it was partly my own fault.'

'How could you possibly have come to that conclusion?'

'Oh, I don't know,' she sighed before carrying on.

'My psychiatrist said that apparently it is pretty common for battered or abused wives to think like that. That the blame lay solely with them. Billy had seen a lot of cruelty during the war and he recognised that pain I was going through. He actually helped me later on. He also said that he'd suspected from the start that you and I were never going to be suited. He said I didn't have the patience to wait for you to make up your mind up about what you wanted to do. I wanted stability from the outset. Philip came along with pots of money and I thought, right, he says he loves me, offers me a huge ring and a lovely house. I thought he was stable and hadn't a clue as to his real character.'

'I suppose I did mess about with my early life,' Richard replied ruefully.

'Yes you did. You played around, did a couple of ski seasons as a chalet boy cum barman and then qualified as a dinghy sailing instructor. Both jobs were fun and self-indulgent but they would never have paid for a mortgage nor help raise a family. Philip promised me he would. Your own business came a little too late. Though as Billy said we were never really compatible in his opinion anyway.'

'He was incorrigible at times. He always thought I was a bit of a waster.'

'Maybe, but he had such a good sense of what was right and what was wrong. We got on so well, as I've already told you. He told me something of his escapades and hinted about the more harrowing stories.'

Miranda suddenly shivered.

'You're cold. Let's move. Would you like a hot drink? What about some hot chocolate with a slug of something in it?'

'Mmmm sounds good.'

They both stood up and stretched their cramped limbs. Richard turned to go towards the kitchen and then faced Miranda. She stood before him looking small and embarrassed and thoroughly shattered.

'Look it's so late now. Why don't you stay the night? You look all in. The guest's room is all made up and I think you need a hot bath and a good night's sleep. Do you have to get back to work or anything?'

'No. I actually have tomorrow off.' She hesitated and then agreed that maybe what he was suggesting had a good deal of common sense to it. It was late and she was tired. Besides she was probably now way over her alcohol limit.

Richard led her upstairs to the bedroom. The room was decorated in cream and terracotta undertones, neither masculine nor feminine; it was all perfectly cosy and welcoming. He drew the curtains and switched on a couple of lamps. Their warm glow pooled on the soft carpet.

'Bathroom's here, plenty of towels and bath stuff in this cupboard. There's a new toothbrush and paste too. Please help yourself to anything you need. There's a towelling-gown on the back of the door if you want one. I'll bring you a drink in a jiffy.'

Richard left Miranda to run her own bath as he slipped downstairs to put the kettle on.

***

Later. Alone in his own bed Richard couldn't sleep. Miranda's story had upset him more than he had realised. Some men were so foul to their fellow human beings. If there was a God in this world it appeared that he had left us long ago.

What was he going to do about her? He couldn't just let her go back home without doing anything, not now. He could let her lean on him, by offering her the support she needed. He still felt something there for her.

God! What a trying world.

But don't we have to try all the time he thought.

From that very first resentful, pimply adolescent age, and then passing through the awkwardness of perhaps university or the first job. On the surface seeming so cocksure of oneself, but underneath being so riddled with self-doubts. We are really just being the same as everyone else. The whole business of living is really so hit and miss, and flawed through and through. We make such good intentions and we try our best. But, so often we fail first ourselves, and then all the others around us. What do we do then? We get up, and try again.

He sat up and thumped the pillow, turning the hot side over to the cooler fresher underside before lying back down again. His door suddenly clicked open and he realised that Miranda stood on the threshold. She slowly walked over to where he lay. In the pale light he could discern the trace of tears running down her stricken face. Her feet stood white and bare against the carpet.

'Richard. Please Richard hold me. Can I stay with you for just this one time. I can't bear to be alone tonight.'

She wanted to say more, to explain but at that moment her face crumpled. The tears were running fast down her cheeks as she struggled to find the words. She gave up and shook as her sobs convulsed her body. Richard got up and crossed over to where she stood. With gentleness he took her hand and led her back to the warmth of his bed.

Wordlessly they fell in together and lay side-by-side, hips touching. Richard put his arms around her and she felt their comfort and protection.

As the dawn rose, Miranda slept soundlessly on. Richard turned his head and stared wide-eyed at the beginning of the new day.

Chapter 28

The relentless sun reflected on the silver wing of the jet as it circled above Washington. Richard leaned over in his seat and caught the flash of the Potomac River as it meandered its way down from upstate and then dumped its muddy teal-coloured water into the mighty Chesapeake Bay. Chesapeake! How he'd longed for ages to explore the inland waters of this unique magnificent bay on the Eastern coast of the US state of Maryland. Now, at last he had been given the chance.

Richard had been caught unawares when he'd picked up the telephone a few days after Miranda's departure. But, straightaway on hearing the faint hiss of static he knew who was calling him. A thread of excitement spread throughout him as he listened.

'Hi, Richard it's Sorrel.'

'Sorrel! How are you?'

'Fine, doing just great. How about you?'

'Not bad. Where are you calling from?'

'Oh I'm at home. I've just spent the last week or so working damn hard putting together an exhibition I have coming up featuring local artists. Now I've finalised the arrangements and things have chilled out a whole bunch. What about you? Dug out any more about your father?'

'Yes, funnily enough I have and from the most unexpected quarter.'

'Great. You'll have to run the details past me. Now the real reason I've telephoned is, how busy are you right now?'

'Well so-so. Do you have something in mind?'

'Yes. Dad has decided that he's really not as keen on sailing as he once was and is planning on selling his boat. I actually think that step-mother number three is less interested in sailing than she is in spending his money on 5 star deluxe hotels, but maybe that's just me being sour. What it means to me is that I have just the remainder of the season to use the boat myself. So, I was wondering, as I know you're a great sailboat fan, whether you would like to come over and spend a few days or a week if you can spare it to explore Chesapeake

Bay. Nothing strenuous, but I'm sure you'd enjoy it. The boat is kind of too big for me to handle on my own, and it's too short notice to ask any of the guys here if they can take time off. Do you think you could put up with me so soon after Germany? Would you be interested?'

Sorrel sounded uncharacteristically young and unsure of herself. She wasn't usually so hesitant.

'Interested? Of course I would love to. When do you plan to get started?'

'Well as soon as you can make it. The sooner the better really as the weather is unseasonably settled right now. It's still very hot, but there are no thunderstorms forecast, which is what usually happens this time of year.'

'OK. I just have to check on flights, but that's a minor detail. Can I call you back when I've got some idea of the available dates?'

***

The undercarriage hydraulics gave their telltale signal that landing was imminent. The cabin staff in business class checked that everyone was safely seated and buckled in securely. The pretty female steward flashed Richard a lazy sexy smile as she collected his discarded newspaper. He smiled back in response and vaguely wondered who was meeting her when they touched down at Washington D.C. Sorrel knew his flight number and landing time, she had promised to be there to pick him up on his arrival. Relaxed and only moderately weary he leaned back in his seat. He was greatly looking forward to spending a week in the States and more than a little excited at the thought of seeing Sorrel again. It was a lot sooner than he had anticipated after their goodbyes at Hamburg Airport.

His luggage appeared almost as soon as he had reached the conveyor belt himself and for once immigration had been a breeze. He had been prepared for a lengthy wait as since 9-11 he had assumed that security would have been paramount and somewhat tedious. Soon he was striding under the "Welcome to the US of America" sign and casting his eyes for his first glimpse of Sorrel.

A little laugh behind him made him spin round on his heel and there he espied Sorrel leaning nonchalantly against a column.

Her unusual face was just as alluring as he remembered, more so. On her home territory she looked tanned, relaxed and delighted at his prompt appearance. He held her to him and they laughed and embraced with his luggage caught between them.

'Hi! You look great. Good flight?'

'Hello. So do you. Not bad, good film for once. These,' he held out a fat package to her, 'are for you, as I know you have a very sweet tooth, despite all that fine expensive dentistry work.'

Sorrel unashamedly pounced on the discrete chocolate box wrapping, exclaiming that they were indeed her favourites, and hang the dentistry work and her figure too for that matter. She justified it by claiming to have missed breakfast anyway.

Later, sitting in her convertible with the hood down and the sun-blazing overhead Richard congratulated himself on making the right decision to come. The promise of perfect weather, a weeks sailing in a gorgeous yacht and with an engagingly lovely girl for company was nothing if not paradise.

Recent events had given him much to ponder over and Sorrel was more than a welcome diversion. Later, he'd probably tell her something of the past week; when the time was right and he was ready. Right now, he was happy to join in with her infectious laughter and accept her amused teasing when she mocked him about being so "bloody British" in an atrocious put on Oxbridge accent.

Somehow she bought out the best in him and he knew with a warm feeling inside that he was going to enjoy this week in her company. It was a pity that they lived thousands of miles away from each other in different countries.

Sorrel expertly gunned the car along the highway, meanwhile keeping a close watch on her speed and fellow drivers. Richard watched her covertly through his sunglasses; he enjoyed how she handled the powerful car with her slim tanned arms and the way her hair was escaping from its thick ponytail in the wind. She said something and he had to apologise and ask her to repeat herself. She laughed and told him to sit up and pay attention.

Briefly she outlined the week ahead. She'd planned a cruise around the rivers and shores of Chesapeake. The names of the rivers and villages tripped rapidly off her tongue and Richard recalled with some relief how he'd spent the previous day exploring a map on the

Net that detailed the whole area. He was glad to have at least some basic familiarity with their proposed cruising grounds. Sorrel made it sound like a perfect week of sailing and exploring. He was a little startled to realise that perhaps the best part of all was that he had her company all to himself.

The fast car rapidly ate up the miles between them and Annapolis. Soon they were swinging off the highway and down the leafy suburbs of the sailing town. Richard was surprised at how pretty the little historical town was, and how some of the minor roads with their century-old cottages reminded him of the south coast seaside villages back in England. Sorrel slowed the car as they entered a sleepy cul de sac and pulled to a halt in front of a tall redbrick house, three storeys high. A thick deep pink rose clambered up alongside the front door, its perfume spilling into the air.

'This is it. Home sweet home for just tonight,' she said. 'Let's get you in and settled and then we'll discuss dinner plans.'

The front door was half panelled with a multi-paned jewel of different coloured glass. As the sun hit the colours the result in the small hall was a stunning kaleidoscope of colour. As they closed the door behind them a pretty white and black cat rushed up and greeted them with a loud meowing, pushing her head hard against them as she wound her way between their legs. Sorrel scooped her up in her arms.

'Richard. Do you like cats? I'm sorry I forgot to ask. Yes, good. Well in that case meet Toast. Say hello.'

Toast nuzzled Richard's hand and he was rewarded by a loud purr and a rough-tongued lick. He was puzzled over her quirky name and said so. Sorrel laughed and explained.

'Toast? Ah that's because she very nearly was. I originally found her as a half-drowned kitten a couple of years back. I brought her in and dried her off in front of the fire. She loved it so much she would hardly leave the warmth and one day she badly singed her fur. She was fast asleep and oblivious to everything. When I came into the room I could smell what could only be burnt cat! See, one side of her whiskers have never grown as long as the other. So, as she nearly became toast that's what she's always been known as. I know, I know. It's corny right? But anyway it seems to suit her.'

The house was charming. Each room was surprisingly light and airy and Sorrel had obviously spent many hours scouring bric-a-brac and antique shops for the right kind of period furniture and light furnishings. She had an eye for colour and the overall effect was one of good taste. In each room she had hung just one painting, so as not to detract attention from it by another. The Logan she had bought with him, he noticed with satisfaction she had hung in pride of place in her sitting room. Richard complimented her on having a comfortable house with such a welcoming and nice feel to it.

Whilst they sat over coffee outside in the sheltered, sunny courtyard she told him some more about her father's yacht, or sailboat in American speak. *Lady Mischief* was moored in the town marina and Sorrel had already victualled her up ready for their weeks cruising. The first night they would spend in the house as the neighbour who was to look after Toast wouldn't be home from Washington until tomorrow. They could either eat in here tonight or try one of the many restaurants in and around Annapolis.

'We'll have an early dinner as I know you'll soon be bushed once the jet lag hits you. After breakfast we'll head down to the marina and I'll show you the boat.'

***

Later, over dinner they caught up on each other's news. Richard told Sorrel the latest he had found out about Billy. He mentioned Miranda and how she had been able to fill him in with lots of gaps and put right the odd guesses and assumptions Richard had made. He didn't of course mention that night spent together or anything she had told him about her ghastly marriage.

He did say how happy he now was since most things fitted into place. He could finally understand and connect to his father and it helped explain his single-mindedness in relation to Penny. Richard could now imagine how he must have felt when he had come home and had to pick up the pieces and start an almost new life. Penny and Megan had been his cornerstone and together they had lived, loved, supported and cared for each other; so building themselves into a close-knit little family. Sorrel gravely listened to Richard. She was both astute and careful. She had heard and understood all that Richard both said and left unsaid.

Skilfully she judged the right moment and then steered the conversation back to the coming week. It was roughly nine months since Richard had aborted his Atlantic crossing and the hell that he had gone through immediately after. He told her how much he was looking forward to this week of new adventure for him with a gleam in his eyes. She knew he had steered clear of yachts or indeed boats of any size up until now, and Chesapeake would be the final challenge as far as sailing went. He said that he'd either slip back naturally into the routine of living aboard once again or else he'd soon discover that he had lost the pull of the sea. Whatever happened Sorrel wanted to be there when he took his first step on board and she was determined that it would be *her* that got him sailing again.

***

Next morning Richard awoke to the early harsh call of seabirds and couldn't fathom where he was for a brief moment. The sun was already rising above the maple trees outside his bedroom window and the light filtered through the gauzy material of the curtains. With a smile, he remembered and lazily stretched his long limbs under the bedclothes. He lay with his hands under his head and thought about today and about the extraordinary woman that he would be spending it with.

Not only was Sorrel very pretty, she was obviously clever and witty. He liked the fact that she was kind hearted and he found her undeniably, an extremely sexy lady. He looked back to their first meeting when he had thought her noisy and shallow. How wrong could he have been? Naturally he wondered why she wasn't either attached or married. So far he had had the good sense not to question her on the subject, neither had she volunteered any information. He would leave well alone; if she wanted to let him into her private life then he felt she would do so in her own time.

The previous evening had simultaneously been both a relaxing and yet exciting time spent in her company.

Richard had watched in amusement as she put away a plateful of salad, a substantial steak with a huge jacket potato, and vegetables. She had looked up and caught him watching her and had had the grace to blush and declare that she was famished. She rarely ate red meat she said, but she had been so busy lately with work and had missed a whole bunch of meals. She was only making up for it after all. When the admiring waiter flashed the dessert menu at her she declined and then immediately relented, to demolish a huge slice of key-lime pie. Richard sat back sipping his espresso but, not without some amazement and admiration.

She was funny, and despite her obvious good looks didn't take them too seriously. She obviously could eat what she liked without worrying about putting on weight. Richard had to admit that she wasn't the stereotyped American. Most girls from the US that he had previously met were unhealthily obsessed with their looks and body. Sorrel knew what she liked and what she could get away with. Life to her was too exciting to worry over trivialities. She turned down Richard's offer of cream with her filter coffee, saying she had to make *some* effort. As he smiled at her she wickedly grinned back in response and he realised just how much he had enjoyed her company the other times they had met. It suddenly seemed incredibly important that she continued to look at him and smile.

A soft knock on his bedroom door broke into his reverie and an already dressed for outdoors Sorrel stepped lightly in carrying a tray of tea things. Toast was at her heels and jumped with a loud purr onto Richard's bed.

'Good morning! Did you sleep well? Oh good. Now I know you prefer tea first thing, so I just hope I have made it right for you. There's cream and sugar if you need them. Oh and if you want to take a shower there's plenty of hot water. Come down for breakfast when you're ready, there's no hurry. Come on Toast.'

As they left his room Richard once again stretched lazily. He noticed that she had only briefly flicked a quick glance at the bare top half of his body as he lay in bed. It was probably her good manners. Feeling smutty he wished that he didn't have any himself.

He quickly drank his scalding tea and then sprang out of bed for his shower. It was too nice a day to waste lying there on his own and he was eager to get down to the marina. He pulled on a pair of light sailing trousers and a polo shirt. It was already feeling warm and he knew that later he would be digging into his sailing kit bag for a pair of shorts. He thrust his feet into his old well-worn deck shoes and then hurriedly repacked his bag. He was ready for a week of sailing.

***

The marina staff clearly knew Sorrel as they waved her through the entrance into the marina's private car park and wished them both the banal greeting 'have a nice day.' They had looked keenly at Richard with open curiosity and he noted with some amusement that Sorrel wasn't going to introduce him.

'Let them guess,' she said with a mischievous grin as they walked down the pontoon, 'they never have enough to do as it is. Why should I make it easier for them.'

Lady Mischief was situated near the end of B dock. She lay there, her fendered side quietly resting against the wooden pontoon. There was no swell to speak of and only a light-teasing breeze blew from a south westerly direction.

Richard stood still savouring the moment. He stared at the yacht with obvious admiration. Then after a minute he slowly walked down her side and then turned back to Sorrel with a low whistle.

'She is beautiful. I've never been on a Hinkley before, let alone sailed one. This is going to be a brilliant trip!'

Her topsides gleamed in the sun and her varnish-work along the toe-rail and coach roof was perfect. Richard noted the distinct Hinkley characteristic touches, the dark blue hull, the cut-away in the cockpit and the discreet use of stainless steel. She was drop-dead gorgeous and worth a pretty penny. With impatience he waited for Sorrel as skipper to give him the permission to go onboard.

Below, she was a mixture of old and new. Traditional was the appropriate word he thought.

Sorrel was the perfect hostess and insisted that Richard have the master aft cabin. She was perfectly happy and at home in the forward cabin.

'Dad always has the aft cabin and I can be more relaxed at anchor at this end,' she said when Richard had protested at her generosity. 'Go ahead, I insist.'

He hurriedly unpacked his toiletries and stowed his bag away in a cabin locker. He was ready for a run-down on the yacht's workings; he wanted to know where everything was kept and how it all operated. He was keyed up with excitement and couldn't wait to get out into the bay and hoist the sails!

Chapter 29

They were under engine as they left the confines of Annapolis. Sorrel at the helm, as she knew the channel well. She was sure that Richard would prove to be an accomplished and trustworthy crew but she wanted to clear the busy thoroughfare of motorboats and sailing yachts before she let him take responsibility of the wheel. They passed the yachts moored outside the marina basin, safely secured to sturdy looking buoys that stated, 'up to 45 feet only.' On the right-hand side there was a muddy slip where a father and small boy were preparing to launch a dinghy from a trailer. Boats of all sizes whizzed to and fro and Richard felt a warm glow of satisfaction as he watched the busy scene spread out before him. Sorrel swung the bow of the yacht slightly to port still in the marked channel, and the Naval Academy now off to their left hand side. The grounds were frantic with activity, as the Naval Cadets were put through their paces in an energetic yomp.

'It's always kind of interesting at this time of day,' a smiling Sorrel said to him as they passed. Richard didn't know whether she meant all the boats activities or the young men.

At a moderate five knots they made their way out into Chesapeake Bay proper. The tea-coloured water frothed in their wake and Richard could see that the bay stretched away for miles both north and south before them.

'Wow! I never realised just how big it was,' he enthused open-mouthed in amazement as he stood on the side-deck. Sorrel smiled at the look on his face. She was glad that he was relaxed and taking it all once again in his stride. At the moment with the weather being so calm and benign, the sea was flat and calm. She knew however that during bad times the wind kicked up into a stiff, choppy sea that could become positively dangerous. The waves were often big and destructive, washing away any unprotected parts of the shoreline. For the moment she decided that she would keep this information to herself and let Richard enjoy the day as it was.

They continued to motor until Sorrel was happy that they were well clear of all other craft. Out in the open water she suggested putting up a sail.

'I suggest we head north as we have a south westerly and try just with the headsail. There's no point in using the main, as with these light winds it will just flap. The genoa is a good size and should be just perfect for these conditions.'

Richard nodded in agreement and stood prepared for action in the cockpit.

'What would you like me to do?'

'If you can just free the genoa line and make that starboard winch ready. Good. Now we'll use the electric winch just to get the sail out and then go manual when we want to trim. Saves on the battery and it's a good workout for the upper body muscles. OK?'

'OK by me.'

The line ran out with practised ease and the sail whipped forward. Richard took a turn off the fat winch and adjusted the sheet until the sail filled. It billowed lethargically and then suddenly went taut as it caught the wind blowing from the port quarter.

'All right!' Sorrel cried looking up at the sail.

'Mmm. That looks OK to me.'

'Perfect. Just perfect. It's my idea of sailing. With a gentle breeze on a flat calm sea, with just the headsail gently pulling us along at what 5–6 knots? Great. No stress, no problems. A clear blue sky and sun. And a handsome companion. What more can a girl ask for?'

Richard didn't know what to say. She was constantly joking with him and loved to tease; especially at what she called his "Britishness." He was only too aware of her a sexy, beautiful woman, but –. But what? He was free and as far as he knew so was she. True, he'd recently made up with Miranda and he was fairly certain without being cocky that she wanted to rekindle their relationship. She too was lovely to look at and sexy with it, but did he really want Miranda and all her baggage? What's more did she truly want him? Or was she still hankering for a convenient and safe, trustworthy partner. He hated the idea of letting her get hurt once again; she had had one breakdown.

Getting back to Sorrel, the biggest but that was holding Richard back was the disparity in their ages. He was nearly fifty for God's sake. Or was he purely imagining things? Was she interested or just flirting for the fun of it?

Playing safe he smiled back and told her that she was indeed very lucky.

They sailed up the bay for about four leisurely hours. They were in perfect harmony with the boat, the sea and weather conditions and between themselves. The sea was a glittering mirror spread all around them and the light winds created only the tiniest of waves. *Lady Mischief* slipped along, the water gently chuckling along her sides leaving only a faint wake behind her stern. The perfect afternoon slipped away and before they knew it they found themselves heading up into a largish river mouth.

Under Sorrel's watchful eye, Richard slowly nosed the yacht's way in between the many crab pots, until they found a secluded gorgeous spot in a bight of the river. The trees along the bank ran down to the river's edge and overhead they caught the flash of kingfishers as they dived for their afternoon's catch. It was breathtakingly lovely and perfect for an overnight's anchorage.

As soon as Sorrel was happy with their position in relation to the shoreline and the water depth she prepared to run out the ground tackle. The anchor chain clattered noisily as it passed over the yacht's bow roller and then there was a silence as they sat and waited for it to settle.

***

'This is the life. Who needs to work!' said Richard later as he lazily pulled the tab on his second can of beer. 'I have really enjoyed today. I didn't realise just how much I had missed my sailing. When I get back home I think I will look up a few friends who have their own yachts and offer my services to them as crew. That way I can ease myself back in and who knows maybe I'll buy another boat in a year or so. Cheers!'

'Cheers! I'm glad you feel that way about sailing again. It's a good idea to take it slowly. You mentioned work before that. I agree wholeheartedly. But, well, I do have to work at least for a few more years. I have to build up a pension some more. Oh, I know I can leave the running of the gallery to my assistant for holidays and stuff but I'm not yet totally financially independent. But hey, I'm working hard on it!'

Sorrel laughed as she took a sip of her ice-cold Chardonnay. She was comfortably stretched out on deck cushions in the cockpit. She had changed earlier into a yellow bikini top and miniscule shorts that she claimed she only wore in the privacy of the boat or her back yard. She wore dark glasses and had pinned her glorious hair up into a loose topknot. Richard's fingers itched to pull out the pins and watch her hair cascade down over her shoulders.

He turned his thoughts to what she had just said and was silent for a moment. He hadn't meant to pry in any way especially over money. He'd never presumed she was wealthy but had thought that she was probably comfortably off. Sorrel continued.

'When grandpa passed away he did leave me his house. I haven't decided yet what to do with it. It's fairly big with a large river-frontage. The house is old too and has quite a history, which is kind of neat. The thing is, do I want to be tied to a big house and all its upkeep, or do I sell it? If I sell it then I'll have no money worries at all. But, I remember spending all my childhood holidays there and I guess deep down I just love it. It would be a great wrench to part with it, I have so many great memories.'

She looked at Richard, her lovely face troubled. It obviously meant a great deal to her.

'I understand. Do you have to decide soon?'

'No. I can leave it for a while, a few months possibly a year or so. But you know, it was always a 'happy house.' I spent the best days ever there. Every day that I can remember was long and sunny with never a cross word and never any boredom. We had picnics down by the river and swimming parties with all my friends. When I graduated from college, Grandpa threw me a huge barbeque with a band. It was much more my home than the ones I lived in with my own parents. That was when they were together. It was just great then.' She paused to sniff and take a quick sip of her wine. Richard was sure that a tear was threatening to escape as she remembered her beloved grandpa.

'Do you think all people look back and remember only the good things of their childhood? Not every day could really have been quite so perfect could it?'

'I think happy, contented and loved children probably do just that. They remember all the good, fun things in their memories. That has got to be good, surely? There's just so much misery in the world and every child has a right to have at the very least, a happy and secure childhood.'

Sorrel nodded her agreement and refilled her glass. Richard still had at least half a can of his beer to finish. She put her cool glass on her forehead saying,

'Phew it sure is hot today. I was telling you about the house. It needs a bit of work doing on it. If I do decide to keep it I'll have to get a few estimates for repair and stuff.'

'Yes but give yourself a little while. Your grandfather's not been gone long. Leave it and when you feel you're ready then think about either selling it or keeping it to live in. I take it you would live in it? Whereabouts is it anyway?'

'Oh, not too far from here actually so I could commute quite easily to work. Would you like to see it?'

'I would, very much.'

'OK, probably tomorrow then.'

The afternoon sun was making them drowsy. The anchorage they had chosen was typical of the upper Chesapeake. Despite the number of boats that had accompanied them out sailing that day it was still fairly easy to find a creek running off a main river that was deep enough to navigate up until a peaceful, secluded spot was found. The river bottom was soft, silty mud, which held the anchor really well. As there was no wind to speak of the yacht would quietly lie facing the direction of the river current. Around them was a canopy of deep green trees still covered in thick foliage and alive with birds. Later, during the fall, Sorrel told Richard that these trees would turn the most beautiful colours running from pale ochre and umber, to deep gold and right through to the russets and bronzy-reds. It was a favourite time of hers, with cooler sailing weather, emptier waters and long languid evenings spent safely at anchor gently rocking to the water's ebb and flow.

'Perhaps you should try it,' she said.

'Perhaps I will, it's certainly tempting enough.'

He couldn't read her eyes through her sunglasses as she turned to lie on her stomach. Five more minutes lying in the sun and they would both be asleep. It was too hot to read and although the water was probably clean enough the natural colour of it put him off having a swim. Somewhere an osprey made its urgent call; they were as common here as magpies were back home he thought. They were prettier though and more interesting. Sorrel was too he thought drowsily as he drifted off.

***

The black gardener had parked the old pick-up truck outside the front door of the house and he ambled slowly round to the front of the vehicle.

'OK Miss Sorrel? When you wanna go back, you just gimme a holla now. Ahm a going to be down by the big old live oak. You know where ah mean?'

A big crooked delighted smile was on his wide black face. Jemm had known Sorrel since she was a baby and both he and his wife Meena adored her.

'Thank you Jemm. Indeed I do. We'll come and find you when we're ready.'

Sorrel and Richard watched as Jemm shuffled over to where a dilapidated old wheelbarrow was resting on the edge of the drive; garden tools poked out from within it. He hitched up his patched dungarees and then put his weight behind the wheelbarrow as he pushed it around the side of the house.

Sorrel watched after him fondly.

'Old Jemm. He's a honey! He and his wife Meena have been part of the household for years. He does all the heavy things around here - or what he can still manage I should say. He must be eighty at least. He splits the logs, saws up the fallen trees, painting and mowing the grass and stuff. You name it he does it. Meena takes care of inside. She cleans, and used to shop and cook for Grandpa. You should taste her Southern fried chicken and apple pie. I know it's a cliché, but she sure does know how to cook! They come with the house. If I keep it then they stay. They're part of it and besides where would they go at their time of life? I don't suppose they have nearly enough put by for their own place.'

'Where do they live?' Richard turned back to face her.

'Oh, there's a small log cabin round the back. It's kind of sweet really. Nice and snug in winter and cool under the shade in summer. They've always lived there as long as I can remember. Come on, welcome to the family home.'

They turned back to face the house before them. Earlier, as they had entered the large white painted gates and began the ride up the drive, Richard had become aware of a weird feeling beginning in the pit of his stomach. The drive was long and shady from the overhanging willows and oaks either side. Here and there he caught a flash of colour beyond, that eventually expanded into immense flower beds; a riot of colour in an oasis of lush green grass. The grounds were simply astonishing and Richard had been totally unprepared as to what to expect. With a sudden gasp, it was the sight of the house as it emerged in view that took his breath away. It was pure antebellum; Gone with the Wind. He thought that these were more usually found further down in the Deep South.

Wide sweeping steps led up to a huge door under a porticoed overhang with round gracious pillars either side. The house was painted brilliant white, so white that it hurt his eyes, relieved only by the shuttered windows that were a deep pleasing green. Flowers in ancient huge stone pots hugged the steps and around the deep veranda. The building looked massive. Richard was momentarily speechless as he gazed at this amazing house standing in front of him. Still stunned he slowly dragged his eyes away and turned towards Sorrel. His face was a picture of amazement as he found himself stammering,

'This is your Grandpa's house? This is now yours'?'

Jemm had let out a chuckle of pure glee from the driver's seat.

'Yes Sir. Now this all belong to Miss Sorrel's here. Yes Sir.' He jerked the hand break on and they came to a stop. Richard once again looked back at the house. She could have told him instead of letting him gawp like a tourist!

He felt a light touch on his hand that was gripping the seat in front.

'Richard. Shall we get out?'

He nodded and recollected himself quickly. For God's sake he was acting like some gauche boy. It was only a house after all. But, what a house. He had to say though he had been totally unprepared as to what to expect.

A sudden giggle at his side told him that Sorrel understood only too well. She had planned to surprise him from the start. She really deserved a smacked bottom. He grinned at her in response. 'Lead on then. Show me your little pad.'

As Sorrel had led him from room to room he realised what a dilemma she was in. It was a huge undertaking to even consider taking on. The basic structure of the house looked sound. It did however, need modernisation here and there; new bathrooms, kitchen, the heating looked pretty much defunct and not robust enough to do a proper job. Doing all this would inevitably lead to more and more hitherto invisible problems.

But maybe the biggest problem was its sheer size. Richard let his mind drift as he imagined the old families that had lived here. There was a chandeliered ballroom; a small band would have played in the corner. Ball-gowned, bejewelled ladies with handsome, suave and correct Southern gentlemen as partners would have been swept around the dance floor. Small black boys loaded with round silver trays bearing cooling drinks for the hot participants; mint julep, whisky sour, rum punch and French Champagne. There would have been tiny canapés to keep appetites at bay before they had all sat down to a sumptuous dinner in the long dining room lit by a thousand candles. Outside the dining room windows there was a courtyard that contained a tinkling fountain playing over water nymphs. Flunkies wearing smart uniforms would have served dinner at the huge table laden with snowy white linen, sparkling crystal glass and silverware that shone so dazzlingly bright.

The kitchen was a huge square affair, with deep walk-in pantries and massive china sinks. The floor looked like it was the original black and white tiles and the plumbing was remarkably ancient; gigantic baths and faucets. Richard was shown a comfortable sitting room, a parlour, a library complete with floor to ceiling full book shelves, a gun-room cum land office, a games room with a billiards table, more store rooms, bathrooms, a galleried landing and bedrooms; he hesitated to ask how many. The furniture was mixed, period, pre modern, well used but mostly tasteful. Many rooms were shut up and their contents covered in dustsheets.

It was a little mind-blowing and at first a bit bewildering. As Richard wandered around following Sorrel, he felt the excitement that he got whenever he discovered a gem of a house that needed restoration. He walked from room to room, his heels first ringing on the well-polished wooden floors before sinking into the deep rugs from far-flung lands. It was definitely old money. Whatever occupation had her grandfather had?

'Well. What do you think of it? Like it huh?'
'Like it? It's amazing. Fantastic! I am staggered and can understand how you feel. If it was mine – well. Uh, I don't know. My initial thought is that you couldn't possibly sell it. But, I do understand, it is so big. Just incredible.'
He walked round his arms slightly outstretched gazing up at the beautifully moulded ceiling in the formal drawing room. He repeated to himself 'incredible' once or twice.
'Mmm. I know.'
Sorrel stood looking around the so familiar room. Almost wistfully she went on,
'It needs people. Children.'
'You're right. Lots of them.'
Richard stopped what he was saying. He was unsure how to continue; it was none of his business really anyway.

***

She had been married. Once before and only briefly. It hadn't worked out. A familiar story that had run along the lines of; they had met at college, fallen in love, finished their education and got married immediately after. He'd become a corporate lawyer within a big firm. Soon Sorrel had noticed how the hours had accumulated downtown, there were long late meetings, endless dinner parties for the 'right people', being seen in the 'right places.' It just wasn't her. In vain she had argued that it had never been her and never would be. Her husband Max expected her to be available as the dutiful East Coast wife. Look pretty; be exceptionally adept in entertaining important clients or the senior partners of his firm. He had to maintain a good impression especially as he was ambitious in becoming a senior partner himself. Children were not on his agenda, or at least not then anyway. He was too busy as a high flyer to become a regular dad. Maybe later when he could use it to his full advantage. Sorrel managed to stay sane for a couple of years until it all became too much. Too many personal outings and engagements had been cancelled at short notice and she was particularly fed up at keeping Max's so called senior partners at arms length. The clients were often boorish, spoilt and petulant and she began to dread the evenings when they had to escort particularly important clients to the opera and ballet. Although she had always had a love of the arts the over exposure to both began to rapidly pall. She eventually lost her patience and one day she chucked the few items that she valued into her car, left the house keys on the hall table and took herself off to fume at her grandparents' house.

At first Max had been both miffed and heartbroken at her departure. When he realised that she was no longer at his beck and call the pleas for her to return home quickly turned to anger. How irksome! How dare she walk out on Maximillian Symmonds the third? A swift divorce followed (à la firm) and Sorrel considered herself well out of it.

Since then she had stayed well clear of lawyers, corporate or otherwise. Richard listened with some surprise as she explained all this over an early dinner one night later in the week.

Satiated with the days puttering around the lower Chesapeake; there had been no wind that day, too much sun, a good barbeque and probably too much beer and wine, they had both crashed down on the soft cushions of the *Lady Mischief's* cockpit. Richard had kept Sorrel's glass charged as she kept him entertained over the inadequacies of said departed husband. He said little about his own views on the subject but privately he considered that Max must have been a first-class prat in allowing his occupation and ambition to thwart his marriage. But, as he well knew himself it took all sorts to make a world and he himself wasn't necessarily right. Well not always anyway.

They were moored up in a particularly secluded area of the Rappahannock River, well into the Corrotoman River really. They had motored under the enormously high bridge at the river's entrance and had kept going until they found a favourite spot of Sorrel's. There were plenty of set crab pots around to foul their rudder or prop and Sorrel was concentrating hard not to run aground in the shallows at the same time. Richard hadn't realised the significance of the white plastic pots dotted around the bay until Sorrel explained to him.

'The pots are set with a thin nylon line running between them and are placed there by the 'Chicken-neckers.' Every morning and evening the chicken-necker comes out in his boat to his patch. He runs the line over a big winch on the back of his boat and at intervals he attaches a chicken neck to the line, which he then drops back into the water. Am I explaining this OK?' she asked anxiously with a frown. Richard nodded, enjoying just watching and listening to her. She continued.

'The chicken is bait of course. The fisherman then starts back at the beginning of the line and hauls it up over the winch. If he's lucky practically every chicken neck will have a blue crab attached to it by a claw. He takes his catch to a local crab and fish factory or restaurant where he sells them. The local crabs are delicious and crab soup is to die for. If you like we can have a go at it ourselves just with a line and a bit of bait. It's real easy and good fun and the crabs are running well this year.'

Later they had done just that and they spent the afternoon picking the crabmeat off the shells that they had bought and then cooked. Richard was appalled at the quantity of butter and thick evaporated milk that Sorrel put into the pot for the crab chowder. But, as he took his first mouthful he said that it had to be one of the tastiest things he had ever experienced. It was thick and wonderfully creamy, but a certain recipe for blocked arteries and a massive coronary.

***

It was still hot after the day's sun and the humidity was making it uncomfortable. They had eaten a light early dinner, washed the dishes and once again made the boat shipshape. Below decks it still felt too hot to be comfortable and they decided that the cockpit was the coolest place to spend the rest of their day. The sun was going down and the lengthening shadows were gathering in the darkened trees around the shoreline. Standing to catch a whisper of a breeze Sorrel lifted her heavy hair off the back of her neck with her arm. The brief respite felt cool momentarily against her skin.

Richard was seated on the opposite side to her and watched. She fascinated him. Being in her company, she made him feel different. Back in England he only chugged along, fairly content but it was hardly what you would call exciting. With a start he realised that when she was around he felt *alive*.

A rivulet of sweat ran down behind her ear and disappeared down the front of her thin cotton dress between her breasts. He imagined the droplets journey and wished that he could follow its path with his tongue.

'Look come over here, it's amazingly beautiful. So perfect and so peaceful,' she suddenly whispered, not wanting to break the silence as Richard quietly joined her on her side of the boat.

He nodded agreement and then involuntarily caught his breath when he looked down at her. The low sun was slanting down through the branches of the trees; the rays casting their light into her eyes and making them sparkle. The long lashes fringing her eyes caused feathery dark shadows on her cheeks and her lips were pink and slightly moist. The heat had brought forth a slight damp patch on her brow, which she wiped away with a hand. He noticed the covering of fine gold hairs along her cheek line. She raised her arms again to lift her hot thick hair from her neck, her breasts thrust and emphasised their shape against her dress. She turned towards him, noticed his attention and let her arms fall to his shoulders. When he did not protest she encircled his neck moving in close, their bodies lightly touching.

'Richard?'

He raised his hands to her waist and tentatively kissed her lips. She tasted of honey and of sunshine. As one they moved closer, harder. Their light kiss deepened as she opened her mouth and he explored her with his tongue. Slowly he kissed her eyelids and neck. He ran his hands down to her firm buttocks, pulling her gently against him. She moaned in his ear and pulled his head down to her breast. Reaching behind her, he felt for the zipper and pulled it down in one swift movement. The straps of the dress fell from her shoulders and encouraged by her low moaning, he continued to kiss the valley between her breasts. Her dress slid down over her hips and pooled around her ankles. She stood before him in a lacy white bra and knickers. Again he found it hard to breathe. She gently moved away from his embrace and unclasped her bra and let it fall to the deck. She hooked her thumbs into her knickers and, bending down stepped out of them. Her creamy-skinned buttocks glowed in the half-light and a groan escaped his lips as his groin responded.

'God Sorrel. You're so beautiful.' Gently he stroked the soft skin of her shoulders and down her back.

She pulled his polo shirt free from the restraining belt and shorts and drawing it over his head let it slip to their feet. His torso was lean and hard and only slightly less tanned than her own. She traced her tongue over his chest and teased a nipple between her teeth. She released it and looked up at him, smiling, and ran a finger over his mouth. She then pulled his head down to her beautiful pale naked breasts. She arched her back and gasped as he tenderly took her soft breasts in both hands. Her breasts were perfectly formed, high and well rounded with hardened aroused nipples. The skin felt like velvet under his touch.

He knew that if they continued he would not be able to contain himself. Taking her face with his hands he tenderly murmured her name and then laid her gently back on the soft, springy cushions of the cockpit.

He kissed her; a long deep kiss before he put his head down between her smooth taut-skinned thighs. His excitement increased when she began to moan and writhe her hips to meet his exploring mouth and tongue.

Suddenly, their excitement began to overtake them. They could contain themselves no longer. Their eyes locked he swiftly moved up and over her body, his manness eagerly probing and then slipping inside her. The feeling was immense. She slowly moved beneath him, drawing him tightly, deeper inside her. Their movements became a rhythm. Long drawn out strokes, that suddenly became more urgent. Their rhythm increased to frantic hard thrusts. The sweat trickled down between his eyes and fell onto her breasts. Their climax when it came was deep and total. So deep that it was almost painful in its release. She arched her back as she engulfed him and let out a low scream. She felt that she was falling, deep down into a bottomless abyss. His groan was an echo of her fulfilment. Their shudders were almost feverish, as they lay there spent, panting with exhaustion and completely and utterly satiated.

***

It was later. They lay drowsily curled together; arms and legs entwined in the darkened cockpit. The tall shadowy willow trees gently swayed their pale fronds in a slight evening breeze. The river continued on its long way to the sea.

Richard opened his eyes and traced a finger down the curve of her cheek. 'That was beautiful. You are a beautiful darling girl,' he said and tenderly kissed her brow.

Sorrel opened her eyes and squinted up at him trying to read his face in the dark. 'Mmm. It was,' she turned towards him snuggling deeper into the comfort of his arms and after a pause quietly asked, 'It wasn't totally unexpected was it?'

'Nooo.' He replied slowly, 'I had fantasised about your beautiful body and what I would do to you if I got the chance. I can't remember the last time I made love in a secluded country setting. It makes me feel like a teenager! I've obviously missed out lately, so I'd better make up for it.' His smile lit up his face and Sorrel realized, not for the first time just what a good looking and sexy guy he was.

She smiled at him in return. 'For me it was amazing, and felt like, well so totally perfect. It's been a long time since I've –.' She stopped, feeling slightly shy and embarrassed. She looked as if she was going to continue her sentence, then instead said, 'well we're both free agents, not hurting anyone. So, something so good can only be right!' she finished simply as she leant over him on one elbow. She played with a stray hair on his chest and playfully pulled it. Richard winced in mock pain and slapped her hand away as he suddenly rolled over and imprisoned her beneath him. He gazed lazily down at her as she struggled half-heartedly to escape.

'Pack it in. You know you can't win. But, yes you're right. The funny thing is I don't feel in any way guilty. Perhaps this was meant to happen. Connie's been dead for over nine months now and I have to get over her and her death sometime. Maybe I can now start to get my life back together and really start living again. For that I have you to thank. You are brilliant company to be with. Not to mention a body that's not too bad!' He ducked as she aimed a cushion at him. 'Come on we'd better get below, somebody's bound to come along here sometime. I don't want to be arrested in the States for indecency.'

***

The week was nearly over for them. *Lady Mischief* had entered the river mouth that headed up towards Annapolis. The previous day they had visited the tiny island of Tangier. It was a weird, but fascinating place that seemed to be populated entirely by Crockets and Pruets. Their men folk all fished as they had over the centuries since they had first arrived from England. The weirdest thing was their accent. Richard was amused when addressed by a stout lady of middle age in what could only be a West Country burr of Devon or Cornwall. It was bizarre to say the least. The one restaurant that the island boasted was at best an ice cream parlour. The local teenagers hung about the premises until they left to go courting around the island in their electrically powered golf carts. You couldn't get a meal after about 8pm as the whole island closed down early on account of the fishermen getting up and away by about 3am.

Now, the sky was streaked with long trails of orange and yellow as the sun once again sank down on what had been another perfect day. Richard had fallen in love with the sailing ground of Chesapeake. It was undeniably beautiful and had been the best place for him to test the waters of sailing once again so to speak.

A cloud formation was gathering in the South East. Perhaps it would bring rain later. Sorrel had been saying all week that it was long overdue and even the sweet corn had suffered and shrivelled away to nothing due to the draught.

Lady Mischief nosed her way on the final trip upriver back towards her berth, a creamy bow wave pushed before her. Other craft were heading in for their marina berths and river moorings. The scene was excitingly chaotic as boats scurried here and there creating a wash. Richard suddenly didn't want to go into the marina. Not yet anyway. He was still in a bit of a shock after last night and couldn't either keep the grin off his face or the smile from his voice. All day he had tried not to keep touching Sorrel at the slightest pretext, without much success. At first, when they had woken in the soft new morning light they had been slightly shy and hesitant with each other. Each remembered the night before vividly. There hadn't been much sleep; a lot of talking and touching and kissing. Richard had woken before Sorrel and had been content to lie there watching her as she slept peacefully unaware of his gaze.

'Can we not anchor out here for the night?' he asked as she rejoined him at the binnacle, 'off the Naval Academy. There looks like plenty of room.'

He felt ridiculously like a small boy who didn't want to go home from a very good party that was still in full swing.

'It would be a nice finish to the week, one last peaceful night at anchor. I don't know about you but marinas have never done much for me. We could still get in early and clean down the boat before my flight back and get you in on time for work.' He looked at her with an earnest appeal on his face that she couldn't refuse.

She took a look around the anchorage. It wasn't crowded at all, and he was right about it being quieter and also cooler than being tied to a concrete and wooden pontoon with no swing to the breeze. Like Richard she too loved sleeping on board and all too soon the yacht would be sold. Heaven knows when she would get the chance again. Besides, she was looking forward to a repeat of last night's activities. It had been a long time since someone had come along and taken her so totally by surprise.

She agreed.

'I think it's a great idea. The bottom's not perfect, hard packed sand and gravely in places, but we should find ourselves a nice soft patch, knock on wood. We'll anchor slightly more out, away from the others.'

Half an hour later they were nicely dug in and had finished sorting out the boat. The genoa sheets were tidily coiled around the big, fat powerful primary winches. The sails were properly folded to ensure that no ultra violet could damage them. They got ready the mooring lines and fenders for the morning and had a last check that everything else was shipshape and put away.

Once again it was sundowner time and a half-hearted argument as to who would cook dinner that night, or should they launch the dinghy and take a run ashore?

They were both feeling lazy and decided that a good stir-fry of all the contents of the fridge would give them the nourishment that they would need. Or what about a barbeque of kebabs? Another G and T would decide for them and Richard went below to do the honours. He was more relaxed than he had been for a long time. Sorrel's idea for him to come sailing with her had helped him more than he had imagined. He now felt that he could take command of a boat again without any misgivings or self-doubt. His badly shaken confidence was now fully restored.

As he reappeared on deck he noticed how the sky was developing interesting colours. The earlier golden rays from the sinking sun had changed to streaks of red and purple-tipped clouds that were building and looming over the trees and buildings of the town. He pointed it out to Sorrel as she joined him.

'Oh! I don't like the look of that,' she muttered, as she turned round to look at the sky behind her.

'I don't believe that our BBQ prospects are very promising.'

They both checked over the yacht ensuring that there was nothing that could be blown overboard and also that the dinghy was safely secured.

Within minutes the sky was a mass of boiling black-purple angry clouds billowing around and over them. There was a sudden crack as the first lightening bolt shot across the bay.

'Wow! Did you see that?'

There was a second flash and the heavens suddenly opened in a mighty deluge. More spectacular flashes followed by crashes rolled around them accompanied by a sudden wind that set the boat rocking.

The pair of them were drenched through and they fled down below laughing and dripping over the saloon floor. They wiped their wet faces and changed their sopping clothes for large dry towels and then watched in awe at the power of the electric storm from the dry safety of the sun bimini.

Another huge flash lit up the whole anchorage and there was a sharp crack nearby. The boat anchored nearest to them was illuminated and they watched in alarm as the electricity struck its taller mast and ran down to its deck guardrails. Sorrel squealed in fear at the nearness of it. The air seemed to 'fizzle' around them. That same strike hit other nearby moored boats, bouncing across the adjacent masts in some terrifying but fascinating dance.

They could suddenly hear the muted sounds of fire engines on the shore and they watched as the fire fighters leapt from their vehicles and began to train their powerful water jets onto the roof of the Capitol building. Sorrel briefly explained that the building contained the original copy of the signed Declaration of Independence. It was therefore of paramount importance to Americans. If the building burnt down history would be forever lost. The firemen were taking no chances by ensuring that the building was well doused in water. A direct hit would be devastating.

Miraculously, *Lady Mischief* rode it all well. She was untouched by lightening. Richard congratulated Sorrel on her choice of their anchorage site. She had kept slightly away from the other yachts and the strike had hit only those clustered together. An hour later and the thunderclaps rolled away until they were no more than a dim growl in the distance. Sorrel was relieved. She had watched the storm with a slightly sick feel in her stomach. If she had had to impart bad news to her father she felt sure that with the stubbornness of parents he would only have placed the blame on his daughter. She said that life wasn't always fair. Richard agreed with her before gently removing her towel from around her body, taking her by the hand and leading her into the aft cabin.

***

It didn't seem like a week ago, that Richard had arrived at Washington DC and had eagerly scanned the awaiting crowd in arrivals.

Back at the airport he had already checked his bag in and clutched his boarding card in his hand along with his passport. He glanced up at the clock and realised that he had only a few more minutes before the last call for his flight would be announced. He hated airports and everything that went with them. From the intolerable queues, and repeated showing of his flight ticket and passport, through to the flight with its plastic tasteless food served in impossibly cramped quarters. He could never quite understand why in the 21st century a flight shouldn't now be both painless and quick! As far as he could make out standards were nowhere as good as they were back in the early days of air travel. Apart from that, flying itself made him slightly nervous and short tempered with everything.

Sorrel waited patiently by his side. Their last night had been bittersweet. Passion consumed their first coming together with an intensity that had left them both gasping and spent. Later, they had reawakened each other's bodies with slow languorous strokes that replaced their earlier urgent almost desperate need.

They had left little time to get to the airport for Richard's flight and Sorrel had weaved in and out of the heavy traffic on the highway.

In silence they had driven, each lost in their own thoughts.

Now, Richard turned to Sorrel and took both her hands in his. He heard himself saying that it had been a fantastic and brilliant week. He had loved Chesapeake and the yacht. The sailing had been a good reintroduction for him to get back into his favourite sport and pastime. He couldn't thank her enough for suggesting it. He thought that he was uncharacteristically rabbiting on about the fun they had had. What he didn't say was that she had been a huge surprise and that he felt alive in her company. She was fun and utterly delightful to be with, and by far the most amazing woman he'd ever had the pleasure of in his bed. He couldn't say that. It was just too what? Crass? Patronising? Cold?

No. It was more than that. Deep down he knew it wasn't just the sex. She made him feel an entirely different person. He didn't want to leave her, not to just go back to England like this. But, he had no hold on her. No commitment on either side. Both were slightly awkward as they gazed at each other.

'It's been the most wonderful week.'
'It has hasn't it?'
'I'm so glad we managed to find the time.'
'We'll do it again.'

When? Oh when? The thought was there but like fools neither said what they *really* wanted to say. It was all left floating....

'Listen there's the final call for the flight.'

Too late.

'Phone soon.'

Please. Let's not leave it like this.

'I will I promise.'

They held on in a tight hug, swamped in each other's arms as they shared their last kiss. As they drew apart a question was in their eyes. Richard broke the silence. He didn't want to embarrass her by saying something stupid that he would regret later.

'I must go. I'm sorry.

To cover his face he bent down and picked up his bag and jacket from the polished tile floor. When he straightened up Sorrel shook her hair back from her face and smiled brightly at him. She appeared relaxed and happy, nonchalant even. Perhaps she was completely satisfied after their little affair he thought. Had that been what she had wanted? Fantastic sex and then back to business as usual. Get on with one's life without any unwanted baggage. He understood that women could be as hard thinking as men. But, he hadn't thought she was like that really.

'Have a good trip. Got your boarding pass?'

He patted his shirt breast pocket. They touched fingertips and then he was gone, turning on his heel and heading for the departure gate.

Would he look back? She waited breathlessly, as a lump formed in her throat. She fought back the tears that threatened to fall. Keeping them back in check, knowing that they'd cascade down her face as soon as he was safely out of sight.

He reached the inner gate; the attendant checked his card. He moved forward to the last door and stopped. Swiftly he turned, an anxious look upon his face as he met her gaze. He drew himself up straight then smiled and briefly waved as he stepped through the door. He was gone.

Sorrel felt totally bereft as she stood there willing him to return to her. When he did not and she realised that he had indeed gone she slowly turned and stumbled away. She held her head down, her hair falling and hiding her face as the tears slid unchecked down her cheeks.

Back in her car she sat behind the wheel and began to gain control of herself. She found a tissue and blew her nose. Her hands were shaking as she brushed her hair out of her eyes. She felt ghastly. Had she been stupid? She'd done what she'd vowed she'd never do again. Not to go down that path again. She'd invited a man into her private life. To share with him her most precious secrets, passions, dreams and dilemmas. Maybe she was stupid. All she knew was, for a week he had made her feel wonderful. More wonderful than she had ever felt before. Only, somehow she'd not been quite enough for him. She'd let him walk away, slip through her fingers. She had been wrong and had misread everything. She hadn't been able to keep him with her and for that she was heartbroken.

Chapter 30

The days passed. Richard had slipped back into his old routine. He checked his portfolio of stocks and shares; the market was up another eighty points! It was time he made a move towards another restoration project. He'd contacted his manager earlier that day and he agreed with him that the time was ripe for investment. For some time Richard had had his eye on a particularly rather fine old Elizabethan Manor that was begging for restoration work. This week it had come on the market and was going to be auctioned for sale. He wanted to buy it and he needed to set the wheels in motion. It was a glorious old house with a wealth of original features and restored to its former glory would be a testing challenge to Richard and his company. Richard had discussed the property potential with his manager and they had agreed on a mutual top bid price. They were both in agreement that this would be an exciting property for their next project.

However, having made that decision Richard was now bored. Money made money it seemed. Richard's manager was so diligent Richard could almost have left the entire running of his company to him. Until the new house project became a certainty he needed something else to occupy his energy and mind.

Moodily, Richard pondered whether he really should have another cup of coffee. He knew too much caffeine wasn't good for him. The telephone rang just as he was refilling the coffee machine. The call came from an old friend that he'd known for years and he presented Richard with the possibility of doing something completely different than he was doing now.

Stephen, his friend, had the opportunity to purchase the agency of the yachts that he was currently representing and selling. At present the manufacturer and owner of the company employed him as the UK sales manager. This owner, with a catalogue of new ideas and plans had decided to change the goalposts and offered Stephen the UK agency to buy.

Richard and Stephen went back a long way. They had both been dinghy sailing instructors in their late 20s and early 30s. Together they had shared the same taste in ridiculous jokes and above all a passion for sailing. Stephen had married and with a wife and young family to support had soon given up his more carefree bachelor lifestyle. He changed jobs and became very adept at selling larger boats and most importantly of all he made enough money as a sales manager to keep the wolf from the door with his growing family.

Now, he had been presented with a whole new scenario. An agency meant capital outlay, which he didn't have. As with most of the other agencies worldwide he needed to have a new boat fresh from the manufacturers in order to show to potential customers. In effect this was a new stock boat and this meant a lot of money to be paid up front. He knew he had the expertise to make a go of it; he was a superb salesman after all, but he had nothing like the money behind him to purchase a brand new yacht.

Cautiously he approached Richard with a tentative offer. He knew he had the money and Stephen promised he would repay it back with the current market price interest. Alternatively, Richard could come in as a partner. He could if he wished put up the capital for the boat and have a share in the agency. Richard was both intrigued and excited in the prospect of a new venture. He would dearly love Stephen to succeed with an agency and for himself he saw it as a good chance to become once again involved in his favourite sport.

Since returning from the States he had been doubly restless. He had been a total wuss and contacted Sorrel only by email. He had thanked her for her hospitality and a great week. Hospitality! He felt a complete fraud. He promised himself that he would telephone her soon.

Now Stephen had come up with a tentative proposal that had a nice feel to it. Richard had plenty of spare capital to invest. He had always had time for his friend and if he could help him in any way then why not? It would be no hardship for him to buy a brand-new boat for use as a demo. Richard could involve himself as much or as little as Stephen wanted or needed him. He felt the familiar rush of excitement course through his body at the prospect of a new venture.

He agreed to meet Stephen down at the Hamble office right away, as they needed to act fast to secure an order for a new yacht.

***

By the end of that working day the deal was done and dusted. A new 50 foot yacht from the factory was theirs. A wealthy Russian who had then changed his mind about buying her had originally ordered the boat. It had recently come on the market and was consequently bought and paid for by Richard at a fair-trade price. Her fitting out was being completed in Sweden, where she was built and she would be sailed over ready for pride of place at the Southampton Boat Show in September. They didn't have long to finalise everything. As was usual in business, things sometimes have a horrible habit of all happening at once. Both partners agreed that as she was a classic blue-water yacht she should be fitted with everything needed for easy long-haul sailing. A good inventory showing the ease of usage and how well she could be kitted out would go a long way to entice potential customers to get out their cheque books. Together they drew up a long list. They included a reliable generator, a water-maker, electric winches, easy running state of the art in-boom reefing (they argued over that one), superb electronic navigational aids, and a well-fitted galley for starters. A suite of top quality Mylar sails was already included and to this they added a cruising chute for light winds and a storm jib, just in case.

Soon Richard was caught up in the heady excitement of it all and promised Stephen that he would be available to help him for the whole run of the boat show. Stephen was over the moon. When the yacht manufacturer had first made his tough proposal to him he had been apprehensive and concerned over just where he was going to get the finance for the offer. There was no way that he would have been able to fund it himself and he had agonised over how he would support his family and their future. As far as the manufacturer was concerned there had been no alternative. Richard had been extremely generous with his offer and he looked forward to their working together again.

They had known each other a long time and Stephen had been upset both when his friend's relationship with Miranda had faltered and then again when Connie had met her death. Apart from Richard's Aunt Mavis, Stephen had been one of the few people that Richard had been able to talk to over the past year and he had listened with interest when Richard informed him that the beautiful, cool Miranda had reappeared in his life in the most unexpected circumstances.

'Sounds like she wants to rekindle your old relationship. Is she still as gorgeous as ever despite what, it must be fifteen or is it twenty years since you broke up?'

'Something like that, but yes she still looks pretty fit. She's kept her figure and her face is older of course but more interesting somehow.'

'She was always a damn good laugh. Good value for money, I thought.'

'Mmm. Only she's more serious now.'

'Well what are you going to do? Give her a second chance?'

Richard thought for a moment. He was unsure just how much to tell Stephen. Miranda hadn't sworn him to secrecy or anything but, there were some things that you just didn't broadcast to the world. Also, he'd not disclosed anything much about Sorrel, and certainly nothing about their last week spent together. He was therefore noncommittal and hedged the question when he replied.

'Maybe.'

Stephen was scathing in his own reply.

'For God's sake Richard you are a berk sometimes! You're not getting any younger, or better looking. If she's still a looker what have you got to lose?'

Richard winced. Maybe, maybe not. Was he being daft? He had finally spoken to Sorrel that week and neither had gone out of their way towards bringing up anything of a personal nature between them. Sorrel had actually even been a bit muted in her conversation with him and there was certainly no question towards commitment of any kind. With regard to Miranda if he turned her away then he was being both cruel to her and losing his chance of possibly rekindling an old but what had been to him a very exciting love affair. Finally as far as Sorrel was concerned she was both younger than he was and bloody miles away to boot.

He also knew that if he told Stephen about his muddle of a love life then he would probably call him worse things than being a total prat as far as women were concerned. Richard was also aware that there were plenty of other guys who'd take full advantage of his situation and happily shag both women silly whenever they had the chance. So why, for God's sake was he being so dammed cautious and correct? Because he had always been that way, the devil inside told him.

'Yeah. I'll probably give Miranda a ring sometime.'

'Make it sometime soon. Invite her down here and we'll make a foursome for dinner. There's a new Thai restaurant in Hamble village that does fabulous food I hear.'

'OK. OK, I'll let you know.'

That had been yesterday. Today the decision was made for him, as when he picked up his telephone mid morning Miranda herself was on the line.

She was friendly, and as bright and chatty as ever. Recently she had started helping out at a hostel for abused women. It was in the town where she lived and she had been amazed at just how many women, thousands, millions of women, were affected worldwide by abuse in the family home. Currently she was working a few days a week but, already she knew she was going to increase her time spent helping out there. After all, she had told Richard with a taste of bitterness she had the perfect hands on experience and hoped to make an impression on some of their sad lives. She considered herself lucky to have rid herself of her charmless marriage and even worse husband.

She had told him that the work was heartbreaking at times, but it could also be rewarding too and they needed her help and support and money too of course. Charities, she said with a little tight laugh, for abandoned animals got far more funding. Abused women were not quite so fashionable or cuddly as our furry friends. Richard found himself offering a sizeable donation and Miranda gasped in delight at his generosity. She promised she'd be over the next day to collect it before he changed his mind. Richard laughed to himself as he replaced the receiver; he had been manoeuvred quite nicely into that one he thought. Not that he really minded as it was a good cause and he could afford it. Like many businessmen, Richard donated regularly to charities of his choosing so another wouldn't harm the balance sheet.

The next day, Miranda arrived as promised. She had brought along a packed hamper with her,

'The least I could do for your generosity is to feed you. I thought maybe a picnic somewhere quiet and scenic? Perhaps along the South Down's way?'

Of course Richard allowed himself to be persuaded by her smiles and pretty ways. As he locked the front door behind them he vaguely recollected at the back of his mind that he had been here before. She was still demanding at times.

Despite all his misgivings they had a fine picnic up on the downs. The views across Portsmouth were fantastic and it was good to be out from the confines of his village for a time. He remembered his mother and father taking him there when he was a small boy. They had piled into their small car with a fully laden wicker picnic basket and a large blanket to sit on the grass. He could almost taste the roasted chicken and tomatoes, followed by small apple pie slices and iced fairy cakes. There was always lots of homemade lemonade as a special treat and maybe a toffee apple to eat in the car on the way home. Small boys were always hungry.

Miranda seemed eager for them to remain good friends. Whether she had further plans in her agenda he had yet to find out. Richard could only imagine what she had really been through when she had been married and there was no way he was going to upset their new but fragile friendship by giving her the cold shoulder. For the moment at least he would let it progress slowly.

***

September was looming fast. The Southampton Boat Show was scheduled to start with a press day on Friday 14th September. Stephen was working all the hours of the day it seemed. The yacht company had already agreed to send another two new boats over for the duration of the show. With the one that Stephen and Richard had ordered it gave three different size boats for customers to view. All three yachts were being sailed from Sweden and Richard had volunteered to help sail their own purchase over. Richard was looking forward to the chance at another long voyage. The week in Chesapeake had firmly rekindled his sailing appetite and he was impatient to get going with this opportunity. He'd sorted out his personal sailing equipment including his foul weather gear. He knew that September in the North Sea could be awful but he was going to be positive about it. He checked over the items of his kit bag; new boots, safety harness, handheld GPS, a few Kronar for shore expenses and his passport.

He had allowed a week for the passage although with good winds it shouldn't take anywhere near that time – so long as there were no snags. Richard knew better than most people about being prepared.

Miranda, although she was no sailor had been very interested in his trip. She'd come down to visit Richard regularly in the last couple of weeks and had made him promise to take good care of himself during the voyage. Without being overly possessive she made him understand that she did care for his health and safety.

In return Richard asked her all about her own work with the hostel and was happy that she had found an outlet for her time and energy. He had been generous with his donation and she'd told him with a slightly wicked smile that he was that most desirous of all males, single, sexy and loaded. She made no bones about what she wanted. Richard thought that forewarned was forearmed; he could still call the tune.

Richard became busier as the days sped past. He found he was juggling his time now between Stephen, Miranda and his own restoration business. He was happier than he had been for months and the only blot was the fact that he hadn't spent as much time talking with Sorrel as he would have liked. They had both said that they wanted to see one another again but time had simply flown by. Now, just as he was literally on the point of leaving for Sweden Sorrel had rung him to inform him tearfully that Lady Mischief had now been sold.

'I'd never have known just how upset I was going to be,' she sniffed over the telephone, 'after all it was Dad's boat really. But I'd used her more than he had lately.'

She blew her nose into a hankie loudly. She was obviously very upset.

'Perhaps you should have bought her for yourself.'

'I couldn't afford to. Besides I haven't told you yet, but I've decided to keep Grandpa's house. I couldn't bring myself to part with it. It didn't feel right somehow. I know he said I could do what I wanted with it and it would have been a fantastic nest egg but something told me not to. And I most certainly couldn't afford to keep both the house and boat.'

'Well that's great. I am pleased that you have decided to keep that. It is beautiful, and a good investment I'm sure. Not that it's any of my business but what will you do about the upkeep and any refurbishment?'

'No that's OK. I'm going to sell the Annapolis house. I may have someone interested already. It'll help pay for some of the repairs and stuff. I'll just have to see. The gallery will just have to sell more paintings.'

Sorrel sounded a bit depressed but as Richard was dashing off practically at that moment there was nothing he could do or say to advise her. The house was certainly beautiful but still a huge undertaking and he hoped that she understood the enormity of the possible expenditure in the future. It would be a labour of love and she'd need to sell a lot of paintings. There again she was obviously intelligent; hardly a teenager needing her hand held whilst being advised on what to do with her own money.

'It's very exciting and I'm sure you'll appreciate the house when you've got it looking magnificent again. The boat, well they all depreciate eventually, even Hinkleys over the years. Besides, who knows you may be able to buy yourself one in a few years time.'

'Sure, maybe.' She sighed.

Richard had already told her of his own exciting news so she wasn't surprised when he said that he was about to leave for Gothenburg.

'I should be back in the UK by the 10th at the latest and then it's all go getting the boats ready and cleaned for the show. We plan to have them in place by the 12th.'

'I've never visited the Southampton Boat Show. I've heard that it's good.'

'Oh one of the best. I much prefer it to London as it's held outdoors and if the weather's good the atmosphere can be brilliant.'

'Mmm. Lots of drinks parties on board I suppose?'

'Ah ha. There are some but, it's jolly hard work too.'

'Oh right! Sitting on expensive yachts talking about your favourite pastime? Very hard work, I don't think so,' she laughed.

'You sound jealous. You're not really are you?' Richard teased her.

'No. I've just got a lot on my mind a the moment.'

'Well, it's just as well that I didn't ask you to crew for me from Sweden back to here then isn't it?'

There was a short silence as both realised what he had said. He had thought of ringing and asking her earlier on but two pals had itched to go along and a bachelor crew had sounded good at the time. He had told himself that it was maybe too soon and that he may appear too eager to see her again after last month's sailing.

Sorrel could have kicked him! Of course she would have come. She would have dropped everything else like a shot. Their week together might have meant nothing much to him but who cared? For once, she felt like throwing caution to the wind and grabbing whatever excitement and happiness came her way. Besides, she didn't truthfully believe that anyone could make love the way they had together and put it all down to simply having a wild sexual casual affair. Could they? Her pride didn't allow her to say any of this as she replied with nonchalance.

'I probably wouldn't have been able to make it. I have too much to do right now with work and Grandpa's will. There's also been a sudden rush of late summer parties. My social life has suddenly taken on a new whirl. You know how these things are,' she lied with her fingers crossed.

Richard felt a prickle of disappointment. He suddenly felt cold and shivered as if the sun had disappeared behind a dark cloud.

'Yes. I understand. Maybe next time. I'm sure there will be plenty of other opportunities.'

'Yeah. Well I've got to run. Work beckons. Have a really swell trip. You know the saying, blue skies and gentle seas. Keep safe.'

Both Richard and Sorrel looked at their dead telephones lost in their private thoughts. Damn! If only I had telephoned earlier. That's another chance that's slipped down the drain.

Sorrel picked up her car keys and headed out of the door for another day at work.

Richard picked up his own keys and kit bag and closed the front door behind him.

The lure of the sea beckoned but had he missed out by not inviting Sorrel to accompany him?

Chapter 31

The last day of the boat show was truly glorious. A hot sun beat down on the decks of the yachts and motorboats at the show. Temperatures had soared today, making it one of the hottest September days on record; it was almost as if the weather was making its last stand against the coming autumn. As the crowds poured through the entrance gates leading into the show it also promised to make it one of the busiest.

The three yachts that Stephen and Richard were marketing were lying snugly against the wooden pontoon. They had been cleaned and polished daily until they gleamed. Their teak decks were a natural pleasing gold hue that gave off that gorgeous smell of warmed wood in the sushine. The stainless steel around the boats sparkled and the little bunting flags hoisted aloft rustled in the breeze.

The show was proving to be a tremendous success and everyone involved had been almost constantly busy. It appeared as if everyone was in the market for a new yacht and Stephen was elated that they had at least one positive sale and another that he felt 95% sure would confirm after a test sail.

'When the contract's signed and the deposit paid,' he said ever cautious, 'then we'll open the second bottle of champagne, not before.'

Richard was delighted too. For himself it didn't matter quite so much as he already had a successful business, but as far as Stephen was concerned he had his large young family to consider and so he had to have a good show. With one sale in the bag already so to speak they were on their way and Richard was extremely pleased for Stephen's sake that he had agreed to come in with him.

Richard had had an extremely busy and memorable last couple of weeks. The voyage back from Sweden and down the North Sea had for once been a doddle. They had had a nice beam-reach across the Skaggerrak until they had swung south. Then they had two days of gentle down-wind running with white sails goose-winged and poled out. The wind had then died and they had run their engine and charged the batteries for nearly twenty-four hours. As they had crossed the

Wash and rounded the south-east corner of England the wind had picked up and they had flown along at a spanking pace nearly all the way to the Solent.

Richard and his crew had a fantastic delivery trip. They had all done their share of watches and galley duties, interspersed with the odd spot of fishing. The new equipment on board had for once, nearly all worked first time with very little drama. Apart from a few teething problems and niggles, Richard was so far very impressed with what he had spent his money on.

Too bad the yacht was going to be a stock boat; at least until they had an offer for her and another one could be ordered from the yard. She had an astonishing turn of speed in the right conditions. It was true that she wasn't yet loaded up to the gunwales but, even so Richard had put her through her paces and she sailed like a dream. With her sails set just right – she got herself in a perfect slot; like in a groove she almost sailed herself with only just the slightest touch on the helm. Sorrel would have loved her.

Richard looked forward to some sailing along the South Coast and had already proposed his services to Stephen for any demonstration trips in the future. Life was looking good; maybe there would be an opportunity to ask Sorrel to come sailing over here some time. It wouldn't be quite so romantic as Chesapeake and the weather would soon be getting colder, but autumn sailing in the Solent had its own charm.

The loud speakers at the show blared out as they introduced the arrival of the demonstration team from Solent Search and Rescue. The helicopter zoomed over the tips of the highest masts as they headed for Southampton water and their 'rescue.' The crowds rushed excitedly forward and craned their necks to get a better look as the winch man lowered the helicopter crew member down towards the stricken yacht to take off the 'injured' yachtsman.

Richard took advantage of the sudden dispersal of viewers from their yachts and poured himself a glass of water. Saturday and Sunday bought out all the 'tyre kickers.' Those people looking for a bargain and 'when I win the lottery brigade.' He had already had to evict a family wearing shiny tracksuits and clodhopper trainers off the yacht when he had found their children running amok and jumping on the main cabin's double berth. He didn't like the look of something suspect, which they had put down the heads either.

He had shaken his head to himself; you needed a lot of patience, good manners and firm hand he thought as he'd pumped the heads clear. He wasn't sure if he had the right attitude for a more permanent job.

He rinsed his glass and put it away in a cupboard. A soft thud on the deck above announced yet another visitor and he emerged from the saloon with a ready smile to greet them.

A radiant Miranda appeared in the cockpit, clearly delighted to find and surprise Richard on his own.

'Miranda! This is a surprise.'

Richard thought back to their earlier time together when he had been mad keen on dinghy sailing. She'd hated everything to do with the water then.

'I thought I'd just pop down and have a look at your new boat darling. Wow! This is divine! So luxurious!' she exclaimed as she gestured an appreciative hand at the rich teak seating.

She was dressed in a pale blue strappy cotton dress with a matching short-sleeved bolero jacket. It showed off her voluptuous figure to perfection and with her summer tan she looked delectable. As custom dictated when going onboard she'd already removed her sandals and had left them on deck. As she descended down the companionway ladder into the saloon, Richard was able to admire her shapely curved calves and trim ankles.

Her delicate perfume filled the cabin as she leant closer, put her arms around Richard and kissed him fully on the lips. She drew back, a smile playing around her mouth as she looked round her with interest.

'I just had to see what your money had bought and whether I approved or not. I can say now that I certainly do. I can almost see myself enjoying the odd sail or two as long as we stay in marinas overnight of course.'

She turned back to him and slipped her arm through his and smiled up at him. 'Will you take me?'

'I'm not sure. You always hated the water. You said it made you feel sick just looking at it. You also were scared to put up the sails and leave the harbour. Maybe a bigger boat would give you confidence. Of course you'd have to learn the basics at the very least. You could do a Competent Crew course and see how we got on together. After all there's no such thing as a passenger on a yacht.'

He smiled artfully at her. He knew her of old. Two could play at that game. He loved anchoring in pretty secluded bays overnight. Marinas were usually a dirty, noisy and over expensive excuse for tying up to a concrete pontoon. He didn't quite see the point.

Miranda pouted and smiled prettily at him. She ran her finger along the varnished mahogany wood panelling.

'You could have the most marvellous parties on board it.'

'Her. A yacht is a she.'

He replied brusquely. For some reason her presence on board was beginning to annoy him. He had been economical with the truth so far. Previously, Miranda had absolutely loathed everything to do with boats and water. She'd campaigned long and hard to get him to change from his earlier career to something a little more 'normal.' Until now he'd forgotten quite how much she had resented his sailing.

'Of course, silly me,' she said as she had a quick look round the other cabins. She exclaimed over the huge double berth in the master cabin and the ensuite 'bathroom.' Quickly she had exhausted the tour.

'Have you got time to take me to lunch? I passed a decent looking refreshment tent on my way here. The menu looks pretty good.'

'Sorry I have to man the fort here. We usually have a simple sandwich on board and an occasional pint of Guinness when we're relieved. We're actually a bit short on staff today, so no I can't leave. Maybe a quick drink later on in the afternoon?'

She looked disappointed as she listened to what he had to say. Then, 'Actually I really wanted to pick your brains too.'

'What about?'

'The hostel. It has run into trouble. Financial trouble.' She paused and when Richard didn't reply she drew a deep breath and then quickly carried on.

'Funding, apart from your own donation this year has almost dried up. The local council hasn't been much help; they're more interested with developing the town sporting facilities so they can make a fortune in their over-priced car parks. Unfortunately, the mortgage on the house has run into arrears. We don't know what to do. If only we could pay it off then we'd be in a stronger position.' Her voice trailed off and she looked at him appealingly.

Richard felt a forbidding feeling growing in the pit of his stomach as he quietly asked,

'How much is the mortgage?'

'Um. Only about two hundred thousand pounds,' she said with an air of false bravado as she looked at him.

'That's an awful lot of money Miranda.'

'It is. I realise that and I wouldn't normally dream of coming to you especially as you've already been so generous. It's just that I can see so clearly the good that it does. All the women have a safe haven, a place where they can stay and recover some of their dignity. A lot use it as a start over place, somewhere fresh to begin a new life without a man in the background bullying them. There are their children too. We have quite a few little ones that accompany their mothers. Often they have been the victims as much as their mothers have been. They suffer in other ways too.'

She didn't have to explain any more; Richard could well imagine the untold horrors and he didn't really want to know the horrible detail anyway, especially if there were children involved. He understood that she was quite blatantly appealing to his good nature and generosity. She continued.

'I'm not asking you outright for money just, well perhaps some idea you can think of to help us. Of course if you did help again we will be forever in your debt.'

'I'll have a think about it and let you know if I can come up with anything.'

'Oh thank you Richard, I knew you wouldn't let us down.'

She threw him a grateful look that was full of satisfaction and hugged him.

'I'm not promising anything yet. Let me think it over.' Gently he disentangled himself and held her lightly by her wrists; a firm look on his face. Of course he knew he would help but he didn't want to seem a complete pushover.

Miranda was about to say something else when there was a light tap on the outside of the hull.

'Sorry, but we'll have to leave it there for now,' Richard said with relief and leapt up the stairs to see who the newcomer was. He stopped on the top step and Miranda heard a cry of surprise. She moved over to get a better view through the port side window and saw a stunning looking girl with a dazzling smile gazing up at Richard as she stood below on the pontoon. It was obviously someone who knew him. Miranda was intrigued and positioned herself for both a better view and clearer hearing. Judging by her accent the girl was from across the other side of the Atlantic. She didn't have the nasal twang of the Deep South nor the harshness from New York. She sounded more refined as Miranda heard her say that she was over here on business and thought she might as well stop off at the Southampton Boat Show.

Stop off? Miranda thought. Southampton was hardly en-route from anywhere. With feminine intuition she decided that there was more to this than the girl was letting on. Miranda joined them in the cockpit and looked at her with studied interest. She narrowed her eyes as she stared at the younger woman. The cut of her casual but smart clothes gave her a poised and confidant look. She was unusually tall with long hair and looked disgustingly fit and healthy. A little spurt of annoyance coupled with jealousy went through her. What a pain interrupting her surprise meeting with Richard!

As for Richard, she immediately noticed that he had hardly taken his eyes off the tall American and had so far completely ignored Miranda.

Aha! This was interesting she thought with relish. What would be the best way to deal with her?

Richard recovered himself from the sudden shock and turned to introduce the two women to each other.

'Miranda. This is Sorrel. She's come all the way over from Annapolis for the show and Sorrel, this is Miranda Barker, a sort of, well cousin by marriage actually and an old-time friend.'

The two women stared at one another and suddenly the slightly frigid air around them thawed as they gasped and laughed together in recognition. But of course they knew of each other already. Richard had forgotten that they had corresponded together earlier that year. In his sudden fluster at seeing Sorrel again he had completely forgotten that it was Sorrel who'd first tracked Miranda down through the family name. As they had exchanged information it was Miranda who had then got in touch with Richard about his father, Sorrel's grandfather and the Bible that had been kept all these years.

He felt his face flame as he realised that once again he was being a bit of a fool. So much had happened that year and with both women arriving at once he had been momentarily thrown off balance. He watched with some bemusement as they hugged each other and then sat down, chatting happily as if they had been friends for years. How did they do it? He thought gloomily. Women totally confused him. They show up out of the blue without a word of warning, look daggers at each other for some unknown reason and then clasp and hug like two long lost sisters.

He was relieved when he had to show a friendly young couple around the yacht. At least he would have time to compose himself again. He left Sorrel and Miranda on deck quite oblivious to him as he took the couple from London below. He felt much more at home going over familiar territory.

The new visitors eventually drifted off. They had been excited and full of praise for the yacht. They would do their sums and who knows perhaps they would place a call through to the sales office on Monday. Richard had carefully taken their personal details down on his pad. Maybe he could arrange a test sail sometime next week or the weekend and whet their enthusiasm further.

He rejoined Miranda and Sorrel on deck. Sorrel glanced up at him and her smile lit up her face. Richard felt his heart do a flip and the butterflies in his stomach made it difficult to breathe. He gave an exasperated look in Miranda's direction and he realised with a sudden jolt that he fervently wished that she would finally go. However, he couldn't be rude, he just needed a watertight excuse to get rid of her and be alone with Sorrel.

She looked good, stunningly gorgeous and Richard devoured her with his eyes. She was wearing an open-necked white cotton shirt with navy pants. Their crisp, tailored formal cut accentuated and only enhanced her overt sexuality. Her hair hung long and loose around her shoulders, and he remembered how he had buried his face in its fragrance and he could almost feel the softness of her neck beneath his fingers.

He suddenly realised that Miranda was addressing him and reluctantly he turned his eyes towards her.

'Sorry Mir, I was miles away. What were you saying?'

'I was just explaining to Sorrel about my involvement and commitment with the hostel.'

'It does sound an admirable venture, don't you think Richard?'

Sorrel was asking him. A slightly dazed look was on her face. She wasn't seeing anything but Richard and hardly knew what she had just said.

Richard held her gaze. He thought that she seemed a little strange, odd almost. She was probably suffering from jet lag.

'Yes very,' he murmured.

Miranda had watched this little interchange with mounting interest. She decided that there was no time like the present and decided to pounce.

'Richard has agreed to help out. He is so generous with his donations. We have a little cash flow problem at the moment, but he's made me promise not to worry, and I won't. Not now. I have such faith in him. Isn't that right darling man?'

'What? Oh yes I have.'

'OK. So do you want to give me your cheque now or arrange for a money transfer next week?' Miranda pressed home her advantage.

Richard didn't answer and Sorrel gave him a little nudge with her foot.

'What? Sorry. What did you say Miranda?'

'I said. Do you want to give me a cheque now or arrange for a funds transfer?' she smiled guilelessly at him.

'Oh, a transfer. I don't have that much sloshing around in my current account. I'll speak to my accountant tomorrow.'

Richard had only briefly looked in Miranda's direction to answer her before resuming his gaze upon Sorrel. So he didn't see the, at first totally stunned, and then delighted look of satisfaction from Miranda at his words.

'You really are a darling, isn't he Sorrel?' Miranda didn't wait and listen for Sorrel's answer as she glanced down at her watch, 'oh is that the time? I really must fly. I have a dinner date tonight and I must get back in good time.'

Richard hardly heard her. He knew that he'd been bamboozled into giving her a huge donation but what the hell. It was only money and he had more than enough and certainly more than most people. He had tried to give his father a new house to live in before he died He had wanted him to be more comfortable and to have no stairs to cope with. But he had turned the offer down saying that it had been good enough all those years for Pen and him and there was no point in wasting good money.

With the hostel project, at least his money would do some good and help unfortunate downtrodden women.

'I hope he's nice,' he heard Sorrel say to Miranda.

'Miranda let out a small sigh.

'Yes he is, very. He's a police superintendent. We've known each other a little while now and he seems kind and we're interested in much the same things. Richard have you been listening to what I've been saying? I must go, I'll speak to you tomorrow.'

Richard had finally taken in what she had been saying. She had a dinner date! There was no longer the need for him to feel responsible for her anymore. She was making her own decisions and building a new life for herself.

Giving her the donation was working its own magic. It was releasing him from her. He watched happily as she hurried to make her departure. She was leaving just as he wanted; he could now be alone with Sorrel.

Sorrel.

He ached to take her in his arms. Maybe later he could persuade her to come home with him and who knows after that? Perhaps she could stay for a day or two and he could get round to saying what he wanted to properly. Unless she was on a tight schedule that is.

Sorrel stood up and went to take a look around the deck while Miranda went below to fetch her handbag. Richard followed to say goodbye properly.

'She's lovely. I hope you're very happy,' Miranda whispered to him.

'What? I don't understand. We're only friends.'

'Rubbish, you can't take your eyes off her. Anyway she's perfect for you and I can see she's nuts about you. She followed you over here didn't she?'

Richard demurred; he could only hope that she had done just that.

Miranda left them in a sudden flurry of pale blue skirts, floral perfume and totally unboaty shoes.

Sorrel and Richard stood and looked at each other. Richard's hands were shaking slightly and he put them in his pockets so Sorrel couldn't see. His heart was pounding again.

'Did you mean to do that?' she asked.

'What? Give her the donation? I don't know really.'

He was confused; his mind was in a whirl over what Miranda had said to him just before she had left.

'Well, it was very generous.'

'Right now I don't really care. It got rid of her! As much as I like Miranda she can be extremely demanding and thick skinned at times. What I really want to know is what are you doing here? I mean I am delighted to see you of course but it's so unexpected. I thought you had a mountain of things to do?'

'I do. But, well I've never been to this boat show and I thought that it would be kind of fun to drop by and see you too. I also do have a meeting in London on Tuesday.'

'Oh right,' he paused and then after a moment continued, 'what about?'

'It's great news actually. A big London gallery is interested in buying me out! They've made me an offer I just can't refuse. I haven't told them yes yet but when I do it will mean a different life. I'll have no money problems but I will have to find something else to do. I'm too young to do nothing else but play golf all day. That would be so totally boring!'

Richard was thoughtful. His stomach continued to churn with almost violent flips.

'Do you want to see over the yacht?'

'Do I? Lead on.'

Sorrel loved the show boat, as Richard had known she would. She was so different from Miranda in almost every way. She was a sailor like Richard and loved everything about the sea. She asked dozens of questions from build composition to weight ratio, the sail plan, diesel and water capacity, engine consumption, battery bank and charging right through to the aesthetic looks of the yacht. She amazed him.

'She is perfect. The perfect Blue-Water Cruising Yacht,' she breathed. Suddenly she burst out excitedly. 'I'm in love!' and laughed happily as she twirled around the salon with her arms outstretched.

'So am I.' His voice was barely above a whisper.

She paused before answering, hardly daring to look at him.

'She's perfect for crossing the Atlantic and sailing through the Caribbean Island Chain. Then going down the steamy Panama Canal, across to the Galapagos and through the Pacific islands. A stop in New Zealand and then a hop across to Australia and then, oh! On up to exotic Malaysia and Thailand. A thrilling sail across the Indian Ocean to Sri Lanka and the Seychelles and then a choice. Either a white knuckle ride up the Red Sea dodging murderous pirates off Aden and Somalia or down to South Africa, through the treacherous Aguilas Current and then across to Brazil. Wow!' Her eyes shone with excitement. 'What a voyage! How long do you think that would take?'

'As long as you want it to.'

'You could buy her,' she said.

'I did,' he replied.

Sorrel looked at him in delighted surprise. Richard then burst out with the question he had been longing to ask her – forever it seemed.

'Would you come?'

'Try and stop me.'

He reached into the fridge and drew out the second bottle of champagne.

THE END

EPILOGUE

The dark haired sailor with the deep-blue eyes drew his arm around the girl at his side and smiled down at her. She smiled back at him and returned her gaze to the open Book at his elbow. He softly blew on its pages and as the Book slowly closed the two again became as translucent as the mist that engulfed them.